THE BARLEYFIELD

SUE SULLY

The Barleyfield

HEINEMANN : LONDON

William Heinemann Ltd
Michelin House, 81 Fulham Road, London sw3 6rb
LONDON   MELBOURNE   AUCKLAND

First published 1990
Copyright © 1990 Sue Sully
ISBN 0 434 75180 4

A CIP catalogue record for this book
is available from the British Library

Photoset by Rowland Phototypesetting Ltd, Bury St Edmunds, Suffolk
Printed and bound in Great Britain by
Richard Clay Ltd, Bungay, Suffolk

For my family and friends

Part One

1

The windows of the schoolroom cast a dusty light on the children. There was a lethargy about them. They were obedient, docile, uncomplaining. She did not stimulate them. How could she, when her own spirits were so low?

Elizabeth did not hear the vicar enter the room through the open doorway behind her. She was startled by the scuffle of the children's boots and scraping of benches as they got to their feet and stood to rigid attention. Robert Munro paused by the door for the ritual exchange of greetings then strode towards her chair. Robert's smile, his pink complexion, and his blond, thinning curls belied the devilish terror he instilled in the children. It was a terror of which he was unaware; for Robert was an insensitive rather than a cruel man.

'Have the children been studying diligently?'

Elizabeth prayed that he would not pick on Johnny Herbert to repeat the catechism. She could comfort the child afterwards with a secretly bestowed biscuit from her pocket, but she could not bear to watch him tremble and shake as he struggled with the meaningless rigmarole.

'We have all studied to the best of our abilities,' she replied as usual.

'Then we shall have to put those abilities to the test.'

What would he say, if he knew that she allowed the younger children, exhausted from helping with the haymaking, to sleep for half an hour with their heads on their desks at the beginning of the afternoon class? 'My dear Elizabeth . . .' he would begin with that condescending smile.

Robert circled the rows of children, a sinister, dark-clothed cherub. Elizabeth's own heart began to beat more quickly. Little Johnny

3

Herbert, pale and still with fright, clung to the side pieces of his smock as if to keep himself from buckling at the knees. Choose Sarah, Elizabeth willed silently, she is word perfect. The vicar halted by one of the benches and turned to confront its end occupant.

'Johnny Herbert,' he intoned, looking up to the vaulted ceiling as though he could see the boy's face up there among the rafters.

Elizabeth nodded to the boy encouragingly. She mouthed the opening words of the catechism to him behind Robert's back and made a silent promise that, when the storm was over, she would give the child all the biscuits in her pocket.

Robert came to meet her from the churchyard. A quiet had fallen over the schoolhouse now that the children had gone. They had drifted off in ones and twos instead of all in a mob as on other days, subdued by the heat and their recent witness of a beating, soon swallowed up in the summer stillness.

'You were too hard on the child,' Elizabeth said, locking the door of the schoolhouse. She dropped the key with an angry movement into the pocket of her sprigged cotton dress.

Robert looked perplexed. 'It's the only way they are to learn the paths of righteousness.'

Elizabeth turned away from him. 'The boy has a poor memory. It is not his fault.'

He repeated the last sentence, as though weighing the text at the beginning of a sermon. 'It is not his fault. Ah, but, my dear Elizabeth, that has been the excuse of all the lazy fellows in the world since time began.' He hurried after her. 'I don't doubt my own brother has employed it at certain moments in his life, when he found himself confronted by his own misdoings.'

'I don't feel inclined to discuss Edward's many failings.'

Elizabeth reached out to open a gate which led into the field beside the church. Robert laid a restraining hand close to hers on top of the gate. Elizabeth was uncompromising in her looks and figure and dressed unfashionably for those times. Her coppery hair, tied in a loose bun, always seemed to be falling from its pins and her large straw bonnet hinted too at eccentricity, for it was trimmed with yellow field daisies, which had been picked for her by one of the schoolchildren that morning and had long since gone into a decline. But the gaze with which the Reverend Robert Munro observed her was one predisposed to worship rather than criticism. His grip upon the gate was white-knuckled. Tension pulled at his full-lipped mouth.

'Robert, I really mustn't delay.' Elizabeth did not disguise her irritation. 'Hannah has a last fitting for her dress before the wedding and Mother gets very fussed if I'm not there to tell Miss Venables our opinion.' In truth, she had been looking forward to reaching home so that she could strip off the cloying material of her frock and fling herself on her bed in chemise and petticoat; the counterpane would be cool, like rippled water against her skin. She moved her hand away from Robert's. She had no illusions about what lay behind his trembling glances, the casually laid hand on her shoulder when he leaned over her to discuss some small problem in the schoolroom, the murmured respectful inquiries after her mother and father on Sundays after church.

'Yes, Hannah's wedding.' Robert blushed. 'Forgive me for delaying you. I only wanted to say that I shall be able to accompany your family to the house after the ceremony. I feel honoured to be so included in what is a very private gathering.'

'I hope Edward will accept my sister's invitation to view the house too, now that he is back from the Continent,' Elizabeth said sharply. 'The invitation was meant for you both.' She recognized too late the unnecessary emphasis she had placed on Edward's name.

Robert frowned. He said that unfortunately his brother's plans were more often than not an enigma to him. 'He has gone to Sherborne, to look at a horse,' he said. 'Yet more expense. It seems he's come home merely to squander his annuity. Since Father died –' He did not finish the sentence; Elizabeth had pushed open the gate, and he was forced to release his hold on it or else fall over. He followed her woefully with his eyes as she passed by him into the field.

The mention of a horse drew Elizabeth back again. Her glance took in a group of stable buildings which lay alongside the schoolhouse. The smell, even at this distance, was unpleasant in the stifling heat.

'I wish that you would speak to Squire Attwell for me about the stench and flies from his horses.' She spoke absentmindedly, as though something other than the stables had been on her mind.

'A stables cannot help but be malodorous.' The words had the ring of a biblical text. 'They are beasts of nature after all.'

'But so close to the school. If he would only get his men to shift the

5

midden to the other side of the yard. Heaven knows, I've spoken to him myself often enough. But if you would just say something in my support?'

If there was any hint of promise in her words, there was none in her eyes. And in any case, Robert's expression had become guarded. He valued too dearly the invitations to supper at Charlford House and the liberal dispensations of the Squire's champagne and brandy to speak up on her behalf. Robert smiled his regret.

Elizabeth turned away again impatiently. 'Farewell then.'

She walked away across the field. Robert was a fool. She could feel his gaze still on her back. How could two brothers be so different? She had known them both from childhood. She and Robert had played together, Elizabeth always the instigator of their games, Robert ever mindful of what authority would say about her wilder ideas. Edward, so much younger, had joined in every escapade with the abandonment of the innocent. He had still been a child, while she had been approaching womanhood. At sixteen he had worshipped her with that same innocence. And Robert had watched the two of them with a glowering jealousy, for which she had felt no remorse.

Elizabeth walked on. She did not look round. Yet, if she could have seen the expression of misery which flooded Robert's face as the distance grew between them, she might have allowed herself a twinge of pity.

Miss Venables, the dressmaker, had refused to add any more false rosebuds to the waist of Hannah's wedding dress. 'It do already look like a pesky flower-garden,' was her professional opinion. Hannah and her mother were in tears. Elizabeth's father, after shouting abuse at everyone, had shut himself in the study. Elizabeth abandoned all hopes of a similar escape to her room and tried to find a solution to the problem. She suggested they add rosebuds to Hannah's bonnet instead of the frock, and honour was satisfied by the compromise. Miss Venables departed to do the necessary stitching. Hannah and her mother dried their eyes, and Elizabeth went into the garden.

The house was in shadow. The windows, square and blank in the grey stone, and the two chimneys set stolidly at either end of the high slate roof gave the building an authority which Elizabeth found oppressive. The house suffocated her with its memories of childhood. And now there was all the excitement of the wedding. She wanted to run away from it, to close her eyes and ears to the fact that her younger sister had made a good match, would soon have a home of her own. She knew what people were saying in the village: Hannah always had been the pretty one, and what hope was there for Elizabeth now, thirty-one next month, and so awkward?

The garden was very still, and filling with shadows; in spite of the heat of the day the earth in the border near the front gate was still dark with moisture from the previous night's rain. Elizabeth plunged her arms in among the leaves of a clump of orange lilies and breathed their faint scent. Whisps of hair fell across her cheek and she brushed them back. She felt restless. A small fear beat out the familiar question. What was to become of her? The answer of course was the answer accepted by hundreds of other single women in her position. She would continue to live in the family home after Hannah had gone. She would care for her parents in their declining years and busy herself with charitable works in the village. She would not lack security. Why should the prospect of such a future fill her with dread?

She began plucking the long-stemmed lilies one by one, aimlessly. After a while the sound of footsteps in the lane broke the stillness. A young man strolled through the open gateway. He was tall and slim and wore a dark-green, soft-brimmed hat and a corduroy coat such as a labourer might wear, yet the rest of his dress and his manner were clearly not those of a farm worker.

Elizabeth looked up and met Edward Munro's boyish grin. It was an expression which never failed to discompose her, causing her heart to beat a little faster and a tremor in her voice to betray the uncertainty of her feelings. It was a reaction of which Elizabeth might approve in a romantic heroine, in the kind of books she read in secret, but which she despised in flesh and blood women of her acquaintance.

Edward took off his hat; his hair was dark and softly curled, a little unruly. He ran a hand through it as if embarrassed.

'I have bought a book.'

'I thought it was to be a horse,' she said, hoping the irony in her voice would disguise her nervousness.

He laughed. 'Robert has been telling tales.'

'Robert is very patient with you, considering the way you upset him. I thought you were supposed to have improved more than your linguistic talents while in France. Your father, Edward, will already be turning in his grave.'

7

He pulled a face, and she returned her attention to the lilies.

'The book was for you.' He took a small parcel from his pocket.

She was startled, unable to hide the fact that she was deeply moved by the gift. He held the flowers she had gathered while she unknotted the string. The volume of Tennyson's poems smelled of new leather. Tears pricked unexpectedly at her eyes. 'It's beautiful.' She fingered the gold lettering on the book's cover and flicked the thin pages until she came to *The Lady of Shalott*.

'I remembered you said that Tennyson was your favourite.' Edward cleared his throat, embarrassed by her reaction to the gift. He had picked it up on impulse from a bookstand in Sherborne, having spotted a pretty woman, an old acquaintance, going into a shop across the street. He had lingered by the bookshop in the hope that the woman would acknowledge him. She had cut him, much to his disgust.

'Listen.' Elizabeth felt an overwhelming pleasure as she read the familiar lines: '*Little breezes dusk and shiver thro' the wave that runs for ever by the island in the river flowing down to Camelot*. Doesn't it make you think of the barleyfield, and the river by the packhorse bridge?'

Edward nodded, but without picturing it. He thought the idea fanciful, hadn't Tennyson been writing from a Lincolnshire landscape, not an obscure village in Somerset? The deviousness of his purchase disturbed him slightly.

'It didn't cost nearly as much as a horse,' he said, as if this might lessen the deception.

Elizabeth laughed. 'I hope not. But I'm delighted with it, Edward. And you shouldn't have been so extravagant.'

An awkward pause fell between them.

'I'm not so fond myself of horses at the moment,' Elizabeth said lightly. She told him about the stench of the midden which invaded the school. 'Your brother won't say anything against the Squire, who insists that we freeze all winter because children need fresh air, and he's too stingy to buy a new stove. And we're plagued with flies all summer because of his horses.'

'The old windbag won't change anything,' Edward said cheerfully. 'Horses are more valuable than children, don't you know?'

'But he should, Edward. The smell is appalling.'

'The children, or the horses?' said Edward with an ironical lift to his eyebrows. 'I wonder that you stay there day after day.'

'I have to.' She was annoyed by his flippancy. 'What else is there for me to do?' She took the bunch of flowers from him, surprised, and a little sorry to see that she had gathered every single lily which had been growing by the gate. She turned and led the way towards the house.

Edward followed more slowly. He watched the sway of her broad-hipped figure in the flowered dress ahead of him, and her red-brown hair falling from a chignon at the nape of her head. A wave of affection swept through him, and a thought, unconsidered until now, stirred in Edward's mind; he dismissed it as absurd; Elizabeth was like a sister to him and always had been. She had taught him to climb trees and how to whistle. They had scoured the lanes round Charlford for blackberries, searched the mud-beds by the river for frogs to play with, made tunnels through the fields of ripening barley, to lie and watch the clouds sail above the quivering heads of corn. He would have followed her anywhere. Her vitality had fired an energy in him and dispelled his natural languor, giving him a sense of purpose which, in more recent years, had been missing from his life. Perhaps he had been more than a little in love with her, he told himself with an attempt at self-mockery. And now? A troubled frown lingered for a while as he followed her indoors.

2

Edward told himself as he climbed the path to Cadbury Castle that men did not fall in love with women like Elizabeth. She was too strong-minded, and, at past thirty, far too old. She should not have worn pink for Hannah's wedding, he decided: the pretty pastel shade made her look fat and billowy. By making such private observations he believed that he could prove to himself that he was not drawn to the swing of her hips and the bouncing edge of her skirt on the path ahead of him.

She turned and swept a hand across her forehead. She brushed back damp strands of hair which had fallen across her cheek. The sun dappled her face with a leafy, liquid light. In that moment Edward was aware of an unwholesome surge of sexual desire. He quickly suppressed the sensation with more acceptable thoughts, the fusion of light and shade on the path, the delicate marriage of colours all around, the plunging of the light through the tree branches.

'It's cooler under the trees,' she called.

He nodded, watching her.

'I really shouldn't have drunk so much champagne. I expect the sun will be even hotter on the hill. I almost wish that I hadn't left my bonnet down at the house.' She chatted, as if she was frightened of the silence.

Edward looked behind, to where the stony track pitched steeply to the lane below. 'I could fetch it for you,' he offered reluctantly.

She laughed, showing her teeth. 'Don't be silly. Is that how young men behave *sur le continent*? I don't want you to be a lap-dog.'

He frowned, unsure of the implications behind such a remark. He felt himself detached from the safety of the roles they had once seemed to fit so easily: Elizabeth, the unsentimental older friend, 'Don't be a baby, it doesn't hurt,' when he cut his knee and she dressed it with a poultice of herbs. Himself, the impetuous youth, 'Let's be explorers. Let's go to China. Let's join a circus,' begging her one summer to go with him to the fair. They had raced like children from stall to stall, sucking on sugar sticks, shouting to one another over the noise of the crowd and the music organs, Elizabeth shrieking with a mixture of fear and laughter when a monkey on a chain jumped on to his shoulder and tore off the brim of his new hat. 'Let's not go home, Lizzie,' he had said. 'Come with me round the world.' And her eyes had shone with a light of wildness, before she had said, 'When you're old enough, I shall be too old. I shall have a stuffy husband who will say, "No, my dear. It isn't proper."'

Elizabeth went on up the path. 'It's a pretty house, don't you think, for a young couple to be starting out in life together?'

'Pretty? I suppose so. I dare say Hannah will soon be filling it up in every corner with china ornaments and frills.'

'Fred will indulge her whatever her taste.'

'They seem very fond. There's something rather repellent about newly wedded bliss.' He exaggerated. He must make it clear that nothing at all about the seductive atmosphere of her sister's wedding day had attracted him.

Elizabeth's skirts swung jauntily ahead. He averted his eyes and laboured to catch her up.

'One day I shall try to paint you,' he said after a while. He had learned, in awkward moments in his more recent past, that art was a useful means of sublimating sexual desire. Reduce a pretty woman to a poem as Tennyson had done, or to a sketch on a canvas, and she was no longer flesh. Except that Elizabeth was not a pretty woman, and that she was flesh was indisputable.

'I should look like a ship in full sail if you were to paint me in this dress,' she said without looking round. 'Pink! It was Mother's choice, not mine.'

'I could have chosen a more delicate image than a great sailing ship. But you're right, the colour doesn't suit you.'

She halted on the path and waited for him. 'I'm not delicate, Edward. I never shall be.'

'You have a kind of beauty though,' he said rashly. 'It's a sort of

11

sensuality.' He flushed scarlet, not knowing how he could have spoken his mind so easily.

Elizabeth too looked confused. 'You know you shouldn't say things like that.'

The trees closed over their heads. The flies buzzed in the green silence. The stillness of the place pressed inward drawing them into a private intimacy, so that there was a brief moment when they might have embraced. Then Elizabeth turned and walked away from him into the sunlight at the top of the hill.

The hill fort of Cadbury Castle rose five hundred feet above the Somerset landscape. The sides fell steeply among tall trees and brambles which almost hid the ancient ditches and fortifications in places. The uppermost rampart formed the perimeter of a large grassy plateau. The July sun beat down upon the two figures walking round its edge.

Elizabeth told herself that it was her duty to restore a proper decorum between herself and Edward. Of course he had not meant to say what he had said. She let him catch her up again.

'What are you going to do now that the summer is halfway over? You cannot paint pictures of Charlford ladies for the rest of your days.'

'My father used to say that the Lord will provide.'

'Your brother is less trusting in divine providence. You can't sponge on him for ever, Edward, now that you have your annuity. And are you really going to buy a horse?'

'Sermons should be left to parsons,' he said. She knew that he was irritated by her lecturing tone. 'Perhaps I should have stayed with the wedding party and listened to Robert spouting.' He thrust his hands into his pockets, spoiling the line of his claret-coloured coat. He left the outside edge of the hill and crossed the corner of the plateau, rejoining the path some way ahead; he walked moodily, pretending an interest in the vegetation on the slopes of the hill.

For a while Elizabeth trailed after him, deliberately letting the distance between them increase. Then she halted. She would ignore him. She raised a hand and put it lazily to the hair bunched against her neck, as though the weight of it wearied her. *Who hath seen her wave her hand? Or at the casement seen her stand? Or is she known in all the land, the Lady of Shalott?* She had read the poems Edward had given her over and over again, stroking the leather binding of the book and tracing the gold-tooled letters on the cover with her fingers. She felt a peculiar affinity for the doomed Lady of Shalott. Though much about Elizabeth indicated a strongly practical nature, a vein of romanticism ran through her. There were times when she wished that she had been born beautiful, or had lived in less rigid times.

She stared down into the green impenetrability of the wooded slope. She thought of the long-ago occupation of the hill. She could almost imagine she saw shadowy figures moving among the trees, and heard whispers close behind her. She broke away suddenly from the spot and crossed the gentle rise of the plateau. She sat down on the grass on the far side of the hill. She spread her knees beneath the awkward hooped petticoat, worn to be in fashion for the wedding. She flapped at the skirt's lower edge to cool herself. The heat of the sun was intense, it had made dark wet patches of sweat under her arms, and she longed to be able to discard her corset. She fanned her face with one hand and admired the smooth folds of the landscape on this more open side of the hill and the way the sun lit the soft brown stone of the houses in the village below. She raised her eyes to the expanse of fields and the horizon, trying to make out the route which they had taken that morning on the carriage drive from Charlford.

Edward was nowhere to be seen. Let him sulk, silly boy. She closed her eyes. When she opened them again and looked around, she saw him walking towards her across the slope of the plateau. Her heart jumped with an uncontrollable surge of joy. She told herself not to be foolish; she was not a naive, susceptible young girl. She reminded herself that he had been sent down from Cambridge before his banishment abroad, that he was fickle, that he was only twenty-two. But still her heart raced with anticipation as he came near.

He sat down close beside her, plucking at the lower edge of his trouser, picking off imaginary bits of grass.

'They say that this is where King Arthur had his court,' Elizabeth said with a false brightness.

'It's not very hard to imagine it. There's something mysterious about the place.'

'You feel it too?' She looked over her shoulder. 'What a strange thing the imagination is. Can't you just picture Arthur and his knights gathering on the slopes? Did they joust and make merry and hold sway over all the land from here?'

'I am at your service, my Lady.' He gave a little bow. 'And, in answer to another question, no, I am not going to buy a horse.'

She laughed and extended her hand to him. 'Good, my Lord.'

Edward took hold of her fingers with mock ceremony, as if he would press them to his lips. Elizabeth held her breath, longing for his mouth to caress her, for him to pull her against him, to touch him and strain him to her and confess that she was wildly and hopelessly in love.

She pulled her hand away. 'Fairy tales, all that business of knights and ladies. Any ancient tribe which lived here would have had to rough it. They wouldn't have had much time for chivalry.'

'You mean they were barbarians.'

'I think perhaps we are all barbarians. Society finds a way of concealing that fact to suit every age. In the old days they called it chivalry and courtly love.'

'And what do they call it now?'

'Now it's all decency, propriety, being respectable.'

'Heaven preserve us from being respectable,' he said lightly.

'I am nearer to that ideal than you are. You have achieved a degree of notoriety, if no other kind of degree, at Cambridge. And no doubt you have made a name for yourself among the ladies abroad. But what could be more respectable than remaining at Charlford? My sister gone and married, my parents growing older day by day, Robert's sermons on a Sunday.' She began to feel at ease with him again. The danger had passed and she could slip into the old familiar role. She was the friend, the surrogate older sister who had watched him grow to manhood, had wished him well at Cambridge, and made excuses for him when the older generation tutted because he had been sent down. She fell back against the grass in an inappropriately girlish, but characteristic gesture of abandon. 'Oh, how it all stifles me! Charlford is so genteel, with our well-behaved matrons and spinsters. Squire Attwell and his horses, and our very proper parson, so different from his brother.'

Her eyes were closed against the sun, one arm was flung back to shade her face. The hill was deserted except for themselves. Edward leaned towards her.

'Poor Elizabeth.'

He kissed her discreetly on the cheek. He had not meant to do such a thing. It was an impulse, foolish, unpremeditated. Elizabeth opened her eyes and they stared at one another. Slowly she put her arms round him, she grasped the silk of his waistcoat under his coat and pulled him towards her. And then Edward was on top of her, his mouth was

14

on hers, he felt the bones of her stays press hard against his ribs and the sun burning his shoulder blades through his coat. He fell upon the voluminous pink skirts as if he had been cast upon a solid but unstable sea. Elizabeth kissed him, she seemed to draw him into her with her embrace, it was passionate, immoderate, and not at all respectable. At any moment they would be locked in the sort of writhing entanglement of male and female limbs such as Edward had all too often dreamed of but, despite his continental re-education, had seen only in books, handed round in secret in his student days. He broke free from Elizabeth's searching mouth.

She whispered, 'We shouldn't be doing this,' with a despairing look which wavered in its conviction. She put the back of her hand to her mouth, as if to wipe away the guilt.

Edward shook his head in agreement, but he could not move. To roll upon the grass, to give themselves up to a wild, grappling union was intensely desirable.

Elizabeth pushed him from her. She clambered to her feet. He caught at her skirt, pulling the cool silk against his face. 'Don't go.'

'It must have been the heat. Or else the champagne.' She looked down at where he lay on the grass. 'What would they say, Edward? Your brother. My family.'

He released her skirt, letting it slide from his fingers. He had not really believed her when she had said that they were barbarians.

The wedding party was grouped, as if by an unseen and artistically prejudiced hand, around the terrace in the garden of Hannah and Fred's new home.

'Ah, there you are. There's my Lizzie. And what have you two been doing?' Henry Thorne's face was alight with a genial pleasure, an expression which would not perhaps have altered very much had he known the answer to his innocently posed question; for Henry's own youth had flourished in more permissive times.

'We have been to the very top of the hill.' Elizabeth stood behind her father's chair and rested her hands on his shoulders. She brushed at the scales of dandruff on the collar of his coat. His scalp was mottled with age under the long whisping hair, the skin seemed paper thin. She sought reassurance from the familiar feel of the cloth coat under her fingers. She must learn to be content, her future was here. She looked up and met Edward's glance from across the lawn, and was at once swamped by a wave of longing which, as it receded, swept away with it all hope of contentment. The truth was out, she thought miserably, she would never know peace of mind again.

The house was bathed in afternoon sunlight. The tophatted figure of Robert Munro stood on the terrace, as if penned in black ink against the warm stone. Edward, on the lawn, leaned against the wall of the terrace and plucked restlessly at little outcrops of grass along its topmost edge. Elizabeth's mother, in a pleasant dove-grey frock, and her Aunt Lydia, black, in bombazine, sat in the shade of a cherry tree. The women smiled at one another, and Mrs Thorne observed to her sister-in-law that the scene would make the perfect subject for a photograph, if only they had such a creature as a photographer in their midst.

'According to Elizabeth, the hill is the ancient home of King Arthur and his knights,' Edward said loudly.

'Camelot!' said Hannah, clasping her hands together. 'How very romantic!' She turned a sweet smile upon her new husband.

That this childlike innocence was a façade, a play-acting designed to flatter the male ego, and masking an intellect which was more than capable of matching her husband's, seemed to have occurred to no one except Elizabeth, whom it profoundly irritated.

'Such speculation about the past seems to my mind to be somewhat frivolous, my dear,' Fred suggested. 'Since no one can either prove or disprove the story of King Arthur.'

'An antiquarian might,' said Elizabeth, for no other reason than that to contradict Fred sometimes seemed very necessary.

Hannah sat on the lawn at her husband's feet. She rested her head tenderly against his knee, and he laid a hand upon her dark curls, as though caressing a favoured spaniel.

'The story goes,' he continued, ignoring Elizabeth's contradiction, 'that King Arthur and his court lie hidden beneath the hill. People round here say that the hill is hollow at its centre. Some of the old folk will swear they've seen Arthur's men ride by on the night of a full moon, or at the very least, that they've heard the sound of his horses in the distance.'

'What splendidly romantic times lie buried in the past,' breathed Hannah. 'All those knights in shining armour, who performed deeds of great bravery for the sake of fair ladies. The ladies waved farewell to them from the castle gates, and knew that their heroes would willingly risk life and limb for them.'

'I should risk life and limb for you, my love,' declared Fred calmly.

'Elizabeth suspects rather that Arthur and his company were a band of ruffians,' Edward said, digging at a patch of lawn with his heel.

'Elizabeth would,' said Fred with a condescending smile.

Elizabeth looked at Edward. Had it been the primitive spirits haunting the hill which had made them behave as they had, or something in their own natures? She felt an echo of the passion which had flowed and burned in her. How strangely it contrasted with her family's careful conversation, Hannah's cheek resting delicately against her husband's knee and everyone's air of pleasant affection.

Robert had finished contemplating a row of potted geraniums on the window ledge. He came slowly down the steps of the terrace. He placed his hands together, pressing the fingertips lightly against one another before he spoke, a habit he had acquired in the pulpit.

'Of course, we all know that the story of King Arthur is a myth. But we would do well to observe the code of chivalry of the knights of old. Our own present-day respect for the weaker sex, our awareness of the nobility of war, and admiration for men of valour, these are all based upon the old values.'

'I would challenge that women were the weaker sex in King Arthur's time,' Elizabeth said. She felt the blood rise to her face. She knew that to argue was out of place on this occasion, but she felt driven, as she often was, by a sense of perversity, to jar them from their complacency. 'The women would have had to fetch and carry, and scrape a living like any peasants. And I see nothing noble, Robert, about war – men hacking one another to little pieces on a battlefield.'

'Elizabeth!' Hannah wailed. 'Why do you have to spoil things so?'

'Why does everyone else have to wrap up the truth in sentiment and falsehoods?'

'Perhaps because we are not all of us so strong-minded as to be able to accept the truth as it stands, my dear Elizabeth,' said Fred.

There was an awkward silence.

Robert took out his pocket watch and studied it. 'The truth, as it stands at present, I fear, is that parish duties call me back to Charlford.' He smiled at Elizabeth, as if pleased with his diplomacy. Like a child who stands waiting to be praised, she thought, and looked away.

The party began to stir. The picturesque scene on the lawn fell into disarray as the figures fidgeted and sought out discarded shawls and hats and canes.

'What a divine afternoon we have spent!' said Elizabeth's Aunt Lydia. She readjusted her bonnet under the cherry tree, then patted Mrs Thorne's hand. 'I think Hannah has managed very well. A perfect match. They make an exquisite young couple.'

The visitors took their leave of the exquisite couple and squashed themselves into the hired carriage for the return journey to Charlford. The rumble of wheels on the road, and the sound of Lydia's voice as she gossiped about the wedding droned in Elizabeth's head. Edward sat at the front of the carriage with the driver. Elizabeth was glad, for she could avoid him while he remained there. Perhaps, after all, they would be able to forget what had happened between them on the hill.

As they reached home, a second carriage passed them in the lane. Its occupant, a square-built man of forty or so, stared as his coachman slowed the vehicle to avoid a collision. Without smiling he raised his hat; his thinning hair merged with heavy side-whiskers, his face was coarse, but handsome, and he was dressed flamboyantly in a maroon frock coat and tartan neckcloth and trousers.

'Good evening to you.'

The wedding party nodded an acknowledgement.

Aunt Lydia, excited by the fine horses and polished coachwork which had borne along the stranger, said, 'My dears! And who is that?'

'He is our new neighbour, called Mr Pengelly.' Mrs Thorne swelled a little with the importance of a piece of gossip. 'They say he's made a fortune at the goldfields in Australia and has come home to spend it all.'

Elizabeth watched the stranger turn the corner past the house.

'On loud clothes and expensive carriages, do you think?'

Edward helped her from the carriage. They avoided one another's eyes.

'Wouldn't we all, if we were wealthy enough?' he said.

3

Elizabeth lay on her bed and nibbled at a biscuit. She stared at the raised pattern of roses and intertwining leaves at the centre of the ceiling. The light breeze from the open window stirred her petticoat, she loosened the laces of her stays and closed her eyes. She was conscious of the bedcover cool against her neck, and of the warm breeze on her bare legs. She tried not to think of Edward, and the way they had kissed on the hill.

A sound of horse's hooves with the light rumble of wheels grew louder in the lane as it passed by. She heard a man's voice call to the horse when the carriage reached a steeper stretch of the lane beyond the house. The sounds drifted lazily on the air, and some familiarity about the man's voice told her that it was their new neighbour, Mr Pengelly. She allowed herself to dwell a little on Mr Pengelly's arrival in the village. It was not unusual for self-made men to aspire to the life-style of the upper classes by establishing a kind of 'country seat' far from London. Mr Pengelly, even without all the rumours of gold-digging, had the distinct look of a *parvenu*, she decided.

Men. They could be fitted into two categories. Either they were unreliable, or they were imbeciles. It was easy to tell which category Edward suited. Edward was not a steady proposition. Robert, on the other hand, was steady, but clearly an imbecile – as was her brother-in-law Fred.

She thought of Fred and Hannah alone together. For a brief moment a technically vague but intensely erotic image of her brother-in-law in a coital embrace with her sister flashed upon her mind. Her own response to Edward had been disturbing. She knew now that she had wanted that gross animal act which men and women did in shame and secrecy together, and that, while she had wanted it nothing had seemed shameful. Once, when she was a child, she had watched two dogs copulate in the lane. Her mother had run out from the garden and smothered her head against her skirts, and when she had asked what the dogs were doing she had been told that she was a wicked girl to show such a vile and unnatural interest. She had been curious about the sexual act ever since – the violence of it, so alien to the mannerisms of social intercourse between the sexes. Animals at least behaved with honesty, they mounted one another openly in the street, or in the farmyard. They didn't have to hide, and perform elaborate artifices in public.

With an effort she prevented her thoughts from sinking deeper into depravity. She sat up and looked at herself in the mirror. She raised her arms above her head and her chemise fell back at the neck and revealed white skin and the swell of her breasts. She surveyed the image before her dispassionately. She was not ugly, though her mouth was too large and her figure too heavy. She would never possess that neat delicacy and charm which constituted everyone's ideal of femininity. Edward's taste was for pretty women, like Hannah, and those fictional women who inspired in a man fine feelings, and a sense of his own superiority.

Hesitantly she put a hand to her breast and with her thumb caressed the cool skin. The face in the mirror looked back at her, like a painting, the eyes unsmiling in the white face, the hair dishevelled, falling in red-brown coils against the pale flesh of her shoulders, and the hand, sinful in its pose. Slowly she removed it. Well then, she must be content with a life devoted to duty, to doing good works, and improving her mind with morally uplifting literature, instead of the various romantic novels which she kept hidden in her dressing table drawer, and fanciful ideas about the Lady of Shalott.

She frowned at her reflection. There was a line across her breasts where her corset had bitten into the flesh. Had the Lady of Shalott worn stays? The real women of a sixth-century Camelot would have gone through life uncorseted, would have given way to the instincts of the flesh freely and without guilt. But the Arthurian ladies of fiction – and of Tennyson's poems – must they always be tightly laced, to accommodate men's preference for pale, fragile, and decorous women?

A ship in full sail, she had called herself, when Edward had said that he would paint her. A ship, however unwieldy it might be, suggested a sense of purpose. It suited her image of herself as a woman of independent mind, who did not care at all about society's conventions. A woman of character.

She pulled a face at herself in the mirror. She was a woman of plain looks and a mediocre intelligence, who had nothing to show for her thirty-one years on this earth, and no future beyond that of caring for her parents in their old age and teaching at the village school until she was dried up and embittered. The knowledge that she might grow old and die in Charlford filled her with a familiar dread. She shifted her gaze away from the woman who looked back at her from the mirror, and the evidence that time and the world were passing her by.

Edward sat with his sketch book by the river. Elizabeth lay upon the bank and watched him through half-closed eyes. He was absorbed in his drawing of her. It was not very good, she thought, with a sense of disloyalty. And he might have flattered her a little. He would never make a living from it.

The river path was deserted. The spire of the village church was the only sign of human habitation among the small rise of trees across the fields. The river moved in slow eddies. Behind Elizabeth a field of barley, the colour of toast, stood hot and dry in the sun. The hum of insects was drowsy in the air. She let her eyes close.

'No. Don't go to sleep.'

She opened them again. She wished that he would discard the sketch and lie beside her on the river-bank and kiss her, as he had kissed her before. She ached for him to touch her.

'I can't help but fall asleep. The air is so still today.'

'The atmosphere suits the drawing.'

'My Aunt Lydia doesn't approve of this,' she murmured. 'She thinks it isn't quite proper. It's not how *ladies* behave in London. She sees you as some kind of bohemian, instead of the thoroughly high-minded gentleman you nearly are. She wanted to come and sit with us.'

'Perhaps she should,' he said. 'Since you're looking particularly alluring today.'

'Edward! You know that I've never been alluring.' She felt a small sense of disappointment when he did not reply. She wriggled her shoulders against the bank. 'Hannah has been married for a whole week.'

21

'Do you miss her?'

'Terribly.'

'Poor Elizabeth.'

He fell silent. She wondered if he was remembering the last time he had said those words.

'I am so bored,' she burst out. 'I feel I'm in a cage.' She raised her head to look at him. He continued with his drawing. She let her head fall back against the grass and closed her eyes again. Her mind filled with the buzz and hum of flies and the rippling of the river by the old packhorse bridge upstream. She drifted in a state between waking and sleeping. She saw behind closed eyes the river's winding path and the shimmering of leaves. She fancied she heard the distant sound of bridle bells, knights riding two and two, like shadows in a mirror.

A deeper shadow fell across her eyelids. When she opened them Edward was leaning over her.

'You must know by now that I love you.'

She nodded. A slow certainty crept through her, a determination almost that what would happen must not be checked by any false sense of what was proper. At the same time she felt a leap of exhilaration. Her heart and her thoughts raced, united for once in their immediate objective. She wanted to draw him close to her, but she made no move to pull him down.

The small distance between them was alive with the tension of their desire. Edward's eyes searched hers desperately. 'What are we to do?'

It was Elizabeth who led the way. She rolled from him. Gathering up her skirts, she scrambled up the bank and made a pathway through the barley. She did not look round to see if he was following, she could hear that he was close behind her and knew that the same wildness was in him as had affected her. She stumbled briefly and they went then on hands and knees as they had done when they were children, gasping with laughter and excitement. The rough stalks scratched their bare hands, the smell of the dry earth filled their senses.

They flattened out a space and made a nest and collapsed into it. There they lay together, solemn now, the heads of corn all around them and the blue sky above.

'I love you,' Edward repeated.

'And I have always loved you.' She knew that it was true. She was lifted on a great tide of happiness by the hot still air of the summer's day, the earth at her back, the pure sky, the faint rustle and drowsy scent of barley and Edward, dear Edward, lying beside her. She reached her hand to caress his face, to touch the eyelashes lying against his cheeks, her fingers tracing his jaw and the smooth, boyish mouth.

He held her and kissed her lips. She could smell the warmth of his face, pleasant, masculine. The tension returned as he pressed himself close against her. For a moment their bodies seemed to swoon together, before the passion of the kiss took them over. Her mouth was locked to his with lips and tongue and wave after wave of yearning, until she felt as if she would drown with the force of it. Their limbs cloyed to one another and became interlocking parts of something infinitely more frantic and powerful. Her hands, moving across the muscles of his back through his shirt, pulled at the material and felt the damp touch of his skin, cool under the thick cotton.

Edward tore himself from her mouth, kissed her throat above the neck of her frock, her breast encased in layers of muslin and her wrists and fingers, gripping them with his own as if he were falling and she were his life-line.

She pulled him back to feed once more on the rapture of lips and tongue. She lifted her lower body to meet him and was intensely aware of that part of him which was pressed hard against the inside of her thigh. And then all was confusion, a fierce struggling with fastenings and shirt tails and trousers, his hands reaching under her, and a terrible need which made her cry out a little as she dragged at her skirts, driven to a frenzy of impatience by the folds of fabric, her only thought to draw him closer, closer.

Edward's breath came in harsh gasps. He entered her awkwardly. 'Oh, Lizzie. Lizzie!'

She grasped at his back, feeling his shirt again under her hand and twisting it to pull him to her, wanting, wanting so badly. She was shocked then by the pain. Her mind cleared and she became alert to each jerk of his body, until he lay exhausted on her. Yet still she tried to drag him closer, for there seemed no end to the want which gnawed at her. Edward rolled aside. He pulled down her skirt for her and she looked away as he covered himself again.

They lay apart without speaking.

The sky still hung above them, blue and distant. Tiny clouds passed across it. Elizabeth watched them, felt the hard earth beneath her shoulders and the barley stalks pricking and itching her back. A clamminess on her skin and the stinging soreness between her legs chilled her, though the sun burned down still. She reached out and snapped off an ear of barley.

It had been a kind of madness. She did not understand it now. Nor had she believed that it would hurt. Shame obliterated the uncomplicated need which had led to what they had done.

'Aunt Lydia would faint, and say that I'm a fallen woman.'

The words jarred. She wished that Edward would turn his face to her and say something. She pulled apart the barley ear and threw the seeds one by one into the surrounding corn.

The horror of the deed was advancing on Edward in ever more mountainous waves. His upbringing, shrouded in moral dogma, had prepared him well for an orgy of post-coital guilt. Though he had flirted with sex before, kissed and fondled a few serving maids, he knew little about women. He recalled all that he had ever heard about the depravity of females who enjoyed unnatural pleasures. It was common knowledge, that decent women might pretend a little, but they did not experience sexual desire. Decent women submitted to a man's stronger passions with a serious and tremulous heart, and then only within the confines of marriage; they found satisfaction through the gentle outlets of affection and self-sacrifice. If Elizabeth wasn't like other women, if she was of a dark and passionate nature, she would possess him, she would drain him, even his soul would be hers. If this was love, suddenly Edward wanted no part of it. He reminded himself that she was older than he was, that she would expect marriage. He told himself with a rush of male egotism that she had planned what had happened from the start. She had tried to trap him. Hannah's marriage had brought too close the prospect of spinsterhood and had made her desperate.

He turned his head to look at her. Her hair had fallen loose; it lay tumbled against the silk of her sleeve; little lines creased and drew down the sides of her mouth. He felt a rush of emotion, and a tender desire, to kiss the lines away. She avoided his eyes and began to search for the pins which had held her hair in place. He wanted to tell her that it didn't matter, that they would pretend that nothing had happened. Instead, he said,

'We ought to return to the village. Perhaps we should abandon the idea of a portrait.'

4

Elizabeth's Aunt Lydia was reminiscing about the wedding, already three weeks distant. Lydia Delahaye was a squat, well-corseted woman, fashionable even in black. She observed a strict code relating to her mourning – her husband had been dead almost two years – and she had now entered what she called her 'jet period'. Jewellery, she said, was such a solace to the wounded soul. Solace, in the form of elegant black pendants, glittered and swung from her ears and hung in coal black strings round her neck; it comforted her bosom, her wrists and fingers; the whole effect was one of massive dignity, with just a hint of being overdone.

Mrs Thorne was not listening to her sister-in-law. She had just returned from reprimanding the cook over the non-arrival of a pot of tea. She took up a position opposite the door, so that she would be the first to see when the woman appeared. She was trembling slightly. After thirty-five years of married life she still found the business of disciplining servants nerve racking.

Henry woke suddenly and noisily in his chair. After a while he said, 'Our friend hasn't been up to the house,' as if he were continuing a conversation which had just been left off. 'Edward ought to pay us a visit. He knows we need him to cheer us up. It's too quiet in the evenings, now that Hannah's gone.'

'I'm not too sure about that young man.' Aunt Lydia looked sideways at Elizabeth, who was sitting upright in a chair by the window. 'Fickle, I shouldn't wonder. The loss of his mother at an early age. And now his poor father in his grave. He has not had a steady influence on him.'

Elizabeth continued to stab silently at the wool-work on her lap. It was a square for an ottoman, it was a project at which she had been working for two years.

'Who, Lydia?' said Mrs Thorne distractedly. 'Who has lost their mother?'

Lydia was extravagantly interested in humankind. She enjoyed burdening herself with the shortcomings of others. She composed her face now in an expression of great seriousness and repeated her belief in the fickleness of Edward's character.

'He is nothing like his brother,' said Mrs Thorne. 'Chalk and cheese. But then, Robert was so much older when old Mr Munro's wife died. And Robert has such a natural respect, so much more like his dear father. He always does the parish credit. After Edward's disgrace at Cambridge, I'm sure the Church wouldn't have him.'

'He doesn't want to be like Robert and his father and go into the Church,' Elizabeth said.

They stared at her, as though they had not been aware that she could hear them.

'It's my opinion it's time that he knew what he did want,' said Lydia, and the jet pear-drop ear-rings swung importantly.

'It's time he came to see us again,' grumbled Henry. 'You just get used to a fellow calling regularly when he's home, and then he throws you over for his plummy friends in Wells.'

Elizabeth jabbed viciously at her sewing.

The cook, staggering backwards through the doorway with a tea-tray, brought a timely diversion. Mrs Booth had a lumbering rather cow-like way of walking, so that she often knocked against furniture and tables, making breakages in the Thorne household an accepted fact of life. She deposited the tea-tray with a crash of crockery on a small table.

'Tea, mam.'

The family knew that Mrs Booth was going through a 'difficult time', though the exact nature of her mid-life difficulties were never alluded to. They led however to 'moods', and the occasional bout of 'hysteria', when everyone would tiptoe round the house, resign themselves to bread, cheese and pickles for dinner, and wait for the crisis to pass.

Mrs Thorne offered Mrs Booth a tremulous smile. 'Thank you, Cook, we are very much obliged to you.'

Lydia sucked air through her teeth with a hiss of impatience.

'You should have trained her years ago,' she said, when the woman

26

had ambled from the room. 'It needs only a little attention at the right time. Now in London –'

Elizabeth interrupted. 'But we are not in London.' She got up to pour the tea. 'And poor Mrs Booth has had a great deal to do, with the wedding and extra visitors.' She handed Lydia a cup and saucer and met her eyes with a defiant stare.

'My dear, if I'm not welcome here.' Lydia pretended to look injured.

Elizabeth was not fooled. But Mrs Thorne was anxious not to offend her sister-in-law. 'You must stay as long as you wish,' she said quickly. She cast a sadly reproachful gaze at Elizabeth, who returned to her seat to stare out of the window.

'I wish our Hannah hadn't gone off,' Henry said mournfully. 'It isn't as if there aren't houses in Charlford. They could have lived here. This house is big enough. Why did they have to go so far away?'

'Fred has inherited his father's house. That must be Hannah's home now,' Mrs Thorne told him.

'Well I miss her.'

Mrs Thorne looked at her husband anxiously for signs that one of his tempers was brewing. Henry had always been a mild-mannered man, too easy-going, she realized now, to have succeeded in the hard-headed world of banking. But lately, attacks of gout had subjected him to an irascibility, alien to his nature, which seemed to frighten him into sudden outbursts of anger, for which he was always mortified afterwards.

'We all miss Hannah,' she said gently. 'But we must be grateful that she has made such a good marriage. It's her duty now to be at her husband's side and serve his needs. That is Hannah's destiny. She was our strength while she was here, but now she is Fred's helpmeet.' She sighed, affected by the sentiment of her own words. 'We must rely on Elizabeth for our strength and support now,' she added. It was a reluctant afterthought.

Elizabeth could not drink the tea on the table beside her. She had made several false stitches in the untidy needlework in her lap. She stared at the misshapen tiger lily with its wilting buds and leaves. What was her destiny? To embroider endless wool squares into her old age? To watch her father become more difficult as the years progressed, squabble with her mother, and be spinster aunt to her sister's inevitable brood of little Hannahs and Freds? Tears of frustration pricked at her eyes as she thought how she would forever move on the edge of other

27

people's lives. She stood up. She made an excuse that the tea was too hot, and escaped to her room, where she threw herself on the bed.

He had used her. And now he had deserted her for some flirt in Wells. She clenched her hands until the nails bit into the palms. She would not allow herself to feel guilty. The words with which society would judge her – trollop, harlot, whore – paraded themselves silently in her mind. Hot tears wetted her cheeks. She would not have Edward judge her in that way too. She hated him. She would make him suffer for deserting her.

The book of poems which he had given her was open on her pillow, where she had been reading it that afternoon. She lay with her cheek against its corner. The print on the page was a blur. She let the lines of Tennyson's *The Lady of Shalott* come into focus. *From the bank and from the river.* And then:

> *'Tirra lirra,' by the river*
> *Sang Sir Lancelot.*

She picked up the book and flung it across the room. She heard a crash as it hit the dressing table. The mirror, where the book had hit it, had cracked across one corner.

It was an omen, she thought. It spelled her doom.

'Mr Munro – we shall have to take you in hand, if all that I hear is true.'

The fair young woman who had spoken looked at Edward over her splayed out cards, as though peeping over the edge of a fan. She was pretty in a thin, edgy way with fine-boned hands and face.

'Several have tried, Miss Fitzroy. I fear that I'm past all redemption.'

'I have a passion for saving lost souls, and I cannot resist a challenge. My trick, I think.' She swept the playing cards on the table towards her. Her smile was bright without being warm and her laugh, though it was not loud, was brittle. 'You should come to London,' she said. 'Wells is all very fine. Staying with my very boring cousins is all very fine, but I, for one, am longing to get back to civilization.'

The musicians could be heard, tuning up in the next room. The young woman took his arm and steered him away from their companions to where there was a general movement of guests through the doorway. Edward looked round amiably for the friends with whom he had travelled to the party. Since he could not see them, he was obliged to let himself be guided by Clara Fitzroy at his side, which on that particular evening, as on previous evenings, did not seem an unattractive prospect.

'You must meet the most charming man in Wells – besides yourself, of course – Jack Harris.' She introduced him to a young man whose smile, while it was too pleasant to be called a sneer, seemed to hint at arrogance.

'Mr Harris is staying with his very boring uncle,' she pretended to confide. 'I suspect he has designs on one of my very boring cousins. Though I like to flatter myself that it's I who have lured him here, all the way from London.'

'There isn't a man in this room wouldn't follow you to the ends of the earth, my dear Miss Fitzroy,' the young man said languidly. He was dressed in a black tailcoat with an elegant white silk waistcoat. He pulled at the end of his moustache humorously with a white-gloved hand.

Clara released a delighted little peal of merriment; it was accompanied by an appropriate sparkle of the eyes and dimpling of the facial muscles, which Edward suspected she had practised in private in a mirror before giving it its public display. He was not foolish enough to mistake the performance for anything spontaneous or natural; and yet, he found himself increasingly won over by the sparkle and the dimples and the pretty, delicately featured face.

He learned that Harris had been studying medicine for a year in London, and that college life was a bit of a lark. Medicine was a lark too, if you didn't mind the gore, and didn't pay too much attention to the professors' obsessions with passing examinations.

After a while, Clara said with a sly tilt to her head, 'Well? What do you think of it for an idea?'

'I detect the beginnings of a conspiracy,' Edward responded lightly.

'But what else can you do? You say they won't have you back at Cambridge. He was sent down,' she confided to Harris. Edward suspected that the young man, with his arrogant smile, already knew this fact.

'It was a misunderstanding,' he protested. 'A doctrinal disagreement which became overheated. Anyhow, if they won't have me back at Cambridge, why should one suppose that they will receive me with open arms elsewhere?'

Harris threw him a more friendly smile. 'Never underestimate the machinations of the fairer sex, my dear fellow. It's clear that you haven't yet heard of Miss Fitzroy's famous powers of persuasion.'

'I'm learning rather quickly.'

Harris waited until Clara had gone a few paces from them and was moving with the other guests through the doorway. Then he drew Edward aside.

'Miss Fitzroy's father is a surgeon. He's not without some influence, and Clara can twist him absolutely round her finger. If she has taken it into her head to make a medical man of you, you have no choice in the matter.'

'But I've no intention of doing any such thing.' Edward adopted a smile which stated clearly that he was not going to let a mere woman take him over. At the same time, an unwelcome memory flooded through him. Guilt stabbed at his conscience, as it had done frequently since that afternoon in the barleyfield: he could not escape the fact that he had behaved badly. Yet it was more than that, there was a terrible yearning inside him whenever he thought of Elizabeth. The cure, of course, was to think of her as little as possible. But he knew that he must talk to her, explain his absence, if indeed it could be explained. The truth was that he was afraid to go anywhere near her again.

Clara had already taken her seat at the end of a row of ladies. Edward watched them, like fragile blossoms in shades of pink and mauve, bobbing and nodding to one another. Clara turned and beckoned to him. He took a seat obediently in the row behind her.

'Well?' she whispered, as the musicians struck out with the opening chord of a Mozart quartet.

'Well, what?' he replied, a little too bluntly.

'Shall I speak to my father for you, when I return to London?'

A woman sitting next to Edward shushed loudly, and he was saved from making a reply. He watched Clara's profile as the music swelled. He noticed the sweep of her eye-lashes, her straight nose, high cheeks, and prettily parted lips, and the little ringlets of golden hair against her neck. She stared straight ahead, as though she was absorbed in the music. But he knew that she was aware that he was watching her. Once, she turned her head and smiled at him, and, with a lurch of dismay, he knew what his answer would be.

5

The pale dazzle of the autumn sky filled the arched windows of the schoolroom. Beyond them was the world outside. Hannah's little house, where Hannah cherished an ideal of wedded bliss and Fred that of master in his own home. And London, where the polite world promenaded, commerce and industry bustled, and where Edward had gone to study medicine. Elizabeth gave an audible sigh. She had promised herself she would not think of him, but with so little else to think of, it was a resolve which was difficult to keep.

The appearance of Robert's face above the window ledge, like the manifestation of a disembodied ghost, startled her and struck terror into the hearts of the children before it disappeared.

'Lor', Miss. 'Tis parson, Miss,' cried out one of the girls.

An apparition worse than supernatural, thought Elizabeth. He haunted her, springing at her when she least expected it, creeping round corners. But Robert was too substantial to be a ghost, he was an ogre, who would devour her if she wasn't very careful, now that Edward had gone.

Robert came into the schoolroom and the children leapt from their benches. Elizabeth too got slowly to her feet and stood waiting for him to approach.

'Have the children been studying diligently?'

'We have all of us studied to the best of our abilities.'

'Then continue with your work, children. I have come to talk to your teacher.'

Robert motioned to her to be seated. He came to stand by her table. His back was to the children and she could see beyond his shoulder that, though their heads were bowed once again over their desks, several pairs of eyes peeped up from under their brows to observe what was going on. She frowned at this mild insurrection, her expression signalled a grim warning and the children's gazes dropped obediently to their books.

'I have just spoken to your mother,' Robert said. 'She has asked me to join you at a small family supper party next week.'

Elizabeth ground her teeth silently and composed a chilling speech to suit this latest treachery by her mother. Robert paused. She realized that he was nervous, and that he had not planned this visit to the school, but had been driven by an inappropriate sense of timing to seek her out.

'I want you to know how much I am looking forward to seeing Hannah and Fred again. It seems only yesterday that we celebrated the happy occasion of their wedding day together.'

'Three months,' Elizabeth replied discouragingly, counting, not from the date of her sister's wedding, but from the day when Edward had abandoned her.

'Yes, indeed. Three months.' Robert fingered the corner of the desk with his plump maidenly fingers. He continued in a low, urgent tone. 'Your family have always been very dear to me – Hannah, your parents, yourself.' He cleared his throat. Elizabeth looked at him with sudden alarm, and with an even greater alarm at the listening children. 'Elizabeth, there is something I had hoped to say to you. I know that, in spite of your maturity of years, you are a little outspoken sometimes. However, the Lord helps us all to correct our faults and in time, with help, I believe you could achieve meekness. It is something we could strive towards together, now that my brother has gone to London.'

'Reverend Munro,' she whispered. 'The children.'

He seemed to remember where he was. He looked confused. 'Will you think about what I have said?'

'Yes,' she returned crossly. She felt rather than saw the interest which this whispered conversation had generated amongst her pupils. Robert turned. Thirty heads cowered over their desks, apparently blind and deaf to everything except the books in front of them.

'Shall I see you in church on Sunday?'

'Yes, of course,' she hissed.

'Well then.' He raised his voice, and said without enthusiasm, 'Who is to recite their lesson for me today?'

A forest of hands rose instantly and obediently. Robert picked out an uncomplicated child, who could be relied upon to give a nearly perfect performance when a perfect performance was required. She began in a monotone.

'What is the way of God? The way of God is a good way. Who are the foes or enemies to God? Bad men are foes to God . . .'

When Robert had gone, a buzz of chatter released the tension in the room. Elizabeth allowed it to continue for some minutes. His words turned over and over in her head. *Something we could strive towards together, now that my brother has gone to London.* She felt a knot of anger tighten in her chest. She would not, could not let him continue his ridiculous pursuit. It was only a matter of time before he would propose marriage. But marriage to Robert – the idea was farcical. She did not know how it had begun.

She called for silence, and the noise subsided. She began a lesson from the blackboard and, as she turned with a piece of chalk in her hand, she saw that one of the children, Johnny Herbert, had raised his arm.

'Yes, Johnny?' The boy, slower than the others and small for his age, always aroused a protective instinct in her.

'Please, Miss. Is you a-goin' to wed Parson Munro?'

A ripple of laughter ran through the rest of the children; they smothered the sound with their hands.

'Who told you that?'

The child looked confused. 'Everyone do say so, Miss,' called out a bolder soul.

'Well then, everyone do say wrong,' Elizabeth said calmly, though the thought, that the whole village might be speculating on the outcome of Robert's advances, chilled her soul. 'And I might add that it is nobody else's business.'

The answer seemed to satisfy the children. They giggled sheepishly. That was not to be the end of the matter however. Johnny Herbert, finding a second run of confidence, gave vent to his feelings. He folded his arms across his smock. 'I did tell 'em. I said you'd never.' He gave her a shy smile. 'But I wor' afraid 'ee might.'

Elizabeth's heart went out to him.

Her mother and Aunt Lydia were sitting in the garden under an arrangement of rustic trellising, where a sickly climbing rose struggled with a virulent species of creeping vine for light and air. Mrs Thorne sidled along the stone seat like a nervous bantam shifting along a perch and signalled to Elizabeth with a little flutter of her hands to sit down next to her.

'And how were the children today, dear?'

'Weary of lessons, and plainly terrified of their vicar.' She sat down heavily between the two women and removed her straw bonnet. 'That man becomes more obnoxious by the day.' She began pulling at a bunch of rosehips which she had attached to the bonnet that morning.

Lydia sighed, as though pained by a burden of immense gravity. 'You really must try to cultivate more charm in your manner, dear,' she advised. Both Lydia and Mrs Thorne frequently used the term 'dear' when talking to Elizabeth. It had nothing to do with a warmth of feeling, nor even convention; but it was laden rather with irritation; in a small way it relieved their exasperation over Elizabeth's disregard for what was expected of her.

'That is no way to talk about a clergyman. You might have said that the Reverend Munro was rather disagreeable today, or something of the kind.'

'But he was obnoxious. He is always obnoxious.' Elizabeth tossed a rosehip into the trellising. 'How could you ask him to supper, Mother? You know he'll sit there making sheep's eyes at me all evening.'

'He's an old friend. Not to see Hannah on her first visit home? It's almost as if he were one of the family.'

Elizabeth looked at her suspiciously. 'Never that,' she said, with more vigour than she had intended. 'Creeping about after me, frightening the children with his tales of hellfire if they can't reel off religious dogma like a railway timetable. You won't push me into marrying him.'

'Has he asked you?' Lydia said in mock surprise. 'You will never marry, dear, if you do not, in the end, learn to cultivate a more feminine manner.'

'Then I prefer the idea of spinsterhood.'

'I'm sure you do not,' Lydia murmured with a tolerant smile. 'Still hankering after his brother, I suppose.'

'I don't hanker.' Elizabeth momentarily hated the dumpy, energetic figure at her side. 'I have never hankered,' she lied.

'You harbour romantic notions, in spite of a pretence at indifference to the marriage game. You must face the facts, Elizabeth. You're no longer in the first flush of youth, and you're ten years older than he is.'

'Nine.'

'There you are then.'

Mrs Thorne was twisting one of the trailing ends of her lace cap between her fingers. 'Robert may be all there is, now that Edward is gone.'

'Then I shall be happy to forgo all there is,' Elizabeth said automatically. She felt trapped and distressed. Lydia and her mother's words filled her with panic.

'What about your inheritance?' Lydia pursed her full lips in a way that was meant to add emphasis to the point. 'It obviously never occurred to your Uncle Willie when he disposed of his money, God rest his soul, that either you or Hannah would end up an old maid.'

Mrs Thorne stifled a wail and wrung the lace lappet of her cap to a piece of rag. Lydia had hit upon the two subjects which caused her the deepest distress: death and money. The death of her only brother Willie, lost at sea fifteen years earlier, was still particularly painful. And money – in this case a settlement of seven hundred and fifty pounds each on Hannah and Elizabeth upon their marriage – seemed to her to be an inexpressibly vulgar subject for women to be discussing.

'You haven't told Robert about Uncle Willie's money!' Elizabeth turned accusingly on her mother who shook her head with a little nervous movement and looked as though she might soon begin to cry.

'I only wish I had had an uncle as mindful of my welfare as to leave me such an inducement to a prospective bridegroom,' continued Lydia. 'Though in my case it wasn't necessary. Mr Delahaye always said that he was so captivated by my face and figure that he would have married me even if I had been penniless.' Lydia's declaration was a faithful adherence to a memory that was perhaps more imagined than real.

'I thought you were practically penniless,' said Elizabeth with a half-hearted attempt at revenge. She threw the last of the rosehips to the ground and stared at the little heap of berries. Their lustre was dulled. They had begun to shrivel. They would still have been hanging in the hedgerow if she had not picked them, warm and shiny in the afternoon sun. And now there was going to be a quarrel.

Lydia had drawn herself up to her full, rather insignificant height. 'If I was penniless, it was because of the gross mismanagement of my brother.' She cast a withering glance at Mrs Thorne. Henry, who had run his family's banking business hopelessly into the ground in the twenties, had made no financial provision for his younger sister. 'Thank goodness, I secured in Mr Delahaye – God rest his soul – a man of means. A man almost related to the nobility. The *French* nobility.'

Mrs Thorne had begun to tremble. 'Oh, Elizabeth. Now look what you've done. Your poor father.'

'I am sorry. It must be said, though he is my own flesh and blood,' continued Lydia, 'Henry has always been an incompetent. You were fortunate you were left with this house and your father's pension, Frances. Or else, where would you have been? On the parish, that's where. And you, Elizabeth,' she rounded on her suddenly, 'should be looking to your future.'

Having started the quarrel, Elizabeth did not now have the will or the energy to enter fully into battle. She got up from the seat with an air of resignation. 'I wish to goodness Uncle Willie had left all of his money to Hannah, or to you, Mother. I'm sure I don't want it. And I don't want a husband either. It's getting chilly,' she said. 'I'm going indoors to read to Father.'

6

Edward told himself that he should never have become a medical student. He was too squeamish. Even the stench of privies and soil heaps, or the sight of dead dogs and cats revolted him. He watched the surgeon in his blood-caked frock coat strutting and pacing before the ranks of students, who waited with that strange mixture of fear and excitement which always preceded an amputation.

Fitzroy was in predictable form, explaining in detail the complications which had arisen from his earlier attempt at a resection of the knee-joint: sepsis of the wound, morbidity, putrefaction of the connective tissue. Not that he was a natural botcher. He had a reputation for being one of the best surgeons in London.

The man on the table below had not been reassured by reputations. Some students had laughed nervously as he fought with the attendants, until the sickening sweetness of the chloroform had muffled, then silenced his cries.

Edward prayed for inner steel against that first cut of the surgeon's knife. A wave of nausea from the ever-present smell of blood in the theatre warned him that he had dismissed too lightly the effect of one of Harris's boozy parties the night before. It wasn't his fault, he would tell them, when they picked him up off the floor, making light of it: 'Not my fault, chaps. Always had a delicate stomach.'

There were always some students who could not take it. They usually dropped out in their first term and were considered to be something of a joke among Edward's new circle of friends. Not that Edward minded a joke, or the carelessly ribald talk among students about the inner workings of the human body. He had already earned a reputation for facetiousness in this respect. And he had learned to conquer his horror of the dissecting room, where at least the inmates had the good fortune to be dead. What he had not been able to overcome was an increasing dread of the surgeon's knife slicing into warm flesh.

Fitzroy stood poised, a half-smile on his face, like an actor about to reward his audience with a favourite scene from a melodrama. Edward wiped the palms of his hands on his trousers. Suddenly he knew that this time he was going to be sick. He stood up and swayed on his feet, and a low cheer rose from the ranks of students. The noise increased in volume as he thrust his way to the end of the row of seats. Dear God, let him get outside, let him not make an exhibition of himself before he left the theatre.

'Sit down, Mr Munro!' roared the surgeon. 'We are all aware, Mr Munro, of your irrepressible desire to keep us entertained.'

Edward hesitated. But a last glance at the leg, bloated and putrid on the table below, sent him lurching to the door. His fellow students stamped and applauded and called out to him. He flung a wave in their direction and escaped from the theatre, clutching exaggeratedly at his stomach.

Outside the hospital, the smell of London on a warm October morning, intensified by the stench from the river and the nearby slaughterhouse, was not pleasant. He leaned heavily against the wall and discharged his breakfast on to the pavement. 'Good old Munro,' they would be saying. 'Always ready for a lark.' The reputation had grown quickly, but it was one which was becoming difficult to sustain.

He rubbed his arms, feeling cold. A girl walked slowly by him on the edge of the pavement. She was dressed in a dirty print frock which was several sizes too large for her. She could not have been more than thirteen. She stopped a few yards from him and turned to see if he was still standing there. She walked back. She did not look at him until she drew level, then she raised her eyes in a question.

'Go away, my dear. I've no money for you,' he said in a manner he imagined Robert might have adopted in one of his more charitable moments. He felt uneasy, and sorry for the girl.

A grin restored a brief flicker of innocence to the child's face. Edward smiled. He turned out an empty pocket in his coat with an elaborately rueful gesture.

'Don' matter,' the girl said. 'Got a 'ankerchief? Or a necktie? Go on,

38

sir. I bin with medical gen'lemen afore. You needn't worry, sir. I ain't got nothin' bad.'

Edward doubted the truth of this assurance, particularly if, as she said, she had been with medical students. He shook his head, and a mixture of sympathy and irritation crossed his face. The girl stopped flaunting her thin body. Her eyes emptied of expression, and she turned away from him and crossed the street. She did not look back. Her secondhand shoes flapped at the heels as she went, making a slapping noise on the stones.

Edward watched her. He wanted to call after her, to give her his necktie or the handkerchief in his pocket, but he did neither. He could taste the sour smell of London with the after-taste of vomit in his mouth. It filled him with a disgust which he could not identify so easily as the nausea he had felt in the hospital. Child prostitutes were a common enough sight, and not confined to cities. The encounter was a reminder, however, of man's baser instincts, and, for Edward, of a more specific guilt.

There was a despair about his mood which he found hard to analyse; except that he knew now that he did not want to be a doctor, any more than he had wanted to go into the Church. He did not want to be in London. Above all, he did not want to be confronted with the sick and hopeless who resorted to the charity of the college hospital. The sights he had seen there had begun a process of disillusionment with society. It was a disillusionment which came all the harder, since he had never before troubled himself with questions of social injustice. In London, he found himself increasingly disturbed by the kind of soul-searching questions which come to most people at some stage in their lives, but which had arrived uninvited in Edward's conscience. He thought of Charlford with a naive longing, and was torn by images of Elizabeth. Did she think just a little fondly of him still? It was a silly, sentimental idea. If she thought of him at all, it would be with loathing. They would have cut the barley in the field by now. The scene of their guilt would have disappeared. He wished that he could excise it as cleanly from his mind.

He shook off the threatening melancholy and made his way to a coffee house in the Strand. The proprietor, wielding a large knife and chopping great wedges from a loaf of bread, reminded him discomfortingly of the scene he had recently left at the hospital. He was going to have to apologize for his swift departure from Fitzroy's

39

performance and he did not relish the interview: the surgeon had a reputation for being as swift with his tongue as he was with the knife.

He met Fitzroy by accident later that day in one of the hospital corridors. It was too late to pretend that he had not seen him, and Fitzroy seemed to be as intent on cementing the encounter as Edward was on trying to avoid it. Edward began to blurt out an ineffectual apology, but the man ignored him. He flung open a door close by.

'Come in here, and stop your dithering. Can't hear a bloody word you're saying.'

Edward sat uneasily in a chair on one side of a huge desk. He was afraid of the surgeon. Most new students were. He was a large, red-faced man, over six feet tall, and more reminiscent of a costermonger than of someone who moved in respectable society and had an elegant wife, and a fashionable and much sought-after daughter.

Fitzroy perched on a corner of the desk in a disconcertingly jaunty manner. Then, as though he was aware that his presence was still too overpowering, he removed himself to a chair and leaned across the desk, folding his arms. He smiled coldly.

'Are you happy with us, Munro?'

Edward could not tell whether, with some rare insight, Fitzroy was aware of his depressed spirits, and so his attitude was designed to be paternal in its concern; or whether, and more probably, the question was a gentle prelude to the too familiar subject of rustication.

'Because if you're not,' the surgeon continued, 'the college could thrive very well without you. I might go so far as to say that the college should not be too sad to see you go.'

'I'm sorry, sir.' Edward said automatically.

Fitzroy clicked his teeth impatiently and leaned back in his chair. He said nothing for several seconds.

Edward felt increasingly uncomfortable. There seemed to be more than his hasty departure from the operating theatre on Fitzroy's mind.

'Why did you decide to study medicine – apart from the fact that, when my daughter met you and took it into her head to adopt you as a cause, it didn't seem a bad idea?'

Edward flinched. His flirtation with Clara Fitzroy had lasted only a few weeks, a little longer than it had taken for them to discover their mutual mistake.

'I don't know why,' he lied. He remembered Robert's response to his decision, a mixture of relief that he would be out of the parish and off his hands, and distaste at the prospect of having a medical man in the family. 'My father was a parson, until he retired through ill-health many years ago. He always wanted me to enter the Church. My brother has the living of a parish in Somerset. It was always expected that I would follow in the family tradition.'

'I've heard that you were sent down from Cambridge.'

'I wasn't exactly thrown out, sir. Aspects of Church thinking seemed to me to be so much humbug. The question of eternal damnation, for instance.' It all sounded rather sober. He was a free-thinker, a radical. It was the first time he had put a name to his weariness of the dry studies at Cambridge.

'The way I heard it, Munro, you spoke your mind at the wrong time, and in the wrong place. Greater men than you have gone under for similar heresies. Perhaps it would have been better if you hadn't thought fit to express your own very personal view about the eternal damnation of a very eminent fellow of the university.'

Fitzroy smiled unexpectedly. The gesture was startling, not to say alarming with its display of tobacco-stained teeth. He leaned forward.

'You know, I had a fear of the knife once. Just the same.'

Edward was further unnerved. He had thought that Fitzroy had interpreted his departure from the theatre as a piece of clowning.

'You have to learn to harden your mind,' the surgeon said.

'I don't think I'm a born doctor, sir.'

Fitzroy clicked his teeth irritably again. 'And what is that supposed to mean, man? That's the sort of hocus-pocus we give to the patients. A doctor can't claim to have been born into medicine. He has to learn, as in any other profession, to become what society expects of him. He is a communicator, a repository of scientific and practical knowledge. But above all, he has to learn to hide his own nature and perform a role. Shall I tell you why I became a surgeon?' Edward nodded feebly, wishing that the interview would come to an end. But Fitzroy was already embarking on his life history. 'I was a sickly child. I saw more than was good for any boy of physicians and quacks. Dyspepsia, that was all it was.' He burped, as if at the memory. 'But the family physician used to be sent for without fail after every bilious attack. He once gave me a book about physiological chemistry – my father was a Calvinist, he believed that any book which wasn't the Bible was the work of the Devil. I read the damn thing from cover to cover, just to spite him.'

Edward smiled at this reflection of his own childhood. Fitzroy seemed encouraged to continue.

'This medical chappie used to tell me stories about the great surgeons who lived in Edinburgh and London, who rode about in carriages, and could earn thousands of pounds a year. I vowed, there and then, I'd come to London and be a surgeon. These were the things which set me on the path to medicine, Munro – childhood dyspepsia, and a lust for money.'

'But I don't really want all that, sir. The fame. The flower-in-the-buttonhole.'

'It doesn't matter what your motive is. That's what I'm trying to din into your numbskull. I soon forgot my ambition to be a great man. I discovered that medicine was fascinating for its own sake. And what happened? I gained a reputation for being a splendid surgeon and driving around in a carriage none the less.' He beamed and nodded, inviting Edward to share in the joke.

Edward smiled, as though he was grateful for the homily. He wondered briefly why Fitzroy had singled him out for this fatherly encouragement. Mad Fritz, the students called him. They said that at the end of the day his frock coat was so stiff with his patients' blood that it stood up on the floor unaided when he took it off. They said that if anyone should ever have the temerity to operate on him, they would find that iced water ran in his own veins. Edward believed himself insignificant among the crowd of students who had begun their first term under Fitzroy's guidance. As the younger son of a country clergyman, he was not quite deserving of the coveted description 'gentleman'. If he qualified as a doctor, he would detach himself from that dubious honour still further. He would be an underpaid medic to some sick club or poor law union, or else a general practitioner, handing out bottles of physic and pills, powders and mustard plasters. He saw now, all too clearly, the future towards which Clara Fitzroy had innocently precipitated him.

He wondered bleakly if his heart could ever be in anything. The motives which had influenced him until now had always been to do with convenience and the easy way out. He did not even know any more what could make him acknowledge that he was happy. Academic success? Fulfilment through the love of a good woman? Certainly not through Clara Fitzroy, nor, since his experience with Elizabeth, through any of the pretty women with whom he had imagined himself in love from time to time.

'I have watched you,' Fitzroy was saying, 'because my daughter seemed to think that there was something rather remarkable about you.' Edward allowed himself to feel temporarily flattered. 'The fact that you are no more remarkable than the next young man and that she now doesn't want to know you from Adam is neither here nor there. I watched you. And I saw a young man who spends too much time entertaining his fellows. But I suspect you have ability. Don't waste it.'

'I cannot bear the sight and smell of blood,' Edward confessed. 'I don't think I shall ever get used to it.'

'Close your eyes. You will, man. We all do. But I meant it, when I said that we shan't hesitate to let you go if necessary. You are on trial, Mr Munro.'

The interview seemed to be over. Edward rose, appropriately chastened, from his seat and made for the door.

The surgeon called after him. 'And don't waste your time mooning after Clara. If she hadn't put an end to the business, I'd have done it for her. I'm not allowing my daughter to fall in love with a bloody medic.'

Edward smiled briefly and closed the door. But it was not of Clara that he was thinking. It was as if he suddenly saw Elizabeth, looking at him reproachfully. 'Love?' she seemed to say. 'I know you. I know now exactly what you wanted from me. And it wasn't love.'

'It isn't true,' he wanted to tell her. But the words echoed hollowly in his mind.

7

For once Edward did not enjoy the music hall performance at the Canterbury that evening. The comic songs seemed too grotesque, the humour was too contrived to merit the exaggerated laughter which rose, almost as though forced by desperation, from the audience. He looked at the figures around him: his friend Harris haw-hawing foolishly at his side, the laughing, joking men and women, all flushed with drink and well-being, a few whores among them, either with an eye to finding a customer, or already in possession of their gentleman for the evening. He felt that a great gulf separated him from the people around him. 'Society is immoral,' he murmured with the pious deliberation of one who believes himself the first to discover the truth behind a familiar truism.

Harris heard the remark and looked at him quizzically; he was aware that Edward had consumed more than his usual amount of porter that evening. Jack Harris wore his arrogance with ease. He was of that class which did not need to question its position in life. His father was a Harley Street physician, his brothers, all three, were officers in the Guards. Harris's future, unlike Edward's, was secure; he would inherit his father's practice in due course. Edward envied him his acceptance of the status quo.

'Where next?' Harris said as they pushed their way through the crowded foyer. Edward, still preoccupied with questions of morality, said gloomily that it was all the same to him, he was out of funds anyway.

'Why did you decide to study medicine, Jack?' he said.

'Didn't fancy the Guards, dear fellow. Scarlet don't suit me. And, I suppose, I fancied earning more than five hundred a year. Fleecing

44

a duchess or two for repairing her bunions seems a very acceptable way of getting into the best society to me.' They had reached a quieter space near the stairway.

'Perhaps we are all affected by selfish interests,' said Edward. 'How many of us really care about those poor devils at the hospital, for instance?'

'Very true, dear fellow,' Harris said over his shoulder. He began to push towards the door. 'Greed. It's what makes the world go round. I say, it's a bit crowded tonight. It's not going to be easy to get a hansom.'

'This generation will be remembered for its worship of mammon,' Edward said with the exaggerated bitterness of the drunk. 'What do we all want? The five hundred pounds minimum a year? The private brougham? The house in the right area? And, of course, the genteel but not too cloying, educated, but not too intelligent, beautiful, but not too expensive, lady-wife.' He averted his eyes from the prominently displayed bust of a woman in a red dress who had been thrown up against him in the doorway.

'I know what all this is about,' said Harris, when they at last flung themselves into a cab. Edward sat hunched in his coat and stared out of the window. 'You are in the dumps because the fair Clara has decided you are not, after all, her knight in shining armour.'

'She says I have no ambition. She's right. I don't know what I'm doing here. Do I really want a string of rich, hypochondriac clients to my name? Or to be lecturing over some poor devil who will perish from hospital gangrene, like Mad Fritz, with a reputation for bullying students?'

'Sounds agreeable enough to me. I'm all for getting our own back.'

'I'm in earnest,' Edward said. Drink had made him aggressive.

'Well, it don't suit you. What's happened to you, Edward? You're no fun lately, and that's a fact. What about a stroll along the Haymarket? See what's what among the ladies. Only looking, of course.'

Edward nodded. He turned again to the window, taking in the scene of darkened buildings, flaring gaslights, and the shadowy figures which moved between colour and darkness outside the cab. Was the whole fabric of existence built on self-interest? Harris was in search of a fat income, like the rest of his class, like most lesser mortals too, given a chance. Fitzroy was a great surgeon because of a surfeit of indigestion and greed. And he had chosen to become a doctor because of a pretty face and a persuasive tongue, and because he had run away from

Elizabeth. Men married women for their looks, or their money, or their virtue and their housekeeping abilities; they did not marry the kind of woman who offered her body before all other considerations. It was too frightening, to discover that he had fallen in love – not with some suitably pretty and compliant female, but with a woman who was plain-featured, strong-willed, and passionate.

He saw that Harris was grinning at him, his teeth flashing in the sudden flare from a lamp on the pavement.

'Penny for them, dear fellow.'

Edward shook his head.

The lights of the city flickered from over the river as they crossed the dark swell of the Thames.

'What about the Punchbowl?' Harris said. 'It's early yet. Pay me back next week.'

Edward sighed. Then he imitated the jaunty tilt of Harris's hat and grinned. The bravado was artificial, but it was enough to dispel the mutual unease which had settled in the cab.

'You need some naughty entertainment. Something to take your mind off things. My opinion is that a certain Miss Fitzroy knocked you over more than you'll admit.'

'Why did God invent women, Jack?' It was a question Edward frequently posed and Harris had heard it before. One way or another, thought Edward, women had made a hash of his life.

'They exist merely for our admiration and delectation, my dear fellow,' Harris said. 'The good Lord certainly never intended that we should take them seriously.'

There was a supper room at the back of the Punchbowl tavern. The atmosphere was thickened by clouds of tobacco smoke which hung in the yellow air like a choking London smog. The customers, exclusively male, talked in subdued voices over their oysters and kidneys. The impression at first was of having entered some gentlemen's club. Polished mahogany-topped tables, red plush seats, and a lavish display of gilt and glass lent the room a sense of elegant decadence. There was no suggestion of the more indelicate aspect of the Punchbowl's reputation, either in the clientele, or, to the innocent ear at least, in the proceedings on the platform at one end of the room, where a girl was singing about the attractions of her garden.

46

Most young men in Edward's circle of friends found it desirable to cultivate a reputation for being 'fast'. Had he and Harris wanted to visit a brothel, they could have chosen any one of a number of more obvious establishments than the Punchbowl, which jostled cheek by jowl in Piccadilly and St James's. But Edward was frightened of total debauchery. To be seen at well-known dives with a hint of notoriety about them – the Cyder Cellars, the raffish Green Bower tavern in Holborn, or the Punchbowl – was enough to supply the required racy reputation, without disturbing too much a conscience beset by deep-rooted ideas of guilt and sin.

Edward blundered after Harris through a confusion of noise and light and sank into a chair. A student colleague nearby commented briefly, 'You've missed almost all the fun.'

'Plenty of legs to see. Stunning costumes,' added the man's companion, a lank-haired youth who was a clerk in the city, and who felt his lowlier status keenly. He eyed the newcomers with an interest tinged with envy before he returned his attention to the platform.

The girl had come to the end of her song and was bowing and curtseying to the applause. Her frock swept the stage, revealing nothing of her legs and ankles, though the bodice of her costume was cut low at the front to show off her bosom. Her face was pretty, very white, with high spots of colour painted on her cheeks and lips. Her smile was that of a doll, fixed and staring, as she twisted and turned, and blew kisses to right and left.

Edward leaned back in his chair and watched her, drawn uneasily to the swell of her breasts in the tight bodice.

Harris commented. 'I don't believe this one's got legs. She's on castors.'

Edward joined in the laughter. He took another unsteady swig from the glass of champagne which had been set in front of him and the lights of the room swung violently as he returned the glass to the table. The feeling of being tipsy was vaguely unpleasant. He felt hot and dizzy. It seemed that his head would burst with the throb of feet stamping on the wooden floor and fists beating out a tattoo on the tables.

He shouted with unexpected vigour, 'Have you got any legs then, my love?'

The girl at once flicked the hem of her skirt to reveal booted ankles and a glimpse of white legs. Edward hooted his approval along with

47

the shouts of others further down the room. The girl left the stage. He saw her, bobbing like a coloured ball among the seated customers, before she disappeared through a doorway under the gallery. He received the congratulations of his companions, smiling as though he had been excessively clever. Almost immediately he felt a chill of shame creep upon him.

'I suppose you all get blasé about women. Women's bodies, that is,' said the clerk. 'I mean to say, you must see everything at the hospital.' He flushed at his own coarseness.

'They're usually dead,' said Edward. 'It's not the same.'

He was beginning to feel ill. He wondered whether to recount an anecdote from one of the anatomical lectures about female generative organs, and thought better of it. Harris and the student next to him would have heard it, and he doubted whether, in his present drunken condition, he would remember it to the finish for the clerk's doubtful benefit.

There was a time when he had known nothing about female anatomy. When he was a boy women had been mysterious creatures, bound round with stiff bodices and heavy skirts which smelled of old cupboards and hid their legs; the question of whether females really had legs had been a serious problem in those days.

He had already gained a reputation among his fellow-students for being a bit of a devil where women were concerned, fuelled largely by his early success with Clara Fitzroy. But, though Clara had teased and flirted, she kept her lovers at a very proper arm's length. That afternoon in the barleyfield with Elizabeth, instinctive and fumbling, had been his first and only experience of carnal love, and it had left him with only a vague notion of those dark, shrouded places beneath a woman's skirts. His real education had been conducted in the hospital theatre, in the dissecting room, and through the descriptive powers of the professor of anatomy. The brutality of the instruction filled his nights with warped and terrifying dreams. Elizabeth would come to him, opened with a surgeon's knife, or rising from among the rows of cadavers. He would wake and cry out, soaked with sweat, weeping for forgiveness.

'The entertainment ain't bad tonight,' Harris was saying. 'Haven't seen anything so artistic since the Red Lion. Have we, Edward, dear fellow?'

Edward no longer noticed what was happening on the stage. He sat

48

with his eyes half-closed against the light. The room had become a nightmare of noise and colour, full of smoke and sallow leering faces.

A number of women, dressed in a bawdy corruption of French peasant costume, were moving among the diners. The girl who had raised her skirt at Edward's request was leaning over him. She whispered something against his ear. He half understood that she was offering to take him to a room upstairs. He could smell her body, a sour hint of sweat mixed with the strong odour of cheap scent. Her skin was as white close to as it had been on the stage. She smiled at him and he could read contempt in her eyes behind the bright gash made by her teeth and lips. She sat herself on his knee and he wondered how many men she had had in her short life. He put his arms round her waist, disturbed to find himself aroused by the pressure of her body as she leaned more heavily against him. He told himself bitterly that the instinct was the same, the flicker of lust he felt for a whore was the same as the feeling which had been roused in him by Elizabeth. He saw now that his presence at the Punchbowl was a sham. He should be wallowing in the filth of the lowest lodging house in Whitechapel, where he could purge himself of Elizabeth and be done with it. He opened his mouth to speak. He had some intention perhaps of conveying thoughts of a deeply sober nature to the girl, now leaning with her arms twined about his neck and curling strands of his hair round her fingers, while she conducted a line of patter with Harris next to him. He knew that he must be drunk, but it was as if he was caught in a nightmare and could not move. The room swam in a haze before his eyes. A vision of a clean landscape opened out before him, long fields of barley, a winding river. He longed to be there, lying with Elizabeth in the yellow field under a blue sky. He would ask her to forgive him and he would tell her how he had never stopped loving her since that day, and she would smile and, like a mother, comfort him and tell him that the world was a safe and pleasant place again. There was a rushing in his ears. He thought he could hear the river, fast-flowing, swollen. The sound grew louder.

His head hit the table with a thud which shook the champagne glasses and drew a burst of laughter from those sitting near as the girl was flung sideways on to Harris's lap.

'Now there's ingratitude for you,' complained Harris. 'A fellow drinks himself silly at another fellow's expense, and then expects a fellow to get him home.'

8

Elizabeth's sister Hannah had acquired a gratuitous, if false glamour through her marriage. She was now the wife of a respected, albeit country solicitor. She was mistress of a household, with three servants. Her purpose in life was to smooth the path of Fred's career: she had achieved justification for her existence.

Elizabeth wondered if she envied her and decided, after a few days reunited in her sister's company, that she did not. She saw, in the way that Hannah followed Fred with her eyes, echoed his most banal opinions, spoke constantly of their house and its new furnishings and fell into that irritating affectation of sweetness, that she had already surrendered her individuality to her husband's prejudices. If she ever suspected that she had merely exchanged one form of imprisonment for another, Hannah would be quite content to be so incarcerated.

Hannah, delicate throughout their childhood, charming and quick to court attention, had been the favourite with their mother because of her docility, What can be more endearing than a good child? Elizabeth had not begrudged her the attention. Nor had she minded when, at Monsieur Ellabert's Classical and Commercial Day Seminary for Young Ladies, Hannah had overtaken her in all subjects. But Hannah had learned quickly to moderate her accomplishments, limiting herself to a brilliance at the piano and at needlework and playing down her achievements in mathematics. Once, when Elizabeth had speculated upon her one day becoming a famous mathematician, Hannah had said quietly,

'I would rather you didn't mention the idea beyond these four walls.'

She had been seventeen and had fallen in love with a land surveyor, a dull man, vaguely related to Squire Attwell's family.

'Men don't like clever women,' she had explained. 'Women are marked out for a different function in life than exploring mathematics, Lizzie. I see no point in it any longer.' And from then on she had ceased to interest herself in academic study. Instead she had cultivated the art of femininity, involving demonstrations of sentimentality over children and the Poor, sunsets and flowers, and a recognition of male superiority and family duty. The dull surveyor had been superseded by an equally dull clergyman. And then Fred had appeared on the scene, swept her to his dull but manly bosom, and offered her a life where she need never think for herself again.

Growing up, the sisters had not been close. Now that Hannah had acquired the mystique of the married woman, the estrangement seemed complete.

One day, during Hannah and Fred's visit, the two sisters spent some time together, sorting boxes of linen for Hannah to take to her new home. They were busy for more than an hour, folding sheets and tablecloths, stacking them on the bed in Hannah's old room, and dusting out and lining a trunk. Elizabeth was aware of a preoccupation in Hannah's manner. An occasional frown of distress would cross her face, her lower lip would tremble and she would bite it and then sigh, as if inviting an inquiry.

Elizabeth obliged her at last. 'What's the matter?' She handed her a folded set of pillow cases.

'Nothing. You know that I've never been happier.' Hannah's blue eyes filled and grew large with tears. She began dropping piles of linen randomly into the trunk. After a while she said, 'Just be thankful, Lizzie, that you will probably never know how true it is that women are born for suffering.'

Elizabeth tried to puzzle out the meaning of this cryptic remark. 'Surely Fred isn't cruel to you?' she said at last.

'No. He's a good husband. He's kind. He's very respectful of my feelings.' This time the tears threatened to fall.

'Then what is it?' Elizabeth thrust a pile of linen doilies roughly into Hannah's hands.

Hannah began to sob with great hiccups, which were wrenched from her until at last she managed to say,

'I think he sometimes seeks female company elsewhere.'

'A mistress?' Elizabeth threw a sheet into the trunk, it hit the lid and fell in a heap in one corner.

'I don't know.'

Elizabeth felt a ghoulish curiosity amidst her outrage, for it was as difficult to picture Fred in the arms of a mistress as it was to imagine that he might beat Hannah – or worse. 'But you're only just married,' she protested.

Hannah continued to weep without any sound, the tears flowing down her cheeks in her shame. She let the doilies in her hand fall and they scattered on top of the linen in the trunk. Elizabeth watched her helplessly.

'I hoped to be everything to him. I thought that I could make him happy. I see now, it's not enough just to be a good wife. There are things –' she lowered her voice almost to a whisper '– to do with the bedroom, which are so distasteful to me, Lizzie. If only you knew. Men, they have such strong passions. We women can't understand the temptations which afflict a man, even the kindest of men, like Fred. I can't hate him for it. I don't think he's any different to other men, in that darker side of his nature. It's his burden.'

Elizabeth ignored this demonstration of wifely charity. 'Have you any proof that he's unfaithful?' she said in the manner of one getting down to business.

Hannah blanched at the lack of delicacy of the question. She shook her head. 'He sometimes goes to London. To meet with clients, he says. But I know, Lizzie, a wife knows these things –' She began to weep again, quite loudly this time, so that Elizabeth was afraid that she would break down completely and alert the whole household to the crisis.

She was not surprised that Hannah's willingness to please could not convert to passion in the privacy of the bedroom. She remembered their mother's grim warnings during their growing years, her allusions to the humiliation of the marriage bed. Life was duty and suffering: it was the creed all women learned from birth. It was not feminine for a woman to desire anything for herself. A woman should strive to display a simpering fragility in public; in private, she must remain unassertive and surrender to her husband's desires with the stoicism of the spiritually self-sufficient. Woman was the weaker sex, pure, innocuous, wanting nothing for herself but martyrdom. This was the ideal.

Elizabeth had not believed it then, she did not believe it now.

'You must confront Fred.'

Hannah stared at her in horror. 'How could I?'

'It's the only way. There must be honesty between men and women. If it was me I would settle for nothing less.' She remembered Edward's treachery. In the end, he too had expected women to conform to an accepted pattern. She threw the last of the linen into the trunk and slammed shut the lid. 'There must be no pretence, no lies, no false respect, or play-acting.'

Hannah shook her head. She dried her face on a fold of her frock. She became calm.

'You know nothing about how it is between men and women, Lizzie.'

The guest list for the supper party to celebrate Hannah and Fred's homecoming had expanded to include Squire Attwell and his wife, also Miss Hemingale, the Sunday school mistress, Dr Molesworth, the antiquated local practitioner, and the newcomer to Charlford, Mr Pengelly. Lydia had suggested that, since the new neighbour was clearly a man of substance and laden with his winnings from the goldfields, the family should make his acquaintance at the earliest opportunity. 'One never knows where it might lead,' she had said with an astute nod of the head in Elizabeth's direction.

A visiting card had been duly delivered to Mr Pengelly's house, closely followed by an invitation to supper. His acceptance had been returned by a manservant.

Mr Pengelly now sat opposite Elizabeth, dark and heavy-jowled, but with an intelligence about his brown eyes. He was dressed in a dark wool coat and a rather too extravagant waistcoat to fit the occasion. He spoke little at first, and there was an air of reserve about him, which could have been taken for diffidence, discourtesy even. Elizabeth speculated briefly on there being a murky secret behind the unpromising exterior. Some criminal activity had forced his trip to Australia, or an adulterous indiscretion had made him flee from England. Since Hannah's revelations about Fred, adulterous indiscretions had not been far from Elizabeth's thoughts.

She could not look Fred in the eye. She found herself watching him when he spoke or moved, looking for proof of a debauched and lecherous spirit. Fred's body was muscular and well-proportioned.

Those features which she had previously dismissed as uninteresting – a blandness about the face, a coldness of expression – now seemed to disguise a hidden voluptuosity. What had drawn Hannah to him originally, if not those animal qualities which so distressed her now? Elizabeth watched Fred's hands holding his knife and fork. The fingers were heavy and smooth, and she imagined them, for a moment, caressing her shoulders. Her gaze rested on his mouth; the lower lip was firm and fleshy. The upper lip, under a silk-smooth, dark moustache, parted from the lower to reveal white and evenly spaced teeth. There was a small chip from the corner of one of the lower teeth. The slight imperfection was not unappealing.

'Would you care for some more green beans, Elizabeth?'

Fred's expression was genial, slightly patronizing, because he guessed that she had been day-dreaming; though his amiability might have faltered, if he had guessed what she had been thinking about. Elizabeth, no longer able to sustain the image of her brother-in-law in a carnal light, gave her attention to the supper of roast mutton and green beans.

'Your brother Willie was very fond of green beans, Frances, I remember,' Aunt Lydia said, as if plunged into an affectionate memory. Elizabeth looked at her sharply, wondering what lay behind the apparently innocent remark. Lydia was a natural schemer; she could not resist manipulating a situation, eager to prove that she was effecting some modest influence over how the world was organized. 'Green beans and eel pie,' Lydia remembered. 'But he was a sea-faring man, so that isn't surprising. Mrs Thorne's brother was a sea-captain,' she told the assembled company. 'An entrepreneur. Not unlike yourself, perhaps, Mr Pengelly.' Lydia offered the stranger a smile. 'A much-travelled man. A wealthy man. But a bachelor all his life.'

'A wise man then, I should say,' declared Dr Molesworth and chortled for a long time at his own wit.

'A wise man, in that he thought to provide his nieces with a dowry.'

Elizabeth looked at her aunt in horror. Lydia returned her gaze and smiled. I am looking to your future for you, said the smile. Here is a man, not too ugly, a little wooden perhaps, but respectably well-off. Why not make the best of things?

'Uncle Willie knew the importance of a dowry,' Lydia declared. 'He knew about a good catch in the matrimonial sense, even though he never fished in the sea of matrimony himself.' She beamed around the table, and with particular emphasis at Mr Pengelly.

Mr Pengelly, feeling that some comment was expected of him, said wrily, 'For myself, I'd rather a good joint of mutton to a piece of fish,' and subsided into silence.

After this there fell one of those little desperate pauses in the conversation which can cause a social situation to take a turn for the worse, unless it is rescued swiftly. The silence lengthened. One or two of the guests began casting secret glances at the clock on the mantel shelf, as if to calculate how long it was before they might decently depart.

It was Squire Attwell who picked up the conversation, only to send it lurching immediately towards a further small crisis of embarrassment. He leaned across the table to Robert.

'Heard anything from that brother of yours in London yet?'

Elizabeth sat very still and prayed that someone would again change the subject.

Robert said that he had not. His pale eyes studied Elizabeth as if searching for something; they blinked miserably at what they found.

Dr Molesworth cackled humorously and stroked his side-whiskers. 'Courting the ladies, I don't doubt. No time for penning letters. What a fellow your brother is, Robert. We never know what he'll do next. I was thunderstruck when he upped and went off to be a medical man. Never would have guessed it.'

A more deeply awkward pause followed. It seemed to Elizabeth that they were all looking at her. She was sure that Mr Pengelly must be scornful of the halting conversation.

Robert said suddenly, 'I know very little about my brother's affairs, it seems as if he has forgotten us all.' He offered Elizabeth a little smile; whether it was commiseration or malice, she could not tell.

'That's the way with the young these days,' said the Squire perceptively. 'Edward was always here a-visiting if I remember. The attraction of a certain lady, eh? At one time, Mrs Attwell and I used to say –' His wife kicked him under the table. A look of pained surprise came over his long, weather-beaten face. He stopped in mid-sentence. 'Taboo subject, eh? Never mind. Nod's as good as a wink.'

'I liked Edward,' said Henry Thorne wistfully. 'He always brought a bit of life to the place.'

Mrs Thorne fingered the edge of the tablecloth. Dr Molesworth coughed noisily. Hannah pulled a sympathetic face at Elizabeth.

'Well,' said Mr Pengelly diplomatically. He dabbed at his chin with

55

a napkin. 'I should say that was the best bit of tucker I have had since coming back to England.'

Miss Hemingale, the Sunday school mistress, explained in the rather uncertain pause which followed, that 'tucker', in Australian parlance, meant food. '"Tackle", folks round here might say,' she added brightly.

'And so should I have, one time,' Mr Pengelly said. 'For I come from round these parts. Tucker. Tackle. It's all the same to me. It all goes down the same way. And very welcome too, I must say.'

This was the longest speech yet attempted by Mr Pengelly and it caused consternation among some of the party. Mrs Thorne looked anxiously at Lydia. Mr Pengelly, in spite of all his rumoured wealth, did not seem to be quite a gentleman. Once again the company lapsed into an embarrassed silence.

'I wonder how the affair between Russia and Turkey will end?' mused Fred. 'Shall Britain too enter into a war with Russia, do you think, if the Czar refuses to withdraw from the Danube principalities?'

Hannah looked at him admiringly, proud of his conversational diplomacy.

Squire Attwell happily addressed himself to the question. 'Of course, we must support Turkey in a war. If Palmerston were prime minister, we'd soon be showing these red-haired barbarians in Russia how to behave. Aberdeen is too milk and water. No stomach for a fight.'

A lively discussion began on the rights and injustices of the current quarrel with Russia, as they were only half-understood by those present. The women were not expected to offer an opinion, nor to declare themselves for or against a war, though Mrs Thorne ventured to say that she hoped it would not mean that brave British soldiers were killed, if the prime minister decided that they should enter the fray.

'Our army will not shrink from its duty,' Squire Attwell said. 'Remember Waterloo!'

Though none of those present had actually been at Waterloo, some indeed had not been born when the battle took place, they did their best to recall that great victory. 'Damn the Czar!' declared Squire Attwell, warming to his theme. 'That's what I say, with apologies to the ladies. Damn the Russian despot. Nicholas may rule his serfs, but Britannia rules the waves, eh?'

How ridiculous he is, thought Elizabeth. How ridiculous we all are. As if we have some God-given superiority over all other nations.

'I knew a Russian once,' Dr Molesworth volunteered. 'He was a little chap. Red hair. Nice fellow though. Not a bit war-like.'

Elizabeth could no longer hold back her opinion. 'I am sure they're every bit the same as everyone else. Russians. Turks. French. I mean we are all flesh and blood.'

'I shall say aye to that,' said Mr Pengelly in her support.

Everyone stared at him. It seemed there was a touch of vulgarity in the way he had been slumped in his chair and when he sat up and leaned his elbows on the table.

'It takes all sorts,' he said, as though deciding to adopt a philosophical attitude. 'And I came across all sorts when I was working on a station – sheep station, that is – and at the goldfields. Frenchies, Chinamen, Aboriginals.'

The word 'Aboriginal' caused a flutter of excitement to run round the table.

'Mr Pengelly!' said Lydia. 'Surely you haven't met such wild and dangerous people as natives in Australia!'

'All sorts,' he repeated. 'Blacks, Irish. A proper mixed bag. The women too – and there's some mixed baggages amongst the women in Australia, I can tell you. Though it wouldn't be proper to tell you, I daresay.' He winked at Elizabeth. Delighted, she smothered a laugh. Mrs Attwell, sitting at Mr Pengelly's left side, looked apprehensive and edged herself away from his elbow, so that Dr Molesworth next to her, finding it difficult to raise his spoon to his mouth, edged to his left also, giving that side of the table a list as if they were at sea.

'Did you meet any ex-convicts in Australia, Mr Pengelly?' asked Hannah rather too eagerly. Fred frowned his disapproval and she looked confused, aware that she had allowed her natural curiosity too free a rein, and that the conversation had taken an unusual, perhaps even an improper turn.

'Plenty at the diggings,' Mr Pengelly said. 'Not all bad, neither. I've been grateful enough in a scrap for a ticket-of-leave man on my side, against some great Irish gold-hunter, bent on splitting my skull with a pick handle.'

'How frightful,' said Mrs Thorne, plucking at the collar of her dress and wishing that she did not always give way to Lydia, or that at least she had insisted they find out a little more about Mr Pengelly before inviting him to her table. She glanced at Elizabeth. She feared, from her expression of rapt attention, that she was attracted by the man's indelicacy. How like her, to be impressed by bad taste.

'Such strange company you did keep, Mr Pengelly,' remarked Miss Hemingale.

'True enough.' Pengelly beamed happily. He leaned back in his chair. Elizabeth watched him linger over a sip of wine and felt that he was enjoying the disturbance he had caused.

Fred decided he would try his skill as a diplomat once more. 'Tell me,' he said. 'Mr Pengelly mentions the Irish. Would we not agree that there's such a thing as a national character, which distinguishes one people from another? A wild ungovernability among the Irish, for example, a deviousness in the Russian character, a certain sense of honour which sets the British above other nations?'

Mr Pengelly, believing that the question had been addressed to him, considered it with a little frown.

'I should rather have it, that folk have their own peculiarities, but that all folks are equal in the sight of God. What do you say, Parson Munro?'

Robert opened and closed his mouth and looked alarmed.

'So long as we are to exclude the Russians, the Paddies, and the lower orders from this egality,' said the Squire.

Mr Pengelly regarded him for a moment. The good humour had left his face. He leaned further across the table. 'I've come across a good many folk on my travels, sir. Believe me, wickedness isn't the mark of the foreigner, no more than goodness is that of an Englishman. And, for sure, virtue was never the best concern of an English gentleman.'

'No need to get insulting,' blustered the Squire. 'No need at all, I'd say.'

'Well!' declared Lydia. She pursed her lips, relishing the heated silence. She felt no responsibility for Mr Pengelly's presence at the supper party. She had already transferred the blame to her sister-in-law, who had enthused about the new man's house, the wagons full of furniture which had arrived there, the stylish carriage and rumours of his great wealth.

Support for the stranger came from an unexpected quarter.

'I agree with Mr Pengelly.' Robert blushed and looked at Elizabeth for approval. 'Are we to say of a man, "Poor fellow, it's not his fault he's wicked, he's a foreigner"? For then where does responsibility for one's own soul and all notion of vice and virtue go?'

'My husband was French,' said Lydia, as if daring anyone to attack her on the point.

'Nevertheless, God has made all of us here English,' Fred said mildly. 'In our character, feelings, education and awareness of duty. There is a certain pride to be derived from that fact.'

'We are what we are. We cannot change it,' said Miss Hemingale.

'It's certainly more comforting, if every member of society accepts his lot. Englishman or foreigner, master or servant, rich or poor,' Mrs Attwell said.

'Comforting for whom?' murmured Elizabeth. 'Does the farm labourer feel comforted by being an Englishman, scraping together a meal of bread and potatoes in his cottage?'

Mrs Attwell looked at her in dismay at being thus challenged.

'The Englishman has always been aware of his duty,' the Squire informed them. 'Which is to maintain the natural order of society, rich and poor. And an English gentleman considers it his duty to defend the weak against the oppressor. To be English is, in a word, to know the true meaning of chivalry.'

'You reckon on such a thing as chivalry these days?' Mr Pengelly seemed to sneer.

'I do indeed,' bridled the Squire. 'At least among *gentlemen*.'

'You should try a spell amongst our countrymen in the colonies.'

Elizabeth waited eagerly. She felt tense with excitement. Mr Pengelly was like a breath of cool night air blown into the stuffy atmosphere of the room. He was able to shake them out of their complacency in a way which she had always longed to do. She tried to imagine the life he had known in Australia, so unconventional, so far from the parochial concerns of Charlford.

Mrs Thorne, feeling her role as hostess fall onerously upon her, and deciding it might be advantageous to go back several places in the conversation and begin again, suggested nervously,

'I'm sure, if it *should* come to a war with Russia, our soldiers will prove that they are Englishmen and be very brave and chivalrous.'

'Surely, surely chivalry towards the ladies still thrives – even out in the colonies, Mr Pengelly,' said Robert. It was a reproof. Pengelly looked unsure of himself, as if he was aware only now that his outspokenness had bordered too much on incivility. 'Is there a man here,' Robert continued, 'who wouldn't strive to imitate the Christian knights of old, who were gentle and courteous towards the

59

fairer sex, brave and enterprising in adversity, and, above all, gentle-men?'

Mr Pengelly knew he was beaten. He fell into the gloomy silence which he had observed at the start of the evening.

'Well, I for one shall strive to be like those knights of old,' Fred enthused. 'Seeking no higher goal in life than to be judged worthy by that fair sex, which we all worship and adore.' He turned worshipful and adoring eyes upon Hannah who blushed prettily at the speech.

'A toast. A toast,' Henry urged. 'To the fairer sex.'

Relief was evident among the guests as the toast was drunk. The small unpleasantness seemed to be over.

Elizabeth looked from one to another: Fred the perfect husband, Hannah, the epitome of the fair sex, awash with happy modesty, her tears of anguish over Fred's suspected infidelity might never have been. Squire Attwell thumped his knee and declared something or other to be 'capital!' Elizabeth's glance was intercepted by Mr Pengelly across the table. He raised an eyebrow, a small gesture, but it was one which seemed to link them both suddenly against the rest.

9

The ladies had retired for the obligatory female chat in the drawing room. They ignored the clamour coming from the kitchen, where Mrs Booth was having hysterics and threatening to leave, or else to kill herself. Mrs Thorne whispered urgently to Elizabeth to go downstairs and do something.

Elizabeth found the cook seated at the kitchen table with a meat cleaver in her hand and with her face buried in a teacloth; she sat down beside her without alarm, for the scene of Mrs Booth having one of her turns was not an unfamiliar one.

''Tis that daft maid,' the woman sobbed. ''Er doan know what 'er's doin' 'alf the time.'

Elizabeth looked at Flo from the village, who cowered in the corner by the scullery door. It was true that Flo was slow-witted, but given potatoes to peel or pans to scrub she could generally be trusted to get on with things without any trouble; they often employed her when extra help was needed in the kitchen.

'Family I can do for,' wailed Mrs Booth. 'But when 'tis all they extra – Squire, and 'is missus, an' all – it do take it out on a body, Miss Elizabeth. I bin at it all day, an' I be bellowsed out.' She gave a shuddering sigh. The worst of the storm, it seemed, was over.

'I'm sure you are,' soothed Elizabeth. She took the meat cleaver from her gently. She was glad to escape for a while from the gossip in the drawing room, which she knew would be all about the behaviour of Mr Pengelly. She felt weary now of the whole business. She wished that Edward had been there, and wondered briefly whose part he would have taken.

61

'It was an excellent supper,' she said. She looked at the stack of dirty pots in the scullery and signalled to Flo to make a start on them.

'"Tweren't nothin' special. 'Twere only a roast.'

'But cooked to perfection,' Elizabeth persisted.

'You always d'say that, Miss Elizabeth.'

'That's because it's always true. Mr Pengelly, the gentleman from The Red House, made a particular point of complimenting the roast. He said it was the best bit of roast lamb he's had since coming home to England.'

Mrs Booth sniffed. 'Well.' She straightened her apron and looked at the teacloth in her hands. ''Twere good on 'n to say so.'

'We all thought so.' Elizabeth put her arm round the woman's shoulders. They remained like that for some minutes. The only sound was from Flo, patiently clattering knives and forks and dishes in the scullery sink.

'He been't no gentleman though,' Mrs Booth said at last. 'I know'd 'n when 'e were a glove-cutter. Arthur Pengelly's mother was a Cornish woman, and no better than she ought to be, some say.'

'He is very *interesting*,' said Hannah.

'He is low and uncouth,' sniffed Aunt Lydia. 'The man is a barbarian.'

'Because he's honest and speaks his mind?' said Elizabeth, returning to the drawing room and squeezing herself between Lydia and Mrs Attwell on the sofa.

'Because he has no notion of how polite society conducts itself. I don't know what you were thinking of, Frances, to have him here to supper.'

Mrs Thorne opened and shut her mouth in mild protest.

'They do say he's very rich,' murmured Mabel Hemingale.

'But not a gentleman,' said Lydia. 'No breeding, you see. You can spot breeding at once when you've moved, as I have, in elevated company for so many years. It's in the bearing, the tilt of the head. Mr Delahaye, my late husband, had breeding. But there, it's the kind of thing one sees more and more these days. Tuppenny ha'penny upstarts. Commercials aping their betters. I blame it all on the railways.'

'Mr Pengelly didn't find his gold at the new town railway station,' said Elizabeth. 'I expect he worked very hard prospecting for it.'

'It's such a pity,' sighed Mrs Attwell. She leaned closer to Elizabeth. 'I must confess, when we heard about him, I hoped, for your sake, dear –' She patted Elizabeth's hand confidentially. 'But, never mind. Your mother has settled for Robert, and I think she may be right. I saw him looking at you with quite a *reverential* attention, shall we say, during supper.'

'That would be all very well,' said Lydia loudly, 'if only Elizabeth would make herself more agreeable. Men don't like opinionated women. It isn't feminine.'

'This is ridiculous.' Elizabeth, mortified by the sudden turn the conversation had taken, threw Lydia a look of hatred and went to the piano.

'Well, somebody has to pay attention to these things,' complained Mrs Thorne.

'Bosh!' Elizabeth replied.

'I think, Elizabeth, that you are really a romantic at heart,' said her aunt. 'It is a distinct disadvantage when one is looking for a husband.'

Elizabeth banged out Mendelssohn's *Wedding March* at a brisk and uneven tempo on the piano keys to drown the women's chatter.

'I expect we have all at some time wished the perfect knight would ride by and sweep us away from all our troubles,' said Hannah quietly.

Later, while Hannah was entertaining the reunited company with a more sensitive performance of one of Beethoven's sonatas, Elizabeth slipped from the drawing room into the garden.

The women's matchmaking had brought back thoughts of Edward. She walked restlessly along the garden path, her arms folded against her breasts, holding in the ache which threatened to escape from her in a great sob of anger and frustration.

After a short time she returned to the house. A figure moved from the shadows near the French windows.

'Are you not enjoying the music, Miss Thorne?' Mr Pengelly's form was very solid in the light from the house. He was smoking a cigar; she caught its scent as he came towards her. She saw that he was smiling. 'The piano sounds more mellow from here, I was thinking,' he said.

She felt annoyed. She had wanted to be alone. But she thought she must not snub him after the friction during supper. She smiled and made a remark about the proficiency of Hannah's playing.

'Do you play, Miss Thorne?'

'Oh, yes. I was taught all the accomplishments necessary for a lady who wishes to shine in the best society.'

'It's a pity you sound so scornful of the idea.'

She did not answer.

'Do you mind my cigar?' He held it as though about to cast it aside, as if he had suddenly remembered the rules of propriety.

She shook her head. 'I don't mind.'

She looked at the lighted drawing room. Mrs Attwell, now seated next to Fred on the sofa, was imparting a story which was evidently of considerable moral worth, from the grave expressions on both their faces. Her father was in his favourite chair by the fire. His hair, newly washed, stood in wings at either side of his head; his eyes were closed. Squire Attwell, standing against the hearth, unaware that he had lost his audience, was delivering a tirade against something or other.

'It all seems so pointless,' she said. She turned to Mr Pengelly. 'You can have no idea how much I admired the way you spoke out against the Squire.'

'I thought in the end I had spoken out of turn.'

'And what's wrong with that? Shake us all up, Mr Pengelly. We need shaking up. I wish I'd been brave enough. But we women mustn't have opinions, it isn't feminine, you know.'

'I can't believe you wouldn't have an opinion of things, Miss Thorne. I think a woman should speak her mind when she wants. I don't hold with those silly, empty-headed ladies, who make their talk nothing but fashions and tittle-tattle.'

'Oh, I agree.' She responded with hearty, almost girlish enthusiasm, excited by the unconventional style of his conversation.

'I did meet a few of the sort in Sydney,' he said. 'All silly talk and that.'

'Were you a long time away from England?'

'Ten years.'

'And all that time prospecting for gold.'

'Lord, no. I tried my hand at farming, and felling for a year or so. Then I thought, Why not try the diggings? Other folk are making their fortunes, why not I? So I gave it a try, and I struck lucky first time off.'

'Would you go back to Australia?' she asked.

'That all depends.' He looked guarded. 'It's a great chance, if you can get a living.'

'I should love to go to Australia. Once, when I was a little girl, I told them that I was going to travel and seek my fortune. It brought a violent reaction from Mother. She said, young ladies didn't indulge in such unfeminine pursuits.'

'It's a great pity, the way things are.'

'Oh, yes,' Elizabeth replied vigorously. 'It certainly is.'

She pretended to examine the berries on a honeysuckle twined against the window frame. She did not want to return indoors, though she knew that there was something a little improper about prolonging her stay outside in the dark; she knew how it would be construed by the occupants of the drawing room.

'You'd like the life in the bush,' Mr Pengelly said. 'You wouldn't need to play the lady if you didn't want it.'

'Why did you come back?' she said.

He shrugged. 'There wasn't a month I didn't feel homesick for England.'

She looked at him in surprise.

'I'm not a young man,' he said. 'I always had this idea, I should come back, maybe start a business. I've got a good head for business, Miss Thorne. Though that wasn't all.'

She looked at him inquiringly.

'I reckoned on settling down,' he said, and there was a creeping tension after the words were spoken. 'A man reaches a certain age, he starts looking out for a wife.'

Elizabeth looked quickly away. She saw her mother, peering anxiously out towards the garden. 'We'd better go indoors,' she said.

Mr Pengelly threw his cigar to the terrace and crushed it slowly into the paving with his foot. He watched Elizabeth's broad-hipped figure appraisingly before following her into the house.

10

Edward's collapse at the Punchbowl tavern had had more to do with a low fever which was sweeping that area of London than a surfeit of alcohol. For several days he was confined to his lodgings.

Clara Fitzroy, hearing that he was ill, made up her mind to forgive him his lack of ambition and became all at once a ministering angel.

'You really should take care of yourself, Teddy.' She flitted elegantly about his room, plumping up cushions, flicking back the curtain to look out of the window, and examining sketches done by Edward in moments of melancholy boredom. She addressed the occasional remark on the state of Edward's health to her companion. Miss Fennimore, perched on the edge of a chair, was aware that she was only required to be there in her capacity as chaperone; she was also aware that in Clara's vocabulary 'chaperone' was very much synonymous with 'gooseberry'.

'It's my opinion you've not been eating enough. And you've been drinking far too much champagne and porter.' Clara looked him up and down seriously, as though judging a piece of furniture which might yet suit the drawing room if only it were a bit more stylish. Clara was no fool, and if she was going to take up with Edward again she must be sure that she could make something of him. She tossed her fair curls and narrowed her eyes. 'You're not so handsome today. You're too pale. You must have more fresh air. Meanwhile, you can fill in your time with some studies and a little sketching while you recover. But not these gloomy things.' She looked with distaste at Edward's paintings of a river flowing sluggishly between sombre willows. 'I shall bring you some of Mama's blackberry cordial next time we visit.'

Edward, remembering a cordial which Elizabeth used to make,

66

imagined her bending near him, urging him to try a sip to ease his throat. He thought how reassuring her large, warm, untidy person would be, here in the intimacy of his room. He wanted to tell Clara that he did not need her there. But he did not know how to do it with the least trouble. And so he did nothing, and Clara continued to visit, bringing with her the silent, doe-eyed Miss Fennimore. They watched over his recovery with a possessiveness which was only alleviated by Jack Harris's more welcome visits.

'Rumour has it that you will be betrothed before long, if not to one then to t'other of them,' Harris commented. He and two fellow students, Rawley and Howitt, had converged on Edward's lodgings some weeks after his return to full health. Harris had come supplied with bottles from his father's cellar. Edward, accepting a third beaker of champagne, remembered that he was due at the Fitzroys for dinner that evening. He groaned at the thought of the awesome trio of Clara, Mad Fritz, and Clara's, by reputation, no less fearsome mother.

'Women!' declared Howitt, an owl-eyed, sunken-chested young man. He pronounced the word as if he were weary of the whole species. 'They're forever harping on the subject of marriage. Mothers, daughters –' He tailed off, evidently remembering some recent, perhaps not altogether pleasant experience.

'In Paris, I'm told, a medic can dispense easily with marriage,' Rawley said. 'One can get oneself kept by a loose woman and live very well by it.'

'And what is your definition of a loose woman, my dear fellow?' said Harris languidly. He poured the dregs of a bottle of hock into Edward's beaker.

Edward looked at it foolishly. He was vaguely aware that if he was going to give a good account of himself at the Fitzroys, he must not drink any more of Harris's wine.

'A loose woman?' Rawley considered the question briefly. 'A loose woman is one who has none of the refinements of class and respectability.'

'Then you must include the entire female portion of the lower classes in your definition,' Harris sneered.

'I've known some of the female lower class to be tight-arsed as a tortoise,' complained Howitt. He peered over his spectacles into his empty beaker.

'Then I shall redefine,' Rawley declared. 'A loose woman is one

67

who is acquainted with all the unnatural acts; moreover, she is content to be the lewd plaything of man's natural vices.'

Howitt was still reflecting on past experiences. 'I've also known women of the wealthier class who have demonstrated a marked delight in the titillation of their private parts,' he continued, 'and who assert that the clitoris is a source of great pleasure during the act of copulation.'

The others stared at him with a mixture of envy and disbelief.

Edward heard himself saying, 'But women like that, whatever class they belong to, must be unnatural. Some deformity, or clinical malfunction must be at the root of their behaviour.'

'True,' said Howitt amiably. 'I would advocate excision of the clitoris in extreme cases of nymphomania.'

They laughed. But Edward was confused. His own remark had been a question rather than a statement. A clinical depravity? Was that true of Elizabeth?

'Why are we so afraid of women?' he said.

'The clap, dear fellow,' said Harris prosaically.

'No,' said Rawley. 'We are afraid to admit that women might be sexual creatures by natural disposition, because it would make them powerful. It might lead to excesses. Hence, we insist that the true woman is merely compliant. If she were to be stimulated by the sexual act it would lead to a weakening of the male species in time.'

'Talking of a weakening of the male species.' Harris yawned. 'I saw as bad a case of elephantiasis yesterday as I shall ever see. The operation for removal of part of the scrotum was perfectly hideous.'

'Not now, old fellow,' protested Edward. 'I, for one, am expected to dine within the hour.'

'Big as a man's head,' added Rawley, who had been present at the same operation. 'Blood everywhere. Dabbed one poor fellow right in the eye.'

Edward laughed with the others, but he was sickened by the anecdote. The delight in indecencies, and stories of blood and gore which were a part of student life secretly appalled him. He remembered how, on one of the rounds of the wards at the hospital, the doctor in charge of the group of students had halted by a bed in which lay a woman infected with syphilis.

'Here we see God's punishment for a life of debauchery,' the man had said. 'In diseases of this nature we can recognize the moral value of suffering.'

68

'Sir, I only went with him for a month,' the woman had protested.

The doctor had ignored her. 'Syphilis, we note, is not so virulent as it once was. We do not see examples of the loss of the palate or part of the cranium as was formerly the case. Treatment?'

'Ingestations of mercury in the more advanced cases,' Edward had replied automatically, trying not to meet the gaze of the woman in the bed, with her teeth blackened and her body disfigured by swellings. 'Withholding of fluids, sweating, application of leeches to the inflammation.'

'I had two buboes lanced yesterday, sir,' the woman had said with pathetic helpfulness. 'I do hope I can soon go home.'

'And contaminate those around you?' the doctor said severely. 'Woman, you are a deadly stinking weed. You are poisoning the very life-blood of this nation.'

'No, sir,' the woman had said seriously. 'It was my man what give it me.'

'Congenital liars, all of them,' the doctor had murmured to the students as they moved away from the bed. And they had laughed.

Edward repeated the scene to his companions, giving a fair impersonation of the doctor, who was a 'character' at the hospital, renowned for his insensitivity.

'It's such a bore, the ward rounds,' said Harris. 'To be thrown among the unwashed Poor before lunch is a nauseous business.'

'They can't wash themselves if they're sick,' Edward said. 'And very often the domestics haven't changed the sheets from one patient to the next. If they have some friend or relative to bring in washing or the occasional luxury they're considered privileged.'

Harris looked at him in surprise. 'If they can afford luxuries, should they be scrounging on the charity of the hospital?'

'The Poor are all scroungers,' said Howitt. 'Ask my father, who is a Guardian of our Parish Union at home.'

'The Poor are no better or worse than ourselves,' said Edward. He was uncomfortably aware of an element of priggishness in the stand he had taken, but felt compelled to continue with it. 'Is it a crime to have fallen on hard times or be born into poverty?'

'He has been reading the works of our great social reformers,' suggested Rawley.

'His fever hasn't yet worked itself out,' laughed Harris. 'Edward, I have noticed signs that you are fast turning into a Radical.'

The truth was that Edward was increasingly troubled by the ranks of humanity which filled the hospital, or hacked the smog from their lungs in the foul air of the outpatients' waiting room. Each had his or her own story of hardship from bereavement, lost employment, or lost dignity. Edward found it harder and harder to dismiss them as the 'Poor', who had latched on to the charity of the hospital. They were individuals, some pathetic and complaining, some indeed congenital liars, but most had a resignation about them. They feared the workhouse above everything else and clutched their letters of recommendation to the Hospital Board with a grip that was close to panic. He recalled the story he had heard that day from a man who had lost a leg in a street accident, how he had been sacked by the manufacturing company which employed him, and had come to the hospital with a tumour growing under his arm, from supporting himself on a crutch. There had been a stoicism about him which Edward had found humbling.

'I merely conclude that a society which condemns the evils which stem from poverty, yet does nothing to strike at the root of the misery, which can allow such inequalities between the rich and the poor, has to be corrupt at its heart,' Edward said.

'How I detest speeches,' said Howitt, pulling out his pocket watch. He began in a slow, drunken fashion to line up beakers on the table, and blinked stupidly through his spectacles, looking for his hat.

'Edward, admit it,' Harris said reasonably. 'For the most part, the Poor are dirty and improvident. They drink away their wages, instead of saving for their old age and sickness. The women spend their husband's money on booze, instead of buying meat to feed their children. No wonder they're all half-starved.'

'I think that I would take to drink, if I was condemned to live in all the insanitary filth of a hovel in Shadwell, or if I was laid up in hospital, or lost my employment, or I felt that things were beyond my control,' Edward said.

Howitt prepared to leave noisily. He called out that he would consider greeting Edward civilly when he next saw him, so long as Edward was in a more satisfactory frame of mind. Rawley also got up to go.

Harris was more inclined to finish the argument. 'But things are never beyond our control, dear fellow,' he said. 'That's where you reformists are misled. The working classes need only the virtues of thrift and cleanliness, and all their problems would vanish in an instant.'

Edward shook his head. Harris was not entirely serious. But even this, his lack of compassion when confronted daily with the evidence, made Edward aware of a distance between them which was becoming harder to bridge.

'Don't let Miss Fitzroy know you're a Radical,' Harris said as he left with Rawley. 'Or she'll throw you over again for more satisfactory meat. Clara knows what she requires from her beaux.'

'And what is that?' Edward said, beginning to feel depressed as he thought of the walk across town and the imminent dinner party at the Fitzroys.

'Excellent prospects, good grooming, charm, a talent for flattery, and fine moustaches,' Rawley said, preening his own moustache.

'Then you fail on all counts, Edward,' laughed Harris.

The November air hit Edward full in the face and made his head reel as he left his lodgings. He turned up the collar of the Prussian blue frock coat he had borrowed from Harris and thrust his hands deep in the pockets. Edward made his way towards the Gray's Inn Road and considered the unlikely prospect of marriage into the Fitzroy family. He saw that he had allowed himself to drift, as he had always drifted, into a situation that was not of his choosing; not quite disliking Clara enough to call the affair off again; nor liking her to the extent that he was uplifted by a vision of a future in which she continued to flit, butterfly fashion, by his side. There were worse things than being betrothed to a beauty like Clara Fitzroy – supposing, just supposing that her father should consent to such a thing. On the other hand, the idea was intolerable while he still could not rid himself of the feeling that he had betrayed Elizabeth. He was a coward. He was afraid of women, afraid of blood, afraid of death; afraid of admitting that there was evil in the world, and of acknowledging the evils in himself.

He would throw himself into his studies. If he had behaved badly in one respect of his life, he could make amends in another. He would become a model student, and set himself the goal of a Junior Scholarship at the end of the spring term. He would renounce the pleasures of the theatre and late night drinking.

With such thoughts he made his way to the Fitzroys' residence, a house which was conscious of its importance in a fashionable area of London. He arrived, having lost his way a number of times, a little

71

befuddled still by Harris's wine, and needing all at once to relieve a full bladder.

The butler showed him to the water closet. It was unfortunately next to the dining room, and its gurgling and clanking announced his arrival more effectively than the manservant's discreet, 'Mr Munro has arrived, sir.'

'You're late, Munro.' They had begun dinner without him. Fitzroy, who was not noted for observing social niceties, scowled at Edward from the head of the dinner table. 'We didn't wait.'

A number of other students at the table turned to enjoy his embarrassment, Edward recognized them only by sight. He smiled nervously and apologized for his late arrival, explaining that he had lost his way.

'Sit down, Munro,' Fitzroy bellowed. 'Don't stand there looking like an amputated limb.'

Someone sniggered. Edward hurried to the remaining vacant seat at the far end of the table, next to a fat student who was eating a plate of oysters, and uncomfortably close to Clara's mother. Mrs Fitzroy stared at him without any sign of pleasure at what she saw. Clara's mother was an older version of Clara. She had what people called 'well-bred' features and was so thin that, whereas in Clara's case the effect was one of fragile beauty, in the mother it was skeletal. There was a chilling evaluation in the expression with which she was studying Edward, and evidently found him wanting.

'Have something to eat, Mr Munro,' she said, and it was an order rather than an invitation.

Clara, sitting next to her father at the top end of the table, smiled at Edward with the same coldness as her mother and looked away. She would demand endless apologies for his crassness in arriving late.

'We are discussing the case for pure water in our cities,' Fitzroy said. 'I have suggested the theory that disease is water-borne. Our young friends here, those who have honoured us by venturing an opinion, contend that cholera is spread by a poisonous miasma. In other words, they uphold the old theory that disease is an air-borne phenomenon. We would value your opinion, Mr Munro.'

Though there was something in Fitzroy's manner which smacked as usual of the theatrical, Edward detected a genuine desire to hear what he might have to say. It occurred to him, that his alliance with Clara was not as unwelcome to Fitzroy as the surgeon had pretended. If this was the case, he thought, with a sudden unshuttering of his

72

mind, a leading career in medicine would be guaranteed. With Mad Fritz's patronage he could fall into a wealthy practice, get on to the fashionable circuits with ease, fame and fortune would be his. He looked at Clara. She was staring at her plate, but he knew that she expected him to agree with her father's opinion. It would be unwise to challenge him. The difficulty for Edward was that he did agree with Fitzroy that disease was transmitted by contaminated water; yet to say so would be laying himself open to the self-accusation of toadying.

He was saved from replying by Mrs Fitzroy.

'Must we forever be discussing medical matters at the table?' she said. 'Disease, poisonous miasma, sanitation. It's all so unsavoury. People fall sick and they die, but we don't want to be reminded of their misfortunes over oysters and partridges. The *foul* does not *fare* well with the *fowl.*'

One or two students laughed sycophantically.

Edward, influenced by his recent argument with Harris and his friends, said, 'But we only have to step outside, into the squalor of the streets to be reminded of the misfortunes of others.' He realized, even as he spoke, that he should have remained silent, or, better, should have acknowledged Mrs Fitzroy's wit with a show of appreciative mirth. But having begun badly he blundered on. 'It was a shock to me, when I first came to London, that so splendid a city should be so rife with misery and disease. More shocking is the fact that the majority of the unfortunates who enter the doors of the college hospital come there to die, and know that they do so. And we, who say that our aim is to save life, can only accept the situation.'

Mrs Fitzroy, who by now clearly disliked him more than ever, said, 'My husband does not accept that death is inevitable, young man. That's why he is a surgeon. Only the other day he was called to the house of a lady nearby, and by his swift action saved her from a horrid and certain death. The subject is delicate and I shall not name her. I shan't say more.'

'And yet,' Fitzroy said soberly, 'if I were to stop to consider how many patients do die after the knife, I should be afraid ever to operate again. We must soldier on, Munro. Not so long ago, a surgeon was considered no more than a "sawbones". Quite rightly too. Medicine was based on a terrifying ignorance. But now, new discoveries are being made every day. We must soldier on. And, as to the Poor, they have an inbuilt stoicism. We cannot begin to understand them.'

73

'I am astonished by their capacity for suffering,' remarked Mrs Fitzroy. 'They seem to be born for it.'

'But the Poor don't suffer by choice,' said Edward. 'You talk about them as if they're a separate species from ourselves.'

'You're not eating, Mr Munro,' said Mrs Fitzroy coldly.

Edward saw that Clara was red-faced and looking at him intently, her eyes were bright with anger. He looked at the untouched food on his plate, and the knife in his hand. He murmured an apology and picked up a fork and began to eat. Edward let the rest of the conversation pass over him. He was aware that another student was speaking in his support, recounting a story of some distant acquaintance of 'noble' birth, who had lost his inheritance through gambling and been reduced to a life of poverty. The man's wife, formerly a 'lady in every sense of the word', had resorted to begging on the streets, the children had been forced to turn to criminal activities of one sort or another.

'It was a punishment by God on the wretched fellow,' someone suggested. 'The family's degradation was a direct consequence of the father's gambling.'

'Surely, if a man or woman goes wrong, there must be something inherently bad in their nature,' said Clara. 'After all, there are charities for distressed gentlefolk; the mother should have found herself some gainful employment, instead of begging on the streets; the children could have chosen to lead a decent and honest life.'

'The children had clearly inherited their father's weak character,' declared Mrs Fitzroy. 'It wasn't the will of God, or force of circumstances, but their own idle or wicked inclinations which brought about their degradation.'

As she spoke, Edward was hit by a kind of revelation. Men and women who fell from grace did so because they were inherently wicked? It was all hogwash. Every beggar, every child prostitute and petty thief was evil by nature. God punished those who were not respectable. Sanitation was not a fit companion for champagne and oysters, partridges, and syllabub. The suffering of the individual was for the common good. It was all no more than social cant.

His heart sang with a feeling of being released from carrying a heavy burden. He was buoyed up by a sense of moral superiority. The instincts which had led him to reject the cant of religion, now revealed to him the hypocrisy of a morality which was imposed by the rich, and impossible for people to live up to without the benefit of material wealth.

He ate the oysters in silence. He munched his way through roast partridge and chestnuts and guinea fowl. He downed the syllabub, the champagne, and after-dinner port. He told himself that he might eat their food and drink their wine, but he was damned if he would be like them and accept the creeds by which they lived.

'Teddy. Whatever came over you at dinner, talking as you did?' Clara said. 'Mother has a great sympathy for the Poor. She sends food parcels every Christmas to the workhouse and the hospital.'

'I'm sure they must appreciate it,' Edward said calmly.

'They do. Edward, if you make an enemy of my mother, I'll never forgive you.' She moved away from him, to talk and flirt a little with a group of students.

Edward watched her, unmoved. He recognized the crude attempt to make him jealous. But he had other things on his mind. His newly found moral freedom did not help him decide what to do about Elizabeth, though he saw even more clearly now what a terrible thing he had done by running away. He did not know what he would say to her.

He would wait until Christmas, he decided.

He watched in a detached way as Clara persuaded her father and the rest to a game of charades.

He could not be sure that Elizabeth still loved him. Could he even be sure that he still would love her, when they were face to face and forced to acknowledge what had happened? His return would be remarked upon in Charlford. There would be gossip, public innuendos about a renewed attachment, and private observations about what had driven them apart, about the incongruity of the match – Elizabeth over thirty, almost an old maid, him with few prospects, no kind of a husband really for anybody.

Clara was coming across the room towards him. She had decided to forgive him.

'Come on, Edward. Are you going to sulk by the piano all evening?' She drew him with her towards the others, saying, 'We are going to play charades. You and I might act out *stick-in-the-mud*. It seems appropriate under the circumstances.'

Above all, he told himself, as he forced a bonhomie on himself, he must not allow himself to be taken in hand by Clara any more.

75

11

There was a coffee house in Drury Lane. The lights and warmth and the smell of hot roasted coffee wrapped themselves round him as he passed it on his way home from the Fitzroys. Edward turned and walked back.

He bought a mug of thick brown coffee at the counter and sat down with it at a table. A young woman was slumped against the wall opposite, but she straightened when she saw him and tidied her shawl, like an exhausted bird which flutters to life when someone approaches. The nature of her trade was implicit in the smile she offered him, part coquette, part business-woman.

'Can I get you anything?' he said. 'Can I get you some coffee?'

'That'd be nice, dear. Plenty of sugar. Though some say I'm sweet enough.'

The weariness in her eyes contrasted with the pertness of her response. Her features were small, quite delicate, again the image of a bird came to mind. Her hands too were small, and clean.

He bought the coffee and returned with it to the table. The woman eyed him shrewdly.

'Do you live near here?' he said.

'Not far. I'll show you, if you've a mind.'

Edward hesitated. He knew that she saw him as a client. He tried to imagine where and how she lived. A faded room in a dingy street. A light burning low, ready for her return with a customer. How strange: he had not intended entering the coffee house, even less of speaking to a prostitute, but he felt a strong curiosity about her. He wondered about the half-world which existed beyond the bright lights and the glitter of the coffee houses and theatres, out of sight of the fashionable squares where people like the Fitzroys entertained promising young students.

'Would you talk to me?' he said earnestly. 'Will you tell me something about yourself? I'll pay you, if you like.'

He flushed as she said, 'If it's indecent talk you want, we'll go to my lodgings. The proprietor here won't stand for that sort of thing. Though he turns a blind eye most nights to me sitting here, waiting for my gentlemen.'

'I just want to know more about you,' Edward said. 'I'm not – I'm curious about how you live. Why did you resort to this?'

Her manner quickly became hostile. 'You a dodger?'

'A dodger?'

'Devil-dodger. A parson. You can bugger off if you're thinking of preaching religion to me.'

'I'm a medical student.'

She looked at him sceptically.

'My brother's a dodger though.' Robert was definitely a devil-dodger.

'If you're a med, you won't have any money,' she said. 'Half a guinea's my fee.'

He put a half guinea on the table and she reached for it with her small fingers and transferred it with the deftness of a conjuror to a hidden pocket under one of the flounces of her skirt.

'Were you born to this sort of life?' Edward began. 'I mean, were your parents poor people, or did they perhaps fall on hard times?' He remembered the story at the Fitzroys' dinner table of the man who had gambled away all his wealth. The Fitzroys' house, with its retinue of servants, the crackling coal fires and party games, the good food and wine seemed so far away as to be unreal.

The girl thought for a moment. 'You want to know how I fell from grace?'

He nodded, feeling a little ashamed of himself.

'If you want details, I told you –'

'No. Not details,' he said quickly. 'I just want to know. I want to understand what led you to this.'

She seemed puzzled, then resigned herself to an easy way of earning her money. 'Well, I'm a seduced governess, aren't I,' she said. 'The gentleman of the house where I worked, he forced me to it. Afterwards he promised he'd set me up in a place of my own, a house in Camden Town.'

77

'As his mistress?' he said, finding her story barely credible.

'Well, he couldn't marry me, could he? Not after what had happened, and me being only a governess. He was one of your higher class of gentlemen, a real swell. Bought me lovely things.' She pulled her cheap shawl closer round her as if remembering better times.

'And then?' he prompted.

'Oh, he grew tired of me.'

Edward felt the guilt of generations of the male species rest upon his shoulders. 'Didn't you regret what had happened, and try to find proper employment again?'

She laughed. 'A girl's got to live. I feel regretful sometimes, course I do, at what it's come to. But I don't think about it unless I can help it. And it's not so terrible as your sort think.'

There was a heavy silence. He watched her trace a spill of coffee with her finger on the table's surface. She put the finger to her mouth and licked it. Their eyes met, and to his dismay he felt his heart quicken with a low excitement. She drank down her coffee, still holding him with her gaze, then she stood up, pulling her shawl round her shoulders.

'You coming then?'

He hesitated.

'Look, dear. If you're so bloody curious about the low life, you should come and see for yourself. I won't eat you.'

The woman went to the door. He glanced at his pocket watch. It was not yet ten. She paused before going out into the street, and let the door swing to behind her. Edward followed.

'Is it far?' he called anxiously.

'Not far.' The slight figure pushed its way with practised agility through the people in the street. Edward's unease grew as they left the lights of the West End and joined the narrow alleys of St Giles. He kept close behind her.

They entered a three-storey building and she paused and tapped on a door on the ground floor, as if signalling her return, before mounting a wooden stair. The shouts of a drunken quarrel they had passed in the street grew fainter; he could hear the muted sounds of conversation and laughter from rooms inside the building. She showed him into an attic room at the top of the house, quiet except for the hiss of gas lamps on either side of the fire.

'Like it?' She seemed pleased with herself. 'Mr Investigator?'

The room was large with a sloping roof and small curtained window. It contained a four-post bed hung with dirty chintz curtains, and a few shabby pieces of furniture, a chair, a washstand, and table. A low fire burned in the grate.

Edward could not honestly say that he liked it. He was nervous still at having come so far through dark, slimy, and unfamiliar streets; and there was a smell in the room which he could not quite identify, a rank, perfumed smell which was faintly nauseous.

'It's very spacious.'

The woman laughed. She removed her shawl, turned up the gas, and took a gin bottle and two glasses from the mantelshelf. 'Spacious. That's it. It's spacious.' She offered Edward a glass. He shook his head.

The woman seemed very cheerful now. She was no longer the pathetic, bird-like creature of the coffee house, but confident, slightly amused by him. She sat down on the bed and took a swig of gin directly from the bottle.

'That's better. Nothing like gin to deaden the senses. I expect it'll do for me in the end. But who cares. Go out blind drunk, eh? It's as good an end as any.'

'Aren't you afraid of dying?' Edward said. Like many people who are afraid of death, he imagined that other people shared his terror. 'Aren't you afraid you might die violently, or from some disease?'

'I'm never afraid of nothing when there's a drop of gin inside me.'

He sat down on a wooden chair and nursed his hat on his lap, trying to feel at ease, but knowing that he was an alien here. His contact with the poverty-stricken people who came to the hospital put him firmly on the side of the charity-bearing philanthropists. Judgements were made: the deserving and undeserving poor, but always 'the Poor', a class, a species apart. He watched the woman throw back her head and drink again from the gin bottle: there, but for the grace of God, went every seduced governess, seamstress, and serving-maid in the country. He told himself that the woman was what she was because of circumstances which were not of her own making: the same fate could have befallen Elizabeth, or Clara and her mother, for they were all women. Yet, somehow he could not believe that Clara would ever lose her carefully preserved virginity should Mad Fritz cast her and her mother

79

out on to the streets after squandering all his worldly wealth. Was it true then that women who gave themselves willingly to sexual pleasure were depraved? And Elizabeth, because she had given herself to him one summer's day in a barleyfield, was an evil woman? Hogwash, he reminded himself determinedly.

He looked at the woman before him and felt miserably confused.

She sensed his disapproval. 'You're a man,' she said defensively. 'You can't never know how it is for us – even when a girl's been brought up with it and never knowed any different.'

A small inconsistency in something the woman had said struck him. 'You told me you were a distressed governess.'

'Did I? Well, perhaps I was. Sometimes it's that, sometimes I'm a milliner, or a Baptist minister's daughter – but you, having a brother in the trade, so to speak, might have spotted that one.'

'So you lied?'

'What odds is it? What's it matter how I started? It all comes down to the same thing.' She drank again from the bottle and got up from the bed. 'Sure you won't partake?' He shook his head, and she returned the bottle to the mantelshelf. She began to unbutton her frock.

'What are you doing?' The fact that she had lied to him seemed to make the situation suddenly unpredictable.

'Now come on, sir.' The woman smiled in a knowing way. 'Don't play the false modesty no more.'

'Please – fasten your dress.' Edward leaped to his feet and put on his hat as if to assure her of his readiness to leave now, this very minute. He glimpsed the curve of her full breasts under the hand which was undoing her bodice.

She came towards him. 'I'm used to shy young gentlemen. Don't fret. I knew all along what you'd really come for.'

He felt distressed, unsafe. Was she right? Was his curiosity about her only a thirst for sexual knowledge? He made a move towards the door, but with a startling speed the woman reached it before him and barred his way. She was breathing quickly, almost as if she were afraid of his leaving.

'Don't you go just yet.' She leaned her back against the door. She placed one of his hands on her breast and smiled; she smelled of gin and onions. He could feel the hard nub of her nipple against the palm of his hand and the soft blowsy warmth of her skin. 'Stay a bit longer, sir. Just a while. Who knows? After a drop of gin you might have the

courage for it. I can have you lickerish in no time once you're willing.'
She kissed him, pulling herself against him with a grinding motion of
her hips and a crude emphasis of her lower body.

More than a little frightened now Edward forced back a revulsion at
the smell and taste of her. If he could get her away from the door, he
could escape. He moved backwards to the bed and she came willingly,
until, at the last moment, as she leaned sideways to fall on to the
mattress with him, Edward thrust her away from him and rushed again
to the door.

Panic rose to his gorge as the knob refused to turn at the first attempt;
his thought was that she had locked it without his noticing. Then, as
the door flew open and he ran out on to the landing, he heard her
shriek out from where she had fallen on the bed.

'Jerry! Jerry, get here quick!'

If Edward had felt insecure before, he seemed now to enter a bizarre
dream. He did not understand that he was about to be set on by the
woman's 'bully', that he had taken on the role of the dupe, and that
in the world of prostitute and protector dupes deserved little sympathy.
He could hear footsteps on the bottom flight of stairs. He stood
uncertainly at the head of the bannister, hearing the same footsteps
coming rapidly up the second flight. He did not know what was
happening, but he felt very sick, and wished himself safely back in the
Fitzroys' company, in his own lodgings, anywhere except where he
was. He ran back into the woman's room and seized a poker from the
fireplace. The woman cried out again.

'Don't do that, sir. Don't you fight 'im. Jerry'll kill you. Just you be
a good boy and do as you're told.'

Edward hesitated, then returned the poker to the hearth.

The man was not large, but he was muscular, and his clean-shaven
face had the look of an inveterate brawler. He smiled as he came
towards Edward, more menacing in the almost urbane manner of his
approach than had he immediately sprung to the attack. He wore grey
moleskin trousers and a lighter grey shirt which was open at the neck
and rolled up at the sleeves to reveal dark-haired heavy forearms.

'So he was bilking, was he?' the man said.

The situation was so far removed from any of his previous experience,
so outlandish that Edward began to feel lightheaded.

'Bilking?' He laughed. These people were foreigners, they even had
their own language.

81

'Bilking, my friend. Leaving without paying your dues.' The man enunciated the words slowly.

'I paid half a guinea,' Edward said, and was at once struck by the farcical aspect of the protest, so that he would have laughed again, close to hysteria, if he had not noticed a sinister alteration in the man's manner.

The man came to stand beside him. He placed an arm round Edward's shoulder in a companionable sort of way, so that it was not until the arm was thrown round further, the stranger behind him and forcing back his chin, that Edward understood properly what was happening. He could not cry out, he could scarcely breathe for the weight of the man's forearm pressing into his windpipe. The woman was turning out his pockets. He heard her swear at what she found. 'Five shillings – and a bleeding pocket watch.'

'We'll have his coat.'

Between them they dragged his coat from his body, forcing his arm back in its socket, the man maintaining a constant pressure on his neck. Edward did not try to struggle, could not, because of the vice-like grip across his throat. The pain was bad, and his blood pounded in his head as if it would burst it apart. He tried to show them that he was no threat to them, that they need not kill him; for he was sure now that that was how it was going to end.

'He told me he was a med, I should have believed him, but he looked like a toff in that rig-out.' The woman threw Harris's coat on the bed in disgust.

'I'll finish him.' The man tightened his grip and forced Edward to the door. Edward's knees buckled, the pressure and the pain became intolerable. He was choking, felt himself losing consciousness. He heard the woman say something, though it was not until afterwards that he realized that she must have spoken in his defence; for the arm around his throat loosened, the room came into focus again, and he saw the woman's face, white, her mouth open, before he was flung on to the landing.

Then he fell. He caught briefly at the bannister and held on to it, but his hands were numb and he lost his balance quickly and crashed down the first short flight of stairs into a door at the bottom. Terror forced him to his feet again. He half fell, half threw himself down the second flight, catching at the stair rails, convinced that his attacker was close behind him and that each gasping, tearing breath would be cut off by that iron forearm again.

He stumbled from flight to flight until he reached the street, and then ran with sobbing breaths until he realized that no one was following. He fell against a wall, let his legs go from under him, and sat in a puddle of filth in the street, his hands cupping his bruised throat.

He did not understand. He had done them no harm. If only they had listened. He could not make sense of the violence of the man against him. His neck and throat hurt with the smallest movement and intake of breath. He became aware of the contact of his trousers with some disgusting substance by his feet. Slowly, a certainty drove out all remnants of goodwill: while the sick and virtuous among the Poor deserved all sympathy, there were others, however much they might have been driven to viciousness by circumstances, who deserved to stew in hell.

12

Charlford wreathed itself in mist and welcomed November. Elizabeth consoled herself once more with *The Lady of Shalott* and became the fair Elaine, the Maid of Astolat, who had died of unrequited love for Lancelot. She closed the book and looked out of the window at the ghost-grey, moisture-laden garden, stroking the tooled leather cover of the book disconsolately, trying to draw some comfort from the memory that Edward had bought it for her.

Of less solace was the Church. The Thornes always attended the village church on Sundays in the morning and evening. Nowadays Henry's gouty leg plagued him with predictable regularity on the Sabbath, and he remained at home in his study, ostensibly to read the great family Bible on a stand by his chair, but more often to doze with his mouth open by the fire.

On a Sunday morning, some weeks after Mrs Thorne's supper party, Elizabeth went to church with her mother and with Aunt Lydia, who, although pronouncing daily on the superior merits of Kensington society, seemed reluctant to return to its bosom.

The trees dripped their blackened branches in the lanes. The damp seeped into the very body of the church and up through the flag-stones into people's boots. Robert's sermon was lengthy as usual. The sermon began with a reference to the Book of Ruth. Ruth, the dutiful daughter, thought Elizabeth. She was becoming frightened of her mother and father's dependence on her. 'What would we do without our Lizzie, now that Hannah's gone?' her father said repeatedly. And, only that morning, Lydia had said, 'Wait until your sister has some good news for us, Elizabeth. Then you'll have plenty to occupy you. You'll learn, as I have done, what a responsibility it is, being an aunt.'

The bleak chasm of despair had widened in Elizabeth's soul. She did not want to be an aunt. Was it too much to hope that one day she might have her own children?

Sometimes she found herself wishing that her union with Edward in the barleyfield had ended in a pregnancy. It happened that way with the village girls, and marriage followed as a natural course. She envied them with their red-cheeked babies in their arms. In a flood of sentimentality she yearned for the serenity of motherhood, the pinnacle of feminine achievement.

And then she thought of Johnny Herbert and his brothers and sisters, with their toes out of their boots, a father who spent his money on gin when he was in work, and who beat his wife whether he was in work or not. Five children, three miscarriages, two stillbirths – what did Mrs Herbert think of motherhood? Then a different kind of yearning affected her, and she knew that there were worse injustices in the world than that of her own frustration.

Robert's sermon had launched into an attack against the worldly and the slothful among the congregation. The pattern was familiar, but his voice, rising in pitch to promise death and everlasting punishment to those who ignored pastoral admonishments, halted her drifting thoughts. Soon he would set to with a diatribe against the neighbouring parish, where a new vicar had recently been appointed, a high church man, who, it was rumoured, had displayed lavishly ornate candlesticks on the church altar and had bowed to them once during evensong. 'Beware, the creeping threat of papism,' Robert would exclaim exhorting his flock to greater spiritual vigilance.

Elizabeth watched Robert's soft lips move above his lofty clerical collar. Did he really believe the rhetoric which blustered from him? His words rang in the chill air and echoed from the walls and vaulted roof of the church. She saw that his pale eyes were fixed intently on her. It was as if he could see right into her soul. She felt trapped. She imagined marriage to those mobile lips and pink scrubbed cheeks and admonitions to guard her soul. His lips would be cold and moist and passionless. She remembered Edward's kisses and the willingness with which she had given herself to him. She shifted in her seat and looked away from Robert. Why was life so unfair?

Lydia, sitting next to her, sensed her inattendance and glanced at her disapprovingly.

What was everyone else thinking about? Elizabeth watched her mother. Mrs Thorne stared straight ahead, as if absorbed by the sermon, but Elizabeth guessed that she was worrying about the household budget, stretched to its limit lately. Her pale, nervous face was pinched up with the effort of doing mental arithmetic at the same time as appearing to pay deference to Robert and her Maker. Her mother would think it extremely wicked to think about love-making while listening to a sermon; it would be wicked to think of such things anywhere. Elizabeth stole a glance at the people near her. She could tell by the occasional jerk of Dr Molesworth's head that he was falling asleep. No indelicate thoughts there. Mr and Mrs Attwell sat in their pew with their sons and daughters-in-law, the men red-necked and sunk in gloom, the women rigid and dutiful under their bonnets. The schoolchildren sat across the aisle, their boredom well-concealed under the watchful gaze of their Sunday school teacher, Miss Hemingale, with her mother beside her.

Mr Pengelly sat in a pew a little distance to Elizabeth's right. A sudden shaft of weak sunlight lit up the empty seat beside him, capturing dust motes in its beam. She could see his profile and bristling side-whiskers, but she could not make out his expression. Mr Pengelly's gaze was firmly fixed on Robert. One leg was crossed negligently over the other, and she noticed that his hand, resting on the pew, drummed silently with the fingers, as though betraying some secret impatience to be somewhere else. Was he really listening to Robert, or had his thoughts perhaps taken flight from righteousness like hers into the realms of intemperate fancies? He had said that a man reached a certain age and began to look out for a wife. In what sense did such a man look for a wife? As a business proposition, to provide him with some comforts? A housekeeper, with the additional service of warming his bed and bearing his children in return for her keep? Or did he long for female company? Did Mr Pengelly yearn, as she did, for the heat of love, the sweet exhilaration of another's body, to know it in every detail, so that a look, a word, a touch was as intense and invigorating as the sexual flame which united them? Elizabeth felt the heat of that remembered flame flicker in the most intimate parts of her. She looked up and Robert's gaze burned into her from the pulpit. She knew then that it was the same fire which inflamed Robert, under the guise of zeal for the guardianship of her soul.

After the service was over she edged along with the rest of the congregation waiting to shake Robert's hand in the church porch. She extended her fingers lightly when her turn came and made to leave quickly, but Robert hung on to them. He had a book in his left hand which he thrust towards her.

'May I speak to you alone very soon?'

Elizabeth, annoyed at the interest which this remark generated among the people around her, was glad that her mother and Lydia had gone too far ahead to have noticed.

'May I also suggest an excellent little book?'

She took the book from him reluctantly.

'Please read it.' Robert's voice was hoarse, either from the exertions of the recent sermon, or from a sudden attack of nervousness. 'It expresses so well my own sentiments.' He seemed to have surpassed himself with this confession: his face and neck had flushed a dark crimson which contrasted strangely with his fair, cherubic curls. He turned from her and seized the hand of the next member of his flock in line, as though greeting a long-lost friend.

Elizabeth walked along the lane, falling further behind her mother and aunt. She held the book Robert had given her idly in her gloved hand next to her prayer book, not bothering to look at the title. She swung her arm, hitting out at the heads of dead cow parsley at the side of the lane. The sun, a haze of yellow light, shone through the mist. Elizabeth breathed in the damp decaying smell of the autumn vegetation. She remembered the leather-bound Tennyson which Edward had given her, and pictured the Lady of Shalott, *robed in snowy white*, floating down to Camelot, while she chanted mournfully with her last dying breath. When he learned of her death, Lancelot would grieve, thought Elizabeth. Except that Tennyson did not make Lancelot grieve. Where was the guilt, the self-mortification for the trouble he had caused?

The air was very still and silent but for the murmurs of people still gossiping near the church.

'Miss Thorne.'

She turned to see that Arthur Pengelly and a large black retriever dog were some yards behind her and hurrying to catch up with her.

She waited for them. She was aware of a small and pleasurable lifting of her spirits.

The animal pushed its nose into the folds of Elizabeth's skirt. Elizabeth, who did not particularly like dogs, concealed her distaste and patted its head.

'Does your dog attend church, Mr Pengelly? I didn't see him.'

'My man was walking the dog,' he explained. 'Merlin's a regular heathen. As his master has been these ten years past, I'm ashamed to say.'

'You probably didn't miss much by staying away if our parson is typical of parsons all over the world,' she said. They walked on together, the dog following close behind. 'Merlin,' she added. 'That's an unusual name.' She was thinking again of the Lady of Shalott, Lancelot, King Arthur and Guinevere.

'He wasn't my dog,' Mr Pengelly said seriously. 'The fellow who sold it me said it was called Merlin. He said it was fitting, what with me being an Arthur. I didn't know what he was meaning, to tell the truth, first off.'

She laughed.

'It's a legend.'

'I know. And I think it's a charming idea.' She turned and the dog wagged its tail. The idea might be a charming one, but the animal was singularly without charm, she thought.

'You look very fine when you laugh,' Mr Pengelly said suddenly.

She was startled.

'Nothing wrong with the plain truth,' he said. 'I thought you believed in plain-talking.'

She felt a mixture of embarrassment and pleasure.

'Tell you what I liked from the start,' he persisted. 'You don't put on airs and graces. Look at the way you're not ashamed to be walking and talking quite natural with me.' He ignored her protest that there was nothing unnatural about walking with a neighbour along a country lane. 'There's some here would say my money isn't so good as theirs because I'm not a gentleman. But I earned what I got, Miss Thorne. Ten years I tried to make something of myself before I struck lucky.'

'Mr Pengelly, I'm not interested in titles.' She felt she had to put him at ease. 'There are some men, who people round here might loosely call gentlemen, who behave without honour of any kind.' She stopped, half afraid, half hoping that he might suspect a meaning behind her words. He smiled benignly; he did not appear to be a man

88

of deep perception. 'I'm sure you deserve your present good fortune,' Elizabeth said. 'And I shall be pleased to be seen walking with you at any time.' They had reached her gate.

'Then might I walk you home from church again some time?'

She hesitated only a moment, then nodded.

They parted very amicably and Elizabeth went indoors to her room to remove her cloak and bonnet. Only then did she examine the book which Robert had given her. She read aloud with ironic deliberation its title: *The Sacred and Sublime Sex.* She flung it in dismay on the bed. A sheet of paper fell from between the pages. Slowly she picked it up.

My dear Miss Thorne,

This treatise on womanhood expresses, so much more exquisitely than could my own humble efforts, the high regard in which I hold your sex, indeed, yourself. It seems to me that you, above all other women, represent the best of feminine virtues, which, if tempered with a true modesty of soul, would provide all that I hope to find in a wife. I humbly hope you will permit me to speak further on this subject.

Your devoted servant,
Robert Munro

Elizabeth crumpled the note tightly in her hand. She felt a sob rise to her throat. She ground her teeth, but she could not prevent the sob escaping. It was followed by another, and then more, until at last she gave in and let a storm of weeping sweep through her with a force of misery and rage which would no longer be suppressed.

In the afternoon she walked across the fields to the river. There she leaned on the stone parapet of the old packhorse bridge, and traced the lines between the stones, and places where lovers had carved their initials. Etched into the centre stone, covered with lichen, was the outline of a hand, where someone had traced their own, or a lover's fingers many years before. She fitted her hand against the outline, feeling nothing except the roughness of the stone, exhausted by her earlier fit of weeping.

A chill wind blew drizzling rain against her face. A few tenacious yellow leaves clung to tree branches across the brown and swollen river. A half-submerged boat lay against the bank downstream. She imagined herself lying in it. If only the broad stream could bear her far away. They would find her later, her eyes darkened, *her blood frozen slowly*, and round the prow of the boat they would read the name, 'The Lady of Shalott'. And Edward would grieve. Oh, how he would grieve, because of what he had brought her to. She gave a shuddering sigh, overwhelmed by a flood of ungovernably morbid and romantic feeling.

They were all gathered in the drawing room when she returned: her father, looking uneasy and leaning for support against the fireplace; Aunt Lydia on the sofa, a little frown creasing her brow, her lips pursed with the importance of some recent happening; her mother hovering and flapping near the doorway.

There was something ominous about the sudden silence which had fallen as she entered the room; as though there had been a catastrophe and they did not know who should tell her the news.

Her mother took a little step towards her. Her hands beat at the air. 'It has come at last. Robert has been up to the house to speak to your father. Oh, I can't tell you how happy I am for you.'

Henry echoed his wife's sentiments with a pretence at enthusiasm. 'Three hundred and fifty a year. That's not bad for a parson – and with your dowry. Of course I have told him that the final word must rest with you.' He tailed off. She thought she detected a plea for forgiveness in his eyes.

There was silence. They waited, as though they already knew what would happen next. Nevertheless, the strength of her reaction startled them and sent her mother fleeing to the sofa for support.

'Do you really think I would tie myself to that idiot!'

This judgement on Robert, hardly fair since he had distinguished himself very ably at Cambridge, excited her further. She paced the floor and wrung her hands.

Mrs Thorne had turned pale. 'Elizabeth!'

'No, Mother. Never. And if Robert is ever man enough to do more than scribble about how he esteems my virtue, I shall tell him to his face.' She trembled for a moment by the port decanter on the sideboard, then turned swiftly to the door, in a departure which was more threatrical than dignified.

Lydia yawned delicately. 'What a bore Elizabeth is becoming. She really will have to learn to curb her tongue. One can hardly make allowances for youth any more.'

Henry mopped his eyes and brow with a large handkerchief.

'Do we have any smelling salts?' whispered Mrs Thorne.

Lydia reached in her carpet bag and handed her a bottle of sal volatile. 'I suppose we can't hold out any hopes for Edward after all this time?'

Nobody was listening. Mrs Thorne lay weakly back against the sofa with her eyes closed. Henry stood by the fireplace. He wound his handkerchief round his hand like a bandage. 'I won't have it!' he burst out suddenly. 'I won't have all this upset in my own house. It's all your fault.' He rounded on Mrs Thorne and Lydia. 'Why don't you go back to London!' Lydia looked alarmed. 'And as for Robert – he's too damned stuffed. He's not half the man Edward is, not half the man.'

Elizabeth, weeping again on her bed, was thinking much the same thing.

When Robert proposed after school the next day, Elizabeth refused him with a surprising restraint in the end. He had backed her into the churchyard and cornered her up against one of the tombstones. Uppermost in her mind at the time, she remembered afterwards, was the certainty that the shortbread which she kept in her pocket would be crushed where she was leaning against it.

Robert's reaction, when she said that no, she would not consider marrying him, was at first one of disbelief. Then worldly pride got the better of Christian stoicism. A petulance, which was neither Christian nor charitable, made him say that she was ungrateful, that she owed it to him, to accept his offer. Consider her parents. Consider her inheritance. Consider what people would say. She was a fool if she believed that Edward gave her a second thought now that he had his friends in London. She had been a fool ever to prefer his brother to himself in the first place. Edward was a fool, come to that. The whole world had gone mad if women preferred to throw themselves at fools and sinners, when they could have a clean-living, God-fearing husband like himself. He left the churchyard without a backward glance.

After a while Elizabeth took the shortbread from her pocket and was relieved to find it intact. *Brief sorrow, short-lived care*, she read from the inscription on the tombstone. But the shortbread was more of a comfort as she walked home across the field.

13

Mrs Thorne remained distraught for several days.

'He told me he revered me,' Elizabeth tried to explain. She had relegated Edward's leather-bound Tennyson to the bottom drawer of her dressing table and had taken to reading books with titles like *A Lady's Life in the Antipodes* and *Travels in Many Lands*. 'He asked me to be the mistress of his home.'

'And what more could anyone want than that?' snapped Mrs Thorne. 'He won't ask you again. Not now. Think what changes you could have made at the rectory with Uncle Willie's money!'

'I don't care about money. I have the money I've saved from teaching at the school – freezing in the winter, bitten by flies all summer. Robert has never supported me against the Squire over the children. How can I even respect a man like that? And I won't marry him just for Uncle Willie's seven hundred and fifty pounds. Which will go straight into Robert's purse, believe me. Robert is one of the old-fashioned breed.'

Mrs Thorne, also of an old-fashioned turn of mind, was out of her depth. 'You have lost your senses. Totally lost your senses. To refuse an offer like that!' A thought occurred to her. 'You're not still holding out hopes for Edward after all this time? After the way he treated you!'

Elizabeth's confusion betrayed her. 'At least Edward wouldn't have talked of reverence,' she protested. Her mother turned away in exasperation. 'But no, Mother. I've resigned myself to spinsterhood. I don't need a husband. I just want to find a way to be myself.'

This Mrs Thorne truly could not comprehend. 'You are very strange sometimes,' she complained sadly.

Elizabeth did not reply.

Certainly she did not mention Arthur Pengelly. And yet, recently he had begun to occupy her thoughts more and more. She found herself looking forward to the times when they might accidentally meet. She would go out of her way to casually bump into him in the village or when he was walking with his dog Merlin by the river. Once, he gave her a lift in his carriage when he passed her on the road. She had been to Yeovil and had missed the return flier, so had decided to walk.

He halted his carriage at the side of the road. There was no one to see them; after only a second's hesitation she had climbed in beside him. She leaned back against the cushions of the carriage. She had never ridden in anything so well-sprung or well-upholstered. Not even Squire Attwell had a carriage so modern as this one. There was something to be said for the comforts which money could buy.

He smiled at her. 'Are you glad I was passing?'

'I enjoy walking,' she said defensively. But she knew that if she had been honest, she would have admitted that she was glad to be there beside him. She closed her eyes to the dizzy passing of tree branches and hedges on either side of the road, and let her mind fill with the smell of new leather, the sour tang of the horses, the rhythm of the wheels on the road and the vibrations of the carriage. The sun was pleasant against the side of her face. She was aware of the warm smell of the man beside her, his sleeve occasionally brushing her sleeve, both of them part of the jostling, swaying movement of the carriage. She opened her eyes and saw that he was watching her. His own eyes were dark and had long eyelashes, she noticed. It occurred to her that he was not so much older than forty as she had at first thought. It was easy to overlook her earlier criticism of his stocky figure, rough manners, and weathered face. And yet, she did not imagine that she was falling in love with Mr Pengelly. Love was something which she had dismissed from her life for ever.

'So, you been out with him in his carriage?' Mrs Booth was gutting and skinning a rabbit when Elizabeth entered the kitchen, flushed from the exhilaration of her recent drive.

Elizabeth rested her hands on the table and leaned towards her confidentially. 'Have you been setting your spies on me?' she teased. 'My Aunt Lydia perhaps?'

''Saw you,' replied the woman laconically.

Elizabeth glanced at the kitchen window. The lane was clearly visible from this side of the house. She prayed that her mother and Lydia had been occupied elsewhere. Flo, the kitchen maid, peeling apples over a bucket in the corner, looked up and gave her a sly smile. Elizabeth suddeny felt irritated by their interest.

'Not a word to my aunt,' she said. 'Or I should never hear the end of it.'

'Anything you say,' Mrs Booth replied.

Elizabeth left the kitchen.

The kitchen maid continued peeling apples for several minutes after she had gone. 'There's somethin' about the way 'e looks at you,' she said after a while.

'Who?' Mrs Booth asked without interest.

'Mr Pengelly. The way 'e do look at a girl. Makes 'n go all trembly.'

'And what would a man like Mr Pengelly be doin' lookin' at a daft maid like you?'

Flo turned sullen. ''E asked the way to the river once. So I told 'n.'

Mrs Booth began jointing the rabbit. 'You said Michael, used to be coachman to the Squire, made you go all of a-tremble. You said Daniel O'Brien the tinker could undress you from top to toe just by lookin'. You'm a dirty mind, Flo. It'll get you in trouble one day.' She brought the meat cleaver down on the table with a crack.

'That's it. Same thing.' Flo jabbed her knife in the air and a ring of apple peel flew from it. She stooped to retrieve it. 'Just like Daniel O'Brien.'

'You ought to be ashamed of yourself, lik'nin' a man like Mr Pengelly to someone as common at flirtin' as Daniel O'Brien,' Mrs Booth said, but without conviction.

The girl sniffed. 'Men's men. They'm all common when it do come to you know what.'

The older woman said nothing, but she did not look as if she disagreed with her. She threw the limp pink pieces of naked rabbit with a vengeance into an iron pot on the stove.

'Seems Elizabeth 'ave given the parson 'is marching orders,' Flo said eventually.

'None of your business.'

'Mr Edward was all right.'

94

'He was another one, if you'm talking about flirtin'.'

Flo giggled. 'Nice though, Mr Edward was.'

Some days after this, Elizabeth, coming out from school, was met by Robert. Johnny Herbert, carrying her books, wavered between his devotion to Elizabeth and his terror of Robert. Elizabeth saw the child's dilemma and took the books from him gently.

'Thank you, Johnny.' She pressed a penny into his hand and closed his fingers over it. 'You'd better run on home.'

Robert watched the child race away. Still looking after the small figure in the lane he said, 'Squire Attwell agrees with me that it might be less embarrassing for everyone, under the circumstances, if you were to resign your position at the school after Christmas. I have asked Miss Hemingale to teach the children in your place.'

Elizabeth did not argue, she made no violent protest but answered coldly, 'Since it seems the whole thing has already been decided, there's not much I can say.'

'I think not.'

Fury boiled up in her and made her blood pound as she walked away from Robert.

As she neared the house she saw Arthur Pengelly coming towards her along the lane. 'I am so very angry, Mr Pengelly,' she burst out. 'Forgive me if I seem a little strange.'

Mr Pengelly's smile faltered. He stood, disconcerted, as she paced in front of the garden hedge, clenching her fists and unclenching them. She came to a halt by the gate and gripped the top rail with her head bowed.

'Shall I fetch someone?' he suggested. 'Perhaps you're feeling faint?'

'I don't make a practice of fainting,' she snapped. 'I said that I'm angry.'

'Perhaps if you were to tell me why you're angry,' he said a little pathetically.

'Because the Squire and his parson are hand-in-glove. Because men can do things high-handedly and escape retribution. Because I, being merely a woman, must do as I am told. Because I have no say, absolutely no say whatsoever in my own destiny.'

'Aha,' he said, as if participating in a guessing game. 'This has something to do with your school.'

'My school.' She seized on the phrase. 'Exactly! But if it were *my* school I should have swept Robert off the premises long ago. And I should have swept out the Squire's horses, his flies, and his insistence on the children's deference to their so-called betters. I have been dismissed, Mr Pengelly. I have been supplanted by Miss Hemingale – much joy may she have. And why? Because I refused the matrimonial advances of our esteemed parson. Now is that fair? I ask you, is that fair?'

He agreed that it was not.

She was silent. As her fury subsided she saw that she had gone too far. She had let her passion flow too freely in front of a man who was practically a stranger to her.

He did not seem offended. 'I can't say as I'm sorry,' he said after a while.

'That I shall no longer be teaching at the school?'

'That you are not to marry Parson Munro.'

She caught her breath. Then she did something she had not done since she was a girl. She blushed deeply, feeling the heat of it suffuse her neck and face. Embarrassed, she pretended to misunderstand him.

'It isn't a light matter, Mr Pengelly. We're not a wealthy family. My mother thinks I've taken leave of my senses to turn a parson down, for I could have had access to a dowry of seven hundred and fifty pounds – and seven hundred and fifty pounds is a fortune to my mother. And why *not* marry the man? A woman has to live. What would you do in the same circumstances? But that's a silly question. You can't know what it's like for a woman.'

'I have known a few women, Miss Thorne. And I've learned that if a woman has spirit, she can do almost anything she wants to.'

'You think I'm wallowing in self-pity.'

'I think you should have tried a spell in Australia along with me. I've known women run stores, catch sheep, trek across country with great packs on their backs. A woman can do anything if she puts her mind to it.'

She felt rebuked, and a little diminished in his eyes. Though she did not know why it should matter to her what he thought. What did Mr Pengelly know about her disappointments? Would he have lectured her about women who had spirit if he knew how Edward had used her and abandoned her? Wouldn't he instead be sympathetic and tell her that Edward was a scoundrel? Didn't he know that what she needed most right now was a friend?

She looked a him and saw then that she had been wrong. There was sympathy in his expression and he had meant what he had said.

'I think that you and I could become friends,' he said, as if reading her thoughts.

She drew in her breath slowly. 'Thank you, Mr Pengelly. I should be very grateful for a friend.'

When she had gone into the house, Pengelly remained a little while in the lane. He paced to and fro, as Elizabeth had done, in front of the hedge; but his agitation was not caused by anger. Pengelly was planning, his thoughts racing ahead into the future. He was a simple man, but he saw the advantages of cultivating a closer acquaintance with Elizabeth.

The fact was, that his money from the diggings in Australia was dwindling fast under the strain of his present lifestyle, and seven hundred and fifty pounds would tide him over nicely for another year. She was a little old, it was true, but not unattractive. And there was a sexuality about her, which led him to believe that, if she didn't love him now, he wouldn't find her unresponsive after a while. He had known women like her before, quick to flare up in temper, but volatile too in bed.

Well, Arthur Pengelly, he told himself. He had come to a decision. He stood still in the lane. You've escaped it long enough, I reckon. It's what you came home for. Just you take the plunge and ask her. She won't refuse. All women want marriage, when it comes down to it.

14

Marriage for Hannah had brought its share of pain as well as pleasure. She sought consolation in making changes in her new surroundings. If Fred spent an illicit night in London he paid for it unknowingly with a set of new curtains or carpets. When he dallied in Bristol or Bath, Hannah would introduce a project for replacing the wallpaper in the dining room or she would decide on the tearing out of the fireplaces in all the bedrooms. She had discovered that such remedies were more satisfying than weeping alone into one's pillow.

The family had been invited to inspect the result of all this interior renovation work. They were to travel over one Saturday, early in December. At the last minute, however, a message was brought from the jobmaster in the village that the carriage they were to have hired had broken a wheel and there was not another to be had that day. Consternation flew about the household. Lydia and Mrs Thorne twittered over what should be done.

'Mr Pengelly will lend us his carriage,' Elizabeth said.

'What are you thinking of!' cried her mother.

'That we have no carriage, while Mr Pengelly has a particularly fine one at his disposal. In fact, he drove me out in it only the other day.'

She ignored their gasps of dismay.

Henry, who had been sunk in gloom in his chair by the fire, became animated. He thumped his stick against the carpet. 'Splendid idea. Splendid. The fellow owes us a courtesy after all this time. Send a message. Tell him it's a matter of urgency. Tell him I've looked forward all week to this visit. He won't want to disappoint an old man. He's an obliging enough fellow.'

'I shall go myself to ask him,' Elizabeth said, tying on her bonnet.

She felt a sense of mission in her errand. She walked with firm, deliberate steps the short distance to The Red House. A slight anxiety had taken over, however, by the time she reached the driveway. It was, after all, presumptuous to ask such a thing after so short an acquaintance. It suggested that there was more than a neighbourly friendship between them.

She was glad, at least, that she did not have to walk up to the great ugly red-brick house and ring its bell, for Arthur Pengelly was in shirt-sleeves in the grounds. He was dragging along a large tree branch from a thicket close by the gates. The dog Merlin was galloping around him, growling and picking up small sticks in its mouth and dropping them again, then racing off among the trees. Mr Pengelly threw his tree branch on to a pile of wood he had already gathered. As he turned he saw Elizabeth. A look of pleasure flew across his face.

'Well, now. This is a fine surprise.'

He came towards her, wiping his hands on the seat of his trousers. His face was red from hauling trees about and his hair curled damply against his forehead. He wore no coat or waistcoat; his waist was thick, his figure heavy in a white shirt; there seemed to be a nakedness about him, so that Elizabeth shifted her eyes away to the pile of branches he had collected, aware that he disturbed her.

'I'm sorry to greet you so.' He glanced ruefully at his hands, stained green with lichen. 'I wasn't expecting visitors so early in the day. You must think me very uncivil.'

'I've come with a very uncivil request. And, if you think it's an imposition, you must, please, not feel obliged to agree to it. But we're in a fix, Mr Pengelly.' She explained the situation quickly, breathlessly. 'We do, of course, hope that you'll stay to luncheon, if you'll drive us.' She felt too stiff and embarrassed. She shouldn't have come. What if he were to misunderstand her motive?

'I doubt I should be a welcome guest, so unexpected,' Mr Pengelly said. 'Though I should be glad to oblige you, Miss Thorne,' he added hurriedly. 'Don't think I'm not willing to drive you.'

The dog had returned from grubbing among the bushes; it faced Elizabeth squarely, its tongue lolling from the side of its mouth. The animal seemed to grin at her; the illusion was not endearing and Elizabeth looked away with a small shudder.

'Hannah's gratitude would far outweigh the inconvenience of setting an extra place at table,' she said. 'In fact, she would revel in the small domestic crisis.' As if to counteract the strained formality of their bearing to one another, she laid a hand on his arm. 'Please do it, Mr Pengelly. For my sake. It's such a pleasure to my father to see Hannah.'

She had not used that sort of feminine trick before. She despised it in others: the soft, wheedling tone, the glance from beneath lowered lashes. She was surprised at herself, and even more surprised at the effect it had on Mr Pengelly. His colour deepened quickly. He thrust a hand through his hair and took a step closer to her.

'I shall have to make myself more presentable than this,' he said.

The dog leered up at Elizabeth and wagged its tail. It turned suddenly and leaped, growling, against its master, so that it almost knocked him off balance and into Elizabeth.

'Merlin seems to agree I should help you.' Mr Pengelly laughed tolerantly and fondled the dog's ugly black head.

Elizabeth, moving aside, met the animal's eye and detected a gleam of evil. 'Whatever does he do if he disagrees?' she said.

'Mr Pengelly has been extremely obliging,' said Mrs Thorne, as though explaining away the addition of a coachman or a mechanic to the luncheon party. The broken axle was explained.

'How very kind. Come in, my good fellow.' Fred swiftly recovered some of his good manners and ushered them into the house.

'You're quite the knight in shining armour, Mr Pengelly,' said Hannah, when they were all settled in the dining room and the matter of Arthur Pengelly's deliverance of them surfaced again. 'And we're extremely grateful to you for donning your armour and saving the day.'

'I wouldn't make much of a knight, I don't think.'

'Oh, come,' Mrs Thorne said. 'It was very noble of you to put off what you were doing and come driving out here at a moment's notice.'

'Almost heroic,' Lydia murmured and dipped her spoon into her soup.

'We're very much indebted to you,' Fred said gravely.

The topic of their gratitude having been twice exhausted, a silence fell on the table. The only sound was that of soup being sipped with varying degrees of delicacy from silver-plated spoons. Sunlight glowed through the polished windows and warmed the dark red curtains. Large vases of dried flowers were silhouetted against the light. The window sills and mantel shelf and numerous side tables were filled with porcelain figurines, enamelled candlesticks, houseplants and arrangements of glued shells. Mirrors in fancy frames and oil paintings of rustic domesticity crowded the walls against a handsome crimson flocked wallpaper. There was a barely detectable smell of fresh paint.

'What a difference you have made to this room, dear,' Lydia said, turning to Hannah. 'You have given me food for thought for when I return to Kensington. Decorations set such a seal on a house. Don't you think?'

They all agreed that Hannah had begun married life admirably. The red wallpaper was praised, along with the hand-embroidered sideboard runner and the fringing on the curtains at the windows.

'It took some stubbornness on my part,' Hannah said. 'Fred is such an old fogey when it comes to the domestic arrangements.'

Fred fingered his moustache and allowed himself a smile. 'A little feminine stubbornness might be excused when balanced against the excellence of the result.'

'I expect Fred has been occupied with more pressing matters,' Mrs Thorne said fondly. 'He's fortunate that he can rely on you to manage the domestic sphere so capably. It's not every man who has a wife who takes such pains to please and provide him with soothing surroundings when he returns from his work.'

'I am indeed a very fortunate man,' Fred agreed. 'Hannah is nothing less than perfection in her management of the house. The perfect wife.'

Elizabeth, watching Hannah, saw her eyes flicker with some hidden thought before she accepted the compliment with a calm smile.

'Hannah has spoken of knights in armour,' Fred continued – he had not yet done with the happy balance of duties between husband and wife. 'I say it's a fortunate knight who can ride out adventuring in the world and know that a loving and virtuous wife waits for him in his castle.'

'Some wives might think themselves fortunate, if they too could ride out adventuring occasionally,' Elizabeth said. 'I shouldn't relish waiting behind virtuously in someone's castle.'

'Oh, Elizabeth!' said Mrs Thorne.

Fred smiled blandly. 'Ever the antagonist, Elizabeth. We were, after all, talking in metaphors.'

'I should allow it,' said Arthur Pengelly.

They stared at him.

'I should allow a wife to face the world, if she wanted it. We shouldn't go putting women on a pedestal, to be looked at. Some aren't up to it anyhow. And some don't want it. And some are a darn' sight better at getting on with things than a lot of men.'

'My dear sir, you are not suggesting that a woman should compete with men in the harsh world outside the home?' Fred stroked his moustache in an amused way.

'I've known women in Australia run stores, catch sheep, trek across country with a pack on her back every bit as good as a man could do it.'

'Well, I'm sure I shouldn't like to try it,' sniffed Lydia. 'Nor any of the ladies of my acquaintance.'

'I should,' said Elizabeth. 'Men like to pretend that women are feeble. It makes them feel superior. They want to tie women to their houses, reduce them to two-dimensional creatures, powerless in any sphere except the domestic.' She saw that Hannah had gone red and realized that she had said too much.

'But the domestic sphere is precisely where women excel,' said Fred.

'Some do,' said Elizabeth. 'But for some, the prospect of endless domesticity seems intolerable.'

'Then they're not true women,' Lydia decided.

'Shall we talk about something else?' suggested Hannah. 'I'm sure we don't want to spoil the day by quarrelling.'

After lunch, Elizabeth, who could not bear the prospect of sitting in the drawing room exchanging inanities about Hannah's taste in carpets and curtains, suggested a walk. She stood restlessly by the window, looking out at the drifts of dark leaves across the lawn. She would have liked to corner her sister alone somewhere, interrogated her about Fred's indiscretions, demanded of her what she was going to do about it. Yet, she could see that Hannah would do nothing. Hannah had settled, like so many others, for passivity.

'Will nobody venture outside?' she said impatiently, when she saw that the women were settling themselves comfortably round the fire.

'But it's so cold,' protested Hannah.

Arthur Pengelly got up awkwardly from his chair by the door and said that he would be happy to go with her for a stroll along the lane.

The sun was very bright. The wind whipped the sides of their faces as they left the house behind. After a while they reached the path which led up the hill. Elizabeth was seized by a sudden fear of retracing the steps she had taken with Edward the previous summer. She stopped and almost turned in the lane.

'Are you tired?' Mr Pengelly said. He had chosen to wear a heavy frock coat; a dark, tight woollen waistcoat, a high white collar and neckcloth, and a black top hat completed his outfit. His stocky figure and expression of grave concern made her think all at once and irrationally of an undertaker.

'We could turn back,' he suggested.

She hesitated. Then she smiled. 'No. Let's go to the very top of the hill. You've never seen such a view as there is from up there.' They set off up the track. 'Do you know that they say this is the site of Camelot?'

'So that is why they talk so much of knights and ladies.'

'You must think them utterly ridiculous.'

'No,' he said gravely. 'Sentimental for my taste. But if it makes them happy.'

'But they're not happy. At least, Hannah isn't.' She paused. 'It's all so much hypocrisy.' She would have liked him to be curious about what lay behind her words. It would have helped to reinforce her feeling about him, that they could talk on any subject without being inhibited by convention. But he merely smiled.

They had reached a steeper part of the path. The wind had dropped and the sun was full out. Mr Pengelly's step slowed to a less athletic pace.

'One could almost imagine it's a summer's day,' Elizabeth said, and her thoughts turned unwillingly to Edward, and a hot day in July.

Mr Pengelly was a little way ahead. He stopped and turned to face her. Perspiration was running down his forehead and cheek. He removed his hat, mopped at his face with a handkerchief, and drew in deep lungfuls of air. He looked faintly ridiculous, she thought, large and sweating in his Sunday clothes. She realized with a little shock that she had perhaps begun to foster romantic thoughts about him.

'It's only a little way now,' she encouraged. 'I shall go ahead, if you like. Are you unwell?' she added with sudden concern.

'I didn't expect it'd be so steep.'

'Let me lead the way.' She walked quickly, as if to show him how easy the climb really was. Sweat soaked her skin and cooled her back, but she did not stop until she had reached the open field at the top of the path. She felt a kind of triumph as she turned and saw that he was several yards behind, yet coming grimly on. He flung his hat to the ground and stood panting, his head bowed, his hands on his waist.

'There, that wasn't so terrible,' she said.

He did not reply.

'There's a wonderful view further on.'

He muttered something which sounded shockingly like 'bugger the view'. She pretended she had not heard. She walked away from him across the hilltop and halted at a small rise near its farther edge. From here she could see the patchwork of fields which in the summer had been green and yellow, but were now a mix of browns. The wind was strong and buffeted her face and ears. She closed her eyes, trying to remember how it had been with the drone of insects in the air. She did not hear Arthur walk up behind her.

'I apologize for my ill-temper.'

'I thought we were good friends,' she said reproachfully. Then, more distantly, 'Did you ever see such a view? You can see the Tor if you look carefully.' She turned and shielded her eyes. The outline of Glastonbury Tor showed faint and blue on the horizon.

'It's very pretty. But you didn't bring us up here to admire the view.'

'I don't know why,' she answered truthfully.

He put an arm round her waist. He was still out of breath. 'I think you do.' He gripped her waist more firmly. 'You feel it, same as me. There's an affection grown between us these past weeks. You and me could do well together.' He gave her waist a squeeze. 'What do you say, Elizabeth? A woman could do worse.'

'I know.'

'Will you think on it?'

She turned to face him. She felt suddenly that it was possible, perhaps even inevitable that she would marry him. She said, 'Did you mean it, when you said that you would allow a wife her independence? Do you believe in an equality between the sexes?'

He was surprised. He hesitated. 'I daresay I did mean it.'

'You were annoyed when I beat you to the top of the hill.'

'Because it seemed you were trying to make me look small.'

'I won't do it again,' she promised.

'Oh, Elizabeth. I do love you.' He pulled her to him and kissed her clumsily, so that she fell back gasping. She put the back of her hand to her lips and tried to smile. His enthusiasm began to alarm her a little as again he crushed her against him. She could smell his sweat and cigars and the wool of his coat.

'Perhaps we should wait a while,' she said with misgiving.

'I've wanted you right from the start.' His voice was thick with emotion. 'Ever since that first night, when you praised me for speaking out against the Squire. If you would do me the honour of being my wife, chance what will, I should love you to the death.'

She looked into his eyes and was drawn again to their depth. She could not pretend that she was not stirred by the straightforward nature of his desire. And there was more. He had tapped an unexpected tenderness in her. She felt as she did when confronted by Johnny Herbert, his eyes wide with love because she had given him a biscuit or a word of praise. She took hold of the lapels of his coat.

'You're as good as any of them,' she said solemnly. 'And if I do marry you, I promise, I too should love you until death.'

15

Edward's throat and injured pride had healed. He did not tell anyone about the incident in St Giles. Harris would have insisted that he find a policeman and hunt the criminals down, would have said superciliously, What did he expect? But the incident had made him strangely ashamed, as if in some way he had been at fault.

Meanwhile, Clara had made up her mind that Edward was going to spend Christmas in London. She said that it was time that he revealed the true depth of their friendship to her family.

Edward protested that Mrs Fitzroy would not be very pleased to see his face across the Christmas dinner table, after the way he had behaved at their last meeting.

'She will have forgotten,' Clara said confidently. 'And Papa won't object. We often have people to stay in the holiday. You can't wriggle out of it, Teddy. It's a *fait accomplis*: I have already asked Papa to include you. And you'll love it, you really will. We have a glorious time, we have games, and *tableaux vivants*, and everything. Papa becomes quite a jolly old thing.'

Edward, blanching at the vision of Mad Fritz in the role of a jovial Santa Claus, heard himself agree to Clara's plan.

He felt sickened by his own inadequacies. Why must he always move with whichever currents flowed most strongly, pulled by a backwash of guilt over Elizabeth, swept along by the tide of Clara's enthusiasm, the ebb and flow of his social conscience tearing him this way and that?

He confessed his most urgent predicament, that of Clara's determination to serve him up at the Fitzroys at Christmas, to Jack Harris the week before the holiday. They walked along the Gray's Inn Road towards Edward's lodgings.

'Half the fellows would let Mad Fritz saw off their right arm to spend Christmas with the lovely Clara,' Harris said.

'But would they want the lovely Fritz for a future father-in-law?'

Harris was thoughtful, then a look of superior intelligence lit his face. 'I have it, dear fellow. You say you're spending Christmas with me. It was all arranged long ago, but it slipped your memory. My mama, unlike Mrs Fitzroy, I suspect, would be cut to the quick if you were to turn us down.'

'Clara will be furious.'

'Better to face the wrath of a lady scorned, than get out of your depth.'

Edward opened the front door to his lodging and called out a greeting to his landlady. He collected his letters from the table in the hall. He opened them as he mounted the stairs. Two were bills. One was a letter from Robert.

'Make yourself comfortable,' he told Harris, pushing open the door to his room. He scanned the lines of the letter in Robert's even handwriting.

'Good news from home?'

'The usual drivel. My dear brother hopes I am buckling to at last. Charlford seems to go on in the same old way. Outrage everywhere at the massacre of the Turkish fleet at Sinope. "The Russian Bear", etc, etc.' He turned the page and gave a little exclamation of anguish.

Harris, in the process of cutting himself a slice of cheese from a dish on the table, waited with knife poised. 'Anything the matter, dear fellow?'

Edward read again the continuing lines of the letter:

. . . I feel it is my duty to tell you, that Elizabeth Thorne has befriended a most unsuitable and uncouth fellow, recently returned from the Australian colonies. I cannot hold back on the opinion that she is in grave danger of losing her good name. What is more, she seems not to care a jot! Perhaps, after all, dear Edward, you were a better judge of character than I thought. You did well to leave well alone where she is concerned, and clearly escaped none too soon . . .

Edward imagined the man as some rough settler from the colonies, a returned convict even, taking Elizabeth's hand in company, smiling at her in a way which acknowledges closer intimacies. He did not believe it. She would not do such a thing. He saw the irony of his jealousy, but could not derive any comforting humour from it. He looked at Harris as if for help. 'Perhaps, after all, I should go home at Christmas.'

Harris laughed. 'I smell a woman, old fellow. Isn't Clara tiresome enough for you? My poor mama will be cut to the quick.'

'I'm sorry. My apologies to your mama.' Edward smiled wanly and cut himself a slice of cheese.

He lay, watching the clouds drift across the square of sky framed by the window of his bedroom at the vicarage. He had lain there many times as a boy, when he had been banished to his room for misdemeanours long forgotten. The hypnotic calm conveyed by the block of light was the same, with its changing patterns, and beyond it an eternity, a vast emptiness in which nothing ever changed.

He told himself that when he saw her everything would be as it had been before. He would show her that in his heart he had stayed true to her. He would sit if necessary on her doorstep. He would perform acts of public penance. In the end she would forgive him.

No such dramatic demonstrations of penitence were necessary when he called on the Thornes that afternoon. Henry grasped him with both hands. He shook him with tremulous energy.

'Good old Edward. I knew we could rely on you to come home. How's life treating you? How does doctoring suit you? See? I knew he'd come back.' He nodded at Elizabeth, and she bit her lip with annoyance and tried to smile.

Mrs Thorne frowned. She had never felt at ease with Edward in the way that she did with his brother. 'Have you been working hard?' she said stiffly.

'Oh, extremely hard, Mrs Thorne. I have set my sights on a scholarship next spring.'

Henry laughed gleefully. 'A scholarship, eh? A reformed character indeed.'

'It's true. I've changed in many ways.' He looked at Elizabeth, as if to solicit her approval, but she turned away from him. She made the excuse that she would fetch them some refreshment and left the room.

Mrs Booth was banging saucepans about on the kitchen range.

''E's back then,' she said without turning her head.

'If you mean Mr Munro – he's come home to spend Christmas with his brother,' Elizabeth said.

'Is that so? Then why be 'e sniffin' round 'ere again?' She turned and waved a saucepan lid at her. 'Men! They'm all the same. Doan you let 'n 'ave any on it, Miss Eliz'beth.'

Elizabeth laid out a ring of biscuits precisely on a plate, she took one from the circle and bit into it disconsolately. She set the plate on a tray with a decanter of wine. Mrs Booth was watching her. Elizabeth gave her a grim smile and picked up the tray.

''Tis a good thing your aunt be gone back to Lon'on. She'd 'a had plenty to say about it.'

'Let us be thankful for small mercies,' murmured Elizabeth.

'I shall say this for Mrs Delahaye. 'Er weren't afeared to speak 'er mind,' Mrs Booth called after her.

There was a pain beneath Elizabeth's breast-bone as she returned to the drawing room; it tightened as she neared the door. He should be more penitent. How dare he expect to find the world just as he had left it, as though nothing had happened?

Edward was telling an anecdote. Her father was laughing; tears rolled down his yellowed cheeks. The tale was about some unfortunate dog, which had found its way off the streets into one of the medical lecture theatres and had reappeared the next day as a subject for dissection. Mrs Thorne was fanning herself rapidly with a newspaper: Edward had always been able to shock her.

Elizabeth stood in the doorway with the tray. For a brief moment, something in Edward's expression, a boyish lack of guile, made her heart leap with longing, interrupting the clear direction of her anger.

'He hasn't improved much in his sense of propriety,' Mrs Thorne complained.

'I'm sure you're right,' Elizabeth said.

'Now that you've become so knowledgeable about medical matters' – Henry lifted his leg on to a footstool – 'you can tell me what is wrong with my ankle.' The foot was puffy and swollen over his slipper.

'You know what's wrong with it,' Edward said. 'Too fond of the port bottle, you and your ankle are. And cream puddings and biscuits.' He took a shortbread from the plate which Elizabeth was silently offering him.

'I think Father expected a less flippant answer,' she said. 'In fact, I think we should all be glad for less flippant answers.' She took another shortbread and bit into it and was gratified to see him flinch a little.

'Time was when a man could enjoy himself,' Henry said. 'No need to worry about the consequences. Cream puddings and biscuits were the thing then all right. And pretty women. No one relished being called a sobersides in my day.'

Mrs Thorne remonstrated with him mildly.

'"Tis true,' he insisted. 'Those were the days. Wellington. Waterloo. Did I ever tell you about the time I met Field Marshal Blücher?'

Edward shook his head. Though, as Elizabeth knew, he had heard the story before and could remember it well enough.

Henry embarked on an account of how, when he was a young man, during the celebrations after Waterloo, a famous Prussian hero with medals on his chest had shaken him by the hand.

'Do you think there will be a war with Russia?' said Mrs Thorne anxiously.

'They are saying that preparations have begun for an expedition in the spring,' Edward said. 'Everyone seems to want it, if only because we haven't been to war for forty years, and people have forgotten what it's like.'

'And what about you?' said Henry. 'Are you looking forward to becoming a physician? You could come back here.' There was a child-like hope on his face. 'You could have old Molesworth's practice. He's just about senile. *He* doesn't know what's wrong with my leg. Thinks he can cure everything with a porridge poultice and sticking a roasted onion in your ear.'

Edward was looking at Elizabeth. 'Who knows? Molesworth's house might be just the thing one day.'

She trembled with rage. Did he really believe that he would one day lure her into Molesworth's dismal little house next to the vicarage? After all that had happened?

'You will be too grand for Charlford, surely,' she said bitterly, 'when you're a rich and famous physician. It was rumoured that you were aiming to be a gentleman – in appearances at least.'

'A toast! A toast!' Henry cried. 'To Edward – the famous physician!'

Elizabeth raised the glass to her lips. Her hand shook. She could not drink the wine. She placed the glass on the table beside her. 'I need some air,' she said. 'I am going for a walk.' She hurried from the room.

Mrs Thorne wrung her hands. 'Oh, now see what has happened. And it's all your fault, Edward.'

Edward felt a chill of unease. 'I'm sorry.' It seemed a foolish thing to say.

'You should never have gone away,' said Henry mournfully. 'Even though no promises were made, she must have thought –'

'We all thought,' said Mrs Thorne. 'And then we heard that you were courting a young lady from London. You behaved very badly, Edward.'

'You're right,' Edward said miserably.

'Well, follow her, dear boy.' Henry cheered up suddenly. 'She goes to walk by the river when one of these black moods is on her. You follow her, eh? Women soon come round if you butter 'em a bit.'

He found Elizabeth at the bridge. She was leaning on the stone parapet, staring at a bare clump of willows on the bank. She had flung on a grey cape in her flight and her hair was falling as usual from its untidy bun.

She seemed self-sufficient, very much alone. He realized that his image of her had altered during the months which had separated them, become blurred at the edges and idealized, making her dignified, voluptuous, yet serene – the more so because of his unworthy treatment of her. The image had become almost comfortable. He had planned what they would say to one another, he would be contrite, she forgiving. He saw now how foolish, how ridiculously naive his interpretation of things had been. But there was no time for reassessment, no decent interlude.

'How is your lady friend in London?' she said without turning to look at him.

'She has said that she will cut me when she next sees me.' He remembered the hysterical scene after he had told Clara that he would not be spending Christmas, nor any other occasion with her.

'She's thrown you over? But, of course. Why else would you come back?' She gripped the top of the parapet. She stared at the brown, fast-flowing river. After a while, she said, 'You were always easily besotted over a pretty face.' She emphasized 'besotted' with some satisfaction.

This was too much for Edward. 'I was not besotted. I admit Clara is very pretty. Very charming, very polished. But I soon saw that all she is interested in is the latest fashions and whether gentlemen should grow moustaches, or swear, or drink porter.'

'That word gentleman keeps recurring. Before you took up with your London friends, you pretended not to care about keeping up appearances and being a gentleman.'

'I don't,' he protested, at a loss against this form of attack.

'You're a worse hypocrite than I thought. How could you do that – go away without a word, after what had happened between us?'

'I know. I should have told you how I felt.'

'How you felt!' she said bitterly. 'I wasn't aware that you felt anything for me. No more than you would if I'd been a whore!' They both flinched at her use of such a word. Tears of self-pity flooded Elizabeth's eyes. 'You're a cad, Edward. You betrayed me, and I'll never forgive you.' She jerked her head with a little helpless movement. She began to walk away from him across the bridge.

There was an ache in Edward's chest. He wanted to run after her, crush her to him, break forgiveness from her. He did not move. He could see the spire of his brother's church among the trees. A plume of smoke rose comfortably from the vicarage chimney. It seemed very far away. Surely, he thought, she was making more of this than need be made? After all, he had come back. She *should* forgive him. Women were creatures given to gestures of mercy rather than attack.

The gap was widening between them on the river path. He hurried after her, slipping on the mud.

'Elizabeth!'

She quickened her pace.

'Lizzie! I'm not proud of myself for what I've done.'

'Nor you should be,' she called.

'Lizzie, wait. I should have written. But I was frightened after the barleyfield. I pretended it hadn't happened. Lizzie, I'm sorry. It's Christmas. Can't we forgive and forget?'

She halted.

Edward's heart thumped against his ribs. As he drew near he did not know what to say. Her hair had fallen in thick coils to her shoulders; he reached out a hand and touched it, as if to readjust it. The small, intimate gesture revived long-buried feelings of desire.

She did not move, though her face was flushed with anger. 'Don't say anything, Edward. We're not the same people we were in the summer.'

'I love you,' he said. 'I loved you before. I love you now.'

She did not draw back, but looked at him with a strange expression, half in hope, half despairing. When he pressed his mouth on hers she responded with a passion which made his heart soar, as if it were a bird released from a net.

His thoughts raced. They would marry as soon as he had qualified, he would take a country practice, in the village, anywhere, it didn't matter as long as they were together. They swayed and clung together on the path.

'Darling Lizzie. My angel. I knew you'd forgive me.' He felt her stiffen in his arms. He touched her cheek and it felt very cold.

'I can't,' she said in a low, almost apologetic tone. He could not be sure that she had spoken.

'Don't you see I'm sorry for it all?'

'Perhaps,' she said. 'But it's too late.' He stared at her in disbelief. 'It's too late. I've promised Arthur.'

Her words rattled in his head, foolish, meaningless, like dead leaves blowing in the wind. With a sense of outrage he said,

'You can't mean the rough, uncouth fellow Robert wrote to me about?'

'I'm sure Robert would write about Arthur in that way. But Robert doesn't know him as he is. Arthur respects a woman as his equal. He's honest. And he's not a hypocrite.'

'I've never been a hypocrite, Lizzie. I didn't face up to the truth. But I'm not a hypocrite.'

'It's too late,' she repeated helplessly. She seemed close to tears.

He forced himself to say, 'Do you love him – this Arthur?'

She avoided his eyes. 'Yes.'

'And what's to become of me?'

To his dismay she laughed. 'Oh, ever the child, Edward. Have you been denied your Christmas present? You'll probably become a famous physician. You'll marry some pretty girl with an opinion on swearing and moustaches. You'll soon forget me again. You managed it very well before.'

Anger and disappointment welled up in him. He felt a sudden violence against her, and against all women. He could not believe that she meant what she said. He had a vague mental image of the man she had chosen, a ruffian, who spat and strode about with his hands in his pockets. He refused to believe that she could do this to him.

And all because of a tumble in the barley – which she had begun, he remembered now. Perhaps she had thrown herself at Arthur with the same abandon as she had shown with him. Oh, yes, it was all very well to talk about his betrayal.

'You're making a mistake,' he said. 'You'll regret it for the rest of your life.'

He was aware, as he walked away from her, that he had cut a peevish figure – though he knew that his heart was breaking.

Part Two

16

Arthur Pengelly's house was tall and gaunt and ornamented with fanciful chimneys, little turrets and church-style windows. The Red House induced in Elizabeth a romantic melancholy from the first moment she entered it.

It was very cold on the day she became Mrs Pengelly. The flagged hallway echoed to their footsteps and with their voices. The sun filtered through the arched windows and cast long shadows into oak-panelled corners.

'I should have carried you over the doorstep,' Arthur said as they climbed the stairway to the drawing room.

'Don't be silly. We're too old for that sort of thing. And I'm too heavy.'

'I like large ladies.' He turned and gave her a rakish kind of wink.

'Why, Mr Pengelly, what are you saying?' she said with a tired flirtatiousness. She followed him through the door into a room as gloomy as the hall, furnished with massively ornate chests and tables and a sofa which looked as if it had been designed as a mausoleum. She untied her bonnet and tossed it on to the sofa. Her feet hurt in the new shoes which pinched her feet; her corset was laced so tightly that she had suffered ferocious pains of indigestion during the marriage service. She felt depressed now that it was all over. None of her family had attended the wedding; an old friend and a passing market trader had been commandeered as witnesses. The event had been shabby and mean. All day she had been trying to quell the doubts which threatened to jog her conviction that in Arthur she had found the ideal partner.

He had been touchingly jubilant when she had said that they could marry as soon as he wished it. Her family, predictably, had been horrified. Only now did Elizabeth begin to take stock of what she had done.

Arthur poured himself a glass of port and sat beside her on the sofa. He kissed her enthusiastically on the lips.

'You're a fine woman, Elizabeth Pengelly. I'm a proud man to have you for my wife.'

She kissed him back and told herself that Edward had deserved to lose her, that she was a lucky woman and that she liked the taste of port and cigars.

Their wedding night was not a success. Arthur had drunk several glasses of port that evening, his face growing redder and coarser by the hour. He was a crude and heavy-handed lover.

Elizabeth lay back, winded, on the pillows of the large four-poster bed and listened to his snores, strange thoughts and memories turning in her mind. It was almost dawn before she too fell into a fitful sleep.

She took on The Red House with a determination to govern it and the four servants and the evil Merlin with the minimum of fuss. She refurnished the rooms from an emporium in Bath, wrote out itineraries for the housekeeper and staff and relegated Merlin to the out-of-doors as often as was possible.

She saw that she had as effectively cut herself off from her old home as if she had gone with Arthur to Australia, instead of only two hundred yards distant. Her mother would not visit or even speak to her. Hannah and Fred refused all invitations to call. Once, secretly, she went to see her father while her mother was out of the house. But the distress the reunion caused him and the conflicts it produced within herself made the effort too great for the pitiful reward it achieved.

Do what she could with changes of furniture and schemes to improve The Red House and its garden, Elizabeth could not occupy her energies as Hannah might have done with the novelty of home-making, and frequently her thoughts would be about the past, and would run dangerously close to regret.

Some weeks after her marriage Elizabeth was with Arthur in the village, when they met Edward. The encounter took her unawares, she had thought him back in London. She clung tightly to Arthur's arm and passed on, nodding to Edward as if greeting an acquaintance of indifferent affections. Yet, the anguished look with which he acknowledged her and the rapid pounding of her heart, were proof, if she needed any, that everything was not over between them.

Then, one day in spring, Arthur announced that he intended to take on a wholesale business on the Dorset coast. They were to move from Charlford.

'I wish you had consulted me first,' she complained.

'I thought you said it was terrible, living so close to your folks all the time.'

'So it is. But before we married I understood that you and I would discuss everything of importance between us. I might not want to move by the sea.'

'Well, do you?'

'Perhaps.'

'What you fussing about then?'

Merlin gambolled into the room. He skidded to a halt on the wooden floor and looked at Elizabeth expectantly, as if daring her to shout and shoo him out, as she would have done if Arthur had not been there. Arthur had been reading the newspaper reports about Britain's declaration of war with Russia and the various accounts of the crowds in London, which had gathered to cheer the troops as they set sail for the Dardanelles. He had several papers spread out on the floor around his chair. It was his intention to improve his mind by reading a fixed number of newspapers and periodicals for two hours every afternoon. Elizabeth could not help despising him a little, not for the attempt at self-education, but for the way he refused to be moved from the study each day, no matter what the circumstances. There were times when the sight of him, buried beneath the *Western Flying Post*, his slippered feet on the fender, irritated her beyond measure.

The dog ambled over to the fire and settled itself down on the rug. Elizabeth met the animal's stare with distaste and turned away.

'Do you need to involve yourself in business?' she said. 'I thought you were well off.'

'I've been living off capital,' Arthur said without looking up.

'Didn't you invest?'

'A little, too late.' He folded his newspaper. 'Truth is, we shan't be able to keep up the rent on this great house for ever. I was flush when I came home to England and full of grand ideas about living like the gentry. But I never counted on how much it'd all cost. We're going to have to be a bit canny until your inheritance is all signed and sealed.'

This news came as a shock. She had not given much thought to their financial situation, assuming that making one's fortune at the goldfields in Australia or California generally set a man up for life and that Arthur had secured an income from investments.

He avoided her eyes. 'It wasn't a big find.' He bent and fondled Merlin's huge black head.

'How much?'

'A few hundred. Enough to buy a carriage and a bit of style for a while. I never expected it, see. It's such a fool's game, the diggings. If I had a guinea for every man that hoped to make a fortune at it, who've gone away empty-handed, I should be a rich man. I couldn't scarcely credit it when it happened. I let it carry me off a bit. And I like the taste of good living now I've known it.'

She stared at him disbelievingly. He got up from his chair and came to her, uneasy, shame-faced. 'It'll be all right. And with your old Uncle Willie's money we shall build this little business into something grand. I told you, I've a head for it.'

'For making money or for spending it?' she said waspishly.

He gave her a little shake, as though cajoling a child. 'Come on, Elizabeth. We shall soon be well set up again.'

'You're planning to invest my money in your business?' she said.

'My money now, Elizabeth,' he said easily, and his hand on her shoulder was firm, so that she could not move away. He laughed. 'Just you wait and see. I shall make you the richest woman in Dorset before five years are out.'

'I don't want you to make me into anything,' she said. 'If I'm to be anything, I want to have something to do with it.'

He frowned. Then he chucked her under the chin and smiled at her with a sudden affection. She did not respond. He shrugged and returned to his paper.

She watched him for a moment. Merlin laid his head on his paws and looked at her unblinkingly.

'I shan't speak to her,' Mrs Thorne declared. 'I shall not.' She set her mouth in a trembling line of resistance and turned her face away from the door.

Hannah wrung her hands. 'They are going away, Mother. Please, for my sake. Fred says this is very bad for me.' She laid a hand protectively on the bulge at her waist. 'He thinks it's time this silly quarrel was over. Fred thinks Mr Pengelly is a decent enough man – underneath.'

For answer, Mrs Thorne picked up a piece of embroidery and pretended to be engrossed in it.

Elizabeth came self-consciously into the room. She had promised herself there would be no sentimental displays of emotion in this farewell scene, but no one had told her, until today, that Hannah was pregnant. She embraced her swiftly and awkwardly, wanting to cry.

Hannah stood with clenched hands. 'Are you well, Lizzie? Is Mr Pengelly well?'

Elizabeth nodded. 'Where's Father?'

'On his deathbed,' wailed Mrs Thorne, forgetting she had decided not to speak and dropping her embroidery. 'Where you have put him. He'll never get over it. You seem determined to kill us all, one way or another. You announce now you're running off to the coast. And to set up in trade! Who is going to comfort your poor father? Tell me that?'

'What's this about Father? Is he ill?'

Hannah shook her head almost imperceptibly.

'He has taken to his bed,' said Mrs Thorne. 'He won't come down. You're killing him. You and this Arthur of yours.'

'"This Arthur" is my husband,' Elizabeth reminded her gently.

'When I think what you could have done at the rectory! And now Robert is going to marry Mabel Hemingale, who may well have attended Monsieur Lapalisse's Seminary, but she hasn't an ounce of good taste in her body.' Mrs Thorne began to cry, alternately mopping at her eyes with a lace handkerchief and attemping to pick up her embroidery.

Elizabeth looked at Hannah, who looked away. She left the room and went upstairs.

Her father raised his head feebly from the pillow. 'Lizzie –? Is it you? It's good to see you.'

Elizabeth detected an element of play-acting. She steeled herself to briskness, but there was an ache in her throat as she entered the room, familiar from childhood, with its great high bedstead, the faded green curtains at the window, tied with a loop of tarnished braid, and the worn patch in the carpet at the foot of the bed.

'Well, I'd rather not have seen you laid low like this.'

'Why should you care what happens to me, now you've cut yourself off from us with this fellow?' He brushed his eyes with the back of his hand and the gesture, though calculated, pulled at her heart. 'I hope you're happy with what you've done. You are happy, aren't you, Lizzie?' he added with sudden anxiety.

She did not answer. She went to the window and looked down at the garden. The grass under the apple tree was scattered with little splashes of pale pink blossom.

'Edward is home again,' her father said.

She forced herself to reply calmly, 'I haven't seen him in the village.'

'He came to visit me. That was good of him, wasn't it? *He* comes to see an old man. You should have married him, instead of this chap Pengelly.'

'It's no good to talk like that.' She turned to face him wearily, leaning against the window sill.

'Edward never got his scholarship,' her father said. 'He came through his examinations just well enough to continue another year. He was all talk of the war with Russia and how some of them have gone for medical posts with the Army.'

Fear gripped her chest and made her heart beat faster. 'Edward hasn't done that?'

The old man shook his head. 'Edward doesn't hold with the enthusiasm for the war. He says all war is a bitter waste. I've a fear he's for the Peace Party. He stood there. Just where you're standing now.'

Elizabeth caressed the window sill as if it could offer some link with Edward. She felt an overwhelming sense of missed opportunities.

'You should have married him,' her father repeated.

She sighed, and came to sit beside him on the bed. She took his hand in her own and stroked the blue and knotted veins.

'They'll have told you Arthur means to make a success of a drapery business. I shall try to visit. If you want me to.'

'Don't leave us.' She watched his eyes fill with tears.

She sat with him a little while. And then she returned, to continue packing up her belongings at The Red House.

17

Edward had felt perversely drawn to Charlford since Elizabeth's marriage. He came home for the summer vacation, but, now that she had gone, the village closed in on him with too many unwelcome memories. A sense of guilt oppressed him; it lay in the slow-moving river and the smell of the August-ripening barley. The dusty heat rising from the fields suffocated him like an airless room.

He saw that his life had no meaning, unless it could be generated by Elizabeth. He reconstructed their final parting, hearing her tell him again and again that he was too late. He returned to the scene as if to an addiction, sickened by the pointlessness of the exercise.

Whatsoever a man soweth, that shall he also reap. Robert was preparing his sermon.

'You're very glum these days, Edward,' he said. 'I hope you're not falling for a fever again. I hear that London has an epidemic of Asiatic cholera. You must take care.'

Edward said restlessly that if King Cholera wanted him he was welcome.

Robert frowned. 'I don't approve of all this negativism. It's anti-religious. I hope you're going to grace us with your presence in church this morning. Miss Hemingale has noticed that you don't attend church. It reflects badly on me. Now that she and I are betrothed it would be nice if you were to sit with her and her mother.'

Edward could not trust himself to reply. He left the house to wander by the river with his sketch book. He stopped by the bridge to draw the willows, but without enthusiasm, and the result was dull and amateurish.

He went to visit Henry Thorne. Henry had aged visibly in the three months since Elizabeth had left Charlford. His hands trembled. His thoughts were vague and composed chiefly of memories of the past.

'Well, this is good. You've come to see an old man.' His eyes were moist with easily won happiness. They clouded as quickly with misery. 'If only Elizabeth was here too.'

'It's you I've come to see,' Edward said. 'How's your leg? Are you eating sensibly these days?'

Henry pulled a face, like a child when it is told to eat up its vegetables. 'Lizzie used to make me eat sensibly,' he remembered. 'Lizzie used to make fomentations out of herbs to ease my leg.'

Edward sighed. He should not have come. It was too painful.

Henry had begun on a string of reminiscences about Elizabeth's childhood: how she had learned to read from the *Sunday Book of Praiseworthy Children*, how she had always loved reading, and her garden. Edward thought back to the day he had bought Elizabeth a book of Tennyson's poems: he had his own trail of fond memories. He wondered if she had kept the Tennyson. He tried not to think about her and to divert Henry's attention.

'What about this war? Is it to your satisfaction?'

'Call this shilly-shallying in the Balkans a war?' Henry rose to the bait. 'What was all the cheering about? Can you tell me? When they waste all this time not knowing what to do next.'

Edward let him grumble about the Army commanders and the government, about the French and the Turks, and the triumphs of a greater war, and of the old Duke who could have shown Lord Raglan and the rest how to conduct a campaign.

After an hour or so he returned to the vicarage. Within a few days he had gone back to London, preferring the risk of cholera to the emptiness of a long drawn-out summer in Charlford.

There was a feeling of panic in the city. It drove people from their lodgings as the cholera epidemic swept through Soho and the East End.

Edward volunteered to help with the extra patients at the hospital. He had not seen the savage effects of cholera before, the sunken eyes, cramped limbs and rapid dehydration of the victims, and the corpses for hasty burial. A smell of vomit and diarrhoea clung to every part of the hospital; it invaded people's clothing and skin, and the air they breathed. At night, in his lodgings, Edward would wake with the stench of cholera still in his lungs and he would be thrown into a panic, imagining himself in a fever, terrified of the violent death which might follow in a matter of hours.

At last the worst of the epidemic was over. Edward learned that Jack Harris was in London and went to visit him.

Harris was obsessed with the war. Had Edward kept up with the latest news? Did he know that cholera had infected the troops in Bulgaria that summer, that the Army were asking for medical help, that they were giving emergency commissions to medical students? He seemed affected by a deep excitement.

'They wasted too much time at Varna,' he said. 'They allowed cholera to get hold and the men's morale has weakened with all this waiting. But what now, Edward? Now that they've decided on an attack against the Crimea and the fighting's going to start in earnest? They're going to want more surgeons.'

Edward's interest in the war was in fact very slight. It was all so far away. What did the Army's problems matter, compared with the squalor on their own doorstep? And what was any war but a throwing away of men's lives?

Harris halted on the path as they walked through Regent's Park. He stood facing him and swung his cane gently to and fro with the gilt knob rested lightly between his gloved fingers. A smile lit his arrogant, good-natured face.

'I've enlisted. I've been offered an assistant surgency. What do you think?' A wave of fear threatened to engulf Edward as the world turned itself on its head. 'My brother Reggie's regiment has already sailed from Varna, may already be in the thick of it for all I know. There's real life going on out there, Edward, and we're missing it.'

Edward forced a flippancy into his voice. 'I thought you didn't care for the uniform.'

'Immaterial, dear fellow. My country has need of me.'

'When do you go?'

Harris paused. He seemed less sure of himself. 'Pretty soon, they say.'

They continued walking. The evening sunlight filtered through the leaves of the trees and dappled them with its warmth. It seemed to

Edward that the last tenuous link of friendship between them had been severed.

'Rather you than me, dear chap,' he said at last.

They turned away from the park and took a cab, then wandered aimlessly among the little shops which peppered the streets near the Strand. They bought picture postcards and a book on mesmerism from a second-hand shop, which Harris said he had taken a fancy to, and deliberately they resumed the habits of their student life; but Edward knew that life would never again be the same. They entered a restaurant in St Martin's Lane, Harris continuing to talk with exaggerated enthusiasm about the war. Edward, thinking of the start of the autumn term without him and with Elizabeth married in Dorset, ate his way stoically and in a depressed state of mind through a macaroni pudding.

Harris wrote from Malta. The expedition was 'a bit of a lark', Edward was missing all the fun.

At home, newspaper reports revealed some of the less larky aspects of the expedition to the Crimea: there were the hundreds of casualties after the Battle of the Alma, inadequacies among the supply and service teams, confusion and squalor at the supposedly magnificent barracks hospital at Scutari, to which the wounded were being transported.

When Harris wrote again, after his arrival in the Crimea, the mood of his letter contrasted sharply with the flippancy of his earlier correspondence.

Edward, listening to the monotonous drone of a physiology lecture on a warm November morning, removed the pages of Harris's letter from his pocket and read them again. It was hard, to imagine the dismay and seriousness from which the words must have sprung, for Harris had never been serious.

No tents. No food . . . This was how the soldiers arrived in the Crimea and were expected to fight the enemy at Alma. Now they are digging in and I believe the siege guns will open against Sebastopol before long, but only half the men seem fit for duty, being worn out, underfed, and affected by disease of one sort or another. The cold is getting bad at nights. Cholera is a killer, but so are dysentery and diarrhoea under these conditions when men have been for days without adequate shelter.

You will think, as I thought, Edward, that all provision has been made for them – there might have been a little confusion at first on landing, a hitch here and there, inevitable in a strange country, but, you will suppose, all major difficulties over organization, in particular of the wounded, must be overcome by now. You are wrong. I have seen for myself the ships in Balaclava, crowded with sick and dying soldiers, crying out for water, and no one to help them. They say that four thousand are at Scutari in a hospital which is filthy and built over a sewer. Five hundred men were sent there after Alma in one ship, with only two surgeons and five men to nurse them, one of whom died on the way. They are desperate for medical men. They are desperate for every kind of comfort. You cannot imagine, Edward, how bad it is.

Edward turned the page in his hand and stared at the scrawl of Harris's words, trying to find in them a relevance to the day to day existence at the college. The rows of dark-coated students around him were seated with varying degrees of attentiveness, as the Professor of Physiology described the uriniferous tubules of the kidney. The scenes in Harris's letter were remote from all this, in a distant piece of land called the Crimea, an exotic place-name on a map.

Oh, he knew about the reality of death. Death stalked his nightmares, parading scenes of decomposition, disease-ridden corpses, the image of a child which had taken three hours on the road to die after being run over by a haywagon, his mother's death, a terrible, drawn-out affair of blood and sputum.

He looked again at the letter. He remembered the afternoon when Harris had told him he had enlisted, his eyes alight with excitement, his hat tilted to the back of his head, a gold-topped cane playing between his fingers.

Some of the old Harris was still there, in the account of finding small luxuries with which to supplement the ration of salt pork and biscuit '. . . Imagine the joy when one of our officers returned to camp with a turkey!' But Harris returned quickly to the bleak tone with which he had begun:

. . . The work of digging trenches and throwing up parapets is hard and the men are exhausted by it. The ground around our positions is poor and rocky, and the Russians have had plenty of time to put up defences and bring in reinforcements, while we have wasted the best of the weather in indecision. The area covered by the siege is very great. Hundreds of horses have perished. Everyone here is weary of the difficulties and, though we say jauntily that we shall soon knock the town to pieces, I am afraid that the Allies are in for a long siege. Heaven help everyone if it goes on through the winter.

The letter finished:

. . . Will you go to see my folks for me? Of course, you will not tell them any of this, but that I am making the best of things and hope to be home for Christmas. I hope it with all my heart, for I don't mind telling you, Edward, I shall be glad when this is over.

Edward folded the letter neatly and returned it to his pocket. He had put off visiting Harris's family, reluctant to involve himself in Jack's affairs, unwilling to concoct a pleasant tale of forbearance in the line of duty and to sound optimistic about a happy conclusion to the Crimean adventure. He would go the next day, he promised himself.

The first thing he noticed was that the household servants were in deep mourning. Afraid that one or both of Jack's brothers had been killed, for the newspapers had been full of accounts of the Battle of Balaclava, he was shown into the drawing room. His fears seemed to be confirmed. Mrs Harris, swathed in black crêpe, her skin a strained and yellowish hue, was resigned to the loss of one of her sons.

'Edward – we have had a letter.' She could not continue. She was not a woman given to excesses, the half-swooning posture, the smelling bottle to hand, the handkerchief pressed to the mouth. With great dignity she poured Edward tea from a large black pot. 'You knew him so well. And he always had such a strong admiration for you.' Tears welled in her eyes.

Only then did Edward understand what had happened. The realization that it was Jack who was dead struck him with a numbing force. He told himself that he had his letter, written only three weeks ago, in his pocket; he was making the best of things and hoped to be home for Christmas.

The woman's voice seemed to come from far away as she explained how her son had become a victim of cholera. 'It's so unfair,' she said

128

bitterly, 'that he went there to care for the sick and wounded and now he's dead, while his brothers have survived much greater dangers.' It was as if she wished that one of Jack's brothers could have taken his place. Perhaps an act of heroism, like that of the cavalry charge against the guns at Balaclava, would have helped to compensate for the death of one of her sons. But to fall to the grip of cholera – he might as well have stayed in England to suffer the same fate.

Edward tried to imitate the restrained quality of her grief. But he could not believe that Harris was really dead. After an hour he made an excuse to leave. He promised to keep in touch.

He walked slowly along Oxford Street, not seeing the people on the pavements or the goods displayed in the shop windows. He could think of nothing, except the fact that Harris was gone. There was no order to the way things happened, no rules, only chaos. Jack's death, like Elizabeth's marriage, was part of some terrible mistake of fate.

'It was me who had nothing to live for. It should have been me.' He did not know that he had spoken aloud. A man, passing along the pavement, turned to stare at him.

He crossed the stream of cabs and horses entering Park Lane and followed the railings of Hyde Park. The leaves had fallen from the trees, a mist hung about the trunks and lay in layers above the grass in the dying afternoon light. He entered the Park and, ignoring the pathways, trudged his feet through the mass of wet leaves on the ground. The air was cold, but he did not notice the damp seeping up from the grass. People passed him, hurrying to reach their destinations before dusk fell.

A private brougham, passing along one of the rides, stopped a short distance from him and a woman's bonneted head peeped out from the window. He glanced up and, as if in some bizarre dream, recognized Elizabeth's sister Hannah.

'Edward? What a very cold, raw afternoon to be out walking,' she called.

He approached the carriage, preparing himself for the necessary polite exchanges. 'How strange to find you in London just now.'

Hannah smiled, as if she was pleased with herself. 'You have met my aunt, Mrs Delahaye.'

Hannah's Aunt Lydia leaned forward and acknowledged Edward

with a gracious little nod of the head, but apparently without much enthusiasm for being reintroduced.

'I am staying with my aunt in Kensington,' Hannah explained. 'Fred had some business to attend to in town. I elected to accompany him. May we take you anywhere? It's so cold, Edward. And you seem so downcast.'

He shook his head.

Lydia said busily, 'I told them. What's the point of visiting in November? Too cold for the baby. And the smog on top of everything.'

'The baby,' murmured Edward. 'Of course. May I offer my heartiest congratulations.'

Hannah, detecting the lack of heart in his words, departed from social niceties and urged, 'What is it, Edward? We were watching you. "I am convinced that is Edward Munro," I said to Mrs Delahaye. "Not cocky enough," Auntie said.'

Edward smiled. 'I suppose I'm not so cocky, but I heard today of the death of a friend in the Crimea.' His voice thickened with emotion, and he saw with a rush of sentimental feeling that there had, after all, been a deep affection between himself and Harris.

'Oh, my poor Edward. How terrible!' Hannah's eyes filled with tears. She had always felt a secret, restrained tenderness for Edward. 'We were on our way to my aunt's house for tea,' she said when she had recovered. She looked at Lydia, who nodded, confirming an unspoken resolution. 'Come and take tea with us, Edward. It will be dark soon. And it isn't far from here. We've been looking forward to toasted muffins.' She looked uncertain then, as though wondering whether toasted muffins were quite the thing under the circumstances.

The invitation invoked an unexpected mood in Edward. It conjured up old memories of nursery teas, images of cosy well-being and bosomy warmth. It occurred to him that feminine company would be comforting. He thanked them and climbed into the carriage.

'What a run of troubles we are having,' said Hannah, when they were seated by Lydia's fireside. 'First we lose Elizabeth. Now you have lost your friend. Though in a very different sense, of course.'

'I doubt that Mr Munro will want to talk about Elizabeth,' said Lydia. 'Not after her disgraceful marriage.'

'We shouldn't think of it as a disgrace, if she has found true happiness, Mrs Delahaye,' Edward said, falling, as he often did when he was embarrassed, into the sort of pious phraseology his brother might have used.

'Is she happy though? Is she? Hannah tells me they are living in extremely modest circumstances. Very cramped and shabby. They have a wholesale drapery business.' She said it as if wholesale drapery were the lowest of occupations on the scale of barely respectable trades.

'Fred and I visited recently with the baby,' Hannah explained. 'But it was very awkward. Her husband is such an ill-bred man.'

'I never could fathom Elizabeth,' Lydia said, intimating that understanding human nature was her particular forte. 'In a way, we must hold you responsible for what happened, Mr Munro.'

Edward flushed. 'I'm afraid I don't understand.'

'Why? By your jilting of her, of course. It's as plain as the nose on her face. Though when you think that she might have chosen a parson, and lived decently and respectable.'

'A parson? You mean my brother?' Edward understood briefly Robert's own peculiar bitterness over Elizabeth's marriage to Arthur Pengelly. 'Robert asked her to marry him?'

'Most emphatically.'

'I think she is happy,' said Hannah. 'You mustn't blame yourself, Edward, for a summer flirtation, which Elizabeth clearly took more seriously than she should have done.'

'I must defend myself against the charge of breach of promise,' Edward said. 'You see, it was Elizabeth who, in the end, rejected me. She turned me down.'

Lydia stared at him with ill-disguised delight at this unexpected twist to the story. She turned excitedly to Hannah. 'There! And we always supposed that he had all but jilted her when he went off to London.'

Edward flushed again at Lydia's bald statement of the truth. It had become so much less troubling lately to believe that, after a few weeks' absence in London, he had returned to Elizabeth as a legitimate suitor and been humiliatingly rejected.

'Mr Munro, we have done you an injustice,' Lydia said.

Edward shook his head, not knowing how to reply, and resorted to drinking his tea. He was conscious of the warm cup in his hand and the heat from the fire on his face. The shock of Harris's death was fading for the time being. But the pain and guilt over losing Elizabeth would always be with him – like an unhealed, self-inflicted wound.

'There must be bad blood on your mother's side of the family,' Lydia said to Hannah. 'Your Uncle Willie was a rum sort too. Look how he parcelled out his money to you girls! Not a thought for his sister.'

'Do let us talk of something else,' said Hannah brightly. 'Elizabeth has made her bed and she must lie on it.' She paused, aware that she had chosen a metaphor which was indelicate. 'As for your friend, Edward. He has perished in a glorious cause. You must let that thought comfort you.'

'What do you think to Miss Nightingale and her ladies?' said Lydia, happy to choose any subject, so long as she might be in charge of it. 'Miss Nightingale, who has gone to help the poor, brave soldiers in their fight against the Russians.'

'I am full of admiration for such women.' Edward was too weary of all the distortions over Elizabeth to offer more than a conventional opinion.

'The Kensington Benevolent Friends' Ladies' Society has begun a Help for our Soldiers in the Crimea Fund,' continued Lydia importantly.

'That is very admirable too.' Edward stirred himself to the necessary enthusiasm. 'Is this your response to *The Times* Appeal?'

'It is. Some of our ladies are knitting socks and blankets. And we are also arranging a Fancy Fair and preparing Christmas parcels – puddings and other little luxuries. It does seem as if it will go on until Christmas?' she said, suddenly anxious that her efforts should not be in vain.

'At least until then,' Edward said, relieved at last to be able to give an honest opinion.

18

Pengelly's Wholesale Linen Draper's was rapidly establishing a name for itself as a supplier of a multiplicity of fabrics, lace and smallwares to suit the drapery trade. The business consisted of a warehouse on the harbour front, with a dusty office above.

It had been Elizabeth's task at first to look after the accounts; this she did at home, since Arthur said it looked eccentric and not quite the thing if she were to accompany him to the warehouse every day. After a short while Arthur decided that they could afford to employ a proper accountant.

'It isn't seemly,' he said. 'It doesn't give the right look to the thing to have a wife doing it.'

'But I like being involved,' Elizabeth protested.

He smiled at her fondly. 'I shall have better things for you to do than keep the books before long. The way things are, we'll soon be living in the style I promised you.'

'I don't know that I want to live in style,' Elizabeth said. '*Style* smacks of putting on airs. *Style* smacks of ladies and gentlemen.'

She had felt trapped and miserable. She was desperately conscious that she had taken a false turning by her marriage. She saw now that she had misjudged Arthur, she had convinced herself that his lack of sophistication hid a desire for truth, she had mistaken gracelessness for honesty. She had read depths in him which were not there.

And now all he could talk about was making a profit and turning himself into a man of substance again. Elizabeth, excluded from the daily affairs of the business, found her function had become that of the wife who smoothed the domestic path towards her husband's success. Arthur did not discuss the business with her. If she questioned him, he would reply with a sort of amused tolerance. If she offered suggestions, he listened with a strained patience and promptly forgot what she had said. She saw herself being eased inevitably into the same straitjacket as her sister Hannah inhabited.

'There is nothing for me to do,' she complained one day. 'I read. I walk along the esplanade and the quay. I instruct the maid over her duties. I'm so bored, Arthur. I've been reduced to those activities which you and I once despised for a woman.'

'We'll move from here soon,' he soothed. 'There'll be plenty for you to do then, in a big house again. You can employ yourself entertaining our business friends and their wives. I shall feel really proud, Elizabeth, to see you sat amongst the best of them, where you belong. Conversing with the topmost folk in the town and dressed as fashionably as any lady in London society.'

Elizabeth could not bring herself to challenge his enthusiasm by admitting that she had no wish to sit fashionably amongst the topmost bores of the district.

As the business expanded, Arthur began to cultivate links with the more affluent tradespeople and dignitaries in the town. He was anxious that Elizabeth too should strike up friendships with the wives of aldermen, magistrates and members of boards and committees of various institutions and charities.

On certain afternoons that summer he would take time from the warehouse to stroll with her along the sea-front.

'To get on in the world we have to be seen,' he told her. 'Leisure must be seen to go hand in hand with hard work.' He paused to raise his hat to a passing carriage, the occupants of which remained invisible to Elizabeth. 'Alderman Beatty and his wife,' Arthur explained. 'Did you see the way he nodded there to me, every bit as if I was as good as him?'

'You *are* as good as he is,' Elizabeth said impatiently. 'You know you are.'

He was not listening.

'Now this lady approaching, Elizabeth,' he said, lowering his voice to a hoarse whisper, 'is the sort I want you to emulate. Her husband owns a manufactory and is a member of the dining club I told you about the other day.'

Elizabeth recognized the woman walking towards them as one to

134

whom she had taken an immediate dislike at a charity bazaar in the town some days earlier. The woman was dressed in a promenade gown and mantel of a green and yellow large-checked silk. It was trimmed all over with velvet bands, fringes and tassels, and she carried a small parasol, reticule and muff which were similarly ornamented. A neat green velvet bonnet, decorated with yellow feathers and tied with a huge yellow bow, completed this walking haberdashery display.

Arthur removed his hat and bowed extravagantly. 'Mrs Willoughby.'

The woman acknowledged him by removing her gloved hand from its muff and inclining it towards him, as if to say, 'You're correct, I am she.'

Elizabeth nodded in as perfunctory a way as courtesy would allow.

They exchanged observations about the breeziness of the sea-front, the fickle nature of the weather in July and the possibility of rain later, and passed on.

'I want you to dress well, Elizabeth,' Arthur said excitedly after some minutes. He studied her plain grey frock. 'Choose yourself some lengths of silk from the warehouse and get them made up in the latest fashions – trimmings and all.'

She laughed, and he looked hurt.

'It would please me, Elizabeth.'

She squeezed his arm; she felt a long submerged tenderness towards him. After all, she thought, where was the harm? And there was a certain satisfaction to be had from knowing how easily she could make him happy.

Some time later, Arthur revealed a conviction he had been nursing, that he was descended from the nobility: his mother had always told him that his father had been a 'proper gentleman'. She was a Cornish woman, who had upped and settled in Somerset, and there had always been some mystery about his birth.

'You mean you were born the wrong side of the blanket?'

'Elizabeth! Don't say such things!' he protested. 'It is possible I might be descended from a very noble line.'

Arthur's descent from quality remained to be proved. However, his desire to appear to have done so began to lead to increasing eccentricities. He would bring home lengths of red velvet from the warehouse and instruct Elizabeth to drape them against the parlour walls, embellishing them with motifs cut from brocade, comprising vaguely heraldic-looking bugles, shields and pennants. Elizabeth complied with all this in a detached way, convinced that the phase would pass, even hoping that when it did and disillusionment replaced his enthusiasm for aping the gentry, they would find a new level of communication.

An occasional flamboyance had always been evident in Arthur's style of dress. Now he insisted on only the most extravagant fabrics and declared that Elizabeth should do the same. His flair for fashion – frock coat, corduroy trousers, tartan cut-velvet waistcoat, at his neck a blue and gold cravat held by a large, jewelled tie pin set in gold – seemed to Elizabeth to border on the flashy. She used what influence she had to moderate his tastes.

His chief obsession was to be invited to join Jack Willoughby's dining club; for an invitation would mean acceptance by the elite of the business community.

He came home one day, early in November, in an apoplexy of excitement and made straight for the brandy decanter on the sideboard.

Elizabeth looked up from the ottoman square she was stitching; she had begun the project some years ago and the thing was almost finished, but she never took it up without the old memories it revived: Arthur's hurried arrival had broken into forbidden thoughts of Edward. Could it really be little more than a year ago that they had lain together in a barleyfield under a summer sun? It seemed a lifetime.

She felt irritated by Arthur's state of excitement, which, she guessed, would be over nothing more than another rise in profits or the fact that Alderman Beatty had taken the time to speak to him in the course of his duties.

'Is anything wrong?' she asked mildly.

'We've been invited to dine at the Willoughbys.' Arthur sat down next to her. His face was red and he was breathing hard.

Elizabeth stifled her response of, Oh, do we have to? and smiled.

'Willoughby has offered me an introduction to his club.'

She hesitated only briefly and kissed him on the cheek; then she continued with her stitching. 'I am so pleased for you, my dear.'

She watched him across the Willoughbys' table. He held his knife and fork delicately. He had grown a moustache and was experimenting with pomading his hair. He looked fat and sleek and happy and as much of a gentleman as did Jack Willoughby at the head of the table or Alderman Beatty, a great walrus of a man, who kept nudging his left knee against her skirts as though by accident.

Elizabeth let the murmur of conversation flow around her. Arthur deserved to be happy. He had ability. He was no fool. But was this what she had wanted, when she had promised to love him?

Arthur was flirting a little with Rowena Willoughby, magnificent in yellow silk, a large cameo brooch at the cleavage of her breasts and a surge of heavy lace breaking against the pale flesh of her shoulders.

Elizabeth looked down at her own, much-beribboned frock; it was rose-pink, the best silk from the warehouse; Arthur had chosen the colour, despite her protests that pink neither suited her complexion nor her figure. She remembered that it had been Edward who had told her that it did not. The fact that Edward had been able to see her as she was, whereas Arthur was undiscriminating and wanted only that she should rival the glamour of Rowena Willoughby, to show her off as if she were additional proof of his rising status, increased her feeling of discontent.

Arthur was telling everyone about the house which he was in the process of buying, which he said was both 'respectable' and 'commodious', and within easy reach of the esplanade.

'Do have a classical style of decor, Mr Pengelly,' enthused Rowena Willoughby. 'You must let us advise you as to staff. We have recently taken on a new house-maid and I believe she has a sister. She's of excellent character. Do you not admire this dining room? Spanish mahogany. Not classical, of course. But very handsome, don't you think?'

'I daresay I shall leave the domestic arrangements to Mrs Pengelly,' Arthur said. 'Staff and furnishings and such. You ladies have a knack in these matters.'

Elizabeth, recalling his obstinacy over the velvet drapes in the parlour and the hours he had spent, cutting and arranging his heraldic motifs, said nothing.

'So, Mrs Pengelly, you are accomplished as well as charming?' said Alderman Beatty. Elizabeth felt the nudge of his knee again and was tempted to repel it with her table fork. 'Mrs Beatty, sad to say, is rather a dunce at the housekeeping.'

Elizabeth offered the alderman's wife a glance of sympathy. Mrs Beatty was a pleasant-faced woman of about thirty-five, with a long face and humorous mouth. She seemed not at all put out by her husband's remark, yet Elizabeth felt compelled for her sake to make it clear that her own skills in household management were limited to baking a decent pastry and being competent with a whitewash brush.

Arthur interrupted her. 'Mrs Pengelly is too modest. She is excellence itself when it comes to the mysteries of housekeeping.'

Elizabeth could suffer this no longer. 'Occasionally, we women might value a glimpse into mysteries beyond those of the domestic arrangements.' She knew that it was neither the time nor the place for voicing her old opinions. She sensed rather than saw Arthur's alarm.

Rowena Willoughby laughed. 'Oh, I disagree. We must leave the greater mysteries of the world to our better halves. Home is where the female heart is.'

'But why should we limit ourselves? My heart is not in the minutiae of carpets and curtains and "shall we have three servants or four when we move to the new house?"'

Rowena shook her head. 'I can never understand a woman who isn't thoroughly contented,' she said. 'It must seem so enviable to our unmarried sisters to be cosseted and protected as we are.'

'Give a woman a husband, a house and pay her a few compliments, and she is happy?' said Mrs Beatty with unexpected irony. Elizabeth wondered briefly if she had found an ally in the alderman's wife.

'It's only natural, that the fairer sex should enjoy the protection of husband and home,' Arthur blustered. 'It's the proper way of things.'

'I've heard you say different,' Elizabeth reminded him. 'In Australia women run stores, catch sheep, trek across the countryside with packs on their backs – every bit as well as a man could do those things, or so I'm led to believe.'

'And what unfeminine, disagreeable women they must be,' said Rowena Willoughby.

'Have you lived in Australia, Mrs Pengelly?' asked Mrs Beatty with interest.

'Mr Pengelly has spent some years in Australia,' replied Elizabeth. 'He once told me how the women there are much less bound by convention than we are in England.'

Arthur looked uncomfortable.

'And what did you think to the new country?' said Willoughby.

Arthur looked at Elizabeth. 'That it's not to be compared with England, was my opinion,' he said.

'Naturally not,' said Alderman Beatty with a self-congratulatory laugh.

'Tell them about the diggings,' Elizabeth said. 'Tell them about the farmsteads, where women are treated as equals, and even kill snakes and herd sheep.'

'My goodness. What excitement,' said Mrs Beatty. 'I'm almost tempted by the idea.'

'It's a rough land,' Arthur said crossly. 'And not one for a lady to contemplate living in.'

'But one where men and women are equal in the sight of God, where women need not play the lady, but can show they've as much spirit as men,' Elizabeth said, desperately reminding him of the opinions he had expressed when she had first met him.

Alderman Beatty laughed. 'Men and women equal? Come, come. How can we fellows match you ladies for charm and beauty? And it's a brave man who would say that women should show as much spirit as men.'

'None but the *brave* deserve the fair,' remarked Mrs Beatty vaguely. She glanced at Elizabeth with a flicker of a smile, as if to say, We have married these men, but we do not have to take them seriously.

'Talking of the brave,' said Willoughby, turning to address Arthur, and apparently dismissing Elizabeth from his mind, 'I read the other day that even the wounded soldiers at Scutari are anxious to get back to the seat of war, in order to qualify to receive their medals when Sebastopol is captured.'

'There is nothing to be compared with the courage of an English soldier,' Arthur said, with the enthusiasm of one who has learned the opinion from somewhere.

'It's a pity that such courageous men have to contend with the mismanagement of their superiors in this war,' Elizabeth said, rather too loudly. 'I've read about the disgraceful conditions at Scutari. I'm not surprised the men are anxious to get back to the front.'

'You shouldn't believe all the scandalmongering in the newspapers, Mrs Pengelly,' said Alderman Beatty. 'There are disruptive agents abroad, determined to undermine the government.'

'In any event, the men will not suffer so much, now that they have Miss Nightingale's nurses to look after them,' said Rowena.

'But, don't you see?' Elizabeth clenched her hands in her lap. 'We applaud the spirit of Miss Nightingale. But isn't she one of those very women who have flouted convention and refused to cling to the protection of the home?'

Alderman Beatty hesitated a mere fraction of a second. 'A freak of circumstances, my dear Mrs Pengelly.'

'And an unmarried lady, you notice,' interrupted Rowena. 'What else is there for them to do but give their lives to good works, poor things?'

There was a pause. Willoughby was regarding Elizabeth with a frown of irritation. She saw that she might jeopardize Arthur's admission to the coveted dining club if she were to pursue the argument further. Arthur did not look at her, his head was bowed over his lap. Elizabeth willed him to glance up, to wink at her, as he might have done once, and reveal by a smile that these people were, after all, nothing to him.

Alderman Beatty asked her a question about the existence of charitable institutions in the corner of Somerset where she used to live. Arthur turned and engaged quickly in conversation with Jack Willoughby.

When, at last, Elizabeth caught Arthur's attention across the table he seemed to have forgotten all about her indiscretion. His smile was broad with satisfaction. She guessed that his membership of the dining club was secured.

19

The rain drifted across the grey Dorset hills and beat against the sides of the coach. There was no comfort in the sound, and none in Edward's journey; but he had to see Elizabeth again. Perhaps she would convey something, by a look or a word, which would settle his conscience, so that he could say to himself, She's happy – you can forget her.

For several hours he walked up and down the quay of the small seaside town. He fingered the piece of paper in his pocket on which he had long ago scrawled her address. The little fishing boats pushed the slate-coloured water in front of them, churning up a foam in the narrow harbour. Edward divided his attention between the boats and the crowd on the quayside, half hoping he might see her walking towards him from among the fisherwomen.

By lunchtime there had been no such chance meeting. The rain had long since stopped, but he was beginning to feel cold and to wonder why he had come. He bought a meat pie from a baker's shop and ate it, leaning against a wall. He stared at the boats and tossed in his mind whether he should return home, or whether, having come this far, he had the courage to seek her out at the address in his pocket. What if her husband should be at home? He had seen Pengelly hardly at all, but in his imagination he had swelled to the proportions of a fairground wrestler, or a man like the bully who had attacked and robbed him, the night he had strayed into the back streets of St Giles.

At last, dusting the crumbs from his coat, Edward turned his back on the sea, and headed for the narrow streets which led away from the harbour.

Elizabeth, dressed in a dark-green frock and apron, was stacking flower pots on a tray in the small backyard outside the house. The maid, a large girl, inappropriately christened Violet, stood in the scullery doorway.

'Somebody t' see 'ee, mam.'

'Who, Violet? You should ask for a name.'

''E woulden' give 'is name. Called hisself a' old friend. 'E's ever so 'ansome.' There was a bubbling of interest in the girl's voice.

Elizabeth's heart jumped with fright. She knew at once that it was Edward. She laid down the stack of flowerpots and wiped her hands carefully on her apron.

'Show the gentleman into the parlour,' she said, forcing a steadiness into her voice. 'I shall be in directly. And, Violet, you may go to visit your mother now.'

'But, mam –' The girl was determined to observe the proper rules. 'I bin a'seed my mother yesterday.'

'And she'll be very pleased to see you again today and for the extra help you can give her at home.' She ignored the girl's look of curiosity. Elizabeth told herself with a wild recklessness that she did not care if she gossiped.

She took off her apron with trembling hands.

Edward stood by the window in the velvety gloom of Elizabeth's parlour. Strangely medieval draperies were festooned against the walls. He looked out at the empty street through the lace-curtained window, wishing he had not come and trying to rehearse what he would say to her. He did not hear Elizabeth enter the room.

'I knew you would come one day.'

Edward swung round quickly. She looked pale in the mysterious light of the parlour. It was nearly a year since they had parted. She was slimmer, her dark, copper-coloured hair was pinned neatly. Her wide mouth trembled a little, and he saw that she was as frightened as he was.

'Well, I'm here,' he said drily.

Elizabeth sat down on a high-backed chair. Edward crossed the room in front of the fire and sat in an armchair opposite her; he picked at a thread on his trouser knee. 'So, this is where you live. I've wondered about it.'

'We are going to move from here in a few weeks. To the other end of the town. He – Arthur – says he wants us to live in style.'

'You don't seem very enthusiastic about the idea.'

'Don't I? I'm sure I should. Arthur's determined to improve our situation. We shall probably become very grand. You might even condescend to come and see us one day, when you get that wealthy practice of yours. Or we could visit you and your lady-wife in London, or Bath, or wherever.'

'I've no lady in mind.'

'I'm sure they're falling over one another to attract your attention, Edward, dear.'

'What am I going to do?' he said. 'Even after all this time, I can't forget you.'

She sat very upright with her back against the chair and her hands clasped tightly in her lap. She opened her mouth as if to say something.

'I wish to God you'd never married that man,' Edward said. 'I wish to God I could be free of you. I can't rid myself of the idea that you married Pengelly purely out of spite against me.'

'That's not true,' she protested. She shifted her gaze from his.

'You aren't happy. I know you're not. Even though Hannah said you were –'

'You've seen Hannah?' For a moment her face lit with a kind of wistfulness.

'Do you ever think of me still, Lizzie?'

She sat in silence. Then she said, meeting the look in his eyes and leaning forward a little towards him, 'There are times when I feel nostalgia for that summer . . . and remember the barleyfield.'

There was a stillness between them. The direction they had taken seemed all at once to lead down forbidden paths. Edward reminded himself that he had come here to finish once and for all what had begun that afternoon in the barleyfield. But to finish it how?

'Arthur isn't a very demonstrative husband,' Elizabeth said in a voice in which she might have discussed the weather. 'It isn't that he's harsh or lacking in affection.' She hesitated. 'He's an honest man. It was because of that I married him. And because of it I think I expected more from the marriage, a closer union between us. Perhaps such a thing isn't possible between men and women.'

'There was between you and me,' he said quickly.

'I don't think so.'

143

Edward felt a sudden jealous impatience to know about her relationship with her husband. 'Do you sleep in the same bed?'

'Edward!'

'Do you?'

'Of course.'

He groaned. 'I can't bear to think of him touching you.'

'You shouldn't be thinking about it.' She looked away. 'If it's of any help,' she added in a small voice, 'the business, and his business friends, occupy a lot of his energies. He has little left for—' She fell silent. She bit her lip. A stifled sob broke from her. 'Oh, Edward, I'm so disappointed at what I've done.' Her face puckered untidily.

Edward thrust his hand through his hair, dismayed to see her exposed in that way and yet secretly exultant. Pengelly was a poor husband: she did not love him.

'You mustn't come again,' Elizabeth said. 'We mustn't meet after today. Knowing how we still feel —' The silence grew heavy with the ticking of a clock on the mantel shelf. The fire cracked in the grate. Edward's body raced with desire for her. She looked away. 'We mustn't,' she said again in a low voice. She did not lift her gaze from her hands in her lap.

Suddenly she stood up, and Edward stood too. It was as if they were in church and a signal had been given for the beginning of an anthem. He was unsure whether she meant that he should leave straight away. Then he saw from her face that she did not want him to go. There was a distance of some three or four feet of carpet separating them. He dared not cross it. He knew that if he touched her he would be lost. Slowly Elizabeth held out her hand to him. He gripped her fingers. He felt the blood pound in his head and rush and tingle through his body.

'What time does your husband come home?' His voice sounded harsh in his ears and too eager.

'Six or seven o'clock. Late usually.'

'Will anyone come to the house?'

'I've sent the maid away.'

This foresight on her part barely registered with him. 'Oh, God —' He was overcome with longing.

'Don't be frightened.' She was like a mother soothing a child.

'Where? Where can we go?'

He followed her into the chilly narrow hallway which smelled of cooked fish. A large black dog came towards them from the kitchen. It wagged its tail on seeing Edward.

'Go back, Merlin!' Elizabeth's voice was sharp. She nudged the animal out of the way with her knee.

Edward waited by the stair. He watched the dog follow her into the scullery. 'I'm going to lock the door,' she called.

He gripped the knob of the stair-rail, almost hoping that in the time it took her to find the key, lock the door, and hang the key again on its hook she would come to her senses, lead him back into the parlour, and give him his hat.

She returned to the hall and brushed past him with a flurry of dark-green silk. She started up the stairs. Edward followed, conscious of the thud of their feet on the treads and the rustle of Elizabeth's skirts as they neared the landing. She turned at the top step, as though to reassure him again, and then she ran across the corridor into the bedroom.

They undressed without looking at one another. The slow procedure of undoing buttons, laces and fastenings produced a terrible modesty and tension between them. She had pulled across the curtains. The room was cast in a greenish light and a thin shaft of sunlight spun dust motes near the dressing table mirror. Elizabeth scrambled under the white coverlet and shivered with cold; the dark tangle of her hair on the pillow and her hunched shape under the cover were all that Edward could see of her. He slipped into the bed and they lay without speaking.

Edward stared at the vertical line of weak yellow light between the drawn curtains and thought that this was where she lay each night with the block of a husband whom she did not love. Her cold foot touched his leg.

'I once thought that I was the Lady of Shalott. I believed I was dying of unrequited love for Sir Lancelot,' she said.

'Was I Sir Lancelot?'

'I thought you were.'

He reached out for her. She moved towards him and the contact of their bodies jerked them simultaneously with a spasm of desire. He tensed himself against her naked body. The touch of her skin was beautiful, softer than all his imaginings. The silken swell of her breasts and the nipples pressing against his chest heightened the ache of his desire. He let his hand move gently over breasts and thighs, exploring the contours of her form, an enigma, a thing of contrasts, of little shocks, her nipples hard and prominent, the mound of pubic hair, so alien to the image of pure female flesh, was warm and coarse under his fingers. The scent of her hair and skin was mingled with the faint camphor smell of cold bedsheets and that other smell of which he had been aware, of tobacco and perspiration, imprinted by her husband on the room.

'I wasn't the Lady of Shalott,' Elizabeth murmured. 'I wasn't Elaine.'

He moved down her body, with mouth and tongue on her breasts and belly, wanting to lose himself in her scent and drink her in.

'Not Elaine – but Guinevere.' There was an exultance in her voice. 'Guinevere, the faithless wife.'

Edward was not listening. He raised himself to kiss her mouth, groaning as his member pressed into the soft moist region between her thighs. Elizabeth pulled him to her, accepted him greedily with a single, convulsive shudder. The blood drummed in his head and through and through him as she gasped and clung and gave an exquisite cry. He moved inside her and was still, his whole being on the point of bursting, yet wanting to hear again her cry of pleasure, wanting the moment to go on and on. He moved again more slowly, held back until he could bear it no longer and Elizabeth's moans grew deeper. Then he thrust and thrust again until she cried out no more.

Edward held her close against him. He smoothed back the dark strands of hair where they clung to her face. She smiled a little in a languorous dreamy way and wrapped an arm round his neck, pulling his head down into the crook of her shoulder. Her skin was cool with sweat. He tried to imprint the taste of it on his lips, drawn by an inexplicable sadness. The joy of these and the moments before them must be sealed into his mind, for they would not be repeated. He started to say something, but she prevented him by pressing her fingers against his mouth.

He lay and stared again at the vertical line between the curtains. The shaft of sunlight streamed into his head, turning the darkness orange when he closed his eyes. The scent of Elizabeth was warm too like the sun, her breath was even and shallow, the curve of her breast against his face was a soft pillow on which to float and float for ever.

When he opened his eyes again the line of light between the curtains had faded. Elizabeth, as if she had been waiting for him to waken, rolled away from him. The space where she had been and the air on his bare flesh when he sat up felt cold. The joy had already gone.

Edward picked up his shirt and trousers from the pile of clothes which they had thrown to the floor.

'They wanted to burn her for the sin of adultery.' Elizabeth sat on the edge of the bed with the cover wrapped round her waist.

'What are you talking about?' he said indulgently. Her skin was smooth, like marble in the dim light. Naked, she was very beautiful. He paused in his dressing to look at her. 'I never did paint you. Like this would be the way to do it.'

'I'm talking about Guinevere. She became a nun. And Lancelot became a priest. They were disillusioned, I suppose.'

'Do you mean to continue the analogy to include your husband?' he said. He began to feel irritated by this persistence with the theme of adultery. 'Arthur, the noble king. Or is he perhaps the barbarian you always pretended to admire?'

He thrust his feet into his trousers and pulled them on. Already he felt the stirring of guilt and the complications and repercussions arising from what they had done. He was aware that nothing had been resolved. By the time he had put on his neck-cloth and tied it he was prepared almost to dislike her.

Elizabeth too had begun to dress. She came to him, heavy-breasted under her chemise and petticoat. She put her arms round his neck. 'Do you wish you'd stayed away?'

'No,' he protested quickly. He kissed her tangled hair.

'But it mustn't happen again,' she said quietly.

Afraid that he might not see her again he said, 'Your husband need never know.'

'For how long? People would soon talk.'

'You can leave him.' Her arms slipped from him. 'If you love me?' he pleaded.

She turned away and pulled her dress over her head. He watched her fasten the bodice. She seemed to have forgotten him in the task of finding and linking each small button and buttonhole.

'We'll go away somewhere,' he urged.

'That's insane. Where would we live? What about your medical studies? And Arthur doesn't deserve it. Besides, you and I decided to part company a long time ago.'

'Because I behaved less than perfectly,' he said bitterly. 'If it was a barbarian you wanted, you'd already found one.'

'I wanted some sort of ideal,' she said. 'I didn't know that ideals are made of dreams and shadows.'

He knew already that whatever he might have hoped for – reconciliation, a turning back of the clock – was impossible. She would not leave her husband. And if she did, they would never be free of guilt.

'I think you will break my heart,' he said.

'That's another myth, Edward. The heart is a tough muscular organ. Don't they teach you that at your medical school?'

20

Elizabeth had made him promise that he would never see her again. For two days Edward could not eat or sleep or study for the hard knot of misery under his breastbone.

After two days he went to the Army Medical Office in St James's and, with the singlemindedness which comes from decisions of an irrational kind, he offered himself for service in the Crimea. When his application was rejected he haunted the corridors of the Medical Office, writing complaints to the Director General, quoting the case of Jack Harris's easy enlistment. He was told by the lower echelons that Harris must have had friends in the right places.

He went to Fitzroy and asked him to speak for him. The surgeon declared that he refused to connive at getting any more of his bloody students slaughtered in a bloody useless war, and that it was time that Edward put in an appearance at a few lectures if he didn't want to be sent down from the College.

Then Edward learned that one of Harris's brothers had been killed in the hand to hand fighting at Inkerman. His resolve to go to the Crimea took on the aspect of an obsession. He went to see Lydia Delahaye.

'What a pleasant surprise.' Lydia was not sure whether the surprise was a pleasant one, but Edward was a very presentable young man and she was excited by the departure from routine. The visit would have been noted by her neighbours, she thought with satisfaction.

'I remembered your enthusiasm for *The Times* Appeal, Mrs Delahaye, I came to the conclusion that I must do something too.'

149

'You want to contribute to our Help for our Soldiers in the Crimea Fund?' Lydia said blankly.

'I should like to work as a doctor in the Crimea. The Army won't have me, so I've decided to go as a civilian. It occurred to me that your Ladies' Society might be willing to fund my journey.'

There was an awkward silence. Lydia considered the idea. It had a certain romantic appeal.

'We shall put your suggestion to tomorrow's meeting,' she decided. 'I'm sure the ladies will find it an interesting proposition.'

The ladies of the Kensington Benevolent Friends discussed Lydia's proposal excitedly. Someone suggested that a resolution should be adopted. Eventually it was agreed: they would sponsor Edward's journey to the Crimea and the money they collected should be used as he thought fit, until such a time as the war was ended.

From here on Lydia referred to Edward as her protégé. The very mention of his name would bring a fond lump to her throat.

Several members of the Society travelled to the docks early in December and one of Edward's last memories of England was of the fluttering of twenty ladies' white handkerchiefs, as his ship pulled away from the quayside.

Elizabeth had sent Edward away. She had preserved her marriage, her reputation and Arthur's position in the town; but her resentment against Arthur had become a more solid thing, feeding on every small irritation.

'We shall call the new house the *Red House*,' Arthur said, as if with a stroke of originality. 'For the time when we were first wed and to remind us that fortune shines on us again.'

'It was my fortune began it,' Elizabeth reminded him sharply.

He looked hurt. This irritated her too. So did his increased eccentricities of taste after the move to the better end of the town. He had bought numerous old pictures and tapestries, which were vaguely medieval in style. All kinds of gothic impedimenta began to fill the house. Stained glass replaced the plain glass in the dining room, wooden panels covered the walls. A suit of armour appeared in the hallway to welcome visitors and Merlin took to lying across the threshold with an arrogant tilt to his head.

Elizabeth could not interest herself in the move. She would begin to unpack a trunk of furnishings which Arthur had ordered and leave off halfway through, with window hangings and chair covers strewn around the hallway. The servants stood by looking perplexed and awaiting instructions, only to be told after a few minutes to hang the curtains where they liked, or else to pack everything away again until another day.

The new house, though less intimidating than The Red House at Charlford, reawoke the old vein of gloomy romanticism in her. She would spend hours reading novels and poetry in the window seat in the dining room, and her mind filled with memories and regrets. The rosy light from the stained glass in the windows streamed across the pages of her book: the Lady of Shalott floated on her barge down the river once more, Guinevere rode through coverts of deer with jingling bridle reins and Lancelot wasted *his whole heart in one kiss upon her perfect lips*.

Arthur had become convinced that there was hidden gentry somewhere in his ancestry; he had settled on a theory that he was descended from the Plantagenets.

'Arthur, it's too ridiculous,' Elizabeth said with a kind of pitying tolerance which barely disguised her exasperation.

'Look scornful if you want,' he said, 'but I mean to make inquiries.'

He had begun a correspondence with a Parson Truscott in Cornwall. He had heard that the parson was in possession of documents, relating to his mother's native village, which dated back to the reign of Edward III. Arthur was determined to prove the noble lineage of a Mr Bone, now deceased, the 'proper gentleman' with whom his mother had been in service for several years.

'A typical philandering squire,' was Elizabeth's judgement. 'I'm sure you grew up more honest and decent without such a father, than you would have with.'

'There's bad and good in all,' Arthur said democratically. 'England wouldn't be what she is today without her peasant blood and her aristocracy. And if I'm to be one or the other, I'd rather it was blue blood than that of the great unwashed that runs in my veins.'

Towards Christmas he announced a plan to leave the business in the hands of his under-manager. He would travel to Cornwall for a few days and examine old deeds and records with Parson Truscott, with the intention of gathering evidence for his claim to the gentry.

'And what am I supposed to do while you're gone?' Elizabeth said.

'Why, amuse yourself here, as you always do, my dear.'

They were seated at the dinner table. The curtains were closed against a gale which buffeted the windows. The candles, which Arthur preferred to the more practical gas lamps on the walls, flickered and guttered.

'But I don't amuse myself. I have absolutely no amusement now we are settled here.'

He smiled tolerantly. He could see that she was playing at being difficult. 'There's parties to be planned for the Christmas season. Invite some of your friends to visit. Indulge in the gossip you ladies delight in. Hold a few tea parties.'

'I do not delight in gossip.' She attacked a lamb chop viciously with her knife and fork. 'I hate tea parties. And I have no friends, they are the wives of your friends. They belong to your life, not mine.'

'But my life is your life,' he said easily.

Elizabeth was silent. She chewed on a mouthful of meat without tasting it. She would probably leave most of her dinner on her plate.

'Now what have I said to displease you?' There was an echo of her own irritation in the little frown which crossed Arthur's face.

'You used not to think like that – your life is my life, the wife is merely an extension of the husband. You promised me independence. You said you wouldn't dominate me.'

'I don't dominate you. Heaven forbid. You're too strong-minded for that sort of thing. You've got opinions. I admired that about you from the start. I can discuss things with you, as if you're an equal.'

She laughed. But he did not know that he had said anything which should have amused her.

'You need something to do,' he decided. 'Why don't you pay a call on Mrs Willoughby or Mrs Beatty? Now, you like Alderman Beatty's wife.'

It was true that she could have made a friend of the alderman's wife; but Arthur's suggestion, which she knew he had made only to humour her, was a lighted match to her anger. She crumpled her napkin in her lap and threw it on the table.

'Why must I always be involved in trivia? I want to *do* something, Arthur. I want to feel independent.'

'You can't be independent,' he said. 'You gave that all up when you married me.'

She stared at him as if he had said something so simple and yet so profound, that, though it had been staring her in the face, it had been hidden from her all this time.

'Perhaps some charity work would be a good idea.' He helped himself to another lamb chop. 'Talk to Mrs Willoughby about getting on the visiting list. There are enough poor families in the town for all you ladies to share between you.'

'Don't patronize me!'

Arthur looked up in surprise. A benign bewilderment crossed his face. 'Perhaps you wish you were a spinster school-ma'am again,' he said quietly and without sarcasm.

Elizabeth remembered with longing the school in Charlford, the hot, still afternoons of autumn, the low murmuring chant of voices as the children recited a text, the smell of dirty bodies crowded together in a small space and Johnny Herbert's tear-stained grimy face.

'It's true, I miss the schoolchildren. It has crossed my mind that I might open a school here one day.'

The idea, though it had only just come to her, lodged in her mind with the ease of an old familiar thought.

Arthur laughed. 'I don't think so, my dear. It wouldn't look right. Besides' – he looked uncomfortable – 'I've been thinking about children of our own before long.'

Elizabeth looked away.

'Well, you're not getting any younger,' he blustered.

She stood up. 'I'm not hungry. Please, excuse me –'

'Elizabeth.' His eyes softened and there was an uncertainty in his voice. 'I want you to be happy. It would mean a lot to me for you to be content.'

'I am content,' she lied.

'Why don't you go to Charlford for a few days come the spring?' he suggested. 'A reconciliation would be a good thing.'

She was surprised. He had not encouraged her before to make any gestures of appeasement towards her family. 'Would you mind?'

'My dear,' he said with elaborate tolerance. 'You're free to do what you wish in this house.'

She smiled.

'About the other thing,' he said.

'The other thing?'

'What I was saying – children and that.'

She paused by the door. 'Perhaps, if you were to pay more attention to the "and that", children would follow as a matter of course.'

'Tonight?' he said, laying down his knife and fork.

'I'm your wife,' she reminded him. 'You don't have to make an appointment.'

21

'How fares our young friend?' Mrs Thoroughgood had not been as whole-heartedly in favour of Edward's project as had the rest of the ladies of the Kensington Benevolent Friends; she made the inquiry sound as if Lydia had taken on a new servant whose progress required monitoring.

'Mrs Waugh tells me we have had some news,' said Miss Marchant, a lady who had been only recently converted to the cause of the Society: having been thwarted in her efforts to bestow love on any one man in particular, Miss Marchant had taken up a general love of her fellow man by way of compensation.

Lydia produced the much-awaited letter and pulled forward her chair a little from the circle of ladies, so that she might be seen better on all sides. She paused, to allow a little suspense to develop among her audience.

'Well? Are you going to tell us what he says?' said Mrs Waugh.

'I was about to do so,' Lydia replied with dignity. 'Mr Munro writes that he has made himself known to the people at the Army camps, and that there is much lacking there in the way of general supplies – due in part to the dreadful hurricane which we were reading about in the newspapers, and the sinking of *The Prince* with so many supplies on board. He believes that a surfeit of Army regulations hampers the movement of supplies from the port of Balaclava to the camps, and that things could be done a lot better without what he calls "petty bureaucracy".'

'I am sure the Army are doing their best,' said Mrs Waugh with a condescending smile.

'He says that the town of Balaclava is a hotchpotch of broken-down houses and all nationalities of people – Turks and French, Armenian, Greek and Maltese – they all call the English "Johnny", and they are all very noisy and villainous. Everyone has to plough through mud and dirt and slush everywhere. He says also that the brave soldiers are touchingly grateful for the little luxuries we were able to provide in time for Christmas.'

'Your Christmas puddings found a home then?' Mrs Thoroughgood emphasized the word puddings in such a way that Lydia wondered whether the knitted pen wipers which Mrs Thoroughgood had herself sent to the Crimea had been in some way superior.

'He mentions the puddings in particular. He also writes that he hopes to make himself more useful, now that he has found a friend in one of the Army surgeons. The surgeon's name is Charles Watkins, and whereas the hospitals will not hear of Mr Munro's working in Balaclava, because he is a civilian, Mr Watkins's regiment has "adopted" him, he says. They have furnished him with a pass, so that he might move freely about the Heights, and he takes up medicine and blankets and food to the camp when the weather is fine; and sometimes he is able to assist the Army doctors in tending the sick in the camp.'

Miss Marchant sighed deeply and her pink cheeks flushed a deeper rose. She had already fallen in love with Edward's romantic mission and was more than a little in love with the man behind it. 'I think it is a wonderful thing that Mr Munro is doing. He is alleviating pain and saving lives so that the soldiers might win further honour on the battlefield.'

'Who is it who said, "A true gentleman is one who is loath to inflict pain on others"?' said Miss Lacey, a woman who was given to generally inappropriate quotations from time to time.

'But doctors have to inflict pain.' Lydia was drawn for the sake of accuracy into an argument.

'And pain is a necessary thing in battle,' asserted Mrs Waugh.

'The doctor himself might be injured in the course of his duty,' said Miss Marchant tremulously and irrelevantly.

'I mean that it is Mr Munro's *intention*, to lessen rather than inflict pain,' continued Miss Lacey, becoming confused.

'My sympathies lie with the fighting man,' said Mrs Waugh, taking her time over the selection of a small cake from a tray of delicacies which Lydia's cook had provided. 'My sister has two boys over there, both have been wounded – one in the Battle of Balaclava, one at Inkerman. She has every reason to be proud of them. Her husband was an Army man too. In India. Macheted by a rabble of natives.'

'How awful!' Miss Marchant turned paler.

'I never knew him show a scrap of fear. They say he cut down six men single-handed before they did for him. A fight brings out the best in a man, I'm sure. My goodness, we needed this campaign. We needed something to cheer for. It makes me go all of a-tingle with pride, to think of those glorious heroes at the Balaclava Battle.'

A few of the ladies applauded. Mrs Waugh was gathering rather too large an audience for Lydia's satisfaction. She felt it necessary to divert their attention elsewhere. 'Mr Munro's decision to go to the Crimea, out of a very proper duty to his Sovereign and his country, may also have been influenced not a little by a broken romance,' she said enigmatically. The diversion had its desired effect. The ladies urged her to say more. 'A little bird has told me, that Mr Munro was devastated when a lady of his acquaintance rejected his suit.'

'How very romantic,' said Mrs Thoroughgood. 'I see it all now. He has gone on a foreign adventure in order to prove to this lady that he is worthy of her.'

'Something of the sort, perhaps,' smiled Lydia, pleased with the reaction she had achieved.

'It's just like in a novel,' said Mrs Thoroughgood. 'A young man proves his valour and wins the hand of a lady of high beauty.'

'Is she a lady of high beauty?' demanded Mrs Waugh.

Lydia hesitated. The truth prodded uncomfortably at the story she herself had almost begun to believe. She could hardly say now that Elizabeth was over thirty and rather plain, and had for the past twelve months been married to a Dorset tradesman. 'She is of *unusual* beauty,' she said. The women sighed with satisfaction.

'There is no doubt about it,' said Mrs Thoroughgood. 'Mr Munro is turning out to be quite a romantic creature in my eyes. I must admit, he is becoming quite a hero.'

If heroes were a breed which sought to shine in deeds of glory, the Crimea was no place for them, and glory was no more than a flight of fancy of deluded poets: Edward imagined Harris dying here at the miserable port of Balaclava.

Edward had arrived just before Christmas. The narrow harbour floated with debris; broken packing cases, straw, and the bloated carcasses of horses bobbed on the water among the transport ships. The quay was scattered with the flotsam of a chaotic supply system. Boxes, cases and bales were roughly covered with tarpaulins, or lay half opened, with their contents spilled into the mud and puddles all around and everything exposed to the rain, which beat down in a cold relentless torrent. Edward made his way along the quayside. Slow processions of carts moved to and from the ships. Some of the carts were filled with soldiers, bearded, filthy and silent, they huddled together like sodden bundles of rags; the heavy rumble of wheels was all that announced their passing. Those who were not too sick to notice stared at him as they went. Edward was very conscious of his new frock coat and the mud-spattered but still shiny boots on his feet.

He stood to one side as a further procession of carts, this time empty, approached from the opposite direction. A man walking alongside the carts broke away from them; his hands were thrust deep into the pockets of his uniform greatcoat and his huge shoulders were hunched against the rain which drove into his back, but he walked purposefully, as though used to the discomfort.

Edward, guessing that the man might have come from the hospital which had discharged the sick for transportation, turned and followed him until he came upon a group of officers slouched in a doorway. The men greeted the stranger and made room for him in the shelter of the building. Edward approached them and explained that he was newly arrived in the Crimea.

'I'd be grateful if you would direct me to the nearest hospital.'

They stared with a discomforting lack of interest at his soaked frock coat and luggage.

'Have you been assigned to a regiment?' said the man he had followed.

'I'm a civilian. The Army hasn't sent me.'

They continued to regard him steadily while he stood in the rain which poured from his clothes and seeped down his neck. They were all roughly dressed and unshaven, with strips of cloth binding their legs like London beggars wore in winter. Two of the men had sheepskins over their army uniform. They all presented a picture more in line with Edward's idea of Russian Cossacks, or Turkish mercenaries, than his image of the natty British fighting man.

'Are you a doctor?' asked one of the men.

'I was a medical student. The Army wouldn't take me as a medic. So I've come out alone.'

'You'll find the Crimea an interesting addition to your medical training,' someone said, and the others laughed.

The first man thrust out his hand. Edward accepted it reluctantly. 'Charles Watkins. Assistant Surgeon. Light Infantry Division.'

'If you'd just direct me to the hospital.'

'I'll take you. Though I warn you, they're not very partial to civilians.'

The man stepped out into the rain. Edward did not miss the burst of laughter from the other officers as they turned away into the building.

The army surgeon who met them at the hospital was a harassed, sallow-faced man, who made it clear that he had no time for visitors. He eyed Edward's shaven complexion and civilian clothes suspiciously. 'Are you a doctor?'

Edward explained again that he had been a medical student.

'Can you perform surgery?'

'I have only watched at amputations.' Edward recalled his terror of the operating theatre. 'But I've worked as a dresser,' he added quickly.

'We badly need qualified surgeons,' the man said. 'We can't allow any Tom, Dick or Harry to take charge of a soldier brought in with his lungs opened or an arm hanging off.'

'I have a letter here.' Edward struggled to pull from his pocket a letter of recommendation with which Professor Fitzroy had eventually been persuaded to furnish him. The surgeon waved it away. 'But there must be something I can do,' Edward protested. 'I've nursed cholera patients. I'm willing to work unpaid.'

'Cholera isn't so bad as it was,' the man said. 'We are doing what we can here, within service regulations. You really should have gone through the proper channels, you know.'

The surgeon's expression was not unsympathetic, yet there was a guardedness about it. Edward was puzzled. He knew that the hospital needed staff; wounds needed dressing, clothing and bedding needed changing, the sickly sweet smell of death pervaded the building.

'Perhaps I should set up a dispensary on the quayside,' he said.

'From what I've seen so far, the men being shipped to Scutari haven't done very well from the care they've received here.'

The man shrugged, and his expression became hostile. 'It's nothing to me what you do. But I can't put you to work in this hospital.'

Throughout the interview Charles Watkins had stood silently by. It was impossible to tell from his expression what he was thinking. As they went down the hill into Balaclava he spoke: 'You can't say I didn't warn you.'

'But why?'

'He wouldn't be able to cope with the extra responsibility. He doesn't want it. Nobody does. It's as much as any of us can do to maintain our own sanity in this hell hole. Besides, for all he knows, you might be one of our sightseers.'

'Sightseers?'

'Tourists. Amateurs. They come out from England to see the fun. You might even have been sent to spy on him, so that you can go home whining to the newspapers about what's going on.'

'Is that what you thought?'

'I've no axe to grind with newspaper correspondents. My first guess though would have been a tourist, or amateur.' He roared with laughter at Edward's look of dismay. He thumped him on the back. 'Come on. I just might know where you can get hold of some transport. You'll be needing a horse or a mule. But first, we'll find you a billet in the town. This place isn't quite so bad as it seems once you know where to get a drink.'

22

There were many impressions of those first days in the Crimea which would stay with Edward for ever. There was the bitter cold, and the smell of dirt and death, which seemed to rise up from the mud and be present in the very rain which soaked everything; there were the narrow streets of Balaclava, noisy, filthy, and seething with people, wagons, camels and mules. And there was the road to the camp, a distance of some seven miles to the Heights above Sebastopol where the regiments were stationed. The way was lined with bullock wagons, axle-deep and abandoned in the mud. Dead mules lay beside the track. The carcasses of starved horses were piled in gullies, left in stinking heaps, some half-eaten by marauding dogs and vultures, some already reduced to skeletons.

Edward fixed his mind on the figure of Charles Watkins, riding at an even pace ahead of him with his head bent against the wind, his face almost hidden by a muffler, worn wound round his head in place of his uniform peak cap. Watkins spoke little on the journey, except to turn and point out here and there a piece of ground over which they might pass to avoid the worst of the mud. Edward urged on his mule impatiently, nervous of the empty carts, the howl of the wind, and piles of decomposing horse-flesh.

Watkins's camp was spread over an area resembling a vast ploughed field lashed by weeks of rain and storms. The tents were like scattered flocks of frail white birds which had alighted for shelter on the hills.

Inside one of the larger tents officers congregated, drinking grog and drying their boots. Edward was offered coffee, a hot, thin grey liquid, by an assistant dressed in an odd assortment of medical uniform and baggy trousers. The coffee simmered on the stove against which socks were drying. There was a steamy, not unpleasant stuffiness in the tent.

But in the hospital tents it was different. Here the men who waited to be taken down to Balaclava lay, ten or twelve together, on the bare ground. They were wrapped in their greatcoats, their feet towards the pole at the centre of the tent. Some were injured, most were suffering from dysentery or the effects of the intense cold. Some had lain for hours in a water-logged trench on the field of the siege, or had suffered the ordeal of amputation and other butcheries at the field hospital.

This was a new horror. There were amputations which had festered, men with senses gone, desolation on the faces of those who had given up hope of seeing any other aspect of humanity than that which haunted them now.

Edward wrote little about the true nightmare of the Crimea to the ladies of the Kensington Benevolent Friends. He might, perhaps, have returned to England at once, disillusioned by his poor attempt to cleanse his soul. He might have returned, suitably chastened, to his studies, older but wiser, found himself a pretty, undemanding wife, a country practice in time and a modest income, and explained away his journey to the Crimea as a period of insanity, his love-affair with Elizabeth an unfortunate chapter in a misspent youth.

Instead, he became involved with the supply problems of Charles Watkins's regiment.

It was Christmas Day. The rain and sleet of the preceding days had eased and there was a light covering of snow.

Edward celebrated by eating one of Lydia Delahaye's Christmas puddings; he sat hunched over a charcoal stove in the attic room which was his lodging in Balaclava. The cold numbed his mittened fingers and seeped through his too flimsy frock coat. The wind blew the sacking blind which covered the square of window and stirred the festoons of black cobwebs which hung from the ceiling laths; a strong smell of horses rose through the thin floorboards from the stable below. He felt very much alone.

He tried to rid his mind of images of festering wounds and corpses and to lessen a creeping sense of desolation by singing carols. But the sound of his lone voice in the small room made him feel worse rather than better.

Later that day, Charles Watkins came to visit him. His large figure seemed to fill the attic. He had brought a bottle of rum. 'Ask no questions,' he said and he poured out generous measures into two tin mugs, which he produced like a stage magician from his coat.

'This must be the divinest pigsty under the heavens,' Charles said, drawing up the roll of Edward's mattress close to the stove and sitting on it.

Edward, affected by his high spirits, felt as cheerful all at once as he had been miserable five minutes before. 'It lacks a certain domestic touch,' he said. 'The old crone next door, who has agreed to cook for me, could take a few lessons from my brother's housekeeper.'

'Ah – home sweet home,' sighed Charles. 'Kensington Gardens. Hyde Park.'

Nostalgia caught Edward unawares. He saw the river at Charlford, winding among flat fields, the yellow-leaved willows and the packhorse bridge.

'How did you meet our benefactresses, the Kensington ladies?' Charles asked.

'Mrs Delahaye is an aunt of –' Edward could not bring himself to say Elizabeth's name. 'She is the aunt of an old friend. She heads a worthy army of determined ladies, blessed with time on their hands and a strong do-gooding instinct. They keep very busy with their charity bazaars and knitting blankets and socks.'

'I know the type,' Charles said soberly. 'Mrs Watkins has a number of similar family appendages. They regularly send me religious tracts to keep my pecker up. Knitted socks would be rather more welcome.'

Edward found it difficult to imagine his new friend, with his tangled red beard and red-veined cheeks and hands, in a setting such as Lydia Delahaye's drawing room; though he supposed that somewhere in his background lay that sort of middle-class respectability.

'Married like me, are you?' Charles said.

'Can a medical student afford to keep a wife?'

'Sweetheart then?'

'A long time ago.'

'Mrs Watkins is a wonderful girl. Three little nippers we've got. They won't know their papa when they see him again.' He fell silent.

Edward said, 'What is it that drives the world to this? At home they give it high ideals, call it love of country and other fantastic drivel.'

'It's a madness, Edward. A leap into the unknown. A craving for experience.'

Edward thought of Jack Harris. He told Charles about him and how he had died soon after he arrived in the Crimea. 'He thought it was all a game,' he said. 'Until the cholera got him. One of his brothers was killed at Inkerman.'

'Either way, you're stone dead. Go home, Edward, before it's too late. I've had enough of all this to last a lifetime, but I can't go home until they let me. If I were a free agent I'd be off home on the next ship like a shot.'

'I suppose you think I'm mad.'

Charles raised his glass in the wool-clad palm of his hand. 'A raving lunatic. I'll drink to that.'

Although the men were badly clothed and fed, and inadequately housed, there was no shortage of supplies in Balaclava. The problem, Edward discovered, lay in obtaining them. As yet there was no railway and the Army had not improved the roads before the bad weather, so that transporting goods to the camps was carried out with great difficulty. Fatigue parties would be detailed to fetch supplies from the port, but the men were weak and the horses half-starved and in poor shape for hauling timber to build huts. The mud on the roads was too deep, the weather too severe, and the wheels of bureaucracy, which drove the processing of dockets and requisition forms via the commissariat, were too slow for anybody to do much to alleviate the problem.

Edward joined the sutlers and other camp followers, haggling for goods in the town and on Balaclava quay. His contribution of medicines and food, paid for by the charitable industry of Lydia's ladies, was small – pathetically so, he would tell himself, on the days when he managed to deliver no more than a few blankets and bottles of quinine through the mud and snow to Charles Watkins's camp – but he invested it with a tenacity, and even in the worst weather he would drive himself to make the journey to the Heights above Sebastopol.

Edward altered during the first weeks of the winter. He lost weight and grew a beard, learned to eat salt pork and biscuit like the army, and bought himself a Cossack coat from a soldier, a trophy from a skirmish with the Russians. He saw that it was not so much the fighting which brutalized the men, who had discovered among dead and dying

Russians an enemy as vulnerable as themselves, as the barbarity of the cold, the smell of death, the mud and squalor. Most wanted little more to do with 'glory', only to get through the winter alive and go home.

Frostbite was common, so were dysentery, cholera, and fever. Edward no longer questioned the military sense of what was happening in the Crimea. His mind was numbed by the horror of all that he saw around him. Each day was the same: the purchase of goods in the town, the ploughing journey to and from the camp. Ashamed of a lingering squeamishness, he made himself spend more and more time among the sick and wounded there. He helped change dressings and steeped himself in all that was hideous. It was as if only by doing the worst tasks could he justify his presence among men who had borne real suffering. They told him about the fighting. 'You think about it all the time – things you couldn't bring yourself to do in cold blood. It seems a great time of madness afterwards.'

'Aren't you frightened?' he asked.

They thought about it. Treading on the bodies of the wounded was the worst. Then there were the horses, screaming with terror, ripped apart by round shot, a man with his head knocked away in front of your eyes. Those bayoneted in the stomach came off worse; the agony looked terrible, but if you were shot in the head or the heart it probably wasn't so bad, you died pretty quickly.

The year wore on into February. Edward took on the peculiar haunted aspect of the men around him and his eyes reflected their suffering. But he felt a dissatisfaction with himself: he was an outsider, a parasite; he had not faced death at the point of a bayonet, or been forced to freeze for twenty-four hours in a trench under fire from the enemy; he could pack his bags and go home whenever he wanted. A sense of his own worthlessness grew stronger.

It was snowing lightly when he started as usual for the camps one morning. He had taken a mule, loaded up with food, lint and bandages. He pulled his greatcoat closer, ignoring the first scurries of snow, used to the way the small fine flakes stung his half-closed eyes. The track was familiar and it was not too difficult, with his head bowed against the wind, to plod his way along.

His mind like the snowstorm was blank but restless, a whirling agitation of tiny disconnected particles, which never settled long enough to form themselves into coherent thought.

After a while the storm became more violent. The track and the familiar landmarks to right and left were soon obliterated as the wind whipped the snow into drifts. Aware that he had wandered off course, Edward turned the mule and retraced their steps, resigned to the fact that the journey was going to take longer that day than usual. He set out again, and the blizzard wrapped itself round him; it blotted out every rock, every slope of hill, every point on which he would begin to fix his attention as a point of reference.

After three hours a small fear gnawed at him, for he had not reached any of the camps, nor had he come upon a single traveller, or tent, or sound that would show that he was close to human habitation. Now and then, great rocks loomed ahead and he would be forced to scramble, dragging the unwilling mule up steep-sided gullies. Soon, he told himself, he would come upon one of the outlying pickets, who would be able to direct him on his way. He prayed that he would not be challenged in Russian, or, if in French, that he would not be shot by an over-eager sentry before he could explain the object of his journey.

His eyes hurt and the skin round them was drawn tight by the wind. His hands and feet felt numb. His coat was caked with ice where the snow had clung to it, and his beard seemed frozen into a wedge. He knew that he was dangerously near to exhaustion and remembered a soldier who had been brought with a train of sick and injured into Balaclava one morning: the man had died, strapped to a pony, frozen solid, his eyes staring out from their sockets.

Above the roar of the storm he heard a different sound, like the distant murmur of water. The idea that if he could head towards it he would escape from this white landscape became fixed in his mind. He used images of a river to force himself on: he pictured waterfalls, a millrace, a millpond beyond it, water running over rocks, a stream tumbling against pebbles. He imagined a narrow stone bridge, warmed by a summer sun, clumps of willows, their bright, sap-filled leaves uncurling in the air. He could feel the sun burning his face. Beyond his closed eyelids lay a barleyfield, it parted before the summer breeze and made a pathway for him. He pictured Elizabeth on the packhorse bridge; she was smiling at him; she seemed to say something, but he could not hear her for the sound of the wind in the barley.

The mule had halted. The roar of water was louder. It filled Edward's

166

head with a muffled sound, too deep-throated to be a gentle Somerset river or even the Tchernaya.

The mule stood trembling and refused to go any further. Edward slapped the animal on its flank but it would not go on. It was at that moment that the wind changed direction and he could see ahead of him.

A more awesome emptiness replaced the blanketing white of the snow. They were close to the edge of a cliff. The sea, dark and laced with foam, pounded against black rocks below. The water sucked and boiled among them.

For a long time Edward stood staring at the sea, its melancholy and endless roar an echo of his own wasted existence. After a while he steered the mule away from the cliff edge. With a last reserve of strength he pushed it hard on the rump, letting go of the bridle. Edward watched the animal trot away across the snow then he turned again to the cliff.

He felt himself drain of free will. He stood at the very end of the world, before a final chaos. The noise of the water pulled him downward. It seemed such a small step, to obey its call and launch himself into oblivion.

23

Elizabeth had travelled to Charlford to visit her parents. Robert Munro met her at the coaching inn in Yeovil. He seemed nervous as he came towards her from among the crowd of waiting people. He had put on a little weight, she noticed; marriage evidently suited him. The cold made his nose and cheeks red – he looked more like a rotund and rosy cherub than ever.

'Have you forgiven me at last then?' she said, as he carried her portmanteau to the trap.

Robert glanced round uneasily, as if afraid that someone might have heard the remark above the noise of friends greeting friends and unloading luggage and the bustle of horses being shifted about on the road.

'I think it's better not to talk about the past,' he said. Only then, as he handed her into the trap, did he turn to look at her properly. She saw his glance drop involuntarily to her waist.

Arthur had said that she must write and tell her family, but she had been reluctant to stir up in advance all the fuss that the news of her pregnancy would cause. He was ecstatic about the prospect of fatherhood. He saw it in terms of an heir to the business; and a child, even if it should turn out to be a girl, was an asset to a man on his way up in the world, who was on the point of discovering that he was in direct line to the Plantagenets of England. She wished for a moment that Arthur had come with her, instead of going off again to Cornwall to pursue his ridiculous delving into his ancestry.

'Your father has grown very frail since Christmas,' Robert said as they set out. 'He has got himself very excited about this visit. He has been looking forward to it for days, Elizabeth.'

She thought she detected a criticism in his words and said nothing.

They talked politely on the journey about her family, about Arthur's business and about Mabel at the vicarage. Elizabeth was tired and she felt the beginnings of a headache. She was careful to avoid references to her pregnancy, nor did either of them mention Edward.

How would Robert behave if he knew whose child she was carrying? More to the point, what would Arthur do if he discovered the truth? The deception was not difficult now. But later, would she be able to keep up the pretence, when he began to do his own calculations, remembered the infrequency of their love-making?

Elizabeth's headache consolidated itself as they drove through the lanes to Charlford.

Robert, concentrating on the business of coachmanship in his new pony trap, was not thinking of Elizabeth's pregnancy. He was wondering how to tell her about the letter he had received and the news that Edward was missing, lost in the snows of the Crimea.

Robert could not grieve. It had been the same when his mother had died, and later his father: outwardly he had mourned, but inside he had been as cold as the family vault in which they lay. There would be no funeral for Edward. The letter had held out little hope of finding a body for burial.

It troubled Robert a little, this lack of feeling in him; a man should grieve for his brother. But the truth was that he had received the news of Edward's disappearance with a sense of release.

He looked at Elizabeth. He decided that it was better to say nothing for the time being.

The Thorne household had worked itself to a pitch of intense activity and Hannah and Fred had been sent for to come and stay for a week during Elizabeth's visit. Mrs Booth could be heard at regular intervals, slamming saucepans about and shouting at Flo in the kitchen.

Elizabeth's pregnancy aroused a wearying excitement. Mrs Thorne was caught between the taboo over discussing a delicate subject and the need to air all the old wives' tales and horror stories regarding her own and anecdotal pregnancies. These conversations took place in a confidential whisper and always out of earshot of Fred and Henry.

Hannah, who had private reason to suspect that she too might be pregnant, listened in a dispirited way to her mother's revelations.

'You would think a woman's chief biological function really is a punishment sent by God,' she said, when she and Elizabeth were alone together.

They were in the garden, the grass was powdered with frost which clung to the hems of their skirts as they walked. The sisters were dressed almost alike in dark woollen frocks and Indian shawls; their hair was pulled neatly behind their ears.

Hannah plucked at a withered berry on a climbing rose under the trellis arch. She seemed weighted with a private seriousness, and more subdued than Elizabeth had seen her since her marriage.

'I am so glad that you're settled at last,' Hannah said. 'I suppose we all accept in the end the role that God has decreed for us.'

'Is yours to be that of martyr?' Elizabeth said quietly. She could see Fred through the window of the house, sleek and self-possessed, and standing leaning with one arm on the back of an armchair as he talked to her father. 'Does he have to go to London as often as he does? You know what he gets up to. Why don't you do something?'

'Because we are happy,' Hannah said without conviction. 'He loves me in his way. And now I have baby Albert.' She regarded Elizabeth steadily and unemotionally. 'You really mustn't meddle, Lizzie. It isn't fair of you.'

Elizabeth wanted to tell her how her own marriage had turned out to be less than perfect, even that she was carrying Edward's child: she badly needed a confidante. But she knew that the scandal of it would be too much for Hannah.

No one had spoken of Edward since she had arrived in Charlford; it was almost as if there was a conspiracy at work against mentioning him; for there were moments when it seemed inevitable, and then Hannah, or her mother or father, would swiftly direct the conversation away.

She wanted to talk about him. She realized that the strain of the last few months had created a tension now that she was here in Charlford, which made her feel unsure of herself. She wanted to ask them how Edward had seemed at Christmas. Was he depressed? She had to know whether his heart had really been broken, as he had claimed; or was he resigned to life in London again? Had he forgotten her? No. If she was honest, she did not want to hear that he had forgotten her. For, if he was free of her at last, he could never know about the child, and there would be nothing but herself and Arthur in the world.

Arthur arrived a few days later with Merlin. He seemed morose and to have put on his old unsociability. Elizabeth discovered that his visit to Cornwall had not been a success: it had turned out that the philandering Mr Bone, who had once offered Arthur's mother his protection, had not been a descendant of the Bohuns of the Plantagenet dynasty, but had come from an obscure line of yeomen, who had settled in Cornwall in the previous century.

'Yeoman stock is very sturdy,' Elizabeth said.

'It's not the same,' Arthur grumbled. 'And I wanted you to think well of me.'

Elizabeth was startled. Was this what had been behind it all – an attempt to better himself in her eyes? It was ridiculous, if it was true. She avoided talking about it; and, after a few hours, Arthur became more good-humoured and seemed to have forgotten his disappointment. He entered into the spirit of the family gathering, bouncing baby Albert on his knee, until the child was sick and Hannah had to remove him from his uncle's rough affection.

Squire Attwell and his wife, and Robert and Mabel, were invited to supper that evening. Someone suggested that the younger members of the party should put on a *tableau vivant*. Old clothes trunks and attic boxes were brought down and raided for suitable costumes.

'The first *tableau* ought to be "The Lady with the Lamp",' said Elizabeth. 'Since the Crimea is in everyone's mind just now.'

Squire Attwell and his wife applauded the idea, but the others looked at one another uneasily and seemed strangely reluctant. Fred and Robert were very solemn as they allowed their arms and legs to be swathed in bandages, to look like wounded soldiers. They lay upon the floor with Arthur, his head cocooned in a torn sheet, while Hannah stood behind them carrying a storm lamp and wearing an expression of saintly, but slightly agitated concern.

The scene drew tears from Mrs Thorne. 'On account of the poor, dear soldiers,' she explained; she patted Robert's hand.

Elizabeth looked from one to the other and intercepted Arthur's amused glance. He raised his eyebrows, and she smiled, united with him briefly in a silent protest at their sentimentality.

171

'I shall choose the next subject,' said Hannah with a forced jollity. '"King Arthur and his Court". It seems appropriate.' She smiled at Arthur, who returned the smile uncertainly. His recent disappointment in Cornwall had left him with a vague paranoia. He wondered whether Elizabeth had perhaps told them about his research into his ancestry and he had become a figure for ridicule.

'The subject is too ambitious,' protested Elizabeth. 'The men need suits of armour.'

'We can improvise from Mrs Booth's pan cupboard.' Hannah was warming to her idea. 'To the kitchen everyone. Fetch the pots and pans. Arthur must be the king, of course. And Merlin – I shall make you a magician's hat.'

'Then I suppose I shall have to be Guinevere,' said Elizabeth. She remembered the last time she had adopted the role. The faithless wife. Guinevere had taken herself off to a convent. Lancelot, grown lean and pale, retreated to a monastery, where he died of grief. Her own fate seemed less romantic.

She began to rummage in a trunk of dressing-up clothes for suitably royal robes and pulled out a length of green curtain.

'What a pity Edward isn't here,' remarked Mrs Attwell. 'He would have made the perfect Sir Lancelot after his recent exploits.'

Elizabeth, who was winding the curtain round her head for a head-dress, halted in mid-flourish and felt sick.

There was a long silence. Hannah, who had reached the doorway on her way to the kitchen, came slowly back into the room.

Elizabeth was unnerved by their grave faces. She looked from one to the other.

'Is anything the matter?' said Mrs Attwell.

Robert cleared his throat. 'I have had a letter. They tell me Edward is missing.'

'Missing?' Elizabeth placed a hand on the back of a chair to steady herself. 'Missing where?'

'In the Crimea,' Hannah told her gently.

'I'm sure there's nothing to fear.' Mrs Thorne looked anxiously at Robert, then Elizabeth. 'After all, Edward would hardly be in the thick of the fighting, and you know what a thoughtless boy he always was. He's probably on his way home and has forgotten to tell anyone.'

Elizabeth could not understand what they were saying. The room

172

had become horribly stuffy. She thought that she would suffocate if she did not have air. She gripped the back of the chair tightly.

'Apparently there was a severe snowstorm,' Robert explained. 'The weather has been very harsh, as we know.' He paused. 'There seems little hope of his being alive.'

'Oh, dear. Oh, dear.' Mrs Attwell rocked to and fro in her chair. 'Why ever didn't you tell us, Robert?'

The Squire looked upset. 'That's a bad do.' His large chin trembled with emotion. 'That's a bad do, my boy.' Mabel had begun to cry.

Elizabeth unwound the curtain from her head with one hand. What was it they were saying – that Edward was dead? She held the weight of the curtain on her arm, staring at the way it fell in a graceful green swirl, as if it was flowing into the carpet. She could not understand why Edward should have been in the Crimea, or why they were saying that he was dead. She looked up. Perhaps she had misunderstood; it was a momentary fantasy; but, no, their faces were frightened, they did not know what to do, and Mabel was still crying. She let her hand slip from the chair which supported her. She could not bear it. How could she go on living with Arthur and the baby? The dark swirl of curtain was heavy on her arm, it dragged her downward. The heat of the room closed in on her, and she fell with a crash to the floor.

Someone brought her a glass of brandy. They fussed round her, said conciliatory things about her 'condition', and, shocks being generally a bad thing, it was understood that pregnant women did that sort of thing. No more was said about Edward. But the spirit had gone out of the evening. The *tableaux vivants* were abandoned, and the Attwells left early.

Arthur did not say very much about what had happened until two days later. An excursion to Glastonbury Tor had been planned and, as she tied on her straw bonnet in the mirror in the bedroom, Elizabeth saw that he was watching her. His expression was troubled.

'Now what's the matter?' she said. 'I told you, I'm well again. Quite well enough for a gentle carriage ride.'

'This fellow,' he said. 'The one they say is missing. What was he to you?'

'We were old friends,' Elizabeth said, taking her time over straightening the bonnet brim and avoiding his gaze in the mirror.

173

'What sort of old friends?'

'We were much like brother and sister.' She felt sick with anxiety and with the effort of keeping up a pretence. She turned and slumped on the bed to wait for him to finish dressing.

Arthur continued to regard her thoughtfully as he tied his necktie. 'Do you have to wear straw? All the fashionable ladies are wearing little silk bonnets these days.'

'I don't care about being fashionable today. We're going for a country drive.'

'I want you to look nice, Elizabeth.'

She was close to breaking point. 'I do dress to please you most of the time. Today – why are you so determined to pick a quarrel? Today I picked up the first bonnet to hand. I had other things on my mind.'

'Such as him – the fellow in the Crimea?'

'He was a friend. I can't help feeling sad.' She reached for her gloves at the foot of the bed and began pulling them on. Her hands were shaking.

Arthur stood, awkwardly fingering the brim of his hat.

'Were you lovers?'

She had not credited him with so much perception. She looked up and met his gaze and was aware of the strength of his feeling for her.

'I remember talk of something. Were you and he lovers before I knew you?' He was trembling violently.

Elizabeth could not speak and her eyes swam with tears. 'You'll only regret it if you persist with this,' she said at last. 'We'd better go downstairs.'

'It always reminds me of a magic, fairy tower,' Hannah said, as the mist-veiled Tor first came into sight across the levels.

Elizabeth, crushed between Arthur and her mother in the carriage, turned her head to view the hill with its tower. She was aware as always of its sense of mystery, linked to something primitive in the landscape.

'Shall we climb it?' said Fred.

'Of course,' said Hannah. 'When have we ever been to Glastonbury and not climbed the Tor?'

'Elizabeth, you'd better stay behind with Father and me in the town,' her mother said.

174

'Nonsense. The exercise will do me good.'

There was a claustrophobia about staying below with her parents to walk among the Abbey ruins while the others climbed the hill. Elizabeth wanted to look across the levels almost to the sea and to let the loneliness of the sky wash through her.

'Is it wise?' Arthur had been silent for most of the journey.

'Wise or not, I want to climb the Tor.'

Hannah and Fred went ahead. Merlin gambolled like an overgrown puppy beween Arthur and Elizabeth as they climbed the steep path.

'Don't fuss. I'm all right,' Elizabeth said, every time Arthur halted to let her pause for breath.

'Are you still thinking of that fellow?' he said once.

She ignored him. She pushed back her bonnet and waved to Hannah and Fred, who had already reached the top of the hill.

Fred was examining the names carved into the stones under the archway of the tower when they reached the summit. Elizabeth joined her brother-in-law without speaking. She touched the cold stones which rose, grim in the shadows, and met the square of pale sky high above. She never liked the tower close to. It lost its mystery and became an unnecessary addition to the hill, square and ugly. She walked past Fred, out into the sunlight, slowly circling the building. She leaned against the wall and closed her eyes, letting the thin warmth of the sun soak into her. She could hear the faint sound of voices on the other side of the tower and the dog barking.

She imagined Edward, frozen to death, or shot by a Russian bullet, or bayoneted, his blood staining the Crimean snow. Her chest hurt with a solid pain which had nothing to do with the exertion of climbing the hill. She had thought he was still the fickle youth who had made love to her in a barleyfield. When he had asked her to leave Arthur and come to him she had not believed him.

'Fred and I are going down,' Hannah said, coming round the corner of the building. 'Are you not feeling well, Lizzie?'

'Tired,' Elizabeth said.

Arthur joined them. 'Elizabeth and me will wait a while before coming down. I told you it wasn't wise to come up here.' His face was strained and unsmiling.

Elizabeth said nothing.

Hannah and Fred left with Merlin, warning Elizabeth to 'take care' and with anxious backward looks. Arthur waited until they were gone.

He walked to the edge of the hill and back. He came to lean beside her against the wall, pretending to examine the band inside the brim of his hat.

'Now, I'll have the truth.'

'Don't make a fuss over this,' Elizabeth said wearily. She turned away from him. He caught hold of her arm.

'I have to know what the fellow was to you.' He was very agitated and his fingers dug into her wrist through her sleeve.

'I told you, Edward was an old friend.'

'Don't lie to me, you hussy!' His face and neck, which good living had turned a florid colour, were flushed a deeper purple. He seemed consumed by an intense and jealous passion.

Elizabeth felt a flicker of fear. 'Arthur,' she pleaded. 'What does it matter now, if Edward and I were once lovers? He's gone. If you care about my feelings–'

'Bugger your feelings.' He flung her arm away from him and her knuckles grazed against the stones of the tower. The pain jerked her from her lethargy. It was as if he had struck her.

'Yes, we were lovers.' She felt a desire to hurt him. 'I could tell you a lot more besides. I could tell you so much more.'

'When were you – for how long?' He was trembling. 'How thick were you, bugger it!'

'When? How long? How much am I devalued because of a past love affair?'

'I gave you my heart. I gave you everything to make you a lady,' he said.

'You gave me nothing. You call a drapery business making me a lady?' Elizabeth did not care now what he did or thought. 'Don't pretend you loved me when you married me. I was convenient. I had a dowry. And you had spent most of your money.'

Arthur opened and closed his mouth, but he could not deny it. He turned away and put on his hat as if to start down the hill. He paused with his back to her. 'Did you never love me at all?' he said at last.

She hesitated. But the hurt of losing Edward was so much stronger than her desire to spare Arthur's feelings. She was tired of him, his ridiculous aping of the gentry, his aspirations, his preoccupation with profits and quality cloth, and dressing her up in finery.

'No,' she said coldly. 'I didn't love you. I married you because I thought you could offer me a kind of freedom, instead of which you've smothered me with restraints and ostentation and decency. I have to tell you something. After we moved to Dorset, I met Edward again. I'm carrying his child. You can do what you like about it – I don't care any more.'

She did not know how she had expected he would react. With violence perhaps. She had not thought about it. She felt only a sense of release because she had unburdened her secret. She waited, looking at Arthur's broad back in his overcoat and top hat. He was very still. He seemed to sway a little, as if from the force of the wind out of the lea of the tower. Then, without turning to look at her again, he started down the hill path.

Elizabeth remained by the wall. The passion of the past few minutes left her and she felt depressed and did not know what to do. After a while she moved away from the tower. As she came over the top of the rise she saw Arthur on the path below her. He was on his knees, his body was bent inwards as if he was winded. When she saw that he did not get up she began to run, picking up her skirts and scrambling down the steep parts of the path, her breath coming in little frightened gasps.

She knelt beside him and held him in her arms. He was very pale and beads of sweat stood out on his face. 'Ah – pain!'

'Where?'

He put a hand to his throat.

She cradled him against her, terrified that he was going to die. She did not know what to do, or how to get him down the hill.

They remained for several minutes, until his breathing had eased and his colour had returned. They sank together against the slope of the hill and she continued to hold him against her, smoothing his hair from his damp forehead.

'You've done a terrible thing to me, Elizabeth,' he said when he was calm. 'I shan't ever forgive it.'

'Don't talk now.' Suddenly Elizabeth began to weep, whether from relief that he was not after all going to die, or guilt at what she had done, or from a more deep-seated grief, she did not know. They stayed there for some time, until Fred came back and helped her get Arthur down the hill to the carriage.

24

They did not talk about Edward afterwards, when Arthur had recovered. Elizabeth was afraid that it would make him ill again, and Arthur became secretive after they returned to Dorset, his thoughts were closed off from her. There were days when they did not speak for hours at a time; and there were times when Elizabeth would see him looking at her with an expression of hatred which chilled her.

Elizabeth held her guilt to herself. Because the developing child inside her had become a bitter thing for Arthur, she was forced to make light of aspects of her pregnancy which might have drawn his sympathy before. She learned to ignore the occasional bouts of nausea, and the fact that she was already becoming clumsier and slow.

Her mother wrote to say that Robert was arranging a memorial service for Edward. Elizabeth did not want to go, and she did not mention the letter to Arthur.

After a few weeks, the strain of bearing a continuous grudge was eased for Arthur by the concerns of Pengelly's Wholesale Linen Drapery, and the day to day trivia of domestic life. He talked sometimes of his years in Australia. He had been happy then, he said. He had been free of marital troubles, the incessant problems of business, and backbiting in trade circles, the effort of keeping up with middle-class society. Elizabeth wondered if he was tiring, just a little, of being a worthy gentleman and member of the small town business world.

And then Merlin died.

The dog had been chasing flies in the garden. It was a warm day, early in April, and Elizabeth was on her knees pulling out weeds from one of the flower beds, enjoying the warmth of the sun on her back and the smell of the damp earth under her fingers. She looked up and saw the dog leap and snap at a bluebottle. Ridiculous, she thought, acting like a puppy, and yet he made her smile. Grudgingly she acknowledged the fact that she had begun to grow fond of him.

Merlin landed awkwardly. He seemed to stagger, and then fell on his side in the long grass. Elizabeth struggled to her feet and ran across the lawn. A solitary fly, tired of the game, landed on the dog's grey muzzle. He was already dead. She pulled him into the shade of a tree and told the servants that no one must move the dog before Arthur came home.

Arthur dug a grave in the garden that evening. He refused all offers from the servants to help. Elizabeth watched him from the window, a little sad that her old enemy would no longer plague her. Arthur stood with his head bowed over the patch of earth, then came towards the house. His figure looked large and lumbering in the growing dusk. He did not glance at the window where Elizabeth was standing as he passed by the house, but walked staring straight ahead of him. She heard him come in through the front door and his footsteps cross the hall, then the sound of the study door opening and closing.

She turned up the gas and drew the curtains. She settled down in an armchair by the fire with a book but did not read. Instead, her thoughts drifted to memories of Edward, which, like a comforting habit – a child sucking its thumb, or relaxing in a favourite rocking chair – lulled her after a few minutes to sleep.

She woke after an hour. The fire had burned low. Then she remembered Arthur.

She crossed the hall slowly and stood, with her shawl wrapped tightly round her shoulders, for almost half a minute by the study door before she raised a hand and tapped gently on one of the oak panels. There was no response. She laid her hand on the heavy doorknob and turned it.

A glass of brandy and an almost empty decanter were on the desk beside him. A candle, close to a pile of books and papers, threw flickering shadows on the seated figure. Arthur looked up. His face was tear-stained and distorted with misery, his hands rested on the desk and he held Merlin's leather collar.

They stared at one another. Arthur began to weep afresh. Elizabeth stepped back into the hall and closed the door.

Some days later Elizabeth went into Arthur's study to open the window and air the room. A heavy atmosphere of stale perspiration, brandy and cigars hung about the furniture. She stood by the window, breathing in the spring air which stirred the curtain folds and cooled her face. Outside, birds squabbled in the sunshine among the branches of a hazel tree near the road. She could hear the clatter and rumble of carriages passing. Everything was busy, in contrast to the mausoleum-like stuffiness of the room.

Elizabeth felt restless, with the small stirrings in her of an undirected energy. She turned to look at the clutter of pens, papers, books and cigar boxes behind her and something caught her eye. She moved away from the window and picked out a piece of paper from a pile of documents on the desk. It was a deed of sale. Puzzled, she read its contents, then read the paper again, to be sure that she had not misunderstood it.

Arthur had sold the business. She stared at the printed evidence. She heard Arthur coming across the hall. She hesitated, tempted to return the paper to the desk and pretend to be occupied at the window. Instead, she held it more firmly and faced him as he came into the room.

'You've sold Pengelly's Linen Drapery.'

He looked guilty. 'I was going to tell you.'

'But why? What will you do instead?'

His gaze dropped to the bulge at her waist, and he shifted his glance to the paper in her hand. 'I'm going abroad,' he said, taking it from her.

'Without me?' He did not answer. 'But what shall I do?'

'What's it to me what you do?' he said with sudden anger. 'I thought to leave you with the house. Fair exchange, don't you think, for that dowry you reminded me I took under false pretences?'

'I didn't say that,' she protested. She tailed off. The enormity of his plan to leave her swept over her. How would she live? What would she do? 'How am I going to exist?' she said.

He shrugged. 'You must manage the best you can. I shall make provision for you until some time after the child is born. But then you must look to yourself. Try some of that independence you once talked so much of.'

'Where will you go?' she said, as he turned to the door.

He smiled grimly. 'Australia,' he said, and left the study, closing the door behind him.

Elizabeth saw now what all his talk of his earlier happiness in Australia had been leading to. *Australia* – the name had a dramatic eloquence about it. The remote sound of it, the implications of adventure and vitality returned to her over and over throughout that day and sent little tremors of nervousness through her. She imagined the vast open spaces where the very air one breathed was freedom. She thought of the opportunity for forging new identities – for herself and her child.

'I want to come with you,' she said that evening. He lowered his newspaper slowly. 'You can pretend I'm your sister. We don't have to stay together.'

He raised his eyebrows cynically, his glance falling on her waist at the word 'sister'.

'We could travel together. And after, when the baby is born, the same financial arrangement you thought of could apply. I won't trouble you.' She smiled, but he did not respond.

'It will take a week or two to settle everything,' he said at last. 'I know of a buyer for the house.'

'You mean you'd consider it?' Elizabeth felt excitement leap up in her, and then fear, because what had been no more than a fantasy a few hours ago was suddenly possible. It seemed almost to be too easy.

'It's all the same to me.' Arthur raised the newspaper again and she could not see his expression. 'Though I should rather we left it that you came as my wife.'

It was not until she lay in bed beside him that night that the thought crossed her mind, that he had perhaps known all along that she would want to go with him.

25

Snowstorms in the Crimea were fickle. They blew up with extraordinary ferocity, and died as quickly, the sun turning the snow to slush and thawing the ice in marshy hollows.

Edward trudged his feet through the mud and melting snow. His hands were thrust deep into his heavy greatcoat, his gaze was fixed on the rough ground, the loose stones and pockets of sludge. Now and then he staggered, but each time he recovered his balance and walked relentlessly on.

He had funked it. He thought about the cliff edge: in the end fear had won. He was not glad to be alive, he felt no relief in the sun playing on his face and melting the ice on his beard. The sun did not warm him. He shivered as he walked, his face felt clammy and his gut was turned to stone.

After some miles he came upon a track. He saw a low stone house set against the hill. He paused and was inclined to walk on, then changed his mind and approached the building through the broken stumps of a vineyard, hacked out weeks earlier by soldiers foraging for firewood. He halted in the doorway of the house, the door swung on one hinge, the farm had long since been abandoned by its Tartar occupants.

The rooms had been looted by the foraging party. Broken glass from the windows, smashed china and pieces of furniture littered the floors. A few items of furniture remained intact, a marble washstand, too heavy and ornate to be worth carrying away, a chest of drawers, with fusty silks and shawls and linen spilled out on to the floor, a bedstead with its feather mattress ripped open, pictures of saints askew on the whitewashed walls.

Edward's brief tour of the building and its outhouses, where the same systematic destruction had taken place, exhausted him. He returned to the first room he had entered, pulled his coat around his body more firmly and sank to his heels against the wall. He stared at the opposite corner of the room, where an ikon hung above the ancient Russian stove. The eyes of the painting stared back at him without forgiveness for the desecration over which it presided, the hand was raised mockingly in a blessing, a gold and silver halo gleamed around the figure's head. Edward's eyes hurt from the blinding effect of the snow. He closed them. Exhaustion swept over him and, after a brief struggle to maintain his position against the wall, he toppled to the floor.

He did not know how long he had lain there. A day? Two days? His face was pressed painfully against the floor tiles when he woke. An orange light stabbed at his eyes and seemed to come from a long way off. Slowly he recognized the flicker of flames, a fire was burning in the stove. A pile of books and broken picture frames had been heaped up beside it.

He stirred and pulled himself to a sitting position. He felt no alarm when he saw that he was not alone.

The woman spoke in French. 'Are you all right?' She was dressed in the red trousers and skirt and blue jacket of an army *vivandière*. She stood in the doorway, as if she had retreated there for safety when she saw that he was conscious.

He nodded and leaned his head against the wall. His eyes were blurred and sore, and there was a sharp pain in his belly.

'Was it you who lit the fire?' he said in her own language. 'Thank you.'

'I have left you more fuel. I must go before it is dark. But someone will come for you. Do you understand?'

He tried to thank her again, but the effort was too great.

She came forward from the door. He saw that she was young. She stood with her arms folded. Her fair hair was drawn under a neat hat. She looked at him with an expression of hardened concern, she had seen worse than an Englishman suffering from the effects of the cold, and not even a soldier at that. Then, unexpectedly, she smiled.

'Some bread,' she said in English. She pointed to a broken plate beside him, on which lay a portion of white bread. Beside it stood an unbroken jug of water. 'Some to drink.'

'You're very kind.'

She stood a while longer. Then, her stock of English vocabulary seemingly exhausted, she said again in French, 'Now, I must go. It is dangerous for me. I should not be away from the camp alone.'

The next moment she was gone, and he was alone, wondering if the whole scene had been a product of his imagination. But there was the bread and the water. And she had promised that she would send help.

He ate the bread she had left him and drank down a quantity of water. He was at once affected by violent stomach cramps. He dragged himself through the kitchen, to relieve himself outside. He returned and threw more fuel on the fire. The effort drained his strength. He curled up close to the stove and watched the growing dusk at the window, until the only light in the room came from the warm glow of the stove. He slept fitfully through the night, with repeated attacks of diarrhoea. By the time the French came for him the next morning he was sweating with a fever. He let the men carry him like a sick child and place him in the seat of a mule litter. There was no sign of the *vivandière* who had found him the day before.

He remembered very little of the weeks spent in the French hospital at Kamiesch. He lay alongside French soldiers with dysentery, fever and frostbite, with severe wounds and gangrenous limbs. He had become one of the casualties of the Crimea, a statistic to be added to the list of those who recovered, or those who died.

For days he lay sweating and freezing in turn. Once, he dreamed or thought that Elizabeth came to him. She stood by his side and stroked his head. But she was only one of the images which he saw, an angel among the sea of devils and death's-heads, of mangled bodies, souls in torment and monstrous apparitions in a private hell.

Afterwards, during the weeks of convalescence, one of the French surgeons, with kindly concern, advised him to go home. 'You have seen enough of this terrible place, the Crimea,' he told him. 'Go home to your loved ones. Sebastopol will never be taken.'

The belief that Sebastopol could never be captured was taking a cynical hold. At home, Parliament had voted a lack of confidence in Aberdeen's government and the government had fallen. In Russia, the Czar died, and was succeeded by another. And still the war went on. The thundering of the battery guns, the sorties by both sides, fighting for possession of a few yards of ground, sent the toll of dead and injured higher. The work of Charles Watkins and his fellow medical officers seemed endless.

Charles would pause to reflect occasionally on Edward's fate. He had gone to look for him when he heard that he had set out from Balaclava in the snow and had not returned to his lodging. Someone said that a mule had been found wandering, loaded up with medical supplies. Several parties had lost their way in the snow that day. When Edward did not return the next day, nor the next, Charles had reluctantly assumed the worst. He cleared up Edward's affairs in Balaclava, wrote to his brother, and to Mrs Delahaye in London. He tried to detach himself from the memory of the stranger whom he had befriended. Friendship during wartime, he told himself, was really rather a luxury.

Slowly the weather began to improve. Men discarded their leggings, turbans and sheepskins. In the ravines and hills around the camp snowdrops, crocuses and wild hyacinths sprang up. Scrubland came alive with the flitting of goldfinches and buntings, thin grass covered over the ground where there had been mud, and in the graveyards the warm weather heightened the smell of the decaying flesh, buried only a few inches below ground.

Vast improvements were taking place in the Crimea. Roads were metalled, huts were built, a railway was nearing completion, the town of Balaclava underwent a 'cleaning-up' operation. Commissions came from England to investigate the claims of administrative mismanagement. For the first time in months, soldiers had enough to eat and were properly clothed.

And then one morning, like a ghost, Edward rode into Charles Watkins's camp.

It was a warm clear day in spring. Edward sat with Charles on a grassy knoll overlooking the field of the siege. In the far distance, the houses of Sebastopol lined the hillside. The buildings shone white, and green copper domes gleamed in the sunshine. The air had been filled with smoke and the noise of cannon earlier, but now there was a temporary lull in the hostilities, and, except for the low ruins of the houses on the outskirts of the town, and the trenches and earthworks below where they sat, there were few signs that a war was being waged. The men, moving about in a battery below, looked like toy soldiers on this picture-book bright day.

Charles drew on a small blackened pipe contentedly. Forgotten for now were the hospital tents, the trench duties – sitting up to his knees in mud for hours with some injured soldier, close to the enemy and the roar of the guns. It was good that Edward had decided to stay. They still needed every man they could get in this interminable campaign.

Edward looked over the scene of the siege to the horizon and the blue sky. A sketch book lay on his knee. His eyes seemed to gaze permanently into the distance, as though wary of too close a contact with detail. His hair was long and thick and his beard untrimmed. He wore no shirt, but a sheepskin jerkin and a baggy pair of red trousers which he had acquired during his convalescence.

Somewhere a bird twittered out a song. It made Edward think briefly of England. The hedgerows would be throwing out bright green shoots. He closed his eyes and tried to remember the smell of the dark crumbling earth, dappled with light and shade beneath the willows. Perhaps he would return. It was not enough, dressing wounds, clearing away the mess and blood of amputations, telling a soldier with his teeth clenched in agony to 'hang on', the surgeons would have him right in a jiffy. There was accusation in their agony: he had not been through what they had been through.

A cluster of dark yellow crocuses grew near their feet. Edward leaned forward and picked one, twisting it between his fingers.

A puff of white smoke rose picturesquely below the hill and the sound of firing started up again. Charles let out a little sigh of regret and knocked out his pipe. Edward studied the crocus in his hand, as if seeing a flower for the first time, wondering at the perfect formation of stamens and petals.

'Don't they say that the stamen of the yellow crocus contains some cure for gout?' said Charles. 'An old man's complaint, Edward. Do you think we shall live to suffer it?'

Edward thought of Henry Thorne, growing old and ill without

Elizabeth near to comfort him. An image of her, with flesh like marble, lingered in his mind. He wished that he could forget her. It was like a sickness, the clinging to the past after all this time.

They left the hill. They passed the edge of one of the French camps on their way back. Two *vivandières* were talking together by one of the tents. They glanced up as the men passed, eyeing Charles's uniform and Edward's sheepskin and the faded breeches, in which at one time he might have thought he cut a dash, a dandy done up in fancy costume. But the trousers, stained with blood and dirt, hung loosely on him, and the jacket emphasized his wasted physique.

One of the women called to him in French. 'Why so sad, young man? You should be blossoming, like your little crocus there.' She laughed, and nudged her companion.

He had forgotten the flower, he still held it in his hand. He looked at the second woman. She stood with her arms folded and her head thrown back. Her fair hair had escaped here and there from under her uniform hat, and blew in fine wisps across her face. He glanced at the crocus. Then he threw the flower to them.

'Thank you,' said the fair-haired woman boldly in English as she caught it. She tucked the crocus into her hat. She looked at him without smiling and a little frown of recognition crossed her face. Her companion dug her again with her elbow and said something which Edward could not hear.

'I think you've made a conquest.' Charles laughed as they walked on. 'Beware of these French mademoiselles. You don't know where they've been.'

It was not until they reached camp that Edward recalled where he had seen the younger of the two women before. He remembered the Tartar cottage and the girl who had saved his life by sending someone to find him.

He hurried back to the French camp, intending to thank her, but the girl and her companion were nowhere in sight, and when he made inquiries about them he was told by an army sergeant to search among the English camps if he was looking for a woman.

Edward was seated with Charles and a number of army medics who were off-duty outside one of the huts, put up to replace the hospital tents on the Heights. He had become accepted as a civilian assistant among the medical surgeons, and had pitched a tent close to the Light Division.

'The French are putting on some races tomorrow,' one of the men said.

Charles puffed at his pipe. 'An excitable lot, the Frenchies. You'd think it was Ascot, or Epsom, the way they're carrying on.'

'Should be a bit of sport though.'

Charles turned to Edward. 'Do you think you shall go along?'

Edward shrugged. Then it occurred to him that the girl from the Tartar cottage might be there. 'Why not?' he said.

He found her serving cups of fruit juice on the edge of the ground marked out for the races. He waited, then smiled at her as he paid for his drink. She returned the smile and turned to the next customer. He stood beside her, watching her ladle liquid into a beaker. If it had not been for her he would have died, he told himself, letting the romantic implications of it steal through him. She was pretty, he observed, though in a graceless, rather bold way. She reminded him of a picture of a milkmaid in a book he had once had when he was a child. Her arms, with sleeves rolled to the elbows, were white. Her face was unfashionably tanned, with high cheekbones and coarsened by the weather. Her figure was angular, he let his gaze wander briefly to her hips and small breasts. He excused her hands, broken-nailed and grimy, and disregarded the way that she chattered with a shrill and ribald familiarity with the French soldiers who came to her table.

'What is your name?' he said, when there was a pause in the demand for refreshment.

'Marianne,' she replied, without turning her head.

'It's very pretty.'

She looked at him with a quick but watchful smile.

'You don't remember me. Do you?'

'Yes, I remember,' she said. 'Did the fire keep you warm?'

'A fever kept me warmer for many weeks at Kamiesch.'

'I'm sorry,' she said. And then, 'I'm glad that you have recovered.'

He waited while she served another soldier. 'Are you enjoying the races?' he said. 'It's good to forget the war for a little while. Don't you think, Marianne?'

'I cannot forget,' she said with a harsh simplicity. 'My lover was killed at Alma.' He felt a shock, a recognition of her pain as she looked at him. 'I thought about you,' she said. 'I asked myself, Why is this young man here? It's clear he's not a soldier.'

He did not answer.

'Come,' he said at last. 'Let's watch the races.'

They met whenever the girl was free. They walked together on the hills. Marianne's harsh chatter, the way she hung on to his arm, laughed with disconcerting mockery at what he had thought of as his competent attempts to speak her language, the way, when she was excited, she flew into impetuous strings of French which he could barely understand, all this charmed him. But there were distances between them which were more than the differences of class or nationality.

'Where did you learn your terrible French?' she said.

He told her about his months on the Continent after being rusticated from Cambridge. He told her about Charlford, and Robert, and the death of his father, about London and his friendship with Jack Harris. He did not tell her about Elizabeth.

He felt that he was close to a kind of normality again when he was with Marianne. He could forget the horrors of the war for a while, and the insidious return of cholera among the troops. He could almost believe too that he had forgotten Elizabeth.

Then one day he was walking with Marianne along the coast, a few miles from Balaclava. They had halted to look down from the cliffs at the waves pounding against the rocks. With a sudden terror Edward recalled that other occasion, in the snow, when he had almost put an end to his life. He turned abruptly from the edge of the cliff. At the same moment he was aware of an inexplicable but very vivid image of Elizabeth. She was naked and heavy-breasted, a smile of regret hovered on her lips.

'What is it?' said Marianne in alarm.

He would not tell her, but walked away from the cliff. She hurried after him. 'Edward?' She shook his arm. 'Edward, what is wrong?'

They walked for a while in silence. Then Marianne said quietly, 'What is it that sometimes makes you sad? Is it a woman?'

'She is married to another man,' he said.

'That is bad.' Then she said in English, 'That is the very devil.'

He laughed and put his arm round her waist. 'Where did you learn your terrible English?'

'Oh, a little 'ere, a little there.' She arched her eyebrows.

'Then I shall have to teach you a little more.'

They were walking along a track, a low whitewashed farmhouse came into view on the hill. They paused.

'I used to walk here often on my own,' Marianne said. 'That is how I found you that day.'

The house looked the same, the broken crockery and glass on the floor, the feather mattress, the linen spilled out of the drawers. Edward wandered from room to room, turning pieces of china with his foot. When he returned to the first room she had set light to some of the wood in the stove, and had found a broom and was sweeping the floor. He leaned against the doorpost and watched her.

'Tell me about her,' Marianne said without looking up from what she was doing. 'Does she know you love her?'

'We loved one another. But I ran away. And so, she married someone else.'

'You ran away – because you loved her?'

'Because she had let me make love to her.' Marianne pulled a face, he knew she did not understand. 'I suppose that does not sound very terrible.'

'It is human nature, I should say.'

'But it was terrible to run away.' She stopped sweeping and looked at him. 'If only I had been honest, Marianne.' He reverted to his own language. 'Why this myth we've contrived – woman is sensual, but she mustn't reveal it, she can be an object of desire, but never desiring? The truth is I behaved badly, and when I came to my senses, she couldn't forgive me.'

'All men behave badly. Mine was a monster,' Marianne said, propping the broom in the corner. 'He drank like a pig. But I loved him. I think your lover has a lot to learn about forgiving. And you have a lot to learn about women.' She removed her hat and jacket and placed them on top of the chest of drawers. Stooping, she pulled a silk shawl from the muddle of clothes on the floor, it was deeply fringed and coloured red and gold. She held it in both hands up towards the window. Her figure was silhouetted against the light and her hair shone in a halo of sunlight, like fine-spun, fly-away threads of gold.

'You are very lovely,' he said, catching his breath at the almost mystic impression of her. 'I wish –'

She put her finger to her lips and came towards him.

'I miss someone too,' she said. 'That is reason enough.'

She stood very still when they kissed. She watched him without shyness or passion as they undressed.

'You are very thin,' she said, and shivered. 'And I am all bones too, yes?'

He drew her close and kissed her again. He said that she was perfect. They pulled the broken mattress from the bed and arranged it close to the stove. They knelt solemnly among the feathers, he wound the red and gold shawl round her shoulders and pulled her gently towards him.

26

The bombardment of Sebastopol was intensified early in June. Word went round in the camps that something significant was happening. The French had launched an attack on the 'Mamelon' fort, the British stormed a number of rifle pits and defences known as the 'Quarries'. The attacks were successful; the casualties had been high, but so were people's spirits.

It was said that the French would now try to take the Malakoff Tower and the British the Redan. These two forts were the strongest Russian defences. Their capture would be more difficult and would require more courage than any of the previous encounters with the enemy. The day which had been chosen for the assault was the eighteenth of June. It had escaped no one's attention that it was the fortieth anniversary of Waterloo.

Edward, affected by the universal excitement, became convinced that Sebastopol would fall. The prospect of an end to the war and of returning home filled him with unease. Whatever he might have achieved here, it had not been his own peace of mind.

Edward woke to the sound of heavy gunfire. It was still dark, the wind slapped at the curtain of his tent. The sound of artillery was unnerving, for the men had been told that the signal for the attack would be closer to dawn. He had slept in his clothes. He put on his greatcoat quickly and breakfasted off dry bread and some ham. Taking his satchels of medical supplies he left his tent.

Groups of spectators were already gathered on the usual vantage points. One man, who fancied himself more informed than the rest, said that he thought the French must have gone off too early. 'Eager fellows, the French,' someone said, and everyone laughed.

They were nervous, thought Edward. And so was he, for no one knew what was happening or how the day would end. He strained his eyes in the semi-darkness, not sure what he was searching for. The sound of guns and musketfire seemed to be concentrated in a ravine to the north of where they stood. Now and then the sky flickered, as if with sheet lightning, as shells burst over the town. Buildings were on fire. He could make out the line of defences, and he could see figures swarming up the steep slopes of the Malakoff.

Edward waited for a while with the other watchers, distancing himself from them a little. Then, as the grey light of dawn grew stronger, he moved away from the rest and picked his way across the ridge.

It was daylight by the time he reached a position overlooking the Redan. The sun broke through the mist on to the scene below him. In the distance hung a pall of smoke, like low cloud on the skyline. Men were swarming from the advanced trenches. The whole scene was like a disturbed ants' nest. It was almost attractive: little puffs of white smoke rose here and there, the figures scurried about in blocks of red and blue, a flash of silver caught the sun occasionally.

There was no mystery to the noise which issued from the picture. The crash of guns, the rapid rattle of musket fire, the yells of men whose blood was up rose in a confusion of sound. There was an energy in it which was compelling, an excitement which Edward could almost grasp. Now, he thought. Now he would understand what it was about, and what it was that gave the whole campaign its driving force. He hitched his satchels more firmly on to his shoulder and set off down the hill.

A picket challenged him and tension pulled his muscles taut as he presented his pass and showed his satchels of bandages. He was allowed to move on.

As he came closer he could see the soldiers in the trenches more clearly, and the men working round the battery guns. Yet, the nearer he approached the individual pockets of activity, the more the larger picture with its sense of artistry disappeared. The groups of ant-like soldiers, the patterns of movement of lines of men, even the solid outline of the Redan, had gone. He saw instead a body, spread-eagled on the ground with its head thrown back and a blue cap, lying blood-stained in the grass. A man with a grizzled moustache ran past him, flinging him a brief stare.

He began to run, catching his foot once on the outstretched body of a soldier. Men were shouting – not the heroic cries of 'Come on lads!', or 'Hurrah!' – but incoherent shouts and obscenities. A round shot ploughed up the ground close by him, sending a shower of earth flying into his face. The guns of a nearby battery filled his ears with noise, which burst upon him like the sound of a steam train. He sought cover in one of the trenches.

There was a sickness in the pit of his stomach. His head throbbed with the din and his heart pounded in his chest as though it would force its way out through his ribs.

The men in the trench ignored him, they were peering over the parapet. The body of each man was tensed, like that of an animal of prey, in the quivering moment of stillness before it leaps to the attack. A shout went up and they tumbled out from the shelter. There was a brief but eerie silence after they had gone. The men left behind peered anxiously after them. Someone broke the tension with an oath. Someone else said, 'Tom's down.' And someone made a joke which Edward did not catch. A burst of laughter contrasted strangely with the renewed gunfire.

'Buggered if I can see anything,' muttered a man close to him. Edward ventured his head over the edge of the trench. Like his neighbour he could not see anything through the smoke. The crash of a shell which exploded close to the battery knocked up a shower of earth and made him draw back his head quickly.

'Near knocked me over, the beauty,' called a soldier who had been hit by flying debris. He got up from where he had been thrown. The other men laughed again.

Edward had fallen back against the side of the trench. 'Are you hurt?' he said.

'It'd take more 'n that.'

Edward clenched his hands to stop their shaking. The coat which he had put on when he set out was hot and too heavy now that the sun was stronger. He laid down his satchels carefully in the mud and removed the coat. The man who had been knocked down was watching him with a cautious indifference.

Edward felt a little foolish. 'Are there any wounded here?' He patted one of his satchels as he replaced it on his shoulder.

'Plenty forward, sir.' The man ducked instinctively as another shell exploded. 'They'll be showing up before long, don't you fret. Lost your way?'

'No.'

'You doan want to get any further forward. You'll get your guts blown out.'

'I thought I could help down here,' Edward said.

'Ah –' The man nodded uncomprehendingly. Then he said, 'It do look like there'll be plenty for you doctors after this is done.'

'I believe you're from my part of the world,' said Edward. He looked at him and saw, under the military hat and beard, a pleasant, round-faced man, who might as easily have been a blacksmith, or a farm labourer, as a soldier. He would have a family, a wife and children who waited anxiously for news at home.

'What part of the world be that then, sir?' the man said.

'Somerset.'

'Well – fancy! 'Tis a small world.' The man uttered a series of little clucks of surprise, as if the coincidence provided more than a passing amusement.

'A strange world. Whatever are we doing here, Sergeant?'

'Tolley, sir. Sergeant Tolley. Ah, er's a funny old world.' Sergeant Tolley was prepared to be talkative. 'Now, I can't say why you, a gen'leman, be asking to get 'eeself knocked over, but us did join 'n for the reg'lar pay, the security, you might say.' He laughed at his own wit, and another shell whistled close to the battery. 'And, to tell the truth, the old woman were glad to be rid of I.'

'What about honour, Tolley? Queen and country, and the nobility of arms?'

'Ah, well. Yes, sir. Do stand to reason. Leastways – 'tis what the buggers what sent us here tells us.'

Edward made his way further along the trench. Every now and then a shell would explode sending a shudder through the bank and throwing up dirt, so that it seemed as if the sides of the trench would crash in and bury everyone. He clambered over broken gabions and pushed among the soldiers crowding the way. Some of them talked crudely about what they would do to the enemy when they got at them. Some were no more than white-faced boys, who vomited from fear, while their officers shouted at them to throw themselves into the smoke and noise ahead. Men swore at one another, and at Edward when he got in the way. They seemed neither heroic, nor brave, nor aware of any noble force, driving them with its mystic purpose.

There were soldiers coming towards him who were wounded, supporting one another. Soon there were others, carried along on stretchers, their limbs smashed, flesh torn from flesh, one with his belly opened, past help, like so much meat on a butcher's slab.

He came upon a group of men clustered round a soldier whose foot had been blown off. They had lifted him on to a stretcher. The foot was attached by a ribbon of skin, blood saturated the canvas of the stretcher.

The men were disputing, with shouts above the gunfire, over who should take the injured man to the lines at the rear. Edward pushed his way among them and they moved aside when they saw his medical satchel. He attended briefly to the wound, but could do little with his few bandages.

'This man must be got to the field hospital,' he said.

They argued that they had not been detailed as stretcher bearers. Edward took hold of the stretcher poles, and one of the men, looking round at the others, stepped forward reluctantly and lifted the other end. They set off on an unsteady course along the trench.

They had covered a distance of several yards when the way became so congested that they were forced to abandon their cover and scramble to higher ground. The temptation to abandon the dragging weight of the stretcher and run for safety was strong. At each burst of noise Edward could imagine a round shot ploughing into his back. He began to stumble in his anxiety to get away from the crash and roar around them. He could hear the grunting breath of the soldier at the other end of the stretcher, labouring to keep up the pace. Once, a shell whistled so close to them that, as it exploded, a fragment of it tore through Edward's sleeve and grazed his arm. The other man let out a hysterical laugh and yelled, 'Give 'em it back! Give 'em it back! The buggers!'

Almost at the same moment, there was a tearing crash. The stretcher poles were wrenched from Edward's hands. He was aware of blood, of screams, of mangled flesh and the body of the other man lying some yards away. The screams had stopped. But the roar of human and mechanical sound continued behind him. Edward stood alone on the hillside. He felt a violence well up from deep inside him. A sob of rage broke from him. 'You buggers!' But he did not mean the Russians.

He scrambled over rocks towards the hills, his breath coming quickly, but he no longer felt afraid.

The cries of the wounded at the field hospital drowned out the noise of the continuing battle. Edward set to work with the surgeons, aware only of a white-hot anger.

'The Frenchies got right into the town,' Charles told them afterwards. 'Right up to the docks before they were driven back.' There were tears of frustration in his eyes.

By mid-morning the slaughter was over. The assault on the Redan had ended in confusion. There had not been enough men, the organization had gone badly. The whole exercise had been a shambles.

'All for nothing.'

'No one can change anything,' Marianne said. 'Men will always kill one another. We are still alive. Isn't that enough?'

Edward watched her gather flowers from the heat-scorched garden of the farmhouse. He sat in the doorway, shadowed by a fragrant honeysuckle. A cloud of little flies swarmed round her figure; the glare of the sun turned the hills beyond into a melting, indistinct mass. Marianne's body took on a slow, hypnotic rhythm, as she stooped and rose in the tall wild grasses.

So many dead. Jack Harris, Marianne's drunken soldier, the casualties of Alma, Balaclava, and Inkerman, the disastrous attack on the Redan, and now, in August, the carnage of the Tchernaya battle. So many thousands. They were just statistics to those who dealt in wars, numbers to put in history books, for future generations to shake their heads at.

'Why do we let it happen?'

'The war will be over soon,' called Marianne. She plucked a daisy and added it to the sparse bunch of flowers in her hand. 'It's as bad for the Russians. I heard some prisoners, who have been exchanged, say that the whole town of Sebastopol is a hospital. The bodies are piled high and they are in a terrible state.'

'But it will not prevent there being other wars. People can't see that the only reality is destruction.'

'People don't want to see, Edward.'

He leaned his head against the cottage wall and closed his eyes. The Crimea was a barren landscape, with its heat, its flies, and its smell of death.

'I try to picture England,' he said. 'Mad Fritz, hoping to frighten a new set of students, people complaining about the noise of the traffic in the Strand, Mrs Delahaye, with her ladies on Friday afternoons. It's as if they were never real. The only reality is what is happening here.'

'Who is Mad Fritz?' She came to sit beside him, leaning her head against his shoulder. 'And who is Mrs Delahaye?' She had been practising speaking English. She attempted to sound the 'h' in a way which once he would have found appealing, but which now irritated him a little.

'Mad Fritz and Mrs Delahaye belong to a different world. Or perhaps it's this world which is the dream.'

'I shall pinch you,' she said, pinching his ribs. 'Then you'll know what's real. I'm real. Our little house is real.'

'I am going home,' he said after a while.

'Will you take me with you?' He felt her body tense beside him.

'You are part of my life here.'

'You can't believe that.' She made him look at her, forcing his head round towards her. 'Do you think I belong here? This isn't my life, I want to belong to you.'

'You do,' he said desperately. 'But everything here is so strange, so heightened. How can we tell what would happen to us in England?'

'So you'll return to England and leave me, put me aside, as if I'm nothing?' Her mouth formed a trembling, threatening line of self-pity.

'No,' he protested. But he did not know whether what she said was true.

He tried to explain. 'Marianne, I have so much to do when I go home. I shall return to studying medicine. But, after that – I owe something to these men. I know what is waiting for them: the prospect of sitting on street corners, war veterans, beggars, a curiosity for a while, until people at home have forgotten all about the Crimea. I think I could try to help them in London. But it would not be a decent sort of life to offer you if you came with me.'

'It's not that,' she said quietly. 'Don't hide behind your moral duty. You can't forget her. The beautiful married lady, who isn't content with one husband but wants you to love her as well.'

'Elizabeth wasn't like that,' he protested. 'And yet, it all seems so long ago. I am not even sure any more if she was very lovable.'

'Then why do you want her still, instead of me?'

'I don't,' he said, taking her in his arms, and he believed that he meant it.

A renewal of the bombardment against Sebastopol dragged the war into September. The cannonade was almost constant, and desperate in its fury.

The Malakoff fell at last to the French, the dead of both sides lay piled feet deep inside its defences.

The Russians, weary of it all, left the city quietly one night and set fire to its buildings and the docks. Sebastopol had fallen.

Edward sat on the hillside below the camp and smoked a cigarette, given him by a dying Russian soldier that day. The man had been distraught with gratitude because he had given him a flask of water.

Sebastopol was still burning after two days. The smoke from the ruined buildings drifted in the early evening across the countryside and the smell mingled with the familiar tobacco fumes from the cigarette in his hand. People were being kept out of the town, but there had been much looting. Every now and then a mine would explode and send them all running for cover.

Edward was glad to have left Sebastopol, not from fear of being blown up by a mine, but because he had been sickened by the unrelieved scenes of horror among the Russians left behind. They had taken them away by the cartload from the hospital near the dockyard: bodies in every state of decomposition and death agony, packed together on blood-soaked and oozing mattresses – and among them the living, and the barely living.

He finished the cigarette and stood up, easing his cramped legs. He would stay a little longer, until the clearing-up of the wounded was over, but after that, however long the regiments stayed to bring the war to some sort of conclusion, he would leave them to it. It was time he went home.

✳   ✳   ✳

It was a month later that he boarded a ship in Balaclava. He stood by the deck rail. Marianne's arm was linked through his own. She no longer wore her *vivandière*'s uniform, but had on a grey dress, a red and gold shawl, and a wide-brimmed felt hat over her fine blonde hair.

She smiled up at him confidently and he felt the warmth of her arm against his own. He thought of the red and gold of October leaves and an English autumn. He realized that he was happy. He smiled and squeezed Marianne's hand.

Together they watched the line of boats by the quay grow smaller, until, as they headed for the open sea, the network of ships' masts behind them looked like a burnt-out forest.

Part Three

27

Elizabeth twisted her wedding ring and edged herself closer to their boxes and bits of furniture. It had been Arthur's idea to move on to Sydney. She watched the faces of the people passing, searching half-heartedly for his black felt hat among the crowds of men, women and children on the quayside.

The wharf was cold at this early hour of the morning, though it would be hot later. 'Winter is far the pleasantest season to be in Australia,' Arthur had told her. She had quickly adapted to the fact that July and August were winter here. Even so, the reversal of the seasons only added to her sense of alienation in this brash and rather awesome country.

Sydney, she had to concede, was beautiful. They had arrived the previous evening and spent the night on the steamer. Arthur, leaning on the ship's rail beside her, had enthused about the fairy-land harbour as if he were coming home. And certainly the sight of the olive-green shores and clear blue water had made her catch her breath with pleasure. But the smell of the sea and of the boat had sickened her. It reminded her of the hours of reeling, sweating and seasickness which had left her helpless and humiliated on the voyage from England, sensitive to every vile odour which had permeated the ship. She had eventually grown accustomed to the ship's rolling, though never to the claustrophobia of shipboard life. She had hated the interested gossip of the women in the ladies' saloon, and the rivalry over who was invited to dine at the Captain's table. Mealtimes had been the worst, over-shadowed by the indigestion and backache which went with her advancing pregnancy.

She shifted her weight uncomfortably, and saw Arthur swinging his way jauntily along the quay. Arthur had not suffered the smallest wave of seasickness. He had spent most of the voyage out in the ship's saloon, drinking beer with a crowd of other men whose background was in trade, playing cards and dominoes, and betting on how long the bad weather would last. Arthur had altered during the voyage, ignoring her for the most part and seeming to thrive on the enforced breathing space afforded by the weeks at sea. His attitude to her, though tolerant, had been distant – to the extent that she had begun to wonder why he had wanted to let her come with him.

She suspected that their money had dwindled considerably since they had left England, and that he had gambled on more than the weather while at sea. Melbourne too had been costly and wasteful, with Arthur flitting from one promise of a business to another, and insisting they stay at the best hotels. She did not know how much they had left. He would not tell her, saying it was 'enough' and not to fuss. He had not even told her what he was planning today.

She saw that he was not alone. A paunchy, middle-aged, bearded man shambled along the quay with him. The stranger eyed the furniture and Elizabeth as if she were part of the jumble of possessions by the wall. The men shook hands and the stranger signalled to another man, approaching with a horse and cart, to begin loading the furniture. All this was done without a word to Elizabeth.

'You'd better get on the cart,' Arthur told her.

'Are you going to tell me where we're going?'

'We're to look at a business I know of. It's some miles into the bush.'

Elizabeth's heart sank at the thought of yet more travelling. First the steamer from Melbourne, and now a long and uncomfortable drive, perhaps lasting for days, along some atrocious track. She felt ill and weary and the baby was kicking her under her ribs.

Arthur did not help her climb on to the cart. The stranger, called Mulligan, locked his hands with a rough gallantry and made a step for her to scramble up beside the upturned table and chairs. 'Up you both go then, my darling,' he said and laughed loudly.

Elizabeth formed a makeshift couch out of a mattress and sat among their furniture feeling large and awkward as she waited for them to be ready to start. She promised herself that once the child was born, Edward's child she reminded herself fiercely, she would no longer be dependent on Arthur.

Mulligan and Arthur sat with their backs to her on the driving seat.

They set off through the narrow streets at a furious jolting pace which, once out of the town, slowed hardly at all in concession to the rough condition of the road. Though only a few inches separated them, she might as easily not have been there for the notice the men took of her. But she preferred her own thoughts to their conversation. She clung to the side of the cart and looked about her, her awe of Australia tempered by curiosity.

The stillness of the bush enveloped them, mile after mile of it, as Sydney was left far behind. Trees with ghost-white trunks rose a hundred feet or more like pillars in a vast green cathedral. Beneath these giant gums grew a forest of smaller trees, palms and tree-ferns, and fresh new growth of wattles and blue gum shoots, their leaves a violet colour with a bloom on them like on a ripe plum.

The stillness was broken by the noise of the horses and the wagon with its load and the whistle and screech of birds. From time to time the sound of distant laughter echoed from rocks and gullies. Elizabeth strained her eyes for a glimpse of the creature which had made the unearthly sound. There were flashes of bright plumage among the trees, blues and greens, white and yellow, a flurry of scarlet finches and once she heard a violent crashing in the undergrowth, as if some large animal had heard the cart approach and was making its escape, but she could not discover the source of the mocking laughter.

'It's a laughing jackass,' said Arthur in answer to her inquiry. He turned his back again, and she did not pursue the question, imagining in her ignorance of kookaburras that it was a wild donkey which had made the sound.

From time to time the men climbed down from the cart to urge the horses over rocks, the cart scraping and groaning as if it would fall apart, their knives, forks and spoons rattling and bouncing in a tin box among their possessions, or to wrestle it up the steep sides of a creek, where the cart wheels clogged with sticky red mud.

The monotony of the eucalyptus trees was interrupted in places, thinning among outcrops of rock, or giving way to springy couch-grass and scrub. Once or twice they passed a cluster of shanty dwellings and single farmsteads, where the land had been cleared for cattle to graze. People would stand and call a greeting to Mulligan and he would halt the cart and exchange snatches of news.

Arthur and Mulligan ignored Elizabeth, telling one another stories about life in the bush, past heroics and narrow escapes from bushrangers. It was the sort of blustering talk with which men tried to impress one another and which might have fired her imagination in England; but now she was here and the adventure was her own, not one of Arthur's second-hand stories.

Three or four hours or more passed. Elizabeth, dulled by the relentless rolling of the journey and by an ache in her back, turned briefly to look at the way ahead and was diverted from her discomfort by signs of human habitation in the distance. They drew nearer and the driver reined in the horses. About fifty yards from the track stood a wooden hut.

The building, though building was perhaps too grand a title for the shack which squatted among the ferns and nettles, had walls and a roof of unbarked timber. The roof swept low to the ground on one side, as if the wall beneath had collapsed; on the other it formed an overhang supported by upright timbers, over which was fixed a broken sign proclaiming that the dwelling was 'O'Hoare's Bush Hut'.

'Does anyone live there?' Elizabeth asked, after staring at the hovel in silence. An obscure thought, that this shanty might be the business they had come to see, made her glance anxiously at Arthur.

He climbed down from the wagon.

'O'Hoare's dead and gone,' said Mulligan. He unharnessed and tied up the horses. 'But there's a township about half a mile along the track.'

Arthur helped Elizabeth climb down from the wagon and squeezed her with a rough and unexpected affection. 'Breakfast. Can you do the honours, my love?'

They left her to unearth potted meat and bread and cheese from the wagon and walked away from her towards the hut. They moved out of sight, where they would relieve themselves, thought Elizabeth. Her own needs must wait. Pregnant or not, equal or not to men in this country, she must pretend she never had to do such a vulgar thing as piss in the open.

'Poor old Tommy O'Hoare,' said Mulligan when they returned. 'A terrible day it must have been when he was found there behind his bar.'

'Died with his hand round a bottle, did he?' Arthur took a sandwich from Elizabeth as she folded it over.

'Sure, he did. Couldn't keep off the booze, O'Hoare couldn't. It was the parson from Yooma found him. Been there two days. Midsummer too.' The man sucked in his breath and pulled a face.

Elizabeth shuddered. She glanced involuntarily at the grim little hut. Whether it was the thought of the bloated corpse of Tommy O'Hoare or the potted meat she was eating, a feeling of nausea swept through her.

'I think I'll take a walk.' She laid down her sandwich.

'Don't be long,' Arthur said. 'We'll be on our way in ten minutes.'

She nodded and left them, walking along the track for a short distance. Crisp curls of tree bark scrunched under her feet and trails of ants followed route marches among them.

She left the track when she was out of sight of the hut, walking on thick, tufty moss and pushing through the cool ferns. The silence, except for the sound of birds and an occasional burst of that mocking laughter, stole upon her eerily. When she stood still the 'bush' seemed to hold its breath too. There was a rustling in the undergrowth a few feet from her. She remembered Arthur's warnings about snakes and glanced down quickly. But she had more to worry about than snake bites.

The ache low in her back had worsened and become a pain which she could no longer ignore, nor had the feeling of sickness left her. She rested her hands on her sides, supporting the weight of her belly, reluctant to move, though the need to urinate had become more urgent.

At first the blood puzzled her. Then she was very frightened. She tried to keep calm but the pain in her back made her sweat. It couldn't be, she told herself. She had not reckoned on the child coming for another two weeks yet. If she walked back slowly to the wagon and sat quietly, perhaps nothing worse than a little show of blood would happen.

The men were loading the food box on to the wagon when she returned. Arthur glanced at her curiously as he helped her over the tailboard and said briefly, 'You all right?'

She nodded, ignoring the low griping pain and trying to smile.

'Your missus looks as if she's seen the ghost of old Tommy O'Hoare,' Mulligan said as Arthur climbed on to the front seat.

Elizabeth held on to a leg of the upturned table and the side of the cart and ground her teeth. She would not have the baby now. Not here. She would die. She gasped as a wave of pain dragged through her. The wagon started into motion.

They had not gone more than ten yards when a jolt over a rut coincided with the next contraction and the violence of it made Elizabeth shout out. She saw Arthur jerk his head round, caught his surprised expression and then heard him curse under his breath.

'Stop the cart. Stop the cart, bugger it. Can't you see her time is come?'

They lifted her from the wagon and set her on her feet. She leaned heavily with an arm about each man's shoulders.

'Can she walk?' Mulligan said, as if Elizabeth had, by going into labour, lost the ability to answer direct questions. 'Couldn't we take her along to Yooma?'

''Course she can't walk, bugger it!' Arthur shouted. 'And she's not going back in that cart.'

They made their way slowly towards the wooden shack. At each stop Mulligan muttered, his voice high with fear, 'Don't drop it here, Missus. Don't drop it here. I've never done this before.'

They reached the hut and Arthur pushed open the door. The interior was dark and foul-smelling. As they entered a flurry of wings beat the air and a black-feathered cockatoo flew past them into the sunlight. There was a high wooden bench across the room, littered with animal droppings, trails of ants and dead beetles. Nettles grew up through the floor. Something scuttled into the corner with a hiss of anger at being disturbed and Elizabeth gave a little scream of terror. Mulligan released himself from her arm which gripped his neck and chased the creature, a large lizard, out through the door with a cry of 'It's only a goanna. He won't hurt you.' But the animal had looked like a dragon, and Elizabeth, remembering all the old wives' tales about creatures crossing the path of a woman in labour and causing terrible deformities, was weak with horror. She begged them to take her out into the sunlight again.

'There should be a bit of a bed through yonder,' said Mulligan in response to Arthur's look of desperation. 'If we can lie her down –' He pushed aside a sacking curtain which divided the bar they had entered from a second, larger room. As Mulligan had predicted, this contained a bed, also a dirty stove and a window, nailed over with a piece of wood, in a half-hearted attempt perhaps to hold back the invasion of the bush creatures from outside.

'Spiders,' said Elizabeth, her teeth chattering with fear. 'There will be spiders.' A smell of rancid cooking was strong in this second room; there were no lizards, nor spiders as far as she could see. But Arthur had told her how they lurked under and inside everyday objects; she leaned against the wall and watched Mulligan pull a filthy mattress from the bed and drag it out into the bar.

'Fetch some blankets and the water,' Arthur shouted after him.

'You can't do anything,' said Elizabeth, knowing that she and her child were going to die here in this filthy hut, where a man had once died before, his body unrecognizable after two days in the Australian heat.

'You're forgetting when I worked the sheep stations,' Arthur said. He did not smile. 'I've helped ewes out of trouble before now. It can't be so very different.'

Mulligan brought a pile of blankets from the wagon and spread them on the bed boards. Elizabeth hugged her arms about her, fighting down the panic which accompanied each successive contraction. She jerked convulsively as she tried to stop the fear from consuming her, but she was weakening. Images of death, of monstrous lizards and creatures which shrieked with hideous laughter were mixed up with her pain.

'I'm going to die,' she whispered as Arthur helped her to the bed. 'I'm going to die here in this horrible country. I know I am.'

Mulligan said something about running to the village and fetching a doctor. Elizabeth did not see him go. 'I'm going to die,' she repeated, moaning with the fear of it. The pain in her back and belly was intense. 'It's a punishment. God's punishing me for Edward and for making you hate me.'

'If you don't keep quiet,' Arthur said calmly, as he sat on the bed beside her and took her hand and began stroking it, 'you won't have any breath to push this old baby out. Now come on, girl, you've got work to do.'

Arthur hid his fear as he spread a fresh blanket to take the infant and saw that the first blanket was already sodden with blood and water. It was going to be a hard birth and he did not know what he was doing; there was a world of difference between easing a lambing and the successful delivery of a human child. He removed his neckcloth and wiped the perspiration from Elizabeth's face with it. 'I don't hate you, Lizzie,' he said. But he did not think she had heard him.

'Poor little scrap,' said the woman by the bedside. She had wrapped the infant in a clean pillow case and placed the bundle in Elizabeth's arms.

Elizabeth smiled weakly. 'Thank you. I don't know your name.'

'Alice McCreery. Your friend, Mr Mulligan, came past my place like a bat out of hell, yelling you were all set to die. And there, it was just a little bit of a babby all the time. Haven't I had ten of my own? 'Course, himself – Dr Kennedy – would choose today to be on a bush trip, just when he's needed. But your man did fine.' She readjusted the fold of cotton round the baby's shoulders. 'And so did you, my darling.'

Arthur moved away from the bed as Elizabeth looked up. She saw that there were tears, wet on his cheeks.

'Thank you,' said Elizabeth again. She did not understand why another human being, let alone a woman, should be in this darkest corner of hell and have come to help her. She had no energy left to understand. But she was alive and so was the child, a girl. A miracle.

Someone had taken the wooden boarding from the window. The sun was warm on her face. She could count the roof timbers lying tightly against one another. A piece of vine had forced its way between them and curled itself under the roof, snaking downwards. Leaves opened from it as if they had only now, with the sun on them, discovered how to unfurl their soft green surface to the light.

Alice McCreery's smile softened the lined, sharp-featured face. She picked up her bonnet from the floor. 'They always send for me. It's a fine little girl you've got there. Now, you take it easy. I'll be seeing you.' She moved away.

Elizabeth heard the murmur of voices as Arthur went with the woman through the hut and outside.

Mulligan stood by the window with his hat in his hands, as if he had stood there throughout the birth and taken root. He grinned at Elizabeth, his teeth flashing in the shadow of his face. Then he cleared his throat and said he would go to look at the horses.

She was alone, with the tiny, old-woman face of the baby against her shoulder. The sun streamed through the window, warming her eyelids, making her feel heavy with sleep.

When she woke the sun had gone. A soft light from an oil lamp cast shadows on the roof. Two large moths battered their wings against its globe. Arthur, with his back to her, was scraping with a knife at the accumulations of grease on the stove. She could hear Mulligan whistling and dragging something across the floor in the next room.

She felt cold. She shivered and eased herself on to one elbow, pulling the blanket further round her shoulders.

A lizard scurried across the floor and disappeared between the floorboards and she remembered the other lizard, which Mulligan had called a 'goanna' and which had frightened her. She glanced anxiously at the baby wrapped in one of the shawls she had packed for her confinement, sleeping peacefully in a wicker basket by the bed. Her anxieties were only just beginning. Her fears would not be for herself from now on but for her child. How could she hope to look after her in this hostile country?

Arthur heard Elizabeth stir and laid down his knife. 'How are you feeling?'

'Glad it's all over.' She looked at him, not sure of him or what he was thinking.

'Looks like we'll not be shifting on. Not for a day or two.'

She nodded. She did not care, as long as her child survived.

'What about the business you were going to see?' she murmured later, when Arthur returned the baby to the wicker basket and Elizabeth had fed her. He lay down on the bed.

'Don't you worry your head about anything.' He squeezed her hand briefly before turning away to sleep.

It was several days before Elizabeth was able to move stiffly about the shack, by which time Arthur and Mulligan had cut down ferns and nettles to let in the light and cleared the hut of rubbish. Mulligan returned to Sydney, but Arthur remained fanatical about making the hut habitable, only pausing to attend to Elizabeth, or to pick up the child when it was restless and take it to Elizabeth to feed.

He had set their wicker chairs outside. Elizabeth sat with the baby at her breast. Alice McCreery had come to visit, bringing with her several children who were eager to see the baby which had been born at the bush hut. They crouched in a semi-circle on the wooden boards, gazing at Elizabeth with rapt attention.

'Tommy O'Hoare could have made more of this dump,' Alice said, nodding her head towards the jungle of undergrowth around the hut. It was evident that the land had once been cleared; there were no tall trees close by, nor behind the hut for several hundred yards up to a point where the land dropped to a stream in the valley below. 'He was a lazy devil, was Tommy. All he cared about was the drink. The hut was always a dump. Folk have kept away since he died. They say it's haunted.'

'Surely the land here's worth using?' said Arthur.

'It belongs to his son. He's another lazy devil. Too lazy to do anything with the place. Too lazy to sell it.'

'Mr Pengelly and Mr Mulligan carried up gallons of water from the stream to scrub the place out,' said Elizabeth.

'You thinking of staying?' said Alice curiously.

Elizabeth shifted her gaze away from the woman's sharp blue eyes, remembering her determination to be independent of Arthur once the baby was born, guilty because she knew she had probably lost him the business he had been going to see. She knew that she was frightened of the future, of staying any longer than was necessary in this primitive hut, where every living and growing thing seemed to want to reclaim ownership of the land, afraid of travelling with the baby over vast stretches of rough country before finding somewhere to settle.

'We shall be moving on before long,' Arthur said, coming out from the hut. 'Drapery's my trade.'

'Yooma could do with a draper's store,' said Alice. 'It's not much of a place, but it's better than some.'

'Shall we go back to Melbourne?' said Elizabeth when she and Arthur were alone. She looked down at the infant in her arms. The baby's face was flushed and swollen with milk, its mouth wet and full as it lolled against her. Edward's child, she told herself. But Edward, his death, and everything that had happened in England seemed too remote.

'Melbourne's expensive. We've not got the money to start in the city.'

'You can't have lost all the proceeds from the business through playing at cards.'

'Not all.' Arthur lifted the baby from her gently. 'You have not given the child a name yet.' He leaned against the rough timber of the doorpost, cradling the baby in his arms.

'A name is the least of her problems.'

Arthur crooned into the baby's ear. 'Agnes, we should call you – because you're pure and chaste. Not like your mother, my little lamb.'

Elizabeth looked at him quickly.

'It's the truth,' Arthur said. 'Isn't it?'

She frowned. He had been behaving strangely since she had started to recover from her confinement. One moment affectionate, like in the old days, at other times cynical, as if the hurt she had done him jabbed its reminder from time to time.

Arthur returned the child, now sleeping, to the basket beside the hut. He came and crouched down beside Elizabeth. She noticed his dark hair and side-whiskers were heavily streaked with grey. 'Don't worry about money,' he said. 'We're a long way off penniless. But it seems like money, wealth – it brought me nothing but trouble in the past. I want to start afresh, Elizabeth. I want to be honest again.'

'You were never dishonest–'

'I mean with you. The baby belongs to your dead lover. We know that. But I feel, if we could be truthful together, live a humble, ordinary sort of life, perhaps something good might come of it.'

Elizabeth was silent. Her plans to leave him seemed to have been made a long time ago. She saw now that she had known for a while that they would stay together. She was aware of a half-forgotten tenderness towards him and she reached out her hand and stroked the lines of his face. 'Where shall we live this humble, ordinary sort of life?'

'I thought about here.'

'O'Hoare's bush hut?'

'I made inquiries at Yooma about the fellow who owns it. It's likely he'll be willing to sell. We could turn it into a store. There's nothing but a makeshift place in Yooma. With passing trade and all we could do well. What do you say?'

The idea was ridiculous. A drapery store in the middle of this wilderness – but she saw that Arthur was serious.

She felt so tired. 'Give me time, a few days.'

The sky was turning a hot orange. The sun set quickly here, one minute a blaze of glory, the next gone and night closing in with its sounds of the nocturnal bush creatures.

'Do you think it stands a chance, Elizabeth?' Arthur's expression was strained. She put a hand again to his face and he pressed it swiftly to his mouth, pulling her knuckles hard against his teeth.

'Yes,' she said, in spite of herself. 'I think we stand a chance.'

28

Yooma was a tiny settlement town composed of log-framed houses, some grouped on either side of a wide, mud-baked track, the rest strung out here and there through the bush. Each had its veranda and its wattle-fenced yard, with chickens, goats and other livestock scratching about in the dirt.

They were not the well-tilled gardens of an English village, reflected Elizabeth, but Yooma's image of itself was one of a civilizing force in an alien land. It had its church and town committee, an aristocracy composed of the better off farmers, the doctor, timber manager and preacher. The people here had waged war on the bush and were winning and they welcomed any newcomers who were prepared to join the battle.

Elizabeth had fed Agnes while the first streaks of dawn lit the sky. She returned the baby to her basket and eased herself from the bed, reluctant to leave the warmth of the rough blanket and Arthur's sleeping body. She rubbed the raised weals on her arm where an insect had found its supper in the night and sought out stockings, shoes and her shift. They were damp with condensation and chilly against her skin as she slipped them on with the dirt-stained frock she had worn the day before; it was already mended at the hem where the bush had clawed its hold on her. She was stiff from chopping out tree roots the previous evening, but she was learning to discount the minor discomforts of insect weals and aching muscles.

She walked softly to the door of the hut and leaned against the doorpost. The mad cackle of the kookaburra carried through the forest, the shrieking of the dawn chorus was deafening. She allowed herself to enjoy the morning briefly, the sweet drifting scent of wattle flowers and the sunlight on the land she and Arthur had cleared between them during the past weeks.

She was adapting, she thought wrily. The truth was that she had begun to enjoy the precariousness of the life here, throwing herself into the physical work with an unexpected energy. If the settlers of Yooma would not let the bush beat them, then neither would she. Here, hardship was not a matter of doing without a new bonnet, or eating bread and cheese because Cook was having one of her 'turns'. It was learning how to bake a flat coarse bread in the primitive stove, fetching up water by the bucket from the creek, digging out tree and nettle roots until her hands became dry and sore and her back was as stiff as a gum tree. She had hitched up her skirts at the waist and entered the battle against the land with the stark, fatalistic philosophy of peasants through the ages. The 'humble, ordinary sort of life' of which Arthur had spoken was already bringing them closer together. All the attitudes which she had once despised, gentility, delicacy and middle-class prudery, were out of place here and it was with relief that she cast them aside.

She had not heard Arthur come through the hut behind her. He slipped his arm round her waist and nuzzled his unshaven chin against her ear.

'Happy?'

'Yes,' she said quickly and meant it.

'I was thinking. It's time we hired some help. The work's too much for you and me together. And, with the plans I've got for this place, I shall need a couple of hands for the building.'

'From Yooma?'

'Better from Sydney. I shall go with the mail coach. It might well take a day or more.'

He was asking her if she could manage without him. Her heart lurched as she thought of several days alone with the baby and the nights in the hut with no one to come to her assistance if she needed anyone. What if Agnes should fall sick, or a snake attack her, or a goanna enter the hut, or a passing traveller turn out to be one of the bushrangers who were rumoured to be in the neighbourhood?

She would not let him see that she was frightened. 'I shall make a garden while you're gone.'

'I'll bring you back some seeds – and a rose-bush.'

'Roses round the door. Who says Australia can't be tamed?'

Arthur was gone for two nights. Elizabeth tried not to let the sounds of the bush prey on her mind, though in the dark the rustle and crash of wildlife round the hut grew menacing, and by day she jumped at sudden movements and the kookaburra's laugh got on her nerves. She worked at making a garden, picturing it growing with flowers and vegetables. She tied Agnes in a shawl on her back and fetched water from the creek. She sat on the mossy river bank, letting the water run over her feet to cool them. She was not lonely, she realized on the second day. Agnes, filling out after four weeks, not only surviving, but growing pink and strong, was all the company she could need. And the bush was too beautiful to be menacing for long. Its stillness induced a mood of calm, which linked the human state with that of the bush animals. Elizabeth was learning to live for the present, neither regretting what had gone before, nor anxious about what might happen tomorrow.

On the third day of Arthur's absence she walked to Yooma to visit Alice McCreery – Alice, whose husband Danny was a sawyer and missed the bush hut for its booze; who had a purple bruise on her face, where Danny had hit her the night before because she had been slow bringing him his tea.

'This is nothing, my darling,' she said, when the story was out and Elizabeth stared at the wound on her cheek in horror. 'Better a bashing or two than him wanting the other.' She laughed. She seemed genuinely to find her situation a cause for amusement. 'Though sometimes it's both I've to contend with. Sure, but it's a hard life.'

That it had been a hard life for Alice was evident, with ten children hanging round her skirts and, from the look of her, another on the way. And yet Elizabeth could see that Alice had once been pretty and, she guessed, was not much older than herself.

She returned to the hut, sobered by her visit, glad that Arthur was a good man and that he had accepted Agnes and that Agnes was not the reminder of the past she had once longed for, but a hope for the future, her and Arthur's future together.

Arthur was back when she reached the bush hut, with a new spring-cart and a load of provisions, and two strangers sitting in the back room, drinking beer at her table.

216

Riley, the older of the two men, rose to greet her, wiping his hands on his shirt before shaking hands. Patrick, Riley's apprentice, stood shyly waiting to be spoken to, a gangling youth who looked as though his clothes were several sizes too small for his rapidly growing frame. 'These are our carpenters from Sydney,' Arthur explained. 'They'll help us with the land and start work on the store in a week or so.'

'But where will you live?' said Elizabeth anxiously. The two men darkened and all but filled the back room of the hut. Agnes, disturbed by the crowd of people, began to squawl. 'I shall have to feed her,' Elizabeth said pointedly.

'Have no fear, Mrs Pengelly,' Riley said with a little exaggerated bow. 'Patrick and myself will pitch a tent in the great outdoors.' He turned to Arthur and gave Patrick a push towards the door. 'And now, the two of us will make ourselves scarce and leave you and your good lady in peace.'

'What do you think?' Arthur said when they had gone. He watched her unbutton her frock and latch Agnes to her breast. 'I know they're a bit rough and ready but they were recommended to me as workers and when Riley saw the plans for this place he was keen as mustard.'

'I'm glad you're back,' said Elizabeth, smiling at him. 'We missed you.'

After a few weeks Riley and Patrick were established as part of the household. They ate their meals with Arthur and Elizabeth, petted Agnes, and drew sympathy from Elizabeth after a rainstorm one evening, so that she persuaded Arthur to let them lay out their bedrolls in the bar. This was now lined with shelves and transformed by the addition of a new door, ready for its opening to the public. The men had already begun work on Arthur's planned extension to the hut.

'Sure, and you're an angel,' said Riley after spending a night on the floor of the bar. 'Just think how me and young Patrick here would be like a pair of drowned rats this morning, if it wasn't for your merciful Christian kindness.'

'You can cut your Irish blarney,' Elizabeth said. 'If you don't get the new house built and lined by November, we shall lose all our potential customers, for they'll think this is still as lazy a good-for-nothing place as it was in Tommy O'Hoare's day.'

The day came at last when Elizabeth and Arthur travelled to Sydney to buy stock for the store. They sang on that first trip back to Yooma, in the new cart packed with bales of calico, sheetings, shirtings and a mix of useful and frivolous goods – penny journals, laces for shoes and laces for stays, ribbons, watch-chains and candles and coffee pots. Arthur was more relaxed than Elizabeth had ever seen him, with his hat perched on the back of his head, bellowing out 'Pop Goes the Weasel'. Elizabeth sat beside him and hugged Agnes to her. She wore a new black straw bonnet and a frosted silver Indian brooch which Arthur had bought her that day pinned to her shawl. A crate of poultry squawked in the back of the cart. She felt ridiculously happy.

It was not true that they were to lose customers because of the chaotic progress of the building at the hut. People walked up from Yooma to see the changes taking place at O'Hoare's Bush Hut, with its new sign over the entrance reading *Pengelly's*. A crowd packed the shop on the day it opened and in the days which followed. Word went round quickly in the district about the store at Yooma and, though the occasional bushman or sawyer rode away in disgust when he found the old bar cleaned up and the shelves lined with nothing more intoxicating than spirits of camphor, most visitors came to admire and to buy.

Elizabeth was seated at a table in the back room cutting up lemons to make marmalade. Mulligan had not forgotten them and had brought Elizabeth a sack of lemons on his way through Yooma one day.

Patrick reached out a hand to take a slice of lemon. Elizabeth watched him eat it, sucking in his cheeks and pulling a grotesque face as the acid reached his taste buds. Riley leaned against the doorpost between the back room and the new part of the house. The day was already hot, though it was still early morning. Riley wiped a patch of sweat at his neck with the top edge of his shirt. 'Sure, the boy's an idiot for punishment.'

'It's cooling,' Patrick asserted good-humouredly.

'You'll need more than that to cool you before you're finished.'

Elizabeth smiled. The men had completed the first room of the new house. For the first time since Agnes had been born she and Arthur had lain together in a proper bed, in a proper bedroom with furniture and with flowers from the bush scenting the air, and they had made love.

The sound of cartwheels outside heralded the arrival of the day's first travellers. Elizabeth wiped her hands on her apron and shouted out to Arthur to take his carpenters off and see they did some carpentering. She shooed the men from the room and went into the store.

She looked forward to the first arrivals of the day. They might be a coachload of people travelling to the mountains, a farming family or any one of the small settlers of the district. They were all nationalities, Dutch, German, Scots, mostly Irish. Elizabeth liked their plain, unmannered conversation and the way people were united by the hard existence in a new land.

The two young women who entered the shop were neither plain nor unmannered. She recognized them at once as the daughters of the Anglican minister in Yooma, a north of England parson who had emigrated with his family five years ago and whose wife and children had spent the past five years brooding with nostalgia for the old country.

The younger of the women leaped to examine a bale of printed cotton with a squeal of joy. 'What do you think, Bella? Isn't this first class?' She held the fabric to her face.

Her sister was more conscious of attention to social courtesies. 'We are so pleased, Mrs Pengelly, about what you are doing to Tommy O'Hoare's establishment. Lucy and I should like to purchase some cloth for summer dresses. We like to try to dress in fashion somewhat, but it's so difficult, don't you think? –' she looked at Elizabeth's plain brown frock '– out in the bush? We heard that you'd got some prints and muslins of quality. In fact, you're becoming quite famous round here, Mrs Pengelly. Where do you find the things you do? Even in Sydney quality seems impossible, unless at a price.'

'Mr Pengelly is very experienced in the drapery trade,' said Elizabeth. 'He was one of Dorset's leading importers.' She was amused to see Bella Symonds's dark eyes flicker with interest.

Lucy brought the bale of fabric to the counter with a thump. 'Our mama was saying you ought to pay us a visit, now that you're settled down properly.'

Her sister interrupted with a determination which suggested a long-standing rivalry between them. 'What Lucy means is we're getting up a little *soirée* on Saturday. If you'd care to join us.'

Arthur had at that moment entered the shop from the back room. Elizabeth followed the young women's gaze. The heavy physical work of the past weeks had made Arthur leaner, the harmony between them had brought a contentment to his face. She sensed the Misses

Symonds's well-developed bosoms swell with anticipation and, for no reason that she could explain immediately, she went to stand beside Arthur and linked her arm through his. She repeated the invitation to the Symonds's *soirée*, hoping that he would find an excuse to turn it down.

'A *soirée*?' he said. 'Well, that sounds very grand. A spot of culture, Miss Symonds, in this wilderness?'

'A little music, Mr Pengelly. A little poetry perhaps.' Bella Symonds dropped her gaze. 'I do hope that you can both come.'

'We'll be delighted.'

Elizabeth dug her fingers into Arthur's arm. 'Arthur, the baby.'

'Nonsense, my love. Riley and Patrick will be here. And the minister's house is not a million miles away. We'll not be gone more than a few hours.'

Elizabeth let go of his arm. She began to unwind and measure out the fabric Lucy had chosen.

She could not say why the Symonds's invitation had unsettled her. But, as she dressed on the Saturday for the visit, putting on her petticoat under a yellow silk frock which she had not worn since leaving England, she was certain that she did not want to enter again that world of English probity. The Symonds girls seemed to threaten the calm she and Arthur had found here.

Arthur was in high spirits as they set out for Yooma. The second part of the house was almost finished, which should have made Elizabeth happy too. Instead, she fretted about leaving Agnes, grumbled at having to wear stays again and sulked when Arthur teased her about being as brown and unrefined as a sundowner's wife.

The Symonds's house was at the far end of the village, about half a mile further along the track and in view of the Reverend Symonds's white-boarded church. The evening was warm and sticky. Insects hummed in the still air. They were biting; something had crawled inside Elizabeth's bodice, making her scratch. Arthur nudged her and raised his eyebrows in disapproval as they drove up to the house.

Several pony-carriages were already drawn up outside and lamps blazed on the veranda, which enclosed all four sides of the house. The company seemed to overflow from doors and windows.

After five minutes of introductions Elizabeth had decided that there were only two members of the whole party whom she would have chosen for their company. The first was the Reverend Symonds himself, a quiet, absent-minded man who reminded her of her father. The second was a Miss McPherson, who, Elizabeth learned, had been the Misses Symonds's governess in England. She was to move to Queensland shortly, to marry the manager of a sheep station; this information Bella Symonds imparted with an attitude of jealous disbelief at the woman's good fortune.

'Have you given a thought to hiring a nursemaid yet, Mrs Pengelly?' inquired Mrs Symonds. 'To look after your little girl.'

'I've not had need of any help,' Elizabeth explained. 'And our living space has been so cramped, it would have been a serious problem where to put anyone.'

'All the same, it's something that must be looked into,' said Arthur quickly.

'Take care, when you do. Get a good solid English girl, or else Scottish. You can't trust the rest.' Mrs Symonds nodded at Miss McPherson, as if to acknowledge that she was one of the superior breed. Miss McPherson let a little smile of apparent – though not precisely definable – gratitude for the compliment play on her lips.

'And as for servants,' declared a Miss Glendenning, whose brother farmed a district east of Yooma, 'wait until you come to engage servants! My dear, in England you wouldn't tolerate for a week the behaviour the Australian-born servant gets away with.'

'It seems I have a lot to beware of in this country,' said Elizabeth.

'Mrs Pengelly, the snakes and mosquitoes are nothing to the treachery of servants.' Mrs Pincher, who had spoken, had suffered on this score more than most. 'The deliberate breakages, the storms of tantrums when asked to do the slightest thing, and the parade of followers I've had to discourage.' Mrs Pincher rolled her eyes in memory of past tribulations.

'They are *all* promiscuous,' mouthed Miss Glendenning.

'What – all tarred with the same brush?' said Elizabeth, echoing the woman's confidential tone. Miss Glendenning narrowed her eyes uncertainly.

'Do you sew?' inquired Mrs Symonds abruptly. 'We need lots of busy fingers for our Fancy Fair next month. We're raising funds to refurbish the church.'

'Oh dear. I've not a single talent for fancy-work,' said Elizabeth with as much regret as she could muster. She sensed a growing hostility among the women. 'Perhaps I might bake a cake instead?'

The vicar's wife smiled with a chilly sort of compliance.

Bella and Lucy announced that supper was laid out in the next room. Elizabeth took Arthur on one side during the crush of handing out plates and filling them with cold meats and pastries. 'I wish we hadn't come.'

He looked at her in surprise. 'It's only sociable –'

'But false. I feel as if we're back in England.'

She was prevented from saying more as Miss McPherson approached. The governess looked embarrassed, as if she saw, too late, that her interruption was badly timed.

'I shall miss all the Yooma gossip when I move to Queensland,' she said.

'I'm sure there's a geat deal of it,' smiled Elizabeth.

'A bottomless supply.' The other woman laughed, then a bleak look briefly crossed her face. 'There's a lot of jealousy in a small community.' Arthur, with a nod to the women, moved away to speak to one of the local farmers.

'I shan't be sorry to escape the Misses Symonds's recitations,' Miss McPherson whispered to Elizabeth. 'They play the piano tolerably well, if the instrument wasn't so horribly out of tune. But I never was able to instil a sense of poetry in either of their souls.'

'Teaching can be a thankless occupation,' said Elizabeth. 'I suffered for years the tyranny of the local squire and the vicar, when I taught at our village school in England.'

'Then I wasn't wrong in thinking we had something in common,' said Miss McPherson with satisfaction. 'And do you like poetry, Mrs Pengelly?'

'I like Tennyson.' Elizabeth remembered the volume of poems which Edward had given her. She had not looked at it since leaving England.

'My life is dreary, he cometh not,' quoted Miss McPherson. 'I am aweary, aweary, I would that I were dead! The lament of every spinster the world over.'

Elizabeth smiled, remembering how she too had once languished for a lover.

'What fools we all are,' said Elizabeth.

'Fools, Mrs Pengelly?'

'To pin our expectations of happiness on a man.'

'I'm sure I shall be happy enough, when Mr Cavendish comes to take me to Queensland,' Miss McPherson said confidently.

Elizabeth saw Arthur returning. He was clearly pleased with himself after his conversation with some of the farmers in the district. Elizabeth smiled too. 'And so am I, Miss McPherson,' she said.

Bella and Lucy had chosen to recite a programme of unexpectedly violent poems, among them *The Charge of the Light Brigade*. This they declaimed, with various wild gestures to represent the plunging into the battery-smoke, the reeling from the sabre stroke, and the cannon to the right, cannon to the left and cannon in front of the noble six hundred. When it was finished, the performers and their audience were exhausted.

Elizabeth looked at Arthur. She raised her eyebrows, to share a secret amusement at the girls' antics. But he seemed depressed by the poem. She wondered, as she squeezed his arm, whether the evening had stirred up thoughts of Edward for him too.

'How frustrating it is, not to have news of what's happening in the Crimea,' said the Reverend Symonds when the recitations and applause and congratulations were over. 'It's the thing I miss most about the life at home. We're so cut off. We don't hear what's going on until months after the event. For all we know, Sebastopol may be taken by now, or the Russian navy may at this very moment be chasing our navy up the Thames.'

'Papa!' said Bella. 'What a horrid thought! The Russians wouldn't dare do any such thing. Our army and navy wouldn't let them.'

'Your patriotism does you credit, Miss Symonds,' said Arthur. 'With you to cheer them, I'm sure the army could capture Sebastopol in a week.'

It was a ritual sort of gallantry, yet to Elizabeth, Arthur's remarks seemed unnecessary, and they rankled. She reminded him of what he had said when they reached home late that evening.

'It was no more than a compliment to the girl,' said Arthur. 'You can't think I meant anything by it.'

'It was false,' complained Elizabeth. She kicked off her shoes and slumped on the bed. The new bedroom was lined with a pretty, sprigged wallpaper, and the light from the oil-lamp threw shadows on the green-painted ceiling. Agnes, in her cot by the bed, stirred and began to mouth at her fist. 'I thought you had rejected all that – the false compliments and buttering of people's egos.'

'Sometimes it's necessary. I did some good deals with the farmers round here tonight, Elizabeth. Save us going all the way to Sydney for potatoes and corn and such.' He paused, irritated when she did not respond with praise for his efforts. He threw his necktie on to the mantelshelf, where it hung, draped over a candlestick. 'You're just jealous, because Bella Symonds is a good-looking girl, and I said you weren't refined.'

'Bella Symonds's idea of refinement is laughable, wouldn't you say?' she retorted. 'You're fooling yourself, if you think she'd be flattered by the attentions of a man your age.'

It was not what she had wanted to say, nor even what she meant. The whole issue was developing rapidly into a quarrel, a petty and demeaning one, if Bella Symonds was to be its focus. Agnes had begun to cry, demanding to be fed.

'A man my age was good enough for you when you feared you were past marrying,' Arthur said bitterly. 'And you weren't above a bit of cradle-snatching once. How old was Agnes's father, eh? A boy barely whiskered?'

Elizabeth gasped as if he had struck her. Her eyes smarted with quick tears. She picked up the baby, who began to scream and squirm in her arms, searching for her breast. She unbuttoned her bodice. 'You're upsetting Agnes.' Arthur turned away with a grunt of impatience.

Their quarrel, unresolved in the morning, left Elizabeth feeling miserable. For the first time since coming to Yooma she felt homesick for England. It was hard, to acknowledge that she would probably never see Charlford and her parents again, and she could not think of Edward without the familiar knot of grief in her throat.

Arthur was reading an old copy of *Punch*, seated on an upturned log. He kept his attention fixed on his paper to avoid speaking to her while she laid Agnes in her basket under the shade of the new veranda.

Elizabeth went down the veranda steps through the weedy patch of garden where she had sown bean seeds and cabbages and planted potatoes. All that showed above the bare earth were a few sets of yellowing leaves. The rose Arthur had bought her grew with its single shrivelled bud defiantly beside the empty rain barrel. Even the wild bush flowers, the yellow wattle and flame-red waratah were wilting under the glare of the sun. The sun and sky seemed so high here, the light so much clearer and harder than in England. And it was still only October. 'Just wait until January,' Lucy Symonds had told her with a grim sort of relish. 'The Australian summers are horrid!'

Elizabeth flapped at the insects with her hand and walked to the end of the garden, where Arthur had fenced off some of the bush they had cleared to use as a paddock. The horses shook their heads at the flies and bent them again lazily to feed among the rapidly regrowing gum shoots and tough grasses. The battle against the bush had only just begun, thought Elizabeth. The native growth had learned to survive here, while European seed would wither. She leaned her arms and chin on the fence, lowering her eyes against the hot bright glare ahead.

In England it would be autumn. Her mother would be dressing for church, her father reading, or pretending to read the great Bible on its stand by his chair, Robert would be rehearsing his sermon. And Edward – she dug her chin into her wrist so that it hurt – Edward would never see Charlford or autumn again. Someone last night had said that they were cut off from news of the Crimea, but the war had never seemed real to Elizabeth, until she had heard that Edward had gone to the Crimea. Now, not only the war, but everything she had ever known before seemed shut off from her, like a once visited room behind a heavy door.

'I think I should write to my sister,' she said to Arthur when she returned to the house.

Arthur did not look up from his reading. 'As you think fit.'

'It's only right that I should let them know we're safe and well. It's six months since we left.'

He laid down the paper. 'I never tried to keep you from your folks, Elizabeth. Any bad feelings were never on my part.'

She hesitated, wanting to remove the obstacle of their quarrel the night before, but she could not bring herself to apologize, and would not be able to bear it if Arthur were to say anything conciliatory. She turned away and went indoors.

They still had not unpacked all their belongings. Clothes and books lay in boxes, in the same state as they had come off the boat. Elizabeth sat on the bedroom floor and began turning out a trunk in which she remembered she had packed a favourite writing case. She found it and laid it on the bed. Beneath the space the case had occupied was a layer of books. She lifted out the green leather-bound volume of Tennyson's poems. For a long time she sat with the book on her lap, staring at the gold lettering tooled on the front and spine. At last, almost reluctantly, she opened it and found again the familiar lines.

'*And moving thro' a mirror clear that hangs before her all the year, shadows of the world appear,*' she read softly. She closed the book and stroked the cover. If he had inscribed it, left some message, it would have been more to remember him by.

That spring and summer were a time of long hot days and dry weariness in the bush, when to go out of doors was like stepping into an oven and to look across the paddock one had to narrow the eyes to slits against the burning sky. The flies were a torment. The dust from Elizabeth's parody of a garden lay thick in the mouth and throat. But the store flourished. People said they did not know how they had managed before 'Pengelly's'. People passing through began to look on Yooma as a likely place to settle.

The house was finished early in February. Riley and Patrick, though no longer employed as carpenters and builders, stayed on as hired hands. Elizabeth took on a general servant for the kitchen work, and Arthur decided that they should employ a nursemaid. And in February at last came rain, bringing with it fresh growth. Elizabeth replanted with beans and potatoes and by March the desolation of the garden had turned to a rich green as if by magic.

Agnes, at seven months old, was an attractive child. Her large eyes, red cheeks and dark curls drew the admiration of anyone sentimentally inclined, and even the new nursemaid, Leila, who had turned out to be more interested in fashions than babies, was won over by Agnes's charm and dimples.

'Are you pleased with the girl?' said Amy McPherson, who still waited patiently to be sent for by the sheep-farming Mr Cavendish in Queensland. 'It was high time you had some of the work taken off your hands.'

'Arthur is pleased to have something rather decorative around the house,' said Elizabeth. They watched Leila, in flounced cotton and extravagant pear-drop ear-rings, carry Agnes up the veranda steps.

Elizabeth turned back to the garden where she and Amy had just chased off a large goanna bent on stealing one of the chickens. Elizabeth had lost her fear of the goannas which inhabited the bush, but not her distaste. She tried to straighten the bean plants which had got trampled underfoot in the excitement. 'Leila's fond of Agnes. And I don't dislike her. However, discipline, according to Arthur, is what Baby Agnes needs.'

'Discipline?' exclaimed Amy. 'That dear, good child needs discipline?'

'All children need discipline, according to my husband. The more so, since one of the Yooma brats absconded with a half pound of bull's eyes behind his back. He took a stick to him the week after, with the mother screaming encouragement – *You beat the wickedness out of him, Mr Pengelly* – and threatening she'd take a second stick to the poor child when she got him home.'

'The Yooma children run wild,' said Amy seriously. 'They're just like young animals. Before I met Mr Cavendish I had a mind to open a schoolhouse here one day.'

Elizabeth was thoughtful.

Amy laughed. 'I can see I've set you plotting. As if you haven't enough to do, Elizabeth! I can hear the mail coach. It's time I was going.'

They turned to the house and saw Arthur come running out from the back of the store. He was carrying a bundle of mail.

'A letter, Elizabeth,' he shouted. 'It's a letter from your folks.'

Elizabeth went slowly towards him. It was several months since she had written to Hannah, long enough to forget the homesickness which had prompted her letter. She felt unprepared for the attack on her emotions which news from home would bring.

'I always find letters upsetting,' murmured Amy, her thoughts on Mr Cavendish in Queensland. 'It seems worse in the summer, when time hangs heavy.'

'It's from my sister.' Elizabeth took the letter from Arthur's hand.

Amy glanced at her, and then at Arthur. 'Letters from home demand immediate attention. I shall bid you farewell.'

Elizabeth sat with Arthur on the steps of the veranda after Amy had gone. She opened the letter with trembling hands. 'I fear so for Father –' She turned to Arthur. 'I should have written sooner.'

She scanned the lines, written in Hannah's small neat hand. When she looked up her eyes were large with tears. She had known in a way, though she had tried to dismiss it only as a fear, that her father would be dead.

Arthur held her against him.

'It's like it says in the Book of Prayer,' she said. 'All those things which we ought to have done and have left undone – Oh, Arthur, I feel such a terrible guilt.'

'I know, my love.' He stroked her hair and wiped the tears which had wet her hand and smudged the page of the letter. 'See here. It's not all sad. You won't be able to read the rest. Your sister has had another child, another boy, and they're to call him Henry. That's like in the Bible too. A time to be born, and a time to die. You couldn't have changed anything.'

Elizabeth held on to Arthur's hand and drew comfort from it. She had done him the greatest wrong of all, and yet he still loved her.

'Read it to me,' she said after a while. She pressed her cheek against his shirt. The sound of his voice was comforting against her ear. He began to read – about the baby, about the difficulties of persuading her mother to uproot from Charlford and live with Hannah and Fred, about a trip to London, her Aunt Lydia's charity work, the return of some of the soldiers from the war. His voice stopped. Elizabeth felt a tension in him.

'Is that all?' She eased away from him, and saw by his face that it was something terrible, but she could not look at the letter.

'No, that isn't all,' Arthur said, and his voice was harsh with emotion. He gave a sudden snort of laughter, the sound was frightening because it was unexpected. He pushed the letter into her hands. 'Seems there's some very good news come out from England. Your fellow Edward has turned up alive.'

29

Edward sat forward in the coach. Marianne, beside him, was silent and clung tightly to his arm. The other occupants of the coach, a man and woman and two small girls, chatted in a low murmur. He watched for each landmark to appear dreamlike through the window, the farmworkers' cottages, a line of grey washing hanging between the bare apple trees in the snow, the public house, its portrait of old King George, crazed with varnish and swinging in the wind, then the gateway to The Red House, as the Thornes' house came into view, glimpsed briefly through a gap in the high hedge bank.

Edward looked away from the window and into Marianne's troubled blue eyes. He pressed her hand.

'I am so frightened to meet your brother and his wife,' she said. 'I hope that they will like me.'

'They'll adore you,' he said. He smiled to reassure her. 'But first, I want you to meet an old friend.'

He banged on the roof of the coach and the vehicle came to a halt by the hedge. Marianne stood awkwardly at the side of the road, while he spoke to the driver, arranging with him for their luggage to be taken on to the vicarage.

Edward's heart quickened with apprehension as the coach moved off. He should have warned the Thornes that he was coming. He could not even be sure that Robert had received his letter, sent from London.

They walked hand in hand to the gate. Edward stared at the boarded windows, in disbelief at first, then understanding and disappointment came over him, and he felt cheated. This was a possibility he had not considered. Clumps of blackened vegetation made little hillocks in the snow, the wind blowing across the garden struck cold against his clean-shaven face.

'This isn't what you expected,' said Marianne. 'A lot of changes can take place in a year, Edward. Coming home is bound to be a little shocking.' She put her arms round him. He accepted her warmth gratefully.

Robert and Mabel had received Edward's letter and were waiting for them when they reached the vicarage. Mabel, excited by the fact that Edward had married a French woman, was clearly expecting something in a more exotic mould than Marianne.

'What a panic you put us all in, Edward,' she said. 'Announcing you wanted to visit like that, and with a wife.' She glanced uncertainly at the wife in question, standing with her fair hair tucked under a plain bonnet in the hall. 'Such a dark horse you always were. And all the adventures you must have had in the Crimea – at one time we'd given you up properly for dead. You're thought of as quite a hero in Charlford, I can tell you.'

'We must be thankful it is all over,' said Robert grudgingly. 'And that the Lord has seen fit to return Edward to us alive.'

Edward looked at his brother and saw the prim mouth and pale, soulless eyes; Robert's hair was receding from the dome of his head, his figure was turning to stoutness, but the antipathy they felt for one another was something which would never alter.

'Has the Lord seen fit to take away Henry Thorne from us?' he asked. 'The house was shut up. Are they all gone?'

'A sad business.' Robert placed the tips of his fingers together and shook his head, as he did when comforting the bereaved. 'The poor man went downhill very quickly after Elizabeth left. And Mrs Thorne, dear lady, has gone away to live with Hannah and Fred.'

Mabel looked eagerly at her husband. 'Does Edward know the whole story? Does he know that Elizabeth –' she pronounced the name rather too loudly and glanced quickly at Marianne, who gave a little frown and looked away. Mabel seemed to wonder if she should continue, but the attraction of relating an impressive item of gossip proved too strong. 'Elizabeth went off to live in Australia last year.'

'With Pengelly?' Edward managed to keep no more than a natural surprise in his voice. He had not anticipated so many changes.

'But of course.' Mabel was a little disappointed. Her announcement had had less effect than she expected.

'The whole business killed her father,' said Robert. 'And her mother is very bitter about the way events turned out.' He frowned. 'Elizabeth always showed a lack of womanly feeling, in my estimation. She was too self-willed. She never had a proper regard for where her duties lay.'

Marianne's cheeks had flushed a deeper colour. She picked up one of the bags from the hall floor. 'Mrs Munro – please, to show me to our room.'

Edward saw that they had hurt her. He took the bag from her hand and put an arm round her waist. 'No more talk about the past.' The shock of Mabel's news was fading quickly, for what difference did it make if Elizabeth was in Dorset or Australia? 'Marianne and I are going to look only at the future.'

'You really intend to proceed with this foolhardy scheme?' said Robert. Marianne had gone to bed, pleading a headache. Mabel was in the kitchen, making arrangements with the cook about the meals the next day.

'I do.' Edward leaned back in his chair. The rectory had altered under Mabel's regime. The rooms had been done up in a modern style, and the low-beamed sitting room was resplendent with layers of varnish and antimacassars.

'You realize you will be exposing your wife to an existence which is barely on the edge of respectability? An infirmary in the East End, Edward! You will be laying yourself open to every beggar and scrounger in London.'

'Mrs Delahaye is convinced it is a worthy cause. She and the other ladies of the Kensington Benevolent Friends have agreed to continue with their charity work to help fund the scheme.'

Robert was not impressed. 'I always did have my doubts about that good lady. Wasn't her husband French?'

'Very suspect, the French,' said Edward gravely.

Robert looked puzzled, then irritated. 'You know I wouldn't intend any slight against your wife.'

There was an awkward pause.

'Will you go to see Elizabeth's mother and sister?' Robert said.

'I shall pay my respects.' Edward hid his reluctance: he had come to Charlford to see Henry, with the old man dead he did not feel inclined to disturb any more ghosts from the past.

When he went up to bed Marianne was sleeping. She was curled up under the bedclothes. Something in the way she lay suggested that she had been crying before she went to sleep. Edward felt a burden of responsibility for her.

He sat in a chair by the fire in his nightshirt and watched the dying fire-flames, thinking of Henry Thorne, and of Elizabeth in Australia. She could not have cut herself off more completely. But perhaps she had planned it that way.

The last ember glowed and faded. Edward climbed into bed beside his sleeping wife. He stroked her hair from her face and kissed her. She stirred in her sleep. No more memories of old flames, he promised. From now on he would do nothing that would make Marianne unhappy.

He went alone to see Mrs Thorne. There had been a fresh fall of snow and the roads were treacherous. Marianne seemed relieved to have an excuse not to go with him, she stayed behind at the vicarage and helped Mabel to arrange dried flowers into bunches for a charity sale – a task for which she showed not the slightest talent, Mabel told Robert afterwards.

'I don't know where your brother found her,' she said, implying that such women lurked in the more secret areas of society. 'But, knowing Edward, I feel very suspicious.'

Edward felt stifled by Elizabeth's family. He did not try to tell them about what he had seen in the Crimea. They talked a great deal about the valour and suffering of the soldiers in the war, but he sensed that their true feeling was for the British victory and 'rule Britannia'.

He had seen the soldiers who had returned, already filling the street corners in London, attracting curious or sympathetic glances to an empty sleeve pinned to a breast, or fold of trouser, neatly wrapped, where a leg should have been. He had recognized the same despair and disillusionment staring from their eyes, as had marked them out in the Crimea. A hero's welcome was short lived once he had been discharged from the service.

Edward outlined his plans to help the disabled soldiers to the Thorne family, and they made polite noises in praise of his Christian calling.

'You have changed, Edward,' said Mrs Thorne, with a suggestion of malice in her voice.

'He has lost weight,' remarked Hannah quickly, in an attempt to invest her mother's comment with more charity. 'We were so frightened when we heard that you had gone missing. Elizabeth too –'

'Elizabeth deserved to suffer a little, after all the suffering she has caused others,' interrupted Mrs Thorne.

'I hear she and Pengelly are in Australia now.'

'She went, believing you were dead,' said Hannah solemnly.

'She doesn't know?'

'She wrote to us from Australia –'

'Australia!' said Mrs Thorne with a downward droop of her mouth. 'Fancy going off to Australia!'

Hannah sighed. 'Mother, if Fred were to decide to go to Australia, heaven forbid, or Timbuctoo – wouldn't you suppose that I and the children would go with him?'

'You weren't such a fool as to marry someone so unsuitable in the first place. She wrote to us from Australia, Edward. She told us she and Mr Pengelly are living in some shanty town in the bush. And there, you might suppose, she expects to bring up her daughter like a lady.'

'She and Mr Pengelly have a little girl,' explained Hannah.

Edward nodded politely, feeling a small shock at this fresh news.

'I shall never see my granddaughter.' Mrs Thorne's bottom lip sagged with self-pity. 'And poor Henry –'

'Now, Mother, don't upset yourself,' said Fred stiffly, but with the automatic response of someone well-used to the brewing situation.

'I can't help it. When I think of all that might have been. If she'd only married Robert, she could have comforted her father in his last years. Instead of which –' She pressed the back of her hand to her mouth.

Hannah gave Edward a tired look of sympathy.

Mrs Thorne began to gather up a collection of items on her knee, embroidery, spectacles case, a small purse, and a bowl of boiled sweets. 'Fred, dear – I think I should like to go up to my room.'

Edward and Hannah waited in strained silence, as Fred took his mother-in-law's arm and walked slowly with her to the door.

'Is your mother right?' said Edward when they were alone. 'Did it all prove too much for your father? It seems to be the opinion held by Robert.'

Hannah shook her head. 'Who's to say? I think he missed her dreadfully. Lizzie always was his favourite. But my father was a sick man, as you know, Edward, before Elizabeth met Mr Pengelly.'

Edward looked at the patterned carpet. 'She has a little girl now?'

'Yes. She seems to have found fulfilment at last. I have written to put her mind at rest that you are alive. And now, you too are married. Do you think you have found happiness?'

'As much as anyone ever can.'

'And Marianne – is she pretty?'

He smiled at what he saw as her interest in the superficial. 'Yes, she's pretty. But not elegant. I think Mabel and Robert regard her as something of a French peasant.'

'Is she honest? That's the thing. Elizabeth talked a great deal about a need for honesty between men and women. I've learned that she was right.' She spoke with an intenseness which led Edward to think that he had perhaps misjudged Hannah in the past. Her eyes were sad, as if a deep unhappiness lay behind her words.

'Marianne is very honest,' he said. 'I'm not so certain of myself.'

'You don't love her?'

He shrugged helplessly. What a strange conversation, he thought, and yet he wanted to continue. He felt a strong compulsion to unburden himself to the calm intelligence of the woman before him. 'Who really knows what love is? I care for Marianne more deeply than I cared for Elizabeth. I have shared more experiences, lived a more real part of my life with her. And yet every day I regret that she's not Elizabeth.'

'You must put Elizabeth out of your mind,' Hannah said after a while. 'It's romantic, and destructive, to wish your life other than what it is.'

They heard Fred returning from upstairs.

Hannah smiled, and Edward felt the warmth of it, like a healing balm. Then, as the door opened, her smile altered, it brightened with welcome. Fred came into the room and looked at his wife, and Edward was presented with a curious analogy. Fred, he thought, was like a man accepting the cocked ears and wagging tail of a dog, which out of pure instinct for survival had learned to deceive its master with a display of devotion.

They found lodgings in Holborn, close to Edward's old rooms near the college. The house was one of a row of gaunt brick buildings. Paint flaked from the lower windows, and a dreary, disused air hung about the front basement steps.

Their rooms were cramped and plain, and a cloying smell of cooked mutton drifted up the stairwell to the top of the building.

Marianne scrubbed and painted, tore down old curtains and bought cheap rugs, bargained for in her halting English, with a thoroughness which awoke in Edward a fresh admiration. When it became obvious that she was going to have a child, he could not believe that he had ever doubted his love for her.

Although more than a year had passed, little had changed at the college. Fitzroy met Edward and told him he was a fool to have involved himself in the debacle of the Crimea, and even more of a fool to have got himself married.

Some weeks after Edward's return Fitzroy cornered him at the end of a lecture.

'What do you do when the little ones come along, eh? How do you intend to support a wife and bairns on the pittance you earn as a dresser, let alone open a dispensary for casualties of that monstrous catastrophe they called a war? Have you anyone to act as patron?'

Edward said that there was Lydia Delahaye and her ladies' society.

'I mean a name, man. Not some circle of twittery old ladies who play at charity work.'

'No, sir.'

Edward knew he should never have confided his plans to Fitzroy who could demolish any idea which was not his own with a few well-chosen words of contempt. He began to feel anxious about Marianne, she would be waiting for him outside. She always complained that the smell from the nearby slaughter houses made her feel ill.

'When do you intend to open this charitable institution of yours?'

'After I've qualified – or, better, next year.'

'You'll be short of money.'

'I still have a pension, left to me when my father died.'

'And the ladies of the Benevolent Friends will supplement this no doubt meagre pension?'

'They have a keen interest in the army veterans,' Edward said defensively.

'If only we could say the same of the government, eh?' Fitzroy said. 'Well, then. What would you say if I were to invest a little financial interest in this scheme of yours, and get up a panel of reliable names?'

Edward was taken aback. 'I should feel very honoured, sir.'

'There are two conditions. You pass your bloody examinations with distinction.' Fitzroy paused. 'And you name this sanatorium, sick club, or home for diseased and decrepit old soldiers after me.'

Marianne was leaning against the wall. Her face was pale, and she was shivering under her wool mantle. Her expression lifted into a smile when she saw him, but her eyes were large and shadowed.

Edward ran the last few yards towards her. He lifted her off her feet. 'The most wonderful thing has happened.' He told her of Fitzroy's proposal.

'That is very wonderful, Edward.'

'The old buffer wants his name on a plaque on the wall, but who cares? He can have his name on posters all over London if it means he'll get all his friends to stump up the money.'

He saw her white face and suffering eyes. When he touched her her skin was moist. 'Marianne? Why didn't you say this morning that something was wrong?'

'I thought it will pass.' She tried to smile. 'It is nothing. A little pain. Indigestion perhaps. But I think, instead of luncheon, perhaps we should go home.'

By the time they reached the house she had begun to miscarry. Edward put her to bed. There was nothing he could do, except wait. After twenty-four hours it was over.

Marianne's grief over losing the child estranged them for a while. Edward's sorrow was for Marianne rather than the baby, and it was mitigated by relief that they had temporarily been spared the burden of another mouth to feed.

Gradually Marianne too seemed to see the loss of the baby as a blessing. She held her hurt to herself. When, in the summer of that year, she again miscarried, she began to say with a bright fatalism that perhaps God did not intend her to have children.

'You're still young,' Edward reassured her. 'Perhaps, in a year or two, when the infirmary's established.'

He was studying the plans for converting a warehouse into a dispensary and a ward to accommodate twenty patients. He did not look up from the papers spread on the table.

Marianne came to stand beside him. She rested her arm on the back of his chair. 'You think about nothing, except that very important infirmary.'

'That isn't true.' He was surprised by the anger in her voice. He put his arm round her and pulled her down on to his knee. Her hair shone in a frizz of gold in the lamplight. Her eyes were dark, and her expression was closed to him. 'Do you think I don't want you to share in it? We shall be working together. You care as much about the soldiers who survived as I do.'

'Perhaps.' She relaxed against him, and he held her, glad that her anger was always short-lived. 'I know always that I will have to share you,' she said. 'But with you I feel so alone, Edward. It's very hard to live that way.'

Shocked, Edward sought in his mind for evidence that he had neglected her. 'It will be different, when you're helping with the nursing.'

'I am not talking about this.' She swept her hand across the table, knocking some of the papers to the floor. She stooped to pick them up. 'The work, it's an obsession. Why? Why do you fill yourself up with obsessions, eh? Why do you go to the Crimea? Why do you marry me? To forget *her*?'

He shook his head. He had been so careful, had censored his thoughts, cast out all the old memories. 'I refuse to live with her shadow forever between us.'

'But it is there. I feel it.'

'Then we'll drive it out. We must.' He caught her hand and pulled her towards him again. 'I love *you*, Marianne. You're my wife. And one day, I promise, we shall have a child, with beautiful fair hair, and rosy cheeks, and blue eyes, like its mother.' She smiled a little, and he kissed her cheeks and then her mouth. 'I love you. Nobody else.'

30

Elizabeth put down her hairbrush and stared at the face which looked back at her from the mirror. She had aged after a year in the Australian climate, her skin had coarsened and there were lines round her eyes. She wound a thick coil of her hair round her finger, pensive, a little sad. Tomorrow she would be thirty-four. She could hear Arthur moving about on the veranda. He called out in the dark to one of the servants. She could hear in his voice that he had been drinking. But he would be cold drunk this time in the evening, not maudlin, like he was when the mood was on him to sit with a bottle into the small hours.

He knocked at the door and waited for her to reply before he came into the bedroom. 'You're ready for bed.'

'I was tired,' she said, looking at him in the mirror. 'Do you mind?'

'It's nothing to me.'

He stood by the bed, looking at her reflection. Her face was framed by her dark copper hair, the skin of her throat and breast were revealed, half shadowed by the white nightdress where she had neglected to fasten the buttons at the neck. She raised a hand involuntarily to the gown. He looked away.

'I thought to go to Sydney tomorrow. Do you want to come with me?'

'Yes, if you like.'

'Not, if I like. Do you want to?'

She hesitated. 'Arthur. You know how I hate the city.'

'That's all right then.'

He came to stand behind her. He put his hands on her shoulders and touched her hair. His fingers were hesitant, as if they were afraid to linger. He had not made love to her since the day of the letter. She referred to it in her mind always as 'the day of the letter', the day when her life had turned itself on its head again.

'And there's Agnes,' she said, though she knew that Leila could well take care of Agnes.

He did not seem to hear her.

She did not know what his mood meant. 'You could get some more tea and sugar, we're running low,' she said. 'And some of the scarlet and black for petticoats. Now that the weather is cooler it's beginning to sell.'

'Do you never tire of the store?' There was curiosity, rather than irritation in his voice.

'Someone has to attend to it. You've done little enough the past six months.'

He did not jump to the bait, hardly seemed to notice. He paused a moment longer, then said, 'I'll be leaving early.'

She heard him go outside.

By the time Elizabeth had opened up the store the next day, Arthur had left for Sydney.

Elizabeth never tired of the shop, nor the life in Yooma. She liked the people – not people like the Symonds and the Pinchers, who threw their energies into visiting and gossip, but people like Alice McCreery, who had been quick to help when Agnes was born and had been as ready to offer advice, or a bottle of home-brewed medicine, when the occasion warranted it since. There was Mulligan, who called in whenever he was passing, to lean on the counter for half an hour and tell her tall stories before he went on his way. And Tom Parrish, one of the bush characters, who drove down once a month from his cottage in the hills to buy tea and tobacco, and would sit on a wooden chair beside the counter for a whole afternoon, talking about his life in the Durham coal mines. People said Tom had found a nugget of gold as big as a man's fist at the Bendigo diggings and had spent the proceeds in a week. And there was Amy McPherson, who waited for her home in Queensland to be ready for her, whom Elizabeth would miss badly when she went.

Agnes had begun walking. Elizabeth watched her stagger across the store on fat legs. She frowned. She had given orders to Leila that the baby should be watched more closely now. There were the hazards of the carts and horses on the road, the river and the chance of Agnes wandering off into the bush.

She picked the child up and patted her legs comfortably against her black dress. She wore mourning for her father still, as a penance rather than from convention; as if the hot and stiff bombasine against her skin, like a hair shirt, could atone for her sins of omission.

'Hello, Aggie. Where's Leila?' She carried her outside.

Elizabeth was not surprised to see Leila, dressed in one of the new, very full crinolines, light green and trimmed with pink ribbon, leaning against a fence post. She was talking to a man on a horse. The stranger was handsome, dressed casually, but with the appearance of a gentleman. He tipped his hat when he saw Elizabeth and swung his horse away. Leila came sulkily across the yard to where Elizabeth stood with Agnes in her arms.

'I have warned you before,' Elizabeth said. She handed the baby into the nursemaid's arms. 'I shan't be so tolerant if you neglect Agnes again.'

Leila's pearl ear-rings swung defiantly. 'I knew just where she was, Mrs Pengelly.'

'You should have been with her. Who is the gentleman you were talking to? You shouldn't be so free with strangers.'

'His name's Cavendish. He's travelled more than eight hundred miles from Rockhampton.' Leila spoke dreamily, her thoughts on the romantic adventures of the long-distance traveller.

'But Cavendish is the name of Miss McPherson's fiancé.' Elizabeth stared after the disappearing rider. She saw Leila's look of disappointment but she was more concerned with what Mr Cavendish's arrival would mean for herself. Amy would be going to Queensland and she, who had come to rely on her, would be left without a friend.

She went the next day with Agnes to visit Amy. She felt nervous as she reached the Symonds's house. She could see them, sitting on the side-veranda, Lucy and Bella in blue silk, Amy dressed in a yellow and red plaid frock, the rider she had seen the day before beside her. Elizabeth was aware of the dowdiness of her black mourning.

Amy jumped up as she saw Elizabeth approach with Agnes. Bella Symonds got more slowly to her feet. 'Mrs Pengelly, what a pleasant surprise – and dear little Agnes.' Bella stroked the baby's dark curls. Agnes obstinately turned her head away.

'Elizabeth –' began Amy. 'Oh, Lizzie. Mr Cavendish has come.'

Mr Cavendish shook Elizabeth by the hand warmly.

240

Amy turned and touched her lover's arm with a tender gesture. 'We're to be married here in Yooma.'

'Miss McPherson has asked us to be bridesmaids,' said Lucy. 'So, we shall be wanting you to order fabrics for us, Mrs Pengelly.'

'White tarlatan, trimmed with blue ribbon,' mused Bella, abandoning her attempt to humour the baby. 'Father is going to give the bride away, and a clergyman is coming all the way from Wollongong to conduct the service. One would almost think it was to be a wedding of some consequence.'

Elizabeth sat on a chair on the veranda and heaved Agnes on to her lap. She flashed a smile of sympathy at Amy. But Amy was absorbed by the man at her side. Mr Cavendish rested an arm lightly along the back of the seat and touched Amy's shoulder, one of his legs was crossed negligently over the other and almost brushed her skirt with his foot, his glance fell repeatedly on her full mouth. Amy trembled, like a butterfly poised on a leaf. Her hands were restless, as if they resisted with great difficulty an urge to touch the man at her side. Her usually sallow complexion was tinged with a pink glow, and her eyes were bright with excitement as a smile hovered again and again on her lips.

Mr Cavendish was a prize, conceded Elizabeth. More dashing close to even than she had thought him yesterday. His build was strong and tall. His face was humorous, with dark, very striking eyes. Elizabeth's pleasure at Amy's happiness was tinged with envy as she observed the intimacy with which she and Mr Cavendish looked at one another.

'When is the wedding to be?' she said.

'In three weeks' time. They won't spare me from the station for longer,' replied Mr Cavendish.

'Oh, so soon?' Elizabeth could not hide her regret.

'I shall write,' said Amy. 'And you must write too, and come and visit us, you and Mr Pengelly – when you can spare the time from the store.'

'Amy has told me what a good friend you have been to her, since you came to live at Yooma, Mrs Pengelly,' said Mr Cavendish.

'Indeed,' laughed Amy. 'I couldn't have kept my sanity without Elizabeth. Though Mr and Mrs Symonds have been extremely kind,' she added with a hasty attention to duty.

Agnes was clamouring to be set down, and Lucy took her, protesting, from Elizabeth's knee, to show the child off to her mother indoors. Bella announced that she would order an extra two settings for tea.

'I shall not stay so long,' protested Elizabeth. 'Mr Pengelly will be returning from Sydney today. I have asked Patrick to fetch me in the dog-cart when he arrives.'

She felt embarrassed to stay here and witness Amy's unashamed exhilaration. Yet the thought of seeing Arthur filled her with discontent. She remained in their company for a further hour, asked politely about Amy's new home, the climate, and the beauty spots around the land which Mr Cavendish farmed, and said that, yes, of course she and Arthur would be present at the wedding.

The afternoon unsettled her more than she had expected. She felt restless on the drive home with Patrick. Agnes, worn out by the Symonds's combined attentions, slept on her lap. Elizabeth stroked her hair, and dried the thumb which had slipped from the baby's mouth and rested against her flushed cheek. The sight of Agnes sleeping moved her, as it always did. The still beauty of the child's face made her want to weep.

She looked away and watched the dark trees passing; night would soon fall. She and Patrick did not speak. Elizabeth told herself that she felt sad because she would soon be losing a friend. But, as she remembered the way Amy and the man from Queensland had looked at one another, a surge of sexual jealousy caught her unawares. She ached for romance, for the arms of a lover round her and for that stirring of passion which she had experienced only briefly in her life. She stared fixedly ahead of her. It was her birthday, she remembered. The warmth of Patrick's arm, which brushed hers now and then as he drove, reminded her of how much loneliness had become a habit. She closed her eyes, so that Patrick would think that she was dozing and not know that the accidental touch of a callow boy of seventeen stirred unacceptable longings in her.

Leila came to meet her and took Agnes from her arms. Her face was flushed, as if she had not expected the dog-cart to return when it did. Arthur came out from the house and a wild thought occurred to Elizabeth. Could Arthur be having a love-affair with Leila? She dismissed the idea as ridiculous, a product of her strange mood on the way home from the Symonds.

'Did you have a good journey?' she said to Arthur, as one might to a stranger.

He nodded. 'Tolerable.' Unexpectedly he took her hand. 'Come –'

'Where are we going?'

'It's your birthday. I've something to show you.'

She let him lead her, like a reluctant child, round the side of the house.

Moths and insects danced around the oil lamp on the veranda. A black retriever puppy stumbled on large paws from its box and wagged its tail at their approach. Her dislike of dogs was tempered by a sentimental attraction to the creature, for it was very pretty, no one could dislike so small and helpless a thing.

Elizabeth picked up the animal and felt its heart beating quickly under her hand.

'This is for me?'

Arthur seemed uneasy and looked away. 'I thought the animal might be extra company.'

She was tempted to say, But you know I don't care for dogs. Instead, she held the puppy against her and fondled the velvet flap of one ear. 'He's beautiful. I shall call him –' She sought for something suitable, remembering Merlin. 'We'll call him *Camelot*.'

Arthur nodded, and seemed pleased.

He left her then, to talk to Patrick. He seemed to avoid her until supper. He was very quiet while they ate. Neither of them mentioned the puppy again, or the fact that it was her birthday.

'Amy has made a very sensible choice of husband,' she volunteered. 'She and Mr Cavendish are to be married in three weeks.'

'You'll miss her,' he said without looking at her.

'I shall look forward to the wedding with mixed feelings,' she admitted. 'We're invited, of course. And Amy says we must visit them in Queensland.'

He looked up then briefly. He seemed to be going to say something, but returned quickly to his former silence.

'Shall we be able to go, do you think?'

'I really can't say, Elizabeth,' he said irritably.

She could not account for his sudden change of humour. 'It would please me very much to think that we might see her again. Riley could manage the store for a few weeks. Perhaps Alice McCreery –'

Arthur scraped back his chair and stood up. Elizabeth was startled by the look of anguish on his face. 'I'm not hungry. You must excuse me, Lizzie.' He turned from her and left the room.

Elizabeth continued eating slowly, trying to puzzle out the reason for his behaviour. She thought about the puppy, Amy's marriage, her request to go to Queensland, but she could find nothing significant in any of it to explain his mood.

She told Riley that she was going to bed early. Would someone tell Mr Pengelly, when he returned, that she had already retired? She walked along the veranda to her bedroom and lit the lamp. She drew the curtains across the window and sat down at her dressing mirror.

Her face was shadowed in the glass. She rested her chin in her hands and let her shoulders sag. Edward had married a French woman, according to Hannah's last letter. He was happily married and a hero of the Crimea. Then why did she still think of him? She stared at her reflection, as if at a stranger, remembered the Lady of Shalott. *'The mirror cracked from side to side.'* She mouthed the words, whispered them, almost believing the curse in the poem.

After a while she opened her dressing table drawer and took out the Tennyson poems. She began reading, pausing at the point where Lancelot rode down to Camelot . . .

> *From the bank and from the river*
> *He flash'd into the crystal mirror,*
> *'Tirra lirra,' by the river*
> > *Sang Sir Lancelot.*

She heard a tap at the door. She replaced the book in the dressing table and went to open it.

'May I come in?'

She stepped aside. 'Of course. I've never shut you out from my room.' She did not add, nor from my bed – but Arthur's glance flew to the counterpane as if she had spoken the words out loud.

Arthur stood in the centre of the carpet, troubled and awkward, his arms by his sides.

'Anyone would think we were strangers,' Elizabeth said.

He smiled grimly.

'Arthur, don't you think this estrangement has gone on for long enough? If we're going to get along with one another for years to come – You might at least sit down,' she said impatiently.

'I'd sooner not talk that way. Not of years to come.'

'I just think that, after six months of this – living like strangers, sleeping apart – isn't it time to try to make things right?'

He did not answer.

'Today I am thirty-four, Arthur. You are forty-five. Do you mean to keep this up for the rest of our lives?'

He sat down heavily on the bed. 'No,' he said. 'I can't.'

She left the dressing table, she crossed the room and hesitated before sitting beside him on the bed. She could smell the brandy on his breath. 'Thank you for the puppy,' she said.

'I meant it, when I said it was meant to keep you company.'

'But I'd rather have your company.' She reached out her hand and let it rest tentatively on his arm. He did not move away. She returned her hand to her lap. 'When I saw Amy and Mr Cavendish today I thought how happy they were. I wished that we could be as happy.'

'You were thinking of him,' Arthur said darkly.

'No, I don't think of Edward still.' His name sounded strange spoken aloud after all this time. 'He's married. He's forgotten about me, and all that is in the past. If only you could put it behind us as well –'

He gripped her wrist. 'I can't, because of your bastard child.'

'Arthur –'

'It's true. Every time I look at little Agnes, it reminds me.'

'But you love Agnes. You couldn't have been a better father to her.'

He looked at her ironically. 'I love her. But that doesn't make any difference when I think of him, and when I know that you still want him.'

'When you thought Edward was dead –'

'When I thought he was dead, it got so as I could bear it. I told myself that you'd forget him, that perhaps there was a chance for us. But when that letter came, and I saw your face when they said he'd turned up again. That was a cruel blow for a man to take.'

He was still gripping her. He saw that his hold was very tight and relaxed it a little.

'I don't know what to do,' she said.

'You can't do anything. It's how things are.'

They were silent. She could feel his hand on her wrist, his thumb joint rested against her leg. He moved it, then moved his thumb again more deliberately, pressing into her thigh. A tremor of sexual excitement ran through her. Again he stroked her wrist and thigh. He laid his other hand on her leg.

'We could try,' she said and closed her eyes as his fingers dug into the fold of her skirt between her legs.

She heard his voice, as if from a long way off, as he laid his head against

245

her breast. 'I want you so badly, Elizabeth. I want you all the time.'

'Then why don't you ever come to my room?'

She moaned as she felt his hands move under her skirt.

'I can't bear it any more,' he sobbed. He buried his face against the skin inside her thigh. He struggled with the fastening of his trousers. Elizabeth fell back on the bed, her eyes closed, her body tense and anticipating the moment of penetration.

He came to her, and she wrapped her legs about him with a greed born of months of frustration. They thrust and clawed at one another, until the urgency of their need was spent. Arthur lay heavily upon her. To her horror he began to weep.

'No. No,' she protested, holding his head against her.

Ashamed, he rolled away.

She waited. She heard him get up from the bed and pick up and put on his trousers. He sat down again on the end of the bed and she pulled her skirts back over her knees. There was no trace of his earlier emotion as he looked at her.

'I'm leaving early in the morning. I'm going to try again at the diggings.'

'But, why?' She sat up, feeling sick with alarm. 'You said yourself once, digging for gold is a fool's game. And the shop is just beginning to pay well.'

'It's not that. I've got to get away. Got to think things out for a while.'

'How will you manage?' She felt an irrational anxiety for him.

'I've not just thought of this, Elizabeth.' He stroked her naked foot with a sudden tenderness. 'I've been planning it for weeks.'

Elizabeth saw then that he was serious, even that he was right that they should part. She thought of the empty space in the darkness beside her, not just in the past months, but for the next months, and the next, perhaps for ever.

'How long will you be gone?' she said, afraid of what he might say.

'Six months? Perhaps a year.'

'You won't see Agnes.'

He stood up and they looked at one another. His body sagged with exhaustion, he looked depressed. But she knew that she would not try to dissuade him any more from going.

She pulled back the counterpane. 'Come to bed, Arthur. Please. Just for tonight. I need you to share my bed.'

31

He would not come back, and she would be alone except for Agnes. Memories of England and Tennyson's poems would console her over the years. The future spread before her on vast and billowing waves into an uncertain emptiness, until, in the first grey hours of daylight, she fell asleep.

She did not stir when she heard Arthur go. He did not say goodbye. When she woke again it was almost nine o'clock. She could hear Leila playing with Agnes on the veranda.

She did not know whether Leila and the servants knew why Arthur had gone, or for how long. She did not care. Her head ached, and her eyes felt sore. She called out to Leila, who came in carrying the baby. Leila avoided looking at her.

'Mr Pengelly has gone away for a while,' Elizabeth said. 'I hope the routine will not alter very much in his absence.'

'No, madam.' Was there a hint of mockery in the girl's reply?

'You can leave Agnes with me for an hour.' Elizabeth felt a need to hold her child. She remembered the store. 'Can Riley manage?'

'We've not had more than the usual customers this morning,' Leila said. Agnes held out her arms and struggled to be set down on the bed. 'She's a bit naughty this morning. I expect she knows her papa is gone.' This time Elizabeth knew she had not imagined the derisive note in her words.

'We shall all have to get used to it.' Elizabeth looked at the nursemaid sharply, searching for something which would tell her whether she had been right to suspect Arthur and the girl.

Leila stared back at her impassively. 'Yes, madam.'

'Thank you. You may go.'

Agnes was pulling the counterpane over her head, demanding to play peep-bo. She whined when Elizabeth did not respond, and clung to her neck, banging her head against her shoulder.

Elizabeth sat her on the pillow and let her handle a glass paper-weight, a crystal hemisphere which encased bright flowers.

She did not know whether she could bring up Agnes alone. She did not know if she could run the store, even with Riley's help. She did not know if she could live alone, without a friend.

She got out of bed and washed and dressed, letting Agnes explore her favourite toy, a hatbox from under the bed. They played at hiding behind a straw bonnet, at pat-a-cake, and making animal noises, but Elizabeth's heart was not in the games. She sat down with the child on her lap at the dressing table, and they looked at one another in the mirror.

'Can we do it, Aggie?' she said. 'Are we independent women?'

The child nodded solemnly at her reflection.

Elizabeth took a picture book from her dressing table drawer and let the baby handle the pages, turning to each illustration in turn, a horse, a cow, a dog, while Agnes shouted the appropriate noises. The child's attention wandered to the drawer beside her, she pulled at a green leather-bound book, fascinated by the gold lettering on its cover.

'A present,' Elizabeth said softly. 'From your father to your mama.' She let the child pull the book from the drawer. They turned the pages together. Agnes grew quiet, copying her mother's reverence.

Elizabeth returned the book to the drawer and closed it.

'Gone,' said Agnes, looking at her in the mirror.

'Long since gone, my darling.'

Riley and Patrick were disturbed by Arthur's departure. Clearly they regarded Elizabeth as a wronged woman. Riley, over-solicitous, ran to shift sacks of grain, or bales of cloth for her, saying, 'I'll attend to that, Mrs Pengelly,' and 'Don't you move a finger, Mrs Pengelly,' every time she attempted to do anything; until, exasperated, she sent him outside to saw logs with Patrick.

Alone in the shop she leaned on the polished counter and surveyed the well-stocked shelves, the boxes of tea and tobacco, bales of cloth, reels of ribbon and threads, soap, china, and baskets strung from the ceiling, alongside aprons and petticoats, boots and tin kettles and bonnets.

All her doing, she told herself. For Arthur had done the buying and the fetching and carrying, but he had left the accounts and the arrangement of the shop more and more to her during the past months.

She would have to drive to Sydney to the warehouses. She would face that when she came to it. Really, very little had changed. A feeling of freedom came over her. It was as if a weight, which she had feared to let go, was being gently lifted from her.

She heard the lunchtime coach which passed through Yooma arrive. Lucy and Bella Symonds entered the shop. They were followed closely by Amy. Word had travelled fast, thought Elizabeth, as she saw the eager look with which Bella and Lucy scrutinized her. She lifted her chin a fraction higher.

'Mrs Pengelly,' said Bella. 'We have persuaded Miss McPherson to choose her wedding outfit.'

Lucy was unable to hold back her curiosity any longer. 'We heard that Mr Pengelly has gone to Victoria. I said to Bella, "It can't be true. Mr Pengelly wouldn't leave his wife and little girl for the temptations of the goldfields."'

'Well, he has,' said Elizabeth, lifting down a pattern book from the shelf.

'When I live in Queensland, I shall expect to spend long spells on my own, when Mr Cavendish is away on business,' said Amy loyally.

'Gold-digging is hardly business,' insisted Lucy, leafing through the swatches of fabric.

'Call it a late hankering after adventure,' said Elizabeth lightly. 'You know how some men hate to settle down.'

'And you don't mind?' said Bella.

'Not at all.' Elizabeth managed to smile.

Bella looked at her from under her brows, and Elizabeth knew she had not put an end to the gossip. The true version of it would already be all over Yooma. Arthur Pengelly had gone and left his wife and child.

They chose a number of fabrics, and Elizabeth made out an order to be collected from Sydney. The women prepared to leave.

'Do you have to go now?' said Elizabeth, drawing Amy aside. 'If you stay for lunch, Patrick will drive you home in the trap.' Amy looked surprised. 'Please. If ever I needed a friend to confide in, it is now.'

'What has happened?' said Amy, as they ate lunch on the veranda. 'Has Arthur really left you?'

Elizabeth nodded.

'But why? I've told Mr Cavendish how wonderfully you work together.'

'It's all rather shocking.' Elizabeth looked into Amy's untroubled face, and knew that she was going to tell her everything, the desire to confess was stronger than it had ever been. She smiled. 'You are just setting out on marriage. And mine is already over.'

'He'll come back. You said yourself. It's a sort of wanderlust.'

Elizabeth shook her head. 'Would it upset you if you learned that Agnes was not Arthur's child?' She watched Amy's expression grow rigid with alarm.

'I can see it would upset Arthur,' Amy said quietly.

'He has tried to forgive me. He tried very hard.'

Elizabeth told her the whole story, beginning with the summer of the barleyfield, and ending with the letter which had brought the news that Edward was still alive.

'I never guessed,' said Amy when she had finished.

'Why should you?'

'Because I'm your friend. I feel somehow as if I have failed you.'

'It asks a lot of a friendship, to share such a guilty secret.'

'Not so much as it asks of a marriage. Poor Arthur.'

Elizabeth felt a vague irritation that Amy should have begun to see Arthur in a sympathetic, perhaps even a rather noble light. She wanted to justify herself, to explain how it had been after her marriage, the disappointments and frustrations and the knowledge that she had made a wrong decision.

'Was he very handsome?' said Amy.

Elizabeth was startled. It was somehow distasteful, to discuss Edward as if she had been attracted by the glamour of a lover. She tried to explain how impossible it had been to marry him, the age difference, the way he had betrayed her, but she saw from the puzzlement in Amy's eyes that she could not understand. A man and a woman fell in love and married. What difference did it make, if the man abandoned the woman for one month, three months, a year even before the wedding, as Mr Cavendish had done by going to Queensland? True love could overcome such separations.

Elizabeth said that Edward had been handsome, that she had loved him and had been too proud to marry him after he had broken their unspoken commitment to one another.

Why? said the look in Amy's eyes. Why, if you really loved him?

Pride had not stopped Elizabeth from marrying Arthur to escape spinsterhood. Pride had not prevented her from coming with him to Australia. Could it be that she had never really loved Edward at all? She shrank from such a conclusion.

She sat for a long time after Amy had gone. She could hear the laugh of a kookaburra, from far away, the sound of the river running over the rocks in the valley and somewhere in the distance came the shouts of children from the village playing by the water.

She tried to decide how she would feel if she never saw Arthur again. She wondered if there was no capacity for deep emotion in her. Her Aunt Lydia had called her a romantic and she had denied it. Romantics were cowards, afraid to commit themselves to reality. Romantic passion had nothing to do with love.

Elizabeth remembered the look in Amy's eyes. She saw how her story must have seemed – a summer flirtation, a lapse of propriety in the heat of a barleyfield and a sordid hour of infidelity which had resulted in an illegitimate child.

She could hear laughter at the other side of the house: Agnes had returned from a walk with Leila. Across the yard, Riley shouted to Patrick. The puppy clambered up the veranda steps and came towards her. She scooped it on to her lap and fondled its ears. 'I love Agnes,' she told the puppy. She looked across the garden to the animal pens, the vines growing on wires, the paddock and the outbuildings. 'And all this is mine, Camelot. From now on I'm answerable to no one.'

Amy's wedding had begun as a modest affair, but the whole of Yooma turned out to cheer her as she and Mr Cavendish drove away.

Elizabeth stood with the farmers' and sawyers' wives to wave goodbye, preferring the company of Alice McCreery, with her children all round her skirts, to that of Bella and Lucy Symonds, who dabbed at their eyes with handkerchiefs, criticized the fit of Amy's going-away frock and hat and complained that they did not know how they would exist without her.

'We shall miss that one,' said Alice. 'We need more of her sort round here.'

'She has been a very good friend to me.' Elizabeth watched the carriage rapidly merge with the dust cloud which followed it. She let her hand drop to her side.

Alice put her head on one side, as if appraising Elizabeth for the first time. 'Amy McPherson was set on opening a school in Yooma one time. Seems a pity no one else has the same idea. Didn't you say once you'd been a school ma'am?'

Elizabeth looked at her sharply. 'But there's the store – and Agnes.'

'Strikes me Riley can run that store a lot of the time,' Alice said, picking up her youngest child and wiping his nose on the corner of her skirt. She shifted his weight to her hip. 'And what do you pay that nursemaid for if she can't keep an eye on a child a few hours a day?'

'You just want me to take your own brood off your hands, Alice,' laughed Elizabeth.

'Sure. And there's plenty in Yooma would thank you for doing it besides me.'

Elizabeth was thoughtful. The idea excited her. But it was imposs- ible.

'Maybe, when Mr Pengelly gets home, you'll have more time to think of it,' said Alice.

'*If* he comes home.'

'That's true. If I let my old man off to the diggings, you'd never see him again. But yours is different. He'll be back. I knew his heart was in the right place when you had your little Aggie.'

The crowd was breaking up. Elizabeth watched the children run whooping and shouting among the trees.

That evening the idea of a school would not leave her alone. There was a seductive nostalgia about recalling her days in the schoolroom in Charlford. She wondered whether her old pupils had forgotten her. Johnny Herbert would have grown tall and left the school, would be working on the land alongside his brothers – and all of them able to read. The children here were illiterate, unless they had parents with the energy or money to educate them at home.

She could set up one of the rooms in the house as a schoolroom. She would drive to Sydney, and order books and benches. Her head

252

was full of suppressed excitement and an urgency to begin straight away. She sat by the bureau in the sitting room, took out pen and paper, and began planning.

The next day she pinned up notices in the shop. The first advertised for an assistant. The second announced the opening of classes at Pengelly's in writing, arithmetic and hygiene at a penny a week and commencing in a month's time.

Elizabeth's school opened on a warm, green morning in October. Thirty-seven children came in a gang from Yooma. They raced through the trees and pulled up outside the back of the store, laughing and jostling one another. They fell silent as Elizabeth came out on to the veranda to meet them. The younger ones were over-awed, the older children waited, remembering the times her old man had given them a clip round the ear. Some had been heard to boast that they were not going to take orders from Pengelly's missis, especially now her old man was too far away to give them a beating. Elizabeth met their defiance with a steady gaze. She leaned her hands on the veranda rail.

'Do you call this ready for school?' she said quietly. 'No one comes into my schoolroom like they're off on a bush picnic. Get yourselves into lines, the smallest at the front. You older children, show them what to do.'

The pause was brief, before they shuffled themselves into some sort of order. Elizabeth waited without moving. Then she smiled. 'Now, we can begin.'

Within a few days a routine had been established. The children were marched to school at eight-thirty every weekday morning, led by the eldest McCreery girl, appointed as head monitor. They sat, as if at a church service, in Elizabeth's dining room, converted to a schoolroom. They went through their lessons. And at twelve-thirty they burst out again into the bush.

After a month Elizabeth had lost only two children to their old ways. The school had become as much part of Yooma as the store had before it.

Pengelly's was fast becoming known to the locals by its nickname of 'Lizzie's Place'. Elizabeth herself was viewed with a respect, which was as much to do with the affection people felt for her as sympathy for a woman who was tackling bush-living on her own. She was a 'good

253

sort', an ear for one's troubles over the counter, and no one doubted that she had worked a miracle on their children.

Elizabeth was aware in herself of a growing dignity. She took a pride in being formidable, even austere. The children were not afraid of her, but they were a little in awe. She enjoyed the natural way in which people accepted her as an independent woman. She told herself that her new life fitted her like a glove.

But there were the times when she was afraid: when a large brown snake slithered through the parched grass of the paddock one day that summer, making Camelot snap and bark and race around in a frenzy of fear, and Riley and Patrick came running at Elizabeth's shout. It was the first time she had seen a snake, except for the grass snakes in England. She scooped up Agnes from the ground and held her to her, rooted with terror as they watched the creature glide away into the bush. By the time Riley reached them it had gone.

And then there were the bushrangers. Rumours were always in the air that bad men had been seen on the road. Elizabeth was taking no chances. She kept a shotgun on the wall of the store-room, out of reach of Agnes, and practised shooting tin cans off the fence posts from time to time with a hat pulled down low to shade her eyes from the searing glare of the sun. And though no one came to the store with any more evil intentions than to hint, with a half-ashamed leer, at the hot and lonely nights, now that she was on her own she was glad that Riley and Patrick were there, and felt safer knowing that she was within reach of the gun.

Agnes was learning to talk. She surprised Elizabeth one day when she looked up from digging in the dry earth with a spoon and said, 'Where Papa gone?'

Elizabeth had not mentioned Arthur to her for several months, and Agnes seemed to have accepted his absence, or to have forgotten him.

She challenged Leila with the incident. 'Have you been talking to Agnes about her father?'

'Her father, Mrs Pengelly?' said Leila with a puzzled frown, and there was a strange, almost imperceptible emphasis in her words.

'Have you spoken of Mr Pengelly to her recently?'

'It's important that the child remembers him,' Leila said.

254

Elizabeth felt an irrational fury. 'How dare you tell me what's important?'

'But when Mr Pengelly comes back –'

'Agnes's father may never come back.'

'But when *Mr Pengelly* comes back.' There was an ambiguous smile on the girl's lips, and again that peculiar emphasis. Elizabeth felt a slow dread creep upon her. Leila could not know – how could she know the truth about Agnes's father?

She hesitated. 'I would rather you didn't mention Mr Pengelly again to her, unless I ask you to.' She knew she had lost the confrontation. She sent Leila away, but for the rest of the day she felt uneasy.

In the way that coincidences seemed to link haphazard events together, persuading Elizabeth that life was really ordered by fate, a letter came the next day from England.

Hannah was reticent at first about the fact that Elizabeth was living alone. She wrote about her mother's increasing eccentricities, her third child, 'yet another boy – how I envy you, Lizzie, having a little girl.' She said that she had been to London with Fred.

. . . And who do you think I bumped into, Lizzie, but Edward Munro? Much altered, of course, since his time in the Crimea, and, to my mind and Fred's, worn down by his charity work in the East End. He has a premises near the river, which he calls the Fitzroy Infirmary, though it is really no more than a few rooms in an old warehouse. I believe the place has the sponsorship of several respected medical dignitaries, etc., but Fred regrets that the charity has no religious foundation; and, for myself, I cannot help but feel disappointed in Edward, having felt sure that he was destined for a more illustrious career. Our Aunt Lydia has become quite a philanthropist, and works admirably for the relief of the poor who attend the infirmary. You would not recognize her, Lizzie. She is a *reformed* character. She hasn't a good word to say for you, yet, I think she would appreciate a letter, which would do much to sweeten her memories of when we were all so much younger. We all have done things we regret, Lizzie. Edward too, I think. But, there, I must not go irritating old sores. And perhaps, by now, Mr Pengelly has returned to you, loaded with gold from the goldfields. I do hope so, Lizzie. As much as I hope one day to see you, my dear, again.

Ever your affectionate sister . . .

255

Elizabeth put the letter in her drawer with all her treasures. The book of Tennyson's poems lay near the bottom, untouched for many weeks. She hesitated as she sat by the open drawer, put out a hand, as if to take up the book, then changed her mind and closed the drawer. She brushed her hair briskly, without looking herself in the eye in the mirror. She buttoned up her nightdress, put out the lamp, and climbed into the high oak bed.

The mattress seemed vast and empty, the pillows too wide, the sheets cold round her body. She stared into the darkness at the invisible ceiling and listened to the night sounds. She thought of Amy, who wrote regularly with news of life in Queensland, unashamedly sentimental about Mr Cavendish's skills as a farmer, relishing the hard and boisterous life on a sheep station, happy. Happy, thought Elizabeth. The word seemed alien, as she lay on her own in the darkness. For the first time since Arthur had left, she acknowledged that she was lonely.

32

Edward had finished at the surgery, the line of patients had thinned to a handful and then vanished, as the lights of the public houses further down the street beckoned in the darkness. Some of them would return in the morning, when the deadening effect of alcohol wore off.

He went into the outer waiting room, to open the windows wide and let the cold air rinse away the smell of sick bodies. He stood in the doorway. Out in the street yellow fog drifted under the street lamps, the sounds of traffic came drifting up from beyond the murky outlines of the buildings. It was always foggy here, so near the river. Perhaps at some stage they would be able to move, but right now it was as much as he could do to keep up with the work of the dispensary, the permanent patients, and his studies at the college, without planning for the future. A weariness swept over him and his head felt light with exhaustion. He turned to see Marianne come through the waiting room from the hospital annexe. She was dressed in a grey frock and white cap and pinafore, the uniform worn by the three women who shared the nursing in the ward. She linked her arm through his and leaned against the doorpost, her cheek pressed against his arm.

'Charles is waiting to see you.'

'In a moment.'

He had met Charles again almost a year ago. Edward had been returning with a group of ex-soldiers from the House of Commons, where he had gone to parade their destitution before an indifferent audience of members of parliament. Charles's rough beard and uniform had gone. He wore a well-cut surtout and silk hat, but the huge shoulders and red hair had been unmistakable.

257

'Charles Watkins! Charles – you old devil,' he had exclaimed, and his friend had greeted him in a noisy embrace.

Edward told him about the Fitzroy Infirmary, had expected no more than a polite interest after Charles had revealed that he had quit the Army and bought himself into a successful practice. But the next day Charles had turned up at the evening surgery and announced that he was ready for duty. Since then he had devoted several hours a week to work at the infirmary. And he had brought Edward's project to the charitable attention of some of his wealthier clientele. 'Make 'em pay up,' had become his motto.

'Charles says the corporal is fading,' said Marianne.

Edward pulled himself to with difficulty. He had almost fallen asleep against the doorpost. He thought of the soldier, Lynch, who was dying slowly from a lung wound which he had received more than two and a half years ago and which had generated a progressive and painful disease. How many people thought of the Crimea now, except those who had been there? And if they did consider Alma, Sebastopol, Balaclava, it was in the reflective glow of a war which had been won. The rest was better swept under the carpet.

He went with Marianne into a room lined on either side with beds which stood out from the walls. A fire burned at each end of the ward, the flames tinting the whitewashed walls and ceiling pink. A nurse, feeding a man from a cup, looked up and smiled and the patient raised a feeble hand to Edward as he passed with Marianne. There were murmurs of greeting from other occupants of the twenty or thirty beds, but most were too ill to bother. Each patient was there because of infection, or a secondary complaint from long-ago sustained injuries. It was no secret that they had gone there to die.

The soldier in the end bed was quiet. He no longer disrupted the ward, as he had done earlier with the violence of his coughing and loud groans. Charles Watkins sat on a stool with the man's hand held in his own, waiting with each low moaning breath for the final death rattle. It came as Edward reached the bed.

Marianne closed the man's eyelids and drew the sheet up over the face on the pillow. Edward looked down at the contours of the man's forehead and nose, forming peaks under the white cover, like an object buried under a layer of snow. The ugliness of the corporal's death was transformed by the sheet into something clean and impersonal.

He turned away. The death would mean a delay of an hour –

arranging for an undertaker to remove the body, searching out the soldier's next-of-kin – which would mean an hour's less sleep after his study that night.

'You look near enough to a corpse yourself these days,' said Charles when the business was over.

Edward closed the Admissions and Discharge book and took his coat from the stand in the surgery. 'Blame an unwholesome fear of failure in the examinations,' Edward said.

'He works too hard,' said Marianne.

'We all work too hard.' Edward linked his arm round her waist.

'If you would take on another doctor –' suggested Charles. 'Get the Board of Guardians to appoint another man.'

'Oh, they'd agree to it.'

'Well, then?'

'It is sensible,' said Marianne anxiously.

'The expense, Charles. Another salary.'

'The charity can support another man. You know that.'

Edward hesitated, steering Marianne towards the door. 'I'll think it over,' he promised, and went out into the street.

Outside the fog was growing thicker. A street lamp lit the corner of the building dimly. As they moved under its light a figure lurched out of the darkness ahead and veered sharply towards them. Edward put an arm about Marianne's shoulders, then withdrew it as the stranger passed them and they continued along the street. Marianne did not speak, she would not nag him about another doctor, but he knew what she was thinking. He knew that she was right. His time in the Crimea had weakened him, he was stretched to his limit by the physical and mental work he was doing, and this year, his last at the college, it was essential that he passed his exams. The Board of Guardians would not support his continuing leadership of the infirmary if he did not get his MRCS.

Edward was reluctant though to admit another medical man. The arrival of Charles, better qualified and older than he was, had caused rumblings on the charity Board about appointing a more senior man. He feared that the project would be taken out of his hands, that at the very least his influence would be weakened. Even the name, dedicated to Fitzroy, irritated him. What did Mad Fritz know about the Crimea and the way that men had suffered?

It was a short walk home. For a while now they had rented a shabby

259

but comfortable villa, close to both the college and the infirmary. Edward unlocked the front door. The familiar smell of closed rooms met them, slightly damp, hinting at fungus secretly growing in the dark below old floorboards.

Marianne shivered. 'Bring your books into the kitchen while I cook the supper. It will be warmer.'

Edward spread his books and papers on the kitchen table, while Marianne set a match to the fire laid that morning and moved quietly about the kitchen. Frequent miscarriages had produced a sluggishness in her movements. Her face had settled into lines of resignation, her once golden hair rarely looked like a halo these days, but was a dull frizz, scraped back into a knot behind her head.

The sound of her was soothing, as she fetched plates, chopped vegetables and shifted pans on the stove. She merged into the background, and Edward was soon immersed in his reading. The heat from the fire crept through the room. The smell of cooking was pleasant. It was not until Edward felt Marianne's hand on his shoulder, heard her calling his name, and felt the hard edge of the book against his cheekbone, that he was aware that he had fallen asleep.

'You do too much.' Her voice was unexpectedly harsh. She cleared a space among his papers and set down a plate of vegetables. 'What will happen to me if you kill yourself?' She sat down opposite him. Her eyes were red, as if she had been crying. She began to eat, then let fall the knife and fork and stared stupidly at her plate, the effort of lifting pieces of potato and onion to her mouth too much for her.

'Marianne–' He was all concern. He saw how selfish he had been not to realize that she too was near to breaking. 'We'll ask for another doctor,' he promised, anxious to reassure her.

'I'm pregnant again,' she said, looking at him with tragic eyes. 'I think I shall go mad if I don't keep this one.'

Edward made an application to the Board and by the spring they had appointed another assistant. Samuels had served as an army surgeon for some years before opting for civilian medicine. He was unobtrusive and dour. Edward no longer saw an extra hand as a threat.

The months passed with increasing anxiety as Marianne's pregnancy progressed without mishap. Edward insisted that she spend less and less time at the infirmary. He threw himself with more vigour into his studies, determined that for her sake he would do well in his finals. They would move away from the drab house by the river. He would get himself a well-paying practice when he qualified and devote half his time to earning a living which would keep a wife and child in comfort.

In the summer he sat and passed the first part of his final exams. They celebrated, drunk with promises for the future.

'No more studying,' laughed Marianne. 'No more propping your eyes open until two o'clock in the morning.'

'A house which doesn't smell of the river. A practice in a swell part of town.' Edward pulled her on to his lap. She wound her arms round his neck and kissed him.

Edward held her away from him a little. He reached a hand to the back of her head and pulled out the pins which fastened her hair. It fell in a cloud to her shoulders, he drew it forward, round her cheeks. 'A family,' he said softly, placing a hand on the hard curve of her belly.

She kissed him again. 'I shall get you some beer.' She struggled free as he pretended to trap her with his arms. She stood up, looking down at him, a light in her shadowed eyes. Her red-veined cheeks were lifted in a smile; for a moment, in the candlelight of the kitchen and with her pale hair floating about her shoulders, she was beautiful. Then a flicker of pain crossed her face. It was brief, but it was intense.

'It is nothing,' she protested at his cry of alarm. 'I felt something earlier. It is nothing.' She turned away.

Edward jumped up to reach her as she caught at the edge of the table and she fell heavily against him.

'My God! Oh – Edward. No!' She pulled at her skirt, lifting it in disbelief to her knees, as she began to haemorrhage, dark gouts of blood splashing the white flesh of her legs. 'Perhaps it will be all right?' She looked up, her eyes pleading with him to say that nothing out of the ordinary was happening.

Edward, helping her to the door, then carrying her upstairs, felt a despair, a certainty of disaster. The blood soaked through her petticoat and her skirt into his shirt sleeve.

'I'm not going to lose the baby?' Her face was white, her hair dramatic against the pillow, like a painting in the light of the lamp. Edward looked down at her, unable to give her the promise she wanted, before he went to fetch towels and water.

The hours which followed were the hardest of Edward's life. He had attended childbirths before, some easy, a little blood, a few hours or so of struggled labour, many like this one, wrung with pain and sweat and pleas for mercy and deliverance from the torment. Childbirth was a natural function he had learned. The task of the *accoucheur* was to let nature take its course. Women were built for suffering. He had learned to accept that a clinical detachment lay at the heart of being a good practitioner.

As he held the laudanum bottle and dripped it between Marianne's clenched teeth, as he bathed her forehead again and again and she writhed and turned from him, his control slipped, his hands began to shake.

'Marianne. Marianne, I love you.' He repeated the words as a contraction made her knees, drawn up on the bed, draw up further and turned her moan into a scream.

'Wait for the next contraction, then push.' He let the instructions pass with their own rhythm through his brain to calm himself as much as Marianne. But the contractions came and went and nothing happened, except that Marianne's cries grew more pitiful, her writhing more violent. And so it went on, the clock on the mantel shelf dragging out the minutes and hours, and Edward, driven to desperate means, slid his hand into his wife's body to locate and manipulate the wet-limbed, bony infant and finally to push and pull, his wrist caught in the vice of each contraction, and drag the baby from its mother.

Marianne lay with her face twisted from him, her arms flung out, her fingers still gripping the rail of the bed. The baby, when it came, was cold and blue and waxy.

Marianne lay still. She did not respond when he wrapped the dead child in a blanket and said, 'My love. I'm sorry,' except to move her head a little so that she would not see him take the bundle away.

Even afterwards, when she seemed to accept quietly that the child was dead, when she lay exhausted, the blood still seeping from her, Edward did not believe that she too would die.

The stillness of the room, the ticking of the clock and flickering lamp-light continued up to and beyond the point where her last breath slipped from her, lightly, too easily, as though death had cheated them and caught Marianne too by surprise. He sat, unable to accept that the person who had laughed and twined her arms round him and kissed him only hours before, no longer existed. The clock ticked on the mantel shelf, its tempo even, like the beating of a pulse, the rhythm of a heart. But only his heart continued its measured tread, unrelenting, pouring scorn on his thin protest that he could not go on living without Marianne.

The sympathy was hard to bear. He did not want their solemn looks, their condolences and expressions of pity. He felt bitter towards Charles, who stood with his wife by his side and wept with genuine grief over Marianne's grave, and towards Samuels, who laid a hand of commiseration on his shoulder and murmured the very phrases which he himself had often used when comforting the bereaved relatives of men who had passed through the infirmary. Fitzroy stood, gruff and silent, with his thin-faced wife. Even Clara was there, sympathetic, but detached, married to a city financier now and content it seemed with her catch. Lydia Delahaye was surrounded by a sea of ladies, black-veiled, wallowing in their tears. He did not want tears, or his brother Robert's false piety, or Mabel with her inappropriate hopes for the future.

They would return to their homes after the funeral, cast off their mourning with relief, talk pityingly of 'poor Edward' for a while, spare him a prayer before sleep, perhaps even shed another tear. But the next day they would begin to accustom themselves to the idea of Munro as a widower. Death was commonplace.

Hardest of all to bear was the thought of the years which had been denied them, in which his and Marianne's love might have gone on growing in strength. He was left with guilt for the years which they had wasted, eaten up by old memories, when Marianne had given all her love, and he not enough in return.

He got into the habit of sleeping at the dispensary, rarely going home to the house which reminded him of Marianne. He could picture her coming to greet him when he opened the front door. He would sit for long hours when he was at home, in the semi-darkness of the kitchen, imagining how their life might have been if she and the child had lived. It had been a girl. They had buried her in the arms of her mother.

Edward immersed himself in work, deliberately taking on duties which he knew could have been assigned to Samuels, and brushing off Charles's offers to spend more time at the infirmary. He was possessive of his Crimean heroes, reluctant to admit casualties from any other source to the hospital, and turning away what he called the 'professionals', the old hands at a life of vagrancy, those who had begged and scrounged since being turned adrift after the Peninsular War.

He knew that people were beginning to say that he was a little mad. Morose, that fellow Munro. Still grieving for his dead wife as if she'd died only yesterday. Obsessed with the Crimea. People wanted to forget, didn't they? All right, so the Crimea had been a bit of a pig's ear, but nobody wanted it ramming down their throats three years after the event.

'You spend too much time alone,' Charles said. 'You must come and spend a weekend with us.'

'I will,' Edward promised. 'But I'm no company, Charles, these days. Ask me again in a month or two.'

Edward used the impartial smile which had become part of his defence armoury. He waited for Charles to put on his coat and hat, pick up his cane, and pause in the doorway. 'I can do tonight's surgery for you,' Charles said as usual.

'You've got a family waiting for you,' said Edward, again with the smile.

Charles shook his head. 'You're wasting yourself here, Edward.'

The words rankled more than usual. It was almost as if the rest of them saw the hospital in a different light. Didn't they think the work was important any more? Had Charles forgotten already the way men had suffered, just as their country had forgotten?

Edward concentrated more intently on the outpouring of troubles from the patients that evening, was more tolerant than usual of the inveterate scroungers, those who came only for the free hand-outs and the bottle of laudanum, 'To kill off bad memories, sir.' 'You're a saint, sir. Who else would remember us poor soldiers, who fought for Queen and country?'

At last surgery was over. He sat for a while, before going through into the waiting room to open the windows to the evening air and let out the stench of the room.

He rested his arms wearily on a pile of bills and papers on the desk. He stared at a painting on the wall, one of his few finished sketches from the Crimea, of four soldiers grouped about a battery near the

Redan. He was getting tired, he could no longer put a name to every face. He stood up and went over to the picture, critical of its execution. He remembered a sketch he had once attempted of Marianne, which she had made him throw away when they came to England.

He turned away from the picture and was startled to see the figure of a woman in the doorway. His mind, already dwelling on vague thoughts of the past, was prepared at first to accept the idea of the supernatural. There was something familiar in the woman's bird-like feaures. He frowned, trying to place her, then dismissed the fancy that he knew her as she hesitated and turned as if to run away.

'Don't be frightened,' he said.

'They told me you treats soldiers.'

'Soldiers of the Crimea. Yes. But not women. This isn't a general dispensary.'

'They said you'd treat my fella. No making us promise we'd go to church nor nothing? No devil-dodgers?'

'That's right.' He looked more closely at the woman, convinced now that he had met her before. 'I know you.' Edward remembered the coffee house, a room in St Giles, a man's forearm forced against his throat.

The woman shook her head, frightened. 'No, sir. I ain't never been here before.'

'I know you,' he repeated. 'You took my father's pocket watch. Though if your friend's a soldier he can't be the brute who half killed me and stole my coat.'

She began to edge towards the door. 'I don't know nothing about a watch.'

She had altered, had aged twenty years in less than six. Her hair was thick with dirt and hung in dark grey lumps from under her torn bonnet. Her cloak was in holes, her shoes open at the toes. By the door she seemed to gather fresh courage.

'If he stole your pocket watch – an' I'm not saying he did – that sod did a lot worse for me.'

It was then that Edward saw a scar, almost two inches long, which ran down the side of her jaw. Her hand flew to her face in an odd gesture of modesty.

'So, your new friend's a soldier?' he said.

The woman nodded. It was clear she did not recognize him. But why should she, among all the other men she had known more intimately, if as briefly, as himself? 'He don't beat me. Though there's times when I think I'd sooner die violent than starve.'

Edward prepared to follow her, packing his medicine bag with little more than morphine, for by what the woman told him as she waited, the man he was to visit was dying.

The basement room was as he expected – the seeping walls, the stink, and filth piled in the corners. The man lay on a mattress, shivering under a blanket stiff with dirt and urine and old semen.

Edward gave the man as much morphine as he judged necessary and promised to return the next day. He knew what he would find and wondered briefly how the woman would exist alone, but knew that she would survive.

The incident unsettled him. Superstition made him search for a reason for this resurrection of the past. It was as if a part of his life which he had thought cut off had risen to challenge him.

He walked back through the dark streets, questioning what he had achieved since those days. Had he altered any of the injustices of society? Who benefited from his charity work except a handful of ex-soldiers, his own conscience, and the consciences of the Board of Guardians – men who lived in comfort, visited the tidy ward of the infirmary twice a year, and convinced their friends that philanthropy was a Christian virtue to be adopted by all gentlemen in society?

Edward headed back to the infirmary, but was sickened suddenly by an image of the bleak camp bed in the surgery and the ward with its sad survivors of a paltry war. He turned aside into a street of shops and terraced houses, and made his way home.

The usual smell of damp mushrooms wafted down the hallway as he opened the door. A small pile of letters lay on the hall table, where the woman who came in to clean and do his washing had left them. He took them into the kitchen, lit the gas, and fetched a plate from the larder on which he placed the meat pie he had bought on his way home.

He considered lighting the stove, but the effort was too great for the small comfort of a kettle of tea. He sat at the scrubbed wooden table, munching the pie, still warm from the shop, and picked up each of the letters in turn.

There was a note from Lydia Delahaye, which he put on one side

266

to open later, a letter from Robert. The third letter had been sent to Hannah's address and redirected. He was curious at its foreignness, and saw that it had come from Australia. A leap of excitement and fear made his heart almost stop beating. His hands shook as he opened the pages and confirmed that they were from Elizabeth.

Ridiculously, his eyes swam with tears. He put the letter down, half rose from the table as if something or someone had called him away. Then, pulling himself together, he reached again to the table and began to read.

33

Elizabeth had resolved not to write at first, when she learned from Hannah that Edward's wife Marianne had died. To send the conventional condolences would have seemed strange and, in any case, by the time a letter reached England her sympathy would be out of place.

And so she did nothing. But the evidence of Edward's child confronted her daily. Agnes was already a sturdy three and a half. The guilt of concealing the truth from him, and the knowledge that Edward had lost a wife and child, gnawed at her. Edward should know that Agnes was his. Behind these thoughts, and harder to acknowledge, was a longing to get in touch with him again. Edward was alone, and it was more than two years since Arthur had gone to Victoria and Amy to Queensland.

Agnes attended the school classes each morning with the other children. Quick to learn, she had already begun to read. She sat at the front of the rows of benches, her face solemn with concentration in the heat, and Elizabeth would feel a wave of love go out to her.

Leila alone treated Elizabeth with a respect which bordered on sullenness. Her duties had dwindled to a few hours in the afternoons. Elizabeth was jealous of Agnes's company, was the first to see the child in the morning, ate all her meals with her, and put her to bed herself at night. The employment of a nursemaid had become an extravagance, yet, self-critical about her motives for wanting to be rid of Leila, Elizabeth could not bring herself to dismiss her.

One afternoon in November Leila asked if she might take Agnes down to the creek. The paddock was crisp and brown and shimmered in the heat; but under the trees it would be cooler, Leila said. Elizabeth, busy in the store, reluctantly agreed.

'Look for fish,' said Agnes, tugging at Leila's hand, as Elizabeth tied on her sunbonnet.

Leila yawned. 'Any fish with half a pinch of sense will lie low today.'

Elizabeth watched them go, shielding her eyes with her hand as she waited for the small figure, trotting beside Leila's swaying crinoline, to turn at the end of the paddock and wave.

She went into the store, wishing briefly that it was she, instead of Leila, who had gone with Agnes. They could have searched for fish together under the stones, lain on the bank and hoped to be quiet enough to see a possum or flying squirrel as they looked up into the high canopy of the eucalyptus trees and watched the bright flight of cockatoos and parakeets.

Elizabeth had been serving customers for an hour when Riley came into the store. He was carrying Agnes on his arm and his face was dark with fury.

'Patrick found her.' He set the child down. 'Come back on her own, if you please.' His voice shook. 'That female is a bundle of trouble. And if it was up to me she'd have had her marching orders long ago.'

'Thank you.' Elizabeth felt irritated by Riley's blustering. But she was angry too as she pictured Agnes returning home alone. Grown men had been known to lose themselves in the bush by wandering too far from the known pathways. It was the season too to be on the look-out for snakes and, though Agnes had been taught, like all children brought up in the bush, not to touch spiders and insects, there was always the fear that she might be bitten or stung. She turned to Agnes. 'Why didn't you wait for Leila? You know you're not to wander off on your own.' Fear made her sharp with the child and her voice was harsh.

Agnes, red with the expectation of retribution and an anxiety to justify herself protested, 'Leila says I can play by myself when she talks to Mr Roberts.'

'Mr Roberts?' Elizabeth looked for confirmation to Riley.

'Overseer at the saw mill. It's been going on some time.'

Elizabeth rebuked herself for not knowing what had been happening, for not playing the role of despotic mistress.

'I'm sure Leila didn't say you were to come all the way home on your own.'

'I was bored.' Agnes's mouth quivered. 'I said, "Can we go home now?" Leila said, "Go away. Naughty girl. Go away."'

Elizabeth drew her breath in sharply with anger. Leila came into the store. Her frock was dusty, her face flushed with the exertion of running. Relief flooded her face as she saw Agnes. She stepped towards her and shook her roughly by the arm.

'You're a bad girl to go off like that. She gave me the slip, Mrs Pengelly. I've been really worried. I ran all up and down the creek.'

'She ran away from you?' Elizabeth spoke calmly.

'She's always doing it. The minute my back's turned. I was showing her where the fish jump. Next thing I knew she was off.'

Agnes looked bewildered, then her eyes narrowed with a look older than her years as she absorbed a small lesson about the adult world.

'Agnes tells me you were talking to Mr Roberts from the saw mill.'

Leila looked frightened. Her expression hardened as she decided to brazen it out. 'The child's a liar. She's overheard some conversation and used it to avoid being punished. She's always inventing things. I'm telling you, Mrs Pengelly, you don't know the cunning of your own child.'

'Agnes is three,' said Elizabeth. 'She hasn't enough years to have developed that sort of duplicity.' She turned to Riley. 'Will you take Aggie to the house?' She waited until they had gone. 'You're dismissed.' She drew twenty-five shillings from the till. 'Pack your bags this afternoon. Don't ask me to give you a reference.'

Leila stared at the coins in her hand. She closed her fingers over them slowly. 'You'll be sorry for this.'

'Don't threaten me.'

'You'll be sorry,' Leila repeated. 'I can ruin you, and your reputation as Madam High-and-Mighty. There's a tale I can tell about your precious Agnes.'

Elizabeth gripped the counter. 'What do you mean?'

'I know Mr Pengelly was worth ten of you. I know why he went away. Because he couldn't bear to live with you. I know how you starved him of affection.'

'He said that?'

'He said all sorts when he'd had a drop from the bottle. You might have stopped him from your bed, but you couldn't stop his mouth when he'd been drinking.'

'Be quiet!' Elizabeth gripped the edge of the shop counter until her hands hurt and the blood pounded in her head.

Leila smiled. 'He made me promise, for Agnes's sake, that I'd keep quiet. But that was a long time ago.'

'You can't hurt me,' said Elizabeth. 'Nor Aggie.'

Leila smiled again. 'I think I can, Mrs Pengelly.'

The story spread quickly in Yooma. There were those who declared they wouldn't believe it, and some who said they couldn't have cared who was the father of Lizzie Pengelly's child – there were plenty who had settled round there with worse than that to hide. But, after a week, trade had become noticeably slower at the store. Attendance at the school had dropped to barely a dozen children.

Elizabeth visited the absentee pupils' houses and was greeted coolly. People shifted their eyes away, said the children were needed at home, that the penny a week had become too much of a drain on their resources. At one house the door was slammed in her face.

Bella and Lucy Symonds took great pains to shun her with the maximum of pantomime. Driving towards Elizabeth as she walked with Agnes to Yooma one morning, they managed to steer their pony-carriage off the road and almost into a gum tree in their anxiety to avoid looking at her.

'That is what they call the *cut-direct*, Aggie,' Elizabeth told her wrily. 'Known only in the politest of circles.' Nevertheless, the incident had upset her.

Agnes skipped along the track, unaware that she was at the centre of a Yooma scandal, pleased because they were going to visit Alice McCreery who had some new piglets to show her.

Agnes asked frequently where Leila had gone. Perhaps hardest of all for Elizabeth was the fact that the child missed her.

'That bitch,' said Alice, pouring Elizabeth a mug of tea. She passed her hand over Agnes's dark curls tenderly. 'Here, my lovely. Mary will show you the piglets.' The girl led Agnes out of the house to the yard.

'Whatever Leila says,' Alice declared after they had gone, 'I'll not believe anything bad of that child.'

'It's true,' said Elizabeth. It was suffocating in Alice's house. Flies buzzed in a dark cloud near the ceiling, filling the air with a constant drone. There was always a smell, rancid and unpleasant, of children and animals and meat which had been left to hang for too long for anyone's good in this heat. The mug of tea in her hands made her sweat. 'What she's telling everyone – it's true, Alice. Suddenly everything seems like a nightmare.'

'Because a silly girl is vindictive after getting her notice? This'll die down, Lizzie. Don't you fret.'

'But I'm losing customers. Riley and Patrick pretend nothing's happened, but they look at me as if I've betrayed them. If it wasn't for you and a few others, the school would have to close.'

Alice cocked her head on one side. 'That's enough of that. What's all this I've heard about Riley going to get himself wed?'

Riley's recent revelation had taken everyone by surprise. Set in his ways, rough and ready and over fifty, Riley, it seemed, had won the heart of a woman half his age.

'He's fetching her from Sydney in a week or two, where she's in service. They're to marry without fuss. "None of your gentrified ceremonials," Riley says.'

'You're taking her on?'

'My kitchen servant's given notice.' Elizabeth looked rueful and fell silent. She smiled. 'She never was much of a cook anyway. And, according to Riley, Honor is the best cook in New South Wales. She sounds a good, warm-hearted girl. Nothing too fancy.' She paused. 'Though whether she'll stay and whether Riley will stay, after this, is another matter.'

Honor stood beside Riley on the veranda, a little apart from him, clearly at ease without his support.

'You'll be wanting to tell me my duties, madam. Can Riley go now? He's been worrying all the way here that you wouldn't be able to manage with him away.'

Elizabeth smiled and nodded. She liked the new woman immediately. Honor's large pink hands clutched a carpet bag to her as if it held the tools of her trade. Elizabeth could imagine it stuffed with wooden spoons and egg whisks and rolling pins. Her frock was plain gingham. Her face was large and pretty, freckled in the deep shade cast by her straw hat. Her brown hair was tucked neatly under it, with a merest suggestion of vanity in the single curl which graced her broad forehead.

'I hope you are going to be happy with us,' said Elizabeth.

'I'm sure I shall, madam. I'm looking forward to meeting your little girl.'

Elizabeth hesitated. The wearying heat, the turmoil of the past weeks, the ostracism of the people of Yooma, swamped her without warning and she felt depressed.

'There is something I must say,' she began. 'There is a lot of gossip being spread here, about my child, and why my husband left Yooma two years ago. You may find it discomforting after a while –'

The girl looked at her without embarrassment. 'Riley has told me all of it, madam. Now, if you'd care to show me to the kitchen quarters.'

'Did Leila go away because I was bad?' said Agnes, when Elizabeth put her to bed that night.

Elizabeth held her closely. 'You're not bad. You're a darling girl. And Mama loves you dearly.'

'I like Honor.' Agnes burrowed down under the covers. 'Do you think Riley likes her too?'

'I'm sure he does, or he wouldn't have married her,' Elizabeth told her, pulling the mosquito net in place. The child became invisible, the pale swathes of net creating a distance between them. Elizabeth slipped from the bedroom and went along the veranda to her own room.

The lamp was lit in Riley's hut. She thought of Honor and Riley together.

Her own bedroom looked bleak, the high bed austere with its single pillow. The lamp, throwing shadows on the ceiling, seemed to reveal only the room's emptiness.

She sat at the dressing table and pulled her writing case from the drawer, intending to write to Amy. But the effort of putting into words all that had happened, and the thought of Amy, reading the letter from the cosy setting of her home in Queensland, perhaps reading passages to her husband and discussing her, made her reluctant to begin. The green-bound Tennyson lay as always in the drawer. She thought of Edward, widowed and childless, somewhere in London. She picked up her pen and began to write.

*

273

It was Christmas. They celebrated with roast turkey and chestnuts, and sweated on the veranda.

Agnes, excited by the games and rich food, was listless the next day. She lay on a chair in the shade of the house. Elizabeth sat close beside her, watching Camelot chase mosquitoes in the garden. She smiled as she looked at Agnes, the child's mouth hung open as she slept.

'She's wore out, poor mite,' said Honor, bringing Elizabeth a cold drink. 'I told Riley. He shouldn't be so boisterous with her.'

'Honor,' said Elizabeth, 'I may have to move from here.'

Honor sat down on the chair beside her. 'Oh, no, madam. Don't you give in to them that easy.'

It was a conclusion Elizabeth had not come to easily. Honor was not the only one who would see it as giving in. But the fact was that the store was losing money. She was beginning to draw on her savings. She would have to move to Sydney, buy a shop, or open a school. Elizabeth looked again at the sleeping Agnes and knew that, alone and with a child, it would not be so simple.

'People is like sheep,' muttered Honor darkly. 'Riley says they were all singing your praises before that woman spread her malicious stories.'

'Things have changed, Honor.'

'I don't care what you done,' the woman said firmly. 'You're a good woman. You've been good to Riley and young Patrick, and to me. If you're going, we're coming with you. If I know them, they'll say the same.' Honor stood up and patted Elizabeth's shoulder, though she was ten years her junior, the gesture was one of motherly reassurance. 'Don't you fret. I'll talk to Riley.'

Elizabeth felt her eyes prick with tears. She could not bring herself to say that loyalty was not going to be enough.

On the following afternoon, Elizabeth left Patrick in the store to attend to the slow trickle of customers. She went with Agnes to the creek, taking a bag of apples and a letter which had arrived that morning from Amy.

She watched Agnes pick grasses. Intermittently she read sections of Amy's letter. Her happiness had become dependent on letters: news from Hannah in England, and the long letters Amy wrote from the sheep station. Both stirred up feelings of nostalgia. She calculated briefly how long it would be before Edward would receive her letter, written before Christmas, and how long before she might hear from him in return. There were no letters from Arthur. He had sent no message to tell her where he was, no word on Agnes's birthday, nor at Christmas. She would not have known whether he was alive or dead, except for news which had come to her through passing travellers. Someone had met an Arthur Pengelly who had struck it rich at Tarnagulla. Someone else had heard that he was headed north.

It was hot and close by the creek. Her head was filled with the sound of bees and the ever-present flies and the water running over the rocks. The air was very still, yet alive with colour, of the butterflies and flashes of brilliant birds among the trees, the sulphur yellow crest and white feathers of cockatoos, the blue and yellow of bee-eaters and blues and greens of noisy budgerigars. Dragonflies skimmed the water with clicks and whirrs of their bright wings.

Every so often Agnes came up with her arms full of long grass and laid it in a little heap, solemnly building a miniature haystack next to Elizabeth's feet.

'Busy?' Elizabeth said.

Agnes nodded without speaking and went off for another bundle of grass.

Elizabeth's heart ached to watch her. She tried not to think of the future and how they would miss the beauty of the bush if she were forced to go away.

The shade of the trees and ripple of the running water were soothing. There was a timelessness about the trees with their straight white trunks, the bark curling down from them in ribbons, like strips of crisp brown paper. She was so content with her life here. She closed her eyes and let the sounds of the creek overwhelm her. It was on days like this that she could picture the river at Charlford without regret or sadness. The present merged with the past: the heat of the Australian sun, the drone of insects, the rippling of a river and the quivering of leaves became the soughing of a barleyfield in the hot summer sun.

The child's cry roused her sharply. Her heart pounded with fear, then slowed as she saw Agnes, some yards off, with a vast bundle of grass and leaves clutched to her chest. She turned to see what had caught Agnes's attention up on the ridge near the paddock and saw the figure of a man coming down through the trees towards them. She shaded her eyes, then caught her breath, her pulse quickening again with fear. 'Arthur!'

Agnes was running, nearly falling, scattering grasses in her wake.

Elizabeth held out her arms and the child came to her, wary of the man's approach.

There was little about him that was familiar. He had lost weight and his hair had thinned, with thick grey tufts merging with heavy side-whiskers. He had on a moleskin coat and flannel trousers which were worn into holes. He did not smile, but searched her face with an apprehension which echoed her own.

Arthur turned to Agnes. 'What's this? Don't you remember Papa?'

Agnes burrowed into Elizabeth and hid her face against her shoulder.

Elizabeth began to feel angry. 'You should have written to say that you were coming.'

'Would it have made a difference?'

'I could have talked to her. Children need more warning for this sort of thing.' She paused. 'And so did I.' She stood up and lifted Agnes on to her hip, feeling a need to protect her from the man before them. She dared not ask if he was back to stay. She did not look at him.

They began to walk towards the ridge, Agnes sucked her thumb and turned resolutely away from Arthur.

'She's grown into a bonny child.' Their eyes met. She felt an irrational quickening of her pulse.

'You've seen Riley – met his wife, Honor?'

'She seems a good sort. Bit of a surprise, eh? The old devil.'

Elizabeth did not answer.

'Leila is gone,' she said after a while. 'I dismissed her.'

He did not question why.

They scrambled up the path to the paddock. Arthur reached out a hand to help her over tree roots, but she refused it and followed more slowly, carrying the dragging weight of Agnes. She reached the top of the bank, her breath coming hard.

'What was all that in the dining room?' said Arthur. 'Desks, chalk-dust. I thought you were done with all that long since.'

'The Yooma children needed schooling.'

He frowned, as if unsettled by something, then said, 'You always said you'd have a school again one day.'

She paused. 'You've seen the shop?'

'It all looks very good.'

'Well, it's not.' Her anger came to the surface, boiling up against him and all that had happened. 'Things aren't very good. And if you've come back expecting a bed of roses, Arthur, you've as much of a shock coming to you as I have just had, seeing you coming down that path.'

She marched ahead of him past the paddock and set Agnes down to run ahead of her to Honor and Riley's hut. Elizabeth walked on to the house. Resentment hurried her steps. She went into the schoolroom, wanting only to get away from him and escape the confusion of emotions which were forcing themselves in on her.

She stood at the pulpit desk by the fireplace and leaned her arms on its cool surface. How could he come back like that, without warning? What did he want from her? This is mine, she told herself fiercely, looking at the rows of benches, the piles of slates and boxes of chalks in the corner, the alphabet cards she had made, the copybooks, the jars of pens and ink pots. She heard his footsteps on the veranda, he hesitated in the doorway. His outline was black against the silver glare of the sun.

'What did you mean, things aren't so good?'

'Everything was fine until a month or so ago. I had money in the bank. I was Yooma's schoolmistress. Pengelly's had a good name round here. And it was all due to me.'

'You've no money left?'

'Enough. Agnes and I are going to Sydney.'

His glance flicked away. 'So, what's gone wrong?'

'I dismissed Leila. She retaliated by spreading the story you told her about Agnes's father and how hard done by you were. No one of a *respectable* class will speak to me in Yooma. They don't send their children to school.' She laughed. 'Pengelly's is less popular that it was when O'Hoare had his bush hut and was drinking himself to death.'

Arthur ran a hand through his side-whiskers nervously. 'Leila – she was nothing to me.'

Elizabeth turned away impatiently. 'I don't care what went on before. The damage is done.'

He came to her and laid a hand on the desk. 'Lizzie, you can't blame me for all of it. You'd done me a great hurt.'

'Oh, your hurt, your hurt! Don't you think I've suffered for it?' She was ashamed of the tears which pricked her eyes. He put his hand out to her and she shrugged him off. The smell of him was strange and yet it awakened old memories. She was aware of the heat of his body through the shabby clothes, the remembered line of his jaw, his mouth and the dark-fringed eyes.

277

'What are we talking about?' he said quietly. 'Do you want me back?'
'I don't know.'
'I'm desperate, Lizzie. Between us we could start up again in Sydney.'
'You want me to feel sorry for you?'
'I want you to take me back. I still love you. I couldn't get rid of thoughts of you all this time.'

She did not know whether to believe him. She was aware of her body's response to the nearness of him, the slow movement of dried up desire.

'You owe me, Lizzie,' he said. 'I kept you with me when we came here. I looked after you and your child.' He waited. He made no attempt to touch her again.

Elizabeth looked at him and saw the despair in his face. The urge to reach out and absorb the touch of his body was unbearable. She moved away from him. 'I must go to Agnes.'

He nodded.

'If I agree.' She hesitated. 'I can't promise I can make you happy.' She avoided the hope in his eyes.

'You won't regret it. I promise.'

Elizabeth turned away, the regrets already beginning as she heard him say,

'From now on there'll be no looking back.'

34

They sold the store and rented a house in Sydney, a villa residence of modest respectability in an unfashionable part of the town. Gone was the massive vegetation of the bush, instead loomed narrow bustling streets of high buildings, with glimpses of the harbour and tall-masted ships between them.

On one side of Arthur and Elizabeth's new home was a boarding-house, whose landlady, Mrs Atkinson, guarded the respectability of her clients jealously. There was a 'refined' lady who sang nightly at the Sydney theatre; a retired Captain of the mercantile Indian navy 'rather reduced in circumstances, but very gentlemanly', who had an addiction to rum; and two young Americans, who had been sent by their parents on a tour round the world, whose tour of adventure had stopped at the brothels and night-life of Sydney. On the other side lived an Italian family, who seemed to conduct the whole range of their affairs in the street. But in Sydney everyone seemed to take to the streets: in the evenings the buildings hummed with the hot sound of cicadas and the local population. People would sit on their balconies, smoking cigars and drinking coffee, watching the passing cabs and carts, enter-tained by the frequent squabbles among the Italians, and the comings and goings from the Chinese opium parlour at the end of the street.

It was the height of summer, a time of dust, flies and humid heat, trapped by the crowded, stuffy houses. The sun glared off brick and yellow sandstone walls and threw the shadows into stark relief. It glittered off the sea, scoring the waves with diamond-hard edges, and lifted a white dusty haze off the streets, which bustled with horses and carriages, cabs and omnibuses and people.

The people! To Elizabeth they were brash and bold and aggressive after the rough but easy-going pace of Yooma. Sydney was unashamedly bourgeois, striving for self-improvement seventy years on from its shameful beginnings. It was common knowledge that more than one of the city's wealthier and more influential businessmen had 'met with a misfortune' many years ago, the current euphemism for 'transported for life', but this was not a subject to introduce into polite conversation. Sydney was building a layer of probity, of banks and business establishments, gaslighting and libraries, to cover its convict origins.

Into this world Arthur leaped with renewed energies, as if the intervening years in the bush and at the goldfields had been a time merely of slumbering. He re-established himself in the trade he knew, supplying small retail shops in Sydney and the neighbouring district with drapery goods imported from Manchester and Birmingham. Demand for European goods in a country greedy for progress was high. Within a few weeks Arthur's plans for an importing company on a grand scale had begun to grow.

Elizabeth opened the ground floor of the house as a schoolroom, exchanging the children of Yooma for the children of the Sydney shopkeepers and the Italians, the Chinese and Irish of the area.

Arthur protested. 'There's no cause to shut yourself up with the ABC and multiplication and a crowd of children.'

'The reason is in me,' she said. 'I have to keep the independence I won at Yooma.'

He looked hurt and she was sorry, but she had her way. She had her way too over Riley and Honor and Patrick, insisting they should all be offered employment with them in Sydney.

It was Agnes who found the move from Yooma the hardest. There was the stranger she must now address as 'Papa', the high house with its several floors and flights of stairs and iron-traceried balconies over the noisy street, the children who came to her mother's schoolroom, with their town ways, foreign looks and voices. She could no longer run with Camelot barefoot out of doors in the mornings, or gather armfuls of grass and flowers. She had to stay indoors because of the traffic and people and could only go outside in the dusty air when led by the hand by Elizabeth or Honor. Camelot too had to be led by a chain, with a tight leather collar round his neck. Riley, who Papa said was a servant, like Honor and Patrick, had to call her 'Miss Agnes', instead of 'little Aggie'. The loss of the freedom of the bush hurt her like a physical pain. Unable to understand, or explain her sense of bereavement, she began to behave badly. Her resentment against Arthur made her sullen towards the stranger who had taken her and her mother away from the country, who shared her mother's bed and who spoke sternly to her when she spilled food, or ran, or shouted.

'The child needs to be disciplined,' Arthur said one day, when he had sent her, screaming defiance, to her room.

Elizabeth, torn between a need to defend Agnes and the knowledge that her child had behaved outrageously, held back her anger. 'She is beginning to settle very well, during the hours when she's with me in the schoolroom.'

'I mean, she needs a governess.'

Elizabeth laughed in disbelief that he could so easily have forgotten about Leila. 'A governess?'

He coloured. 'Why not? We shall soon be able to afford it.'

'I am not having another woman in the house to discipline my daughter. I can teach her myself.'

'The child has run wild too long.'

'I don't remember that you worried how wild she was when you went away to the goldfields.'

'Well, things are different now.' He looked uncertain. 'I don't want this to come between us, Lizzie.'

'You could order me to accept your wishes. I'm your wife. That does, I believe, give you certain rights over me.'

'Elizabeth,' he said unhappily. 'You know that's not my way.'

She sighed. 'Give me time. Before you came back I had Agnes to myself. It's hard to give up all that freedom.' She went to him and leaned her head against his chest. Their physical hunger for one another, urgent in the first weeks, had settled into a less compelling pattern. There was an undeniable barrier between them. Elizabeth, like Agnes, had hated all the changes which came with the move from Yooma.

She tried to enjoy the luxuries which accumulated with the new lifestyle, the ease of shopping and of visiting the music hall and the theatre, the stimulus of the new school and of meeting new people, even the chance to wear pretty clothes. The years in the bush had altered Elizabeth's appearance dramatically, ageing her skin, but also whittling away the flesh of her cheekbones and her figure. Though she despised the fashion, she took to wearing crinolines and, to please

Arthur, wore her hair waved and in a heavy chignon behind her head. They paid social visits, as they had done in the old days in England, although Elizabeth suggested that the people who were so eager for their company now would not be as enthusiastic about inviting them into their homes if they had seen Arthur in his worn-out flannels when he came back from the goldfields, or herself with her skirts tucked up, hacking out tree roots, or if they knew the secrets behind their marriage.

Yet, people seemed to sense a romantic quality about them. The Pengellys fitted in with the entrepreneurial climate of Sydney. Arthur Pengelly was making a name for himself in business circles. His wife was reputed to be quite a character in her own right; had lived on her own out in the bush. Elizabeth Pengelly was a bit of a looker and heads turned when she and Arthur appeared together in public.

Elizabeth did not care for the attention they attracted and treated it with disdain. She had already begun to hate the city with its brash community of speculators. She missed Alice McCreery and her school-children at Yooma and wrote long letters to Amy in Queensland. And when Arthur was not in the house and school was over she would spend hours in the kitchen with Agnes, helping Honor with the cooking and reminiscing about life in the bush.

After six months Arthur had established *The Pengelly Importing Company*. He was talking of investing in property, of building a batch of two dozen villa residences for rent, and, in particular, of moving to a more prestigious area on the east side of the city, where elegant houses stood in handsome gardens and armies of servants tended the aspirations of the new wealthy towards the upper middle-class lifestyle of old England.

Elizabeth resisted the move, suspecting that one of Arthur's motives for leaving their present house was to wean her away from the school-room.

And then the issue was taken out of her hands.

She did not tell Arthur immediately when she discovered that she was pregnant. The certainty, that her independent existence in the schoolroom must end and she would again be imprisoned in Arthur's life filled her with a slow panic, like the first swell of storm waves on a calm sea.

*

They had returned late from a whist party at the home of Ronald Latimer, a Sydney woolbroker. During the course of the evening Elizabeth had had to leave the room because she felt faint. She and Arthur quarrelled a little when they reached home. Arthur was morose after an evening of brandy drinking and grumbled at her for interrupting the game and for her lack of courtesy towards the other players.

'You never feel faint. You were just bored with the whole business and wanted me to know it.'

Elizabeth was quick to retaliate. 'You know how I feel about the false manners of people like that. Tell them about Agnes. Then see how quickly your new friends will disappear.'

'If that's meant to pass for humour, Lizzie, I feel it's in poor taste.'

'I've no time for *respectable* people. I'd sooner spend an hour with Honor and Riley, or Patrick. Those are my friends. They've stuck by me through everything.'

She kicked off her evening shoes and slumped on the bed. Her hooped skirt bounced up, showing her knees. She was tired. She wished now that she had not bitten so hard on his criticism, but the effort of playing cards while nursing a sick headache had been a strain and had left her irritable. She began to rub the circulation back into her feet. She saw Arthur watching her, an expression of distaste pulled down the eges of his mouth.

'You look like any common settler's wife.' He turned away.

Elizabeth's temper broke. 'And weren't you then a common settler!' she shouted. 'With your airs and graces. Your "Yes, Mr Latimer. No, Mr Latimer. Three bags full, Mr Latimer!"'

'Listen!' He seized her wrist and pulled her to her feet. Elizabeth cried out in surprise. 'I don't care how I do it. I shall get to the top here among people like the Latimers. A man must have his pride.'

'And what may a woman have?' she said scornfully.

'You'll have all you could want. Servants. Nice things.'

She shook her head. It was the drink which made him talk like that. 'Don't you remember, Arthur, when we first lived at the bush store? We were happy. All we wanted was each other.'

He laughed. 'Fine talk, from someone who never wanted me in the first place.'

'I took you back, didn't I? Though heaven knows why now.'

'And God knows why I came!'

The quarrel was beginning to slide into unreason. Elizabeth felt the grip of Arthur's fingers on her arm and the throbbing return of her headache. She wanted him to hurt her. 'Why did you – when you hate me so much? Why did you come to me with your, Please, Lizzie, take me back. I still love you, Lizzie?'

'Don't – say that.' He made a move and she thought that he would hit her. She flinched, and he lowered his hand.

'I want to know why you came back to me,' she said more calmly.

'Because I'd run out of money.'

'I don't believe you.'

'Because I was too old to go on breaking my back, hoping to strike lucky again. Panning and surfacing is finished. They're sinking shafts. Men with capital are going in.'

'I don't believe you.'

'Don't then. But it's the truth.'

'I'm pregnant. We're going to have a baby.'

He stared at her foolishly. An expression of pain, as if her words had struck him a physical blow, crossed his face. He looked down at his hand on her wrist and seemed surprised to see it there. He released his hold and sat down on the bed.

'When?'

'Next spring.' She sat down beside him. She did not want the child, growing inside her. Now that she had told him there seemed nothing more to say.

Arthur looked as if he were going to cry. 'This puts an end to your fancy notions of staying a school ma'am, anyhow,' he blustered.

Elizabeth did not reply, waiting for him to raise the subject of moving again. But he seemed exhausted. He sat with his arms resting on his knees, staring for a long time at the carpet. At last he stood up and began to undress for bed.

Elizabeth took off her crinoline and corset and slipped on her nightdress. She left her hair unbrushed and climbed into bed, grateful for the cool pillow against her aching head. She could hear Arthur, still moving about the room. A silence fell, she sensed that he was watching her.

'I don't hate you, Lizzie,' she heard him say.

'I know.'

She turned her head into the pillow and pretended to go to sleep.

*

She guessed the next day that Riley and Honor had heard some of their quarrel. Honor went about her work in her usual way, but she threw her the occasional clandestine glance, as if to judge how she was bearing up under an understood strain.

Agnes, in the way that children sense when something in the adult world is not as it should be, seemed bent on stretching everyone's patience to the limit by acting the part of the spoilt child. She would not wear the dress which Elizabeth picked out for her that morning, teased the dog by pulling his ears and said that Riley smelled of beer: she would not have him near her, when he offered to lift her up to look out of the window at the passing carriages.

The child's observation had not been unfounded, but Elizabeth smacked her and banished her to her room for an hour. She went down to the schoolroom, where Honor was lighting the stove, for it was one of those wet, clammy days of early spring. She debated whether to suggest that Riley should cut down on his drinking, but remembered Arthur's own consumption of brandy the previous evening. She decided instead on an apology.

'I have left Agnes to reflect on her sins. Please tell Riley I'm sorry for her rudeness.'

Honor set down the coal scuttle and wiped her hands on her apron. 'She'll be better when she's got a brother or sister to worry about.' She looked at Elizabeth pointedly and dropped her gaze.

Elizabeth sat down on one of the benches.

'I guessed you were expecting, madam. I'm sorry to speak out of turn.'

Elizabeth fingered the edge of the bench. 'I don't expect things will change very much,' she said without conviction.

'You'll miss teaching the children. But you'll have your own young ones to occupy you.'

Elizabeth wished that she could talk to Honor openly, confide in her as she would a friend. The gulf of mistress and servant lay between them, and Honor would always consider words which bridged that gulf as 'speaking out of turn'.

'Do you and Riley want a family, Honor?'

Honor blushed. 'One day perhaps, Mrs Pengelly. Though I shouldn't like to lose my post.'

Elizabeth was shocked. 'I wouldn't dismiss you.'

285

'You might not, Mrs Pengelly.' Honor picked up the coal scuttle again. 'But the master might think different.'

It was Elizabeth, in the end, who brought up the subject of moving house. She had begun to make plans to close the school, and had discovered a teacher, a down to earth, pleasant young man, who had been tutor to one of Arthur's associates' family. He had joined up with a local non-conformist minister, who planned to raise subscriptions and open fresh schoolrooms in the neighbourhood.

'So, my work won't have been in vain,' she told Arthur. 'I feel so relieved to know that, if we go from here, someone else is to carry on. Mr Appletree, the minister, seems a decent man. He came today to talk to the children. It reminded me of the time when Robert Munro used to terrify the children with his visits. The contrast couldn't have been more striking.'

Arthur was watching her from the opposite side of the fireplace. The firelight shone on Elizabeth's flushed face as she spoke. Her eyes were bright with satisfaction. Arthur said nothing.

'What are you thinking?' she asked. 'I shan't mind any more about leaving this house.'

'I was remembering a long time back, when you met me all in a pet, after you'd been dismissed by Munro from your teaching.'

'You said that you were glad I wasn't going to marry Robert.'

'It would have been very different for you if you had.' His expression was enigmatic in the shadows. 'Or if you'd wed his brother.'

'Arthur –'

'I'm glad you're reconciled to the move,' he said quickly. 'I've found a property. Countrified and with a garden. Agnes will like that.'

'It will be better,' she said. 'For children.'

He nodded. 'I'm pleased about the baby,' he said stiffly. 'It would console me greatly to have a son to carry on the name.'

It was summer again, almost December, and a year since Elizabeth had written to tell Edward about Agnes. The interval was so long, the fact that she could have written at all now seemed remote and a little fantastic.

They had left a forwarding address at Yooma. When the usual

286

bundle of letters came Elizabeth was not thinking of Edward. Honor brought the post to her in the schoolroom. Elizabeth sat at her desk, her feet on a small footstool. She flicked through a past copybook of one of her brighter pupils. Today had been the last school day. There had been a few tears, some of them her own. She felt empty, drained by the heat and her emotions. The smell of children lingered. The rest of the day stretched before her with nothing to do except to wait for Agnes to return from her walk with Riley, and for Arthur to come home from his office.

'You should be sat in a more comfy chair upstairs,' Honor said disapprovingly. 'Postman brought some letters. There's one from England.' She handed the letters to her and peered over Elizabeth's arm.

Elizabeth opened the letter and saw that it was from Edward. She stared at the lines of writing. After so long, how strange, that it should come, just as she had thought one episode of her life was closing.

'Thank you, Honor.' The woman suppressed her curiosity and moved away to the door. 'And Honor –' Elizabeth hesitated. 'About this letter – I should be glad if you didn't mention it to Mr Pengelly.'

35

My dear Elizabeth,
So many times I have begun this letter and failed. You say, perhaps
I will despise you. But if you were to know me now, you would find
me very much changed.

Your letter came at a time when I was at my lowest ebb. My wife
and child had died, I had become disillusioned with my work at the
hospital for Crimean war veterans – just when it seemed I had
nothing and no one to live for, into my life comes a voice from the
past, telling me that I have a daughter.

How can I convey what joy the news brought me? Any feelings
of hurt, that you could have kept her from me, were swept away by
a longing to know more about her. You say she is beautiful. But
how? Is she dark, fair? Is she a strong child? Is she talkative? Will
you tell her the truth one day? You see how much there is I long to
know, now that you have told me?

When you read this, so many more months will have gone by.
Months when I shall nurse images of you, Elizabeth – a solitary
soul, like myself – there in your lonely bush school with Agnes.

I nurse no grievances these days. My life is busy and full. I have
relinquished all but a nominal guardianship of the Fitzroy Infirmary
and now have a general practice, and part charge of a dispensary in
the East End of London. I have been persuaded by loyal friends that

I was fast becoming a recluse, and should live in a greater degree of comfort. And so, with some show of crusty reluctance, I have taken up bachelor rooms in a respectable part of town. Who knows? I may even one day become that rich and famous physician to which you once objected so strongly.

How much has come between us since then, not least, ten thousand miles of ocean.

Write when you are able, and tell me more about Agnes.

Believe me, dear Elizabeth, I remain

Your friend,

Edward Munro

Elizabeth held the pages of the letter close, as if they might escape from her as she sped up the stairs. She unfolded them again in the privacy of her room.

She remembered her own strained and hesitant letter, in which she had told Edward that he had a child. Her chest and ribs hurt with each breath as she read and re-read his inquiries about Agnes. The handwriting was firm, yet she sensed the reserve behind the flow of questions, as if he might perhaps have poured out so much more if he had been sure of her.

She traced the lines of ink with her fingers, tried to picture him as he wrote and the expression on his face as he brought the letter to a close. '. . . I remain your friend.'

She lay down on the bed and held the letter against her face. The paper was warm against her cheek. She tried to detect a scent, a memory of him, but there was nothing, just the warm, faintly pleasant smell of the paper.

How they had abused their old friendship. A vivid memory, of two children making tunnels in a barleyfield, made her squeeze her eyes tight shut and tears wet her face as she remembered that other summer's day, when they had put the innocence of friendship behind them for ever.

She folded the letter slowly under her fingers, pressed it in her hand and got up from the bed. She lifted a wooden box, a present from her sister, out of her drawer. The inlaid pattern on the lid was smooth to the touch, the corn-coloured lining seemed a fitting nest in which to lay the pages. She closed the lid over them and turned the key.

36

It would soon be Christmas. Riley and Honor had gone ahead to prepare a welcome at their new home. Patrick drove Elizabeth and Arthur, with Agnes bouncing with excitement between them.

The two-storey house stood among similar houses in a tree-lined road, far enough from the commercial centre of the city to give an illusion of being, if not in the bush, then in a tamed version of the countryside. A short gravelled drive led through wrought iron gates and green lawns to the wide front door. The house was built of yellow sandstone. A veranda ran the length of the building, its roof supported by delicate pillars and decorated with screens of ironwork, like traceries of thick white lace. A canopy of vines covered the veranda roof, dividing the upper and lower storeys with a band of green. The windows under the veranda were cast in deep shadow and white shutters screened the upper windows, fending off the glare of the sun.

They stepped into the cool and quenching shade of the entrance hall. Elizabeth, long since seduced by the beauty of the house, put her regrets behind her. For Arthur's sake she would be happy.

They toured their new home; Arthur was as excited as a child showing off a toy. Agnes ran ahead of them from room to room, singing out, 'Papa's study,' 'Mama's drawing room,' 'Everyone's dining room,' impatient at their slowness to follow. Elizabeth said Agnes might go and discover her own bedroom, where Patrick had installed her toys. She watched the child climb the curving staircase to the floor above.

'She is going to be content here.' She leaned on the bannister rail at the bottom of the stair and stroked its polished surface. 'And so am I.' She turned to Arthur and smiled.

He put his arm round her shoulders. 'I'm glad.' His kiss was warm against her lips, yet distant. She sensed a detachment in him. His pleasure was in the house, rather than in her or Agnes's contentment. She did not mind. She was pleased for him. He deserved the fruits of his success.

She turned away from him and began to climb the stairs.

'I've been thinking,' Arthur said. 'It's time you had some shares in the importing company.'

Elizabeth was surprised. 'If you think so.'

'It was, after all, your savings from the Yooma store that started us off again.'

'And you had something left from the diggings.' She felt that it was a little ridiculous that they should be apportioning responsibility, as if awarding points of merit.

'Nevertheless, it would please me to see you involved in some way with the business, make me feel I'd put things straight.' He hesitated. 'It would give you back some of that independence you were after.'

'Yes,' she said slowly. 'Thank you, Arthur. I'm grateful.'

In January they went to a photographic salon in Sydney, to mark the anniversary of the founding of the company.

They sat for separate portraits, Elizabeth feeling stiff and uncomfortable, posed against a vaguely Grecian pillar draped with a fringed velvet curtain. She hoped that the camera, which was said never to lie, would not reveal that she was nearly six months pregnant.

'Another year, Elizabeth,' Arthur said proudly. 'The opening of another decade.'

They waited for the photographer and his assistant to change the backdrop from elegant feminine drapery to an imposing chair and writing table, better suited to the image of a man of business.

'I shall have my portrait hung upon the wall, and one of yourself placed upon my desk at the office, where I can look upon you when seeking inspiration.'

Elizabeth smiled, surprised by the pretty speech and tempted to express doubt as to whether her expression, rigidly moulded to a look of grim perseverance, would inspire Arthur to very great achievements.

She tried hard to pretend that this new way of life was fulfilling.

There were Agnes's lessons to occupy her, consultations with Honor and the housemaid, and with Riley and Patrick about the organization of the house and its garden. But her old restlessness had returned. She saw, in the day to day purpose of Arthur's life, divided neatly between home and business, that she and Arthur would always be ill-matched. He loved her, in his way, as she perhaps loved him. But he took what he needed from her, and that was all. And she, who had once wanted to share an honesty in marriage, now needed nothing from Arthur that he could give her.

She watched him sit by the table, his knees planted squarely apart, his chin raised, hair sleeked with pomade on either side of his head; his expression was dignified, though the pose verged dangerously on pomposity. This man, with whom she had on three separate occasions chosen to live, whose child she was carrying, was a stranger to her.

She went over in her mind the letter she had written that morning to Edward. She calculated that by the time she received a reply her second child would be born. She had poured out on paper the loss of her school, the events which filled her days, Arthur's rapid rise in trade circles. Between the lines she had revealed her sense of frustration, because she was not the solitary soul he had imagined, and her independence had come to an end.

She felt the small flutter of the baby inside her. She wished the ordeal of the pregnancy were over. On a more immediate level, she was glad when the photographic session was ended.

'I should like to have some likenesses of Agnes,' she said, as she and Arthur went down the stairs to the street.

Arthur considered the idea. 'Excellent. We shall pay another visit to the studio next week.'

'I can bring her,' Elizabeth suggested as he helped her into the waiting carriage. 'There's no need for you to bother. I'll come with Honor tomorrow. There, it's decided.'

'As you think fit, my dear. I shall look forward to the results.'

The deception excited Elizabeth, with its small risk of discovery, but the fact that one of the photographs was destined for England went undetected. No one knew that she had written to Edward and that her days were often filled with fruitless yearnings; nor that she kept his letter to her, locked in a box, alongside her copy of Tennyson.

*

The birth was a difficult one. 'She is thirty-seven,' confided the physician to Arthur. 'What can we expect? But she must on no account have any more children. Her constitution is far too delicate.'

Elizabeth, too exhausted to complain, nursed the baby's head against her breast. Arthur was solicitous, almost cloying. He had hidden his disappointment well because she had not borne him a son and heir.

'Delicate constitution!' Elizabeth said after the doctor had gone. 'I'm as tough as an ox when I'm not giving birth.' She felt a small and private victory over the two men, physician and husband, because her second child was a girl.

'All the same, we must take care.' Arthur took the baby from her and handed her to the nursemaid, whose employment had, in its turn, been a small victory for Arthur.

Elizabeth was confined to bed for several weeks. She was too ill to protest when it was taken for granted that the woman's position was to become permanent. Miss Grey, with her sensible face, frock and figure, was in any case not to be compared with Leila.

'She is very kind,' said Elizabeth, in response to Arthur's query as to how Miss Grey was settling into the household. 'But I do wish she would allow me to do more.'

'It's what we employ her for, to look after little Katherine.'

'But I see next to nothing of the baby, except to feed her, and even less of Agnes.'

'Agnes's naughtiness would tire you.' Arthur was standing by the window, looking down into the garden. 'For a child not yet five years old, she's very wilful.'

Elizabeth said nothing, but her heart ached for her daughter. Agnes's reaction to her baby sister had been composed of tears and tantrums. 'Send the baby back,' she had begged Elizabeth; and instructed by her father to kiss the tiny Katherine, her response had been, 'I can't, she looks like a frog.'

'I feel very strongly we should consider having a governess for her,' said Arthur.

'No,' said Elizabeth fiercely. 'She's too young.'

'Then what are we going to do about her instruction?' he said, trying to humour her.

'I shall carry on teaching her.'

'But, my dear, you're far from well.'

'I'm not an invalid!' As if to prove the point, Elizabeth flung back

293

the bedcovers and swung her legs out of bed. She swayed on her feet, dizzy from the long bed-rest but roused at last from the lethargy which had kept her passive until now.

Arthur came quickly to the bed and held her. She felt smothered by his embrace. It was as if he wanted forcibly to return her to the imprisonment of the bedclothes. Elizabeth fought against him, beating her arms against his chest until her strength had gone. He lifted her on to the bed, tucking the sheets around her gently. She began to cry, furious at the weakness which frustrated her free will.

Arthur sat on the bed and held her hand, stroking it as if she were a child. 'Now we'll have no more of it. Or you shall make yourself very ill. I've made up my mind. Agnes is to have a governess. When you're well again, you may have some hand in the choice.'

'You'll not select anyone without my approval,' Elizabeth said with a last-ditch defiance, but her former resistance had gone.

'By the way, your shares have done very well,' Arthur said. 'Six months and you've made a tidy profit. Shall I turn it back for you into investment?' He patted her hand. 'Or shall you spend it on something for yourself? There, I'll say nothing in the matter. You can be entirely independent and go on a spending spree, when you're fit again.'

Elizabeth looked at him for a long while; she had forgotten her shares in the company; an idea came to her, which made her head throb with impatience. 'How much?' He did not immediately answer, smiling still with that humouring benevolence. 'How much are the profits?'

'Two hundred and fifty pounds.'

She nodded. 'Not so much as Uncle Willie left me for a dowry.'

'Not half so much. Well? Shall I reinvest it for you?' Arthur's tolerance was becoming strained.

'Oh, leave it for now. Perhaps I shall spend it.' She lay back on the pillow and closed her eyes. '*When* I am well enough,' she added with heavy sarcasm.

She heard him walk softly from the room, and the slow closing of the door. Only when she was sure that he had gone did she pull herself up on the pillow and clamber from the bed.

A letter had come that morning. Honor had remembered her instructions for caution over letters which came from England; she had waited until Elizabeth was alone before handing it to her. Elizabeth took the pages from their box and read them again greedily, trying to piece together a picture of Edward from his words and from elusive snatches of memories, already half forgotten.

She paused and looked at herself in the mirror. Her eyes were deeply shadowed. Her hair was very dishevelled. She lifted her hairbrush to smooth it and lowered her arm again with weariness. How much had they both changed? Edward said that he was 'leaner', also 'wiser'; he talked a great deal in his letter about the injustices of society. '. . . Do you pine for your school, Lizzie? Do you miss your work at Yooma? I sense from your last letter that you let go too easily the fulfilment you once found there. Oh, Lizzie, the mistakes you and I have made.'

She sat with the letter resting in her lap. Then she reached for a pen. She would tell Edward about her latest plan.

One morning in early September, Elizabeth drove out in the dog-cart to Yooma. The servants had gathered anxiously in the hallway before she went.

'Let me drive you,' said Patrick. 'Let me tell Mr Riley – he'll say I should drive you. You're not strong still. What would Mr Pengelly say?'

Elizabeth lifted Agnes on to the carriage beside her and took hold of the reins. Camelot jumped up behind them. 'I'm sure Mr Pengelly will be delighted we have been for a drive.' She remembered Arthur's words the day before: 'You're too quiet, you don't amuse yourself as you should.'

Miss Hastings, the governess, tucked a rug round Agnes's knees in a proprietory way. 'Now, don't you be naughty for Mama, Miss Agnes. Just you be a good girl today.'

Patrick hovered still. Honor looked troubled. Miss Grey turned her back, absenting herself from responsibility. She took the baby indoors.

'Stop fussing, everybody!' exclaimed Elizabeth. 'You may send out a rescue party if we're not back this evening by dark.'

Elizabeth and Agnes sang nursery rhymes on the journey. The early morning sky was high and cool. Elizabeth, remembering the days in Yooma when she and Arthur had made the trip to and from Sydney for supplies, felt the same lightness of heart as she had felt then, with Arthur beside her in a battered hat, laughing and talking and singing. He would be in his office, with his portrait as founder of the importing company framed above the door, portly behind his morocco-surfaced desk, in the red-carpeted, panelled cell of his office. An impatience, to put as much distance as she could between the two images of him, made Elizabeth urge on the horses.

'Will we soon be there?' asked Agnes, as she had asked repeatedly since leaving Sydney, at every sign of a settlement, or twist in the track, or pause to cross a creek or gully.

'Just another hour,' Elizabeth promised. 'Happy, my darling?'

Agnes nodded. After a while she said, 'I'm glad Katherine didn't have to come with us.'

Agnes sat very straight, with her bonnet tipped to the back of her neck and her head lifted to watch the tree-tops passing. She was alert to all the changes in the vegetation and every sudden movement, pointing out a lyre-bird, the sulphur-crested cockatoos and laughing when a flock of lorikeets rose, flapping and squawking through the trees and at a group of kangaroos which bounded for half a mile or more along the track ahead of them before moving away with graceful leaps through the undergrowth. The screech of birds filled the air. The familiar cackle of the kookaburra seemed to welcome them home.

Hardly anything had changed. The store had a new sign above the door. The house looked the same. Elizabeth did not stop but drove on into Yooma.

A few chickens scratched around in the dirt track. People turned, only mildly curious as the carriage passed between the houses. No one recognized her in her peach-striped silk frock and black feathered hat and velvet jacket. A small crowd of children gathered as the travellers pulled up beside Alice McCreery's fence. A girl came out from the house and stood, her expression wary, before a look of wonder crossed her thin features. 'Ma! It's Mrs Pengelly!'

'Glory be! Not Lizzie.' Alice came out from the house, wiping her hands on her apron. 'Well, aren't you dressed the fine lady!' she said as Elizabeth got down from the carriage. 'And is this little Aggie? My, but you've grown tall!'

Agnes jumped up and down, wild with a sense of occasion. Camelot barked and ran round them, hitting their skirts with his tail.

'Run inside, Mary,' said Alice. 'And put the kettle on.'

Elizabeth took Agnes by the hand and, with a little sigh of satisfaction, she followed Alice indoors.

'You have a look of the grave on you, Lizzie. What's been going on?' said Alice, when they were seated in the sitting room.

'I've had another child. Aggie has a sister.'

'There's a blessing.'

'No, it's not,' said Agnes with vehemence. 'I hate her.'

Elizabeth frowned. The McCreery children, crowded in the small room, giggled in sympathy.

'And haven't you grown a bold tongue in your head for your size!' said Alice. 'Out you all go with Mary. Give that dog of yours some exercise.'

'She's too bold for her own good, I'm afraid,' Elizabeth confessed when the children had gone. 'Arthur has decided she must have a governess.'

'It could be the making of her.'

'Or the breaking.' Elizabeth hesitated. 'What of Leila? Is she still in Yooma?'

'Gone. And good riddance too!' Alice banged her teacup in her saucer with feeling. 'All that bad talk has long since died down. People forget. And most folk wish they'd never listened to her. Things haven't been the same since you left. We miss the school.'

'I had a school in Sydney. I miss it too.'

'Sure, but you're too fine a lady nowadays for all of that.'

'I have a plan though, a scheme, Alice.' Elizabeth could not keep it to herself any longer. 'Fine ladies are allowed their charitable projects in the circles my husband moves in. I want to build a proper schoolhouse here. I could provide Yooma with a teacher.'

Alice looked at her steadily. 'The nobs of the village would have to agree.' Her eyes in the thin face were bright with hope.

'I mean to talk to the Reverend Symonds this afternoon.'

'It would be a wonderful thing for Yooma. Sure, Lizzie – and I thought you'd forgotten us all.'

Elizabeth was nervous as she drove the dog-cart on to the minister's house. She could not forget the hostility of her last months in Yooma. She was relieved to see the Symonds's veranda empty, and to discover that Bella and Lucy were not at home.

Symonds stroked his cheek anxiously and glanced frequently behind him, as if expecting his wife to appear at any moment over his shoulder.

'Bella and Lucy have gone with my wife to Melbourne,' he said. 'Mrs Pengelly, you'd best say what you've come to say and be brief. You and I have never quarrelled, but circumstances make me reluctant to accept you in my home.'

'Circumstances about which you know only hearsay and gossip,' Elizabeth reminded him.

The man went pink and cleared his throat. 'True, but –' Again he looked behind him. Reassured by the silence he said, 'Well, then. We can't talk here on the doorstep. You'd best come into the house.'

Elizabeth outlined her plan for a school in Yooma quickly, anxious for his response, aware that if he should decide to oppose it her scheme would be at an end.

But Symonds forgot his caution. He knew just the plot of land, close to the church, he said. 'This is is a very generous plan, Mrs Pengelly. It's one which would, I am sure, re-establish you and Mr Pengelly in the hearts of the people of Yooma.'

'A way for the sinner to atone for past misdemeanours?' suggested Elizabeth.

Symonds looked confused. 'Now, now, my dear. Couldn't we let bygones be bygones?'

'So, you would supervise the progress of the building? If I will raise the money.'

'More than willing.' He went with her to the door. 'Might I ask when Mr Pengelly will be coming to discuss the matter?'

Elizabeth smiled. 'My husband is very busy these days. He has left the entire organization of the scheme to me.'

It began to rain as she left Yooma with Agnes. The sky was bruised with purple. Soon heavy drops of water made dark spots on the road ahead.

Elizabeth welcomed the storm. It seemed to herald a fresh start with its associations of drama. 'We're in for a soaking, Aggie. Up with the umbrella.'

Agnes handed her the brolly and laughed as rainspots made Camelot whine and shiver. She held out her hand to catch them. 'I love the rain,' she shouted. 'I love Mary and the piglets, and Mrs McCreery and everyone. And Camelot. And most of all you, Mama.'

'And Papa,' Elizabeth prompted.

'And Papa,' Agnes said reluctantly.

'And do you still hate little Katherine?'

The child considered the question for several seconds. 'Yes. I'll always hate Katherine.'

Elizabeth fretted for a short while over the baby, guilty at having left her all day in the care of Miss Grey. She was heavy with milk and uncomfortable. She imagined scenes in which the baby had screamed for hours, rejecting the capable ministrations of the nursemaid and the pacification of a rubber teat and glass milk bottle. She shook off her anxieties and concentrated on guiding the horses. She began to fret about other things. The track was quickly softening, making the driving hard-going. She remembered the creek ahead, when its waters were swelled with rain.

An hour later her fears were confirmed. The creek, which on their journey out had been a fordable stream, was now brown and deep and swirling with debris. The horses' hooves slipped on the bank and the animals shied in fear. Elizabeth jumped down from the carriage and held on to the lead horse's head. She backed him away from the water, her own feet slithering and skidding sideways in the mud.

Camelot leaped around the dog-cart, barking with frantic excitement. Agnes, wild-eyed but, as Elizabeth contemplated afterwards, totally unafraid, clung to the rail of the carriage and shouted at the dog to keep calm or they would frighten the horses.

Elizabeth steered the animals away from the creek until the dog-cart was on drier ground. She stood, defeated for the moment by the situation. Alone and on horseback she might have risked the crossing, but with Agnes and the dog-cart it was impossible.

'Aren't we going to make them go through the creek?' Agnes was disappointed.

Elizabeth climbed back on to the carriage, wishing that she had Agnes's simple confidence and that she could tell herself that she was not frightened. They would have to make a detour upstream, to where a bridge took the road northwards. The extra miles would add more than two hours to their journey, and in not much longer than that it would be dark.

'Settle down, Aggie, and get some sleep. It's going to be a long journey home.'

*

299

Night came quickly, but they were on familiar ground by the time Elizabeth lit the carriage lanterns. The rain had stopped. She watched the stars slide across the sky, that huge, empty bowl of the heavens which echoed the vastness of the country.

She was relieved when they neared Sydney, but she was aware in herself of a feeling of anti-climax as the safety of her tidy world gathered them home. The bush was raw, but it was real. The door was flung open as they reached it. Arthur came rushing out on to the drive. The noise and confusion woke Agnes, who, realizing that the adventure was over, decided to cry.

'Where the devil have you been!'

Elizabeth said nothing, but climbed down from the dog-cart, trembling with exhaustion. The carriage wheels were clogged with mud, and the horses in a lather. She turned to Patrick. 'The horses are pretty done up.'

Patrick took the horses off with the carriage, he was straight-backed with anger. Even Camelot was subdued, as he slunk along by Patrick's side.

Miss Grey waited in the hall. She held out her arms to take Agnes and threw Elizabeth a glance of undisguised disapproval.

'Where the devil have you been?' Arthur repeated, following Elizabeth into the house. 'I demand an explanation.'

'For a drive.'

'Patrick says you left this morning.'

'It was a long drive,' snapped Elizabeth.

Agnes, in the comforting embrace of Miss Grey, had stopped crying. 'We've been all the way to Yooma. I was born there, Papa. Mama says –'

'Yooma! Why Yooma, in heaven's name?'

'Really, Arthur!' said Elizabeth. 'We're quite safe. I'm sorry to have caused you so much worry, but we had to make a detour because the river was full. Do stop sounding like something out of a melodrama. Miss Grey, Agnes will be hungry. Would you get her something hot from the kitchen?'

The woman lowered her gaze respectfully and took Agnes off upstairs. Elizabeth started to follow her. Arthur caught hold of her arm.

'I'll have a proper explanation for this.'

'May I change my clothes and see Katherine first?'

'She's been as good as gold, Mrs Pengelly,' called Miss Grey from the landing.

Arthur reluctantly let go of Elizabeth's arm. 'I shall tell Honor to delay supper. I shall be in the drawing room, until you've satisfied me with an explanation.'

Elizabeth turned away from him and swept upstairs. She tightened her jaw with rage. It was then that it occurred to her that she would not tell him. He did not deserve to know about her plans for Yooma. She would tell Edward in her letters, in secret. And when it was done, and the school was built, Arthur would see that he could not demand explanations from her in his high-handed way.

37

Edward was not yet thirty, though he seemed older; people remarked how the Crimea had left its scars. His handsome face was gaunt, his once boyish hair was already greying. He had developed a slight stoop as if continually harassed by the elements.

The April wind was cold in Hyde Park, reluctant to let go of winter. Edward walked quickly, he swung his cane a little and the expression on his face suggested a private optimism. He felt alive for the first time in weeks, was conscious of the spring flowers, the green haze of tiny buds breaking on the trees and the clamour of birds above the sounds of the traffic. He felt that, if he had been in the open country instead of London, he too might well have burst into song.

Edward was going to visit Lydia Delahaye, but this was not the cause for such high spirits. He fingered the letter in his pocket, which he had received that morning. Was it wise, he warned himself, to derive so much happiness from a few letters, counting off the weeks until he might hear from Elizabeth again? You should marry, friends told him, but he knew in his heart that he would never marry again. And the advice was given mostly out of habit. People had grown used to his solitary existence. He was a respected figure in the medical world and a respectable and sober gentleman in club circles. He played the role of bachelor uncle to Charles Watkins's brood of children; and for Lydia's ladies he was a man with a romantic past, who could still occasionally cause female hearts to flutter.

He rang the bell of Lydia's house and waited. Today's visit was a social call, though he was no stranger to the house, as founder of the Fitzroy Infirmary and in his capacity as Lydia's physician. Lydia was getting wheezy with age, and her memory was less sure, her eyes no longer scrutinized him sharply when he met her.

Edward could hear voices as he was shown towards the drawing room. At least, there would not be some well-meaning and unattached lady from the Benevolent Friends' Ladies' Society, sitting blushing and anticipating his matrimonial consideration; Lydia had long ago given up trying to matchmake. His spirits sank a little as he saw that Lydia's drawing room was crowded with company, but rose again as he recognized Hannah, surrounded by her five children. Hannah was unmistakably pregnant again. Her mother, Mrs Thorne, like a half-starved blackbird in her widow's weeds, sat close to the fire with her back to everyone. Fred stood by the hearth with a bored expression. He was making a half-hearted attempt to coax his mother-in-law into conversation.

'Mr Munro! We were just talking about you!' exclaimed Lydia. 'There now, isn't that fortuitous?'

Mrs Thorne twisted round from the fire and screwed up her eyes to see who had come in. 'Who's that? Who is it? Do I know him?'

'It's Edward – Mr Munro,' prompted Hannah. She smiled at Edward. 'We were just saying how, when Fred and I were married nearly eight years ago, we never would have guessed what a great man Mr Munro would become.'

'I would dispute the great,' laughed Edward. 'Stuffy perhaps. A sobersides.'

'Oh, never that,' said Lydia, shifting her corseted figure flirtatiously. 'Whenever you attend our Friday meetings the proceedings are very lively.'

'The ladies' charming company clearly draws out the best in a man,' Edward said, bowing slightly. He accepted a seat, flicking back his coat and resting his hands on his cane. 'But I shouldn't have come today, if I'd known I was going to intrude on a family visit.'

'Nonsense, Edward,' said Hannah. 'How can you say that when I have known you from childhood?'

Lydia leaned forward and patted his hand. 'You're a family friend.' Mrs Thorne, losing interest, turned away again to the fire.

One of the children, Henry, was pulling at Hannah's sleeve. 'Will Mr Munro show me some of his funny animals?'

'He has never forgotten how you once showed him how to draw comical farm animals,' Hannah explained.

'He was very quick to learn.'

'He is an intelligent boy for his age,' said Fred confidently, as if the fact could not be disputed. 'He shares his lessons with his brother Albert, though Henry is not yet six.'

The same age as Agnes, thought Edward. He regarded the boy's delicate face, comparing it in his mind with the portrait he had at home of his and Elizabeth's child, searching briefly for a family likeness. Elizabeth had written that Pengelly kept a strict control over Agnes's lessons with her governess, that he was determined on breaking her spirit. Edward had felt a fierce rage against the man and had cheered when Elizabeth wrote further, that Agnes was just as determined that her spirit would not be broken. 'If only you could see her, Edward, when she speaks out against the smallest injustice. How proud you would be of your daughter.'

'Edward?'

Hannah was speaking. He was aware of the younger child, George, by his chair.

'Will you teach me to make pictures too?' the child said engagingly.

'Of course.' Edward lifted him on to his knee. 'Have you entered the schoolroom yet, like your brothers?'

'Next year,' murmured Hannah fondly.

'Elizabeth wrote that she had engaged a governess for her elder daughter,' remarked Lydia.

'The child leads the poor woman a merry dance, I believe,' said Edward eagerly, without thinking.

'She has written to you too?' asked Fred curiously.

Edward glanced down at the soft strands of fair hair of the child on his knee, afraid to meet Fred's eyes in case the look in his own betrayed him. 'She has written on several occasions. We *were* once old friends.'

'Oh, come, Mr Munro,' teased Lydia. 'Enough water has passed under the bridge to own up to an old romance. We have all had romantic episodes in our past.'

'Who has?' said Mrs Thorne, looking at Fred.

'No one, Mother-in-law.' Fred moved away from the fire, as if the heat had become too uncomfortable. 'I must repeat, under the circumstances, my surprise that Elizabeth should think it proper to write to Edward.'

'Mr Pengelly clearly has no objection,' said Lydia. 'Sometimes, Fred, you carry your solicitor's stickling for propriety too far.'

304

'Ha!' Mrs Thorne let out a shriek of laughter.

Hannah frowned and busied herself with a loose thread on Albert's cuff. The children giggled, making the most of the strained silence, until a gruff 'Ahem!' from Fred warned that further levity would bring retribution.

'It is very interesting for me, to hear about Elizabeth's life,' said Edward. 'How successfully she has become an Australian.' He paused. 'And to hear about her children.'

'She is wealthier than you would ever have made her,' said Mrs Thorne from the fireplace. 'You with those soldiers of yours!'

There was a more shocked silence.

'That is true,' said Edward calmly.

'Edward has moved from the East End now, Mother,' said Hannah.

Mrs Thorne nodded to herself. 'Mr Pengelly is very influential in Sydney. He knows all sorts of important people.'

'A tradesman like Pengelly will always remain a tradesman,' remarked Fred, seizing a small opportunity for revenge on his mother-in-law.

'Certainly, it's not the same as having a profession.' Hannah, eager to smooth over the situation, glanced pleadingly at Edward, as if asking him to forgive them.

Edward felt detached from their embarrassment. He thought of Elizabeth's own comments on Pengelly's rise in society. 'Arthur knows all the right people in Sydney. Wealth has always spoilt him, Edward.' She wrote how much she regretted her husband's obsession with prestige and the pursuit of money, that it would always come between them. 'If it were not for my secret journeys to Yooma, to watch the progress of the school building, I think I should go mad with frustration. But it will soon be finished. What then, with nothing on hand to occupy me? Another year goes by, Edward, and then another, and the thought comes to my mind. Will I ever see your dear face again?'

'Hannah and I are so glad you relinquished your presence at the Fitzroy Infirmary,' said Fred. 'Founding the place was one thing. But to spend your life's work among the riff-raff of society is quite another.'

'But if it were not for the riff-raff of society,' said Edward, 'the more affluent among us would have no opportunities to practise our charitable gestures. Gentlemen would not be able to shake their heads at the *plight of the Poor* and donate a sovereign. The world would be a very dull place.'

'He's teasing you, Fred,' said Hannah. 'You should know that Edward has a soft spot for his charity cases.'

'Spongers and shirkers, most of them. No moral fibre.'

'Mr Pengelly is fond of charitable projects, I believe,' interrupted Lydia. 'He recently donated a large sum of money to an orphanage. Elizabeth sent a newspaper cutting from the *Sydney Morning Herald*. And then, he is going to open a school at that place where they used to live. How very respectable it has all become.'

'I believe it is Elizabeth who is building the school,' corrected Edward.

Lydia laughed. 'She could hardly do such a thing without Mr Pengelly. That's Elizabeth all over. If she has one chief fault, it's an overeagerness to be at the centre of things. She has delusions of a woman's importance in situations where women must take second place as a matter of course.'

'She did rather try to fly in the face of nature always,' said Hannah sadly.

'Unwomanly,' pronounced Fred.

'She was a wicked, ungrateful daughter,' cried Mrs Thorne and thumped her stick on the floor. 'She killed her poor father.'

Edward, unable to keep silent, set the child down from his knee. He stood up. 'I must protest. I don't believe that Elizabeth was any of those things.' They looked at him. He bent down to the child. 'Another time we'll practise drawing. When you next come to London.'

'You are not going?' said Lydia.

'Perhaps. Yes, I think I should go now.'

Out in the street, Edward began to walk quickly, eager to get home and to the task of the letter he would write to Elizabeth, congratulating her on the completion of her schoolhouse. The thought of the quiet of his study, the ticking of the clock and crack of logs on the fire was comforting. He would have the portrait of Agnes before him, and Elizabeth's letters to read over and over.

And then – when the letter was written and posted? He would not think of the months of waiting, the bleakness of the spring and summer, until he received a letter in return.

Another year goes by, and then another. He knew he was fooling himself, reading false hopes into her words, but he clung to them none the less. *Will I ever see your dear face again?*

38

Arthur was late. The carriage had been ready and waiting for an hour. Elizabeth, standing with Agnes and Katherine in the hall, knew that he had forgotten his promise to go for a drive with them that day.

'Can't we have our picnic without Papa?' whined Agnes.

Elizabeth put her finger to her lips; she tapped on the study door.

Arthur was seated at his desk. He looked up from his papers, surprised to see her dressed for an outing, annoyed at being interrupted.

'Arthur, you haven't forgotten?'

'Forgotten?'

'I was going to show you how I have spent the interest on my Pengelly shares today.'

His expression cleared briefly, then darkened with fresh impatience. At one time, thought Elizabeth, turning away, he would at least have tried to hide his irritation.

'Well, what's this all about?' he said as they set out. 'Jenkins seems to know all about it. He gave me a dry look the other morning, when I said you had some scheme up your sleeve.'

'Your accountant has his own ideas about more profitable ways of investing my money. He's been advising me over the past eight months.'

'Eight months – a mystery indeed.'

Elizabeth was not surprised that Arthur did not know of her journeys to Yooma. Jenkins and the whole household had been sworn to secrecy. She doubted anyway whether Arthur ever paused to consider what

307

occupied her. There were days, she reflected, when their paths never crossed at all: trade meetings and dinners with colleagues kept him late in the evenings, and Elizabeth had adopted a habit of retiring early to bed.

She watched him secretly as Patrick drove them. Arthur's face was red and heavy. The frequent dining out had produced a dramatic effect on his figure, which, inclined to stoutness, had become very fleshy during the past year. He visited the barber regularly, his side-whiskers were discreetly coiffured to fringe the increasing baldness on top of his head. His taste for fashion had channelled itself into well-tailored but more sombre outfits than in the past.

It was autumn, nearly winter, and after recent rain the landscape was green. The gum trees were silken smooth under their brown bark tatters. The scent of the bush was damp and fresh and bees hummed in the air.

Arthur's expression relaxed as they left the town behind. At one point they passed a mass of hanging vines, the sun shone through the leaves, as if through a green cathedral window, and Elizabeth saw him smile with pleasure.

He sensed her scrutiny and turned to look at her. He raised an eyebrow in inquiry.

'I was thinking that it's a long while since you and I spent any time together,' Elizabeth said.

'We must remedy that. I'll ask Jenkins to get some tickets for the theatre, if that would please you?'

She said that it would. But it had not been what she had in mind.

'I hope you approve of my project,' she said, suddenly nervous. It occurred to her that she desperately wanted his approval over the school. If he would, just this once, support her, she would try to be content and she would love him. Perhaps she had always loved him. Perhaps love was this uneasy thing which had held them together, which bound her to him when reason told her she should have parted from him long ago.

'I told you you might have free rein with the money.' He looked at her quizzically. 'Is it likely I shall disapprove, like Jenkins?'

She decided to prepare the ground a little. 'You remember your gift to the orphanage –?'

'Aha! You have given the money away to a charity. A gesture designed to raise Pengelly's social prestige.'

'Something of the sort. I believe Jenkins expressed the opinion that the scheme would be good for the reputation of the business.'

'My dear, I was jesting. That money's yours, to spend independently. Not to improve my standing as a social benefactor.'

Arthur began to look puzzled as Patrick took the road for Yooma. He glanced at Elizabeth. She turned her head away, and he fell into an uneasy silence.

'Shall we soon be there?' asked Agnes.

'Soon enough,' Arthur replied grimly. 'And then, no doubt, we'll be rewarded with your mama's grand surprise.'

They drove towards the schoolhouse. Elizabeth looked at the white-painted, weather-boarded building with a string of flags across its doorway and her heart beat quickly with pride. Someone had daubed a banner with the words 'Yooma School' and hung it from the windows.

'It was my money,' Elizabeth said, already defensive. 'You said I might be entirely independent.'

'But a school again, Lizzie! And out here in the bush! I might have guessed it'd be something of the kind – some crack-brained thing! How do you think you're going to keep it financed? How will you pay for a man and his family to come here and run a school? I hope you don't imagine the business is going to pick up the bill.'

'Jenkins thought –'

'Jenkins, it seems, has lost his senses over this thing too. You'll find you can't twist me round a finger so easily.'

'Jenkins thought a voluntary subscription from the pupils, like before, and the regular income from my shares will be enough to cover the expenses of the teacher. I myself shall come out weekly, to supervise the curriculum and look over the children's copybooks.'

'Over my dead body!'

Several people were approaching the carriage, among them the Reverend and Mrs Symonds with Bella and Lucy. Arthur jumped down to greet them with a show of affability. Elizabeth followed more slowly with the children.

The village had prepared a small ceremony, a crowd was gathering by the school. Arthur accepted the keys to the building and the speeches from members of the village committee with a faintly jaded smile. 'I must insist that none of this is my doing,' he said, when invited to make a speech in reply. 'The accountability is all that of Mrs Pengelly.' He bowed slightly towards Elizabeth. He did not smile. 'And to tell truth, I know nothing of the venture. My wife has presented me with this opening ceremony of Yooma School as a surprise.' A gasp of amazement ran through the bystanders. 'An example of the natural deviousness in women, you might say.'

The crowd laughed, though a little uncertainly. Elizabeth lifted her head defiantly. She met the gaze of Lucy and Bella and then saw Alice McCreery wink at her; she smiled.

'And now, I should like Mrs Pengelly to conduct me on a tour of the building,' Arthur continued. The crowd parted for them as they went up to the school. Arthur unlocked the door with an exaggerated flourish. 'I should rather this all had been without benefit of an audience,' he said under his breath as they went into the building.

'I didn't know,' protested Elizabeth. 'It was Reverend Symonds who got up the speeches.' She had not expected that Arthur would be overjoyed. Nevertheless, she felt that he had somehow let her down.

'I'd not the smallest inkling what you'd been doing.'

'Have you ever troubled yourself over what I do each day?'

The Symonds and members of the village committee had followed them inside. Arthur adopted a tight-lipped smile. The little party walked from room to room, pointing out the various features to one another – the modern stove in one corner of the classroom with its chimney pipe reaching high into the gable roof, the fresh green paint on the walls, the provision for coats in the porchway, the rows of well-spaced benches, the generous living quarters for the school's teacher – as if they had not seen all these things before.

'And when is this miracle of education to commence?' asked Arthur as the tour came to a halt outside the school once more.

'The schoolmaster arrives next week,' said Elizabeth.

'No doubt with a wife and a hoard of offspring to support.'

'He is a single man, Mr Pengelly,' interposed Bella Symonds.

'You must be very proud of Mrs Pengelly,' suggested Lucy.

Arthur said stiffly, 'I have nothing but admiration for all my wife does.'

He decided on a strategy of putting a bold face on things; all through the luncheon held on the Symonds's veranda Arthur cultivated an attitude of jovial acceptance of the surprise his wife had planned for him.

On the way home it was a different matter.

'You could forbid it,' Elizabeth said coldly.

'Don't be ridiculous. Things have gone too far.'

'I don't know why you are so angry. You gave me a free rein, to do with the money what I liked.'

'But not squander it on a community of bush settlers. Not to desert your family each week and take off to Yooma!'

Agnes looked at them anxiously, sensing the onset of a quarrel.

'I feel as if I have deserted people like Alice and the children in Yooma,' Elizabeth said. 'I feel it's wrong, that you and I should live so well. We were like these people once. We lived there, just like them.'

'We were never like them!' he said violently. 'And you owe them nothing. Where's your pride? They made an outcast of you once.'

'It's not just for them. It's for me. You know it has never been enough for me just to be your wife.'

The school opened a fortnight later. Arthur complained that Elizabeth would neglect her family duties, that she would overtire herself with so much travelling, that Agnes and Katherine would suffer because of her absence.

Elizabeth was sitting by the fire. For once, she had waited up for Arthur to come home from a business meeting. She guessed from his face that he had been drinking.

'You have engaged a nursemaid and governess specifically to ensure my absence from the children,' she reasoned. 'How can they miss me for one day each week, when in any case they are occupied with Miss Grey and Miss Hastings in the nursery?'

'It's not natural,' Arthur blustered. 'It isn't womanly, to be so interested in people outside your home.'

'There is nothing for me to do otherwise. You have the business, your friends and colleagues outside the home. Why is that so much more natural? Why should I be content with reminding Honor to scold the housemaid because your shaving water was the wrong temperature this morning, telling Riley where to plant roses, admiring all the splendid furniture we have bought, the view from the bedroom window and listening to my children being turned into dutiful daughters from behind a closed nursery door?' Elizabeth felt the frustration of an old pattern repeating itself. She would never make him understand.

Arthur went to the sideboard and poured himself a glass of brandy. 'I wish you'd show a bit of pride in what I've achieved sometimes, instead of talking as if it were a crime to have earned an enviable kind of living.'

'I have never envied it,' Elizabeth said. 'I don't want it. I should have stayed in Yooma when you came back from Victoria.'

'You should have stayed in England, maybe. But you didn't. You knew which side your bread was buttered. Oh, I'm not complaining. You've been a good wife. But don't you pretend you're above all this.' He waved his hand to indicate the crystal chandelier, the decanter and glasses sparkling on a polished silver tray on the tapestried runner on the sideboard. He walked past her to the opposite side of the fire, where he slumped in a chair and drank from his brandy glass. He turned it restlessly between his fingers.

Elizabeth had noticed the usual strong smell of brandy and cigars as he had passed her. But there was a less familiar smell on his clothing, a sweetish smell of perfume. The implications jerked her to attention. 'You have been with a woman! You haven't been to a meeting tonight.'

He drained his glass, but he could not meet her eyes. 'Now don't start that.' He stood up and went to the sideboard. He hesitated before reaching for the decanter and refilling his glass. 'I went to the meeting. And after, we were at the theatre.'

'Who is she?'

'It's not important.'

'Not important?' She caught at his arm as he returned to his chair.

'No. She's a nothing.' He sat down again. His hands trembled on his glass. He half-raised it to his lips, then set it unsteadily on the floor. 'Bugger it, Lizzie! You know the sort of thing.'

'I came to Sydney because I thought you needed me,' she said quietly. 'All I've ever wanted from you was that you should be honest with me. I see myself becoming more and more like my sister. She has a cross to bear – did you know that? Fred and his women. He waited only as long as it took to get her pregnant.'

'You're no better than anyone else, Lizzie,' he said bitterly. 'You were a frustrated spinster when I met you. You wanted a man, any

312

man would have suited. And when I wasn't satisfactory for you, you lost no time taking back your fancy-man.'

'I loved Edward!'

'And you've never loved me.' He stared into the fire flames as they died low in the grate.

Elizabeth opened her mouth to protest, but she did not know what to say.

Arthur leaned forward to the log basket. He selected a heavy chunk of wood and threw it roughly into the fire. A puff of grey ash flew out over the hearth and landed on the rug.

'Now look what you've done!' Elizabeth was near to tears. He was so smug, with his brandy, his business cronies and their mistresses. 'I did a terrible thing, marrying you when I didn't love you. I should never have left them all, Hannah, Mother, my poor father!'

'And your lover! Don't you forget your lover!'

She wanted to escape. The smell of the brandy made her feel ill. She turned away. 'I'm going to bed.'

He did not reply.

She halted by the door. 'I'm going to Yooma tomorrow. I'm taking Agnes. I should like her to have her lessons with me one day a week.'

'No, Elizabeth,' he said quietly.

'Miss Hastings has agreed to it.'

'No. I forbid it.'

She opened the door. 'We'll discuss it in the morning. You'll see, I'm determined on this and Agnes is looking forward to it.'

She was shocked by the speed with which he reached the door. He slammed it shut and fell with his arm against it, trapping her against the wall.

'She'll not go! You'll not defy me any longer!' He moved his arm from the door and Elizabeth thought that he was going to strike her. His fingers were spread wide, the palm tensed. He lowered his hand slowly and stepped back, releasing her from the wall. 'I *will* rule in this house.' His face was very pale. He folded his arms across his ribs, pressing his hand against his chest and leaned with his back to the wall.

'Arthur – whatever's the matter?' She could not understand at first when he did not answer, until he released his breath in an exclamation of pain.

313

Elizabeth ran out into the hall. 'Riley! Patrick!' She returned swiftly to the drawing room. 'Patrick will fetch the doctor.'

He nodded.

Elizabeth felt very calm. She stood by the door until Honor and Riley came, running across the hallway. She turned again to Arthur. 'It will be all right,' she said. She could not bring herself to touch him.

39

Elizabeth did not go the next day to Yooma. Arthur was confined to the house and garden for the next six weeks and ordered to rest.

Elizabeth watched him drive away from the house when he returned to the office, relieved to be free again; he had been a fractious and demanding invalid.

She stood at the window long after he had gone. July, a month of lush growth and flowers in England, but here the garden was saturated with heavy monsoon rain and the wind, blowing strongly from the south, whipped the twining branches of bougainvillaea vine against the posts of the veranda.

'You'll be going back to your visits to Yooma,' said Honor, coming into the dining room to take out the breakfast dishes.

'I suppose I shall,' Elizabeth replied, but she was affected by a lethargy which she could not explain.

'Will Miss Agnes be going with you?'

'Mr Pengelly doesn't want her to,' Elizabeth said, remembering the quarrel which had brought about Arthur's illness. She looked at Honor, who regarded her shrewdly. She wondered just how much the house staff knew.

'You'll be waiting for a letter from England.' Honor carried the tray to the door. 'Mail's late this month.'

Elizabeth smiled. 'You're a wily bird, Honor.' Then, more seriously, she said, 'I'm very grateful for your silence about the letters from England.'

'No point in upsetting the apple cart.' Honor paused. Something troubled her. 'Though there's some upsets can't be avoided.'

'Is there something wrong?'

'It's me and Riley, madam. I can't hide it much more. We're going to have a family.' Honor's pleasant face crumpled with distress.

Elizabeth left the window and sat down at the table. 'Don't worry about it,' she said at last. 'I'll talk to Mr Pengelly.'

'But you can't!' Elizabeth was horrified by Arthur's reaction. 'Where will they go? How could you do such a thing, after they've been so loyal?'

'They might be loyal to you,' he said, 'but neither Riley nor his wife have forgiven me ever for going off and leaving you at Yooma.'

'That's ridiculous. Honor has never shown any sign of hostility to you.'

'Nevertheless, I felt it.' He returned to his newspaper, as if the matter was closed. 'You must give her notice. Riley too. For there's no place for his wife and child here if he stays.'

'I can't believe you are the man I married,' said Elizabeth. 'I won't do it. If you want to dismiss them, you must do it yourself. But I shall oppose you with all my will.'

She slammed the study door behind her. Honor was in the hall. Elizabeth guessed that she had heard what had happened. 'I'm sorry, Honor. I will try again.'

'It's not your fault, Mrs Pengelly.'

'I don't know what to do.' Elizabeth felt helpless. She went to the woman and put her arms round her. 'If the worst comes to the worst, and you have to go, I shall try to help Riley find a situation. If you need anything –' She did not see Agnes on the stairs. Honor's stoicism broke. She leaned, sobbing, against Elizabeth's shoulder.

'I don't want to leave you, Mrs Pengelly. I don't want to leave here. We've been so happy.'

Agnes ran and threw her arms round Honor's skirts. 'Why is Honor leaving, Mama? Who said so?'

Honor dried her eyes on her apron. She shook her head and stroked Agnes's hair. 'There, we mustn't go against your papa.'

Agnes threw Elizabeth a look of horror. 'Has Papa said Honor and Riley have to go?'

'Aggie, this isn't anything to do with you. You don't understand.'

'I do. I won't let him.' She ran to the study door. She did not check herself before opening it. Elizabeth stood in disbelief as Agnes entered her father's sanctuary. 'Papa – how can you be so wicked? You can't send Honor and Riley away.'

Elizabeth heard Arthur's roar of anger. She rushed to the study door, but Agnes stood in front of the desk without flinching.

'Who sent the child in here, meddling in adult business?' demanded Arthur.

'She overheard. She's bound to be upset.' Elizabeth put out her hand, to lead Agnes from the study, but the child held her arms resolutely behind her back.

'I'm not going until Papa promises he didn't mean it, and he won't send them away.'

There was silence. Elizabeth's disapproval of Agnes's behaviour was tinged with a secret pride. 'Come, Aggie,' she said sternly. But Arthur was before her. He laid down his newspaper and left his desk. Picking up Agnes round her waist, he marched with her out of the study, past Honor to the wine cupboard, where he deposited her and shut the door. He turned the key and pocketed it.

'She can stay there until she repents of her wilfulness. I shall speak to her in an hour.' Arthur went into his study and closed the door.

'Oh, Mrs Pengelly, I'm so sorry. It's all because of me.' Honor began to cry again. Elizabeth walked to the door of the wine cupboard. She waited, expecting to hear the child sobbing, but Agnes, inside the cupboard, made no sound.

'Poor little mite. She'll be frightened in the dark there.'

'Agnes,' called Elizabeth through the door panel, and casting a glance towards the study. 'Aggie – are you all right?'

Agnes did not answer.

Reluctantly Elizabeth left her to repent her sins.

After an hour she returned to the hallway. There was still no sound from behind the door. Arthur came out from his study.

'Thank you, my dear, but I shall deal with this.' He stood by the cupboard with his arms folded and rocked backwards and forwards on his heels. 'Agnes. This is Papa speaking. Now just tell me how sorry you feel, and you may come out from the dark.'

They waited expectantly.

'This is ridiculous, Arthur,' hissed Elizabeth. 'Let the child out for goodness' sake.'

317

A small clear voice came from the cupboard. 'I'll not come out 'til Papa says Honor can stay.'

Arthur reddened with anger. He looked at Elizabeth as if for support.

'Very well. We'll leave her until bedtime. We shall see what going without dinner does for her pride.'

Elizabeth picked at her dinner. She could think of nothing but Agnes in the cupboard. There was no light inside, except for what could penetrate the cracks under and around the door. The rows of bottles would be sinister shapes in the dark.

'Arthur, whether she apologizes or not, you cannot leave her there all night.' She could see that he was troubled. 'There's no harm in retracting a little,' she coaxed. 'Aggie has been punished for a whole afternoon.'

Arthur cut a slice from an apple and ate it, then nodded. 'You're right. We'll end the punishment after dinner.'

'Agnes,' called Arthur through the door panel. 'Do you hear me. You may come out now and say you're sorry.'

A muffled voice shouted back from the cupboard.

'What does she say?'

'I think she says that she's not coming out.'

'Agnes!' said Arthur loudly. 'I've decided your punishment is ended. I am going to unlock the door.'

He drew the key from his pocket and opened the door with a flourish. He fell back with a shout of surprise. Elizabeth covered her mouth to stifle a shriek. A wall of wine bottles from the floor to as high as Agnes had been able to stack them blocked the entrance to the cupboard.

'I'm staying here,' called a voice from behind the barricade.

'The sediment!' roared Arthur. 'She's disturbed my best claret! Fetch Riley! Somebody get that child out!'

Elizabeth began to laugh.

Arthur roared again and Riley came running. Miss Grey, carrying Katherine, and Miss Hastings, already hovering on the landing, edged down the stairs to see better what was happening. Patrick and Honor and the housemaid, for whom 'Miss Agnes and the wine cupboard' had been the conversation all afternoon, crowded into the hall.

Riley patiently began to remove the wall of bottles.

Agnes received a beating. Elizabeth knew that Arthur's slipper had driven in her self-will, rather than expelled it. She did not want her to hate Arthur, but she was prepared to let her resent his autocracy.

'Will Papa let Honor and Riley stay now?' said Agnes, when Elizabeth tucked her into bed.

Elizabeth sat beside her and smoothed back her hair from her face. 'I will try to persuade him, my darling. But sometimes we have to accept the way things are.'

'I never will,' Agnes said solemnly. 'Not when it's not fair.'

Elizabeth kissed her tenderly. 'I'm very glad,' she whispered.

Elizabeth rode to Yooma the next day. The school was thriving well without her. The long interval had alienated her a little from the children and the schoolmaster. They were polite to her, they recited their prepared lessons very formally, as they might have done for any passing visitor. She called on the Symonds and Alice McCreery and felt like a lady of charitable intent. On the journey home, she rode, letting her horse have his head, feeling the exhilaration of the wind on her face; the visit had made her restless. The Yooma project was finished. She saw that all that remained for her now was to keep on providing the money. Her real place, as Arthur would tell her, was at home with Agnes and Katherine.

Honor came to meet her in the hallway. Elizabeth guessed from her reddened eyes that she had been crying again. She laid a hand briefly on the woman's shoulder and gave it a squeeze of sympathy.

'There was a letter from England, Mrs Pengelly.' Honor pulled a letter from her pocket and gave it to her.

In all the upset over Honor and Riley, Elizabeth had thought only fleetingly of Edward. In the privacy of her room an hour later her heart quickened with affection as she read the familiar hand. 'The end of another winter in England . . .' Elizabeth remembered Charlford, the winds across the frozen river pathway and the bridge over the river. An overwhelming nostalgia for Somerset swept over her. She missed the gentle landscape, the subtlety of spring breezes, fine summer rain and autumn mists. Edward wrote of London. He had been to see her Aunt

Lydia, had met her mother and her sister's family there. How different they all seemed – her mother, strange and cantankerous; Hannah, 'very matronly, the perfect mother'; Fred, middle-aged at thirty-five, with blinkered eyes, 'who clearly disapproves of our correspondence' – Elizabeth smiled – 'He probably thinks we are conducting a secret love affair across the globe.'

Elizabeth rested the letter on her knee and looked at the inlaid box lined with yellow silk, which lay open in her drawer, inside it the carefully preserved letters and book of Tennyson's poems, which she kept hidden from Arthur. Secrets? Edward must know that she would not show his letters to Arthur. A love affair? With a stab of guilt, she knew that it had become just that for her. But Edward never spoke of love in his letters, and very little of the past. Was it only because of Agnes that he wrote to her?

She folded the pages of the letter and placed it on top of the others in the box. She could hear that Arthur had come home from work. He called to her. Reluctantly she locked the box and closed the drawer. A quick glance in the mirror tested whether her guilt was reflected in her face. Satisfied, she left the room and went downstairs.

Arthur announced that they should spend more time together. People were beginning to talk, he said. A wife who took herself off on outlandish experiments in bush education, who insisted on keeping on a servant who was six months pregnant – Elizabeth and Agnes's combined efforts had secured a reprieve for Honor until the baby was born – 'They'll say next I can't control you.'

'*Control* me, Arthur?' said Elizabeth. They were making a tour of the garden, skirting the perimeter of the lawn. Arthur had planted roses, bed after bed of them; in the colonial tradition he had established a determinedly English garden, with borders of sweet william, sweet peas and geraniums. A pair of black cockatoos sat incongruously on a branch of lilac. A single mimosa, Elizabeth's favourite tree, with its fluffy globes of wattle flowers, splashed brilliant yellow against the darker foliage and released its evocative scent across the garden, a reminder, with the cockatoos, of Yooma and the bush.

Arthur frowned. 'I fear talk of an estrangement. Perhaps we should plan a house party at Christmas, just to show that all's well. What do you think?'

She shrugged. She said that if he supposed a cosy tableau of domestic bliss would stop tongues wagging, she might as well support the charade.

'No charade, Elizabeth,' Arthur said calmly.

She sighed. If only there was not this uneasy pretence between them. 'I've a trade meeting tonight,' he had said, for the second time in a fortnight. And she had replied, 'What a bore for you,' knowing that the Chamber met less than once a month and that he would be going instead to some pleasure house.

They made their way round the top edge of the lawn and past the window, where the maid was setting dinner in the dining room.

'By the way,' said Arthur, 'better tell the staff I shall want no supper. I forgot to mention – we're eating at the Club.' He paused to watch the maid as she bent and straightened by the table on the other side of the glass. Her black taffeta frock swung up over her ankles. The girl did not see him. She was intent on getting the placings correct.

'Will you be late?' Elizabeth watched his attention on the girl.

'I expect so. No need for you to wait up.'

'Arthur –'

The sharpness of her tone surprised him. He turned to look at her.

'Do you ever think of everything we've been through together?'

His expression became shuttered. 'I prefer not to.' He walked on past the window and waited for her by the front door. 'I learned to forgive you for certain things a long time back. Don't go raking things up, Elizabeth. Why don't you come inside? It's getting cold.'

She followed him into the house. They reached his study and she rested her hand on his arm. 'But, do you ever think of me in the way you used to?' She could not bring herself to use the word love. 'Do you really need me for anything any more?'

Arthur sighed, prepared to be tolerant of whatever mood had come over her, making her difficult. 'Of course I do. You're my wife. The mistress of my home.'

Elizabeth's hand slipped from his arm. She felt the last remnant of hope drain from her: she could remember those same words, spoken once with a pious sense of duty, when Robert Munro had asked her to be his wife.

*

321

Elizabeth went to her room early that evening. She had asked the maid to light a fire in the grate. The flames had aready mellowed to a warm red, making the room look rosy and welcoming.

She opened the drawer in her dressing table and took out her book of poems and the box which held Edward's few letters. She made herself comfortable on the bed against a mound of pillows. It was like burrowing into a nest, lined with memories and her treasures.

She was not conscious of time passing, until the clock in the corridor struck ten. She listened to the last sonorous chime, her hand resting lazily on the open pages of Tennyson's *Morte d'Arthur*. The fire had made her eyelids heavy. She was vaguely aware of sounds downstairs and of movement in the corridor. When the door opened she could only stare, her hand still resting on the page. It was as if they were transfixed by that instant, Elizabeth on the bed and Arthur framed in the doorway.

Arthur's face was dark red, either from the cold air or from recent brandy. His silk scarf lay very white against the black of his cloak. He held his hat and cane. Elizabeth was reminded incongruously of the villain in a play they had seen recently at the theatre. Slowly she closed the box of letters.

Arthur frowned a little, as if he was surprised, even displeased, to see her still dressed. Elizabeth tried to judge his mood. Something or someone must have upset his evening.

'I've been thinking over what you said,' he murmured. Elizabeth saw now that he had been drinking. He came further into the room. 'What are you reading?' He dropped his hat and cane on to the counterpane.

'You're back early.'

'The meeting was cancelled. What are you reading?' he repeated. He held out his hand with a smile on his face. 'Let me see.'

Elizabeth held the book against her chest, like a child asked to deliver up a favourite object. 'It's nothing. It's not important.'

'Then why do you look so guilty? What is it – risky stories?' The idea amused him. He giggled for a while about it. 'All right, then. I'll look at this instead.' He picked up the box of letters from the bed.

'Arthur – please don't!' Elizabeth floundered on the counterpane, trying to take the box from him, while he held it above her head. He swung away from her to the lamp and lifted the lid of the box. He seemed puzzled at first by the letters, pulled out one, and set the box down carefully on the bed. Elizabeth's heart rose into her throat, fear dried up her tongue, as he unfolded the pages to read.

'What is this?' He still could not understand. He turned the page, with an empty, uncomprehending smile.

'You have no right,' she protested, as she saw his smile falter.

Arthur stared at her and at the book on her lap. He forced it from her resisting fingers, glanced at its content and threw it back on the bed. 'Poems. Letters. What is this?' He tipped up the box and let the letters scatter. 'How long has this been going on?'

'It's not important,' she repeated. 'It's just a comfort to me. And he wanted to know about Agnes.'

'Not important? My wife getting secret letters from a past lover, mooning over them and reading poetry!' He searched for words to express his outrage and failed. 'I'd come home early, to patch things up between us, Elizabeth. I was going to tell you –' He frowned, trying to remember what he had been going to tell her.

Elizabeth began to gather up the letters and put them in the box.

'Leave them be –' She felt his hand on her wrist. 'Do you think I'll let you keep them!' She tried to wriggle free, but his hand was firm. 'Do you think I'd let you keep them!' he shouted, his face close to hers was bloodshot and smelled of drink. 'These are going on the fire.'

He was by the hearth in a few seconds, tipping the contents of the box into the flames. Elizabeth watched the fire burn up round them with hesitant flickers, as the bundle of paper briefly deadened its heat. Then the paper caught light. It flared, and a yellow blaze lit the hearth. Flames swallowed up the lines of dark ink and white paper, curled over their edges, turned them brown and then black.

Arthur stood with his arm along the mantel shelf, staring at the charred and burning letters. He straightened and seemed all at once very sober. 'God moves in mysterious ways, Elizabeth. You'll thank me one day for what I've just done. You shall learn, as I learned, to cut the past out. No more letters, no more correspondence over Agnes. Cut it out, like you would a canker.'

Elizabeth clutched a pillow to her, hating him with a violence she had never felt before. Arthur came towards her and picked up the Tennyson. Elizabeth released her hold on the pillow slowly, afraid of what he would do next.

'This book.' He flicked through the pages. 'It seems to have some importance.' He looked up, challenging her. 'Is it a keepsake?'

She returned his look coldly. 'Surely, there's no harm in a book of poems?'

He snapped the book shut against his cloak. 'A canker. I'll not let my wife keep this sort of rubbish. It goes on the fire with the rest.'

Elizabeth was frozen into immobility, then she scrambled from the bed. He would not assume proprietorship of her in that way – his wife, his house, his possessions. He would not burn her poems. She reached the fireplace before him and barred his way.

'Lizzie, your frock! Take heed of the fire.'

'If you burn my book,' she cried, 'I'll never forgive you!'

Arthur hesitated, disconcerted by the wildness in her. 'Very well. I'll take it downstairs to the kitchen stove.'

'I'll not forgive you!' she repeated.

He shook his head. 'Words, Lizzie.' He opened the door and left the room.

Elizabeth paused for a moment, not believing that he could mean it. Then the danger of her dress catching fire roused her and she moved from the hearth.

Arthur had reached the end of the corridor before she caught up with him. She flung herself against him at the top of the stairs. He had not seen her coming and fell back with a grunt of surprise against the bannister rail. 'What the devil! Elizabeth!'

Elizabeth's hatred had concentrated itself into retrieving her poems. Fear that he would burn them drove a panic through her. She tried to wrench the book from him, but Arthur pulled it away. He held it at arm's length above the stairwell, leaning back a little over the rail.

'Arthur – please!'

'For God's sake, control yourself,' he panted.

She stepped away from him. 'Please. Give me my book.' She was aware of the servants in the hall below them.

Arthur glanced down and saw Riley. He lowered his arm. He pulled back his cloak where it had fallen from his shoulder. He spoke quietly. 'Now turn round and go back to your room.'

'I will when you give me my poems.'

Arthur ignored her outstretched hand. He brushed past her to go down the stairs.

Elizabeth's fury broke. She would not have it. He would not treat her with such contempt. She let loose a howl of rage. 'No! I won't let you!'

Arthur turned. His expression was almost comical, red-faced, and surprise making him at first forget his anger. Elizabeth lunged for the book and he raised his arm to defend himself. He jerked the other arm, which held the poems, instinctively away from her and was thrown off-balance by the movement.

In the same instant Elizabeth toppled against him, heard him gasp as her weight hit him and he fell back once more against the bannister rail. And then she was fighting for the poems, tearing at the arm which fended her off, straining to reach the book. They were silent except for Elizabeth's stifled sobs of desperation and Arthur's panting breath. He struggled to escape her hands which clawed at him. Their eyes met, but, if there was an instant when Arthur might have wavered, it quickly vanished. His expression hardened to a determination as strong as Elizabeth's own. Their eyes held one another's gaze, their wills were locked in a conflict in which they no longer recognized one another. Hatred burned between them, consuming everything that had gone before.

Honor and Riley watched from the hall, hovering with indecision and disturbed by the indignity of the scene. The clock on the landing struck the quarter hour, its familiar chimes adding an incongruous note of reassurance to the violence on the stairs.

As the sound died away, Arthur's expression altered. He coughed and his arm tightened across his chest. The book of poems slipped from his hand and fell, bouncing against the stairs.

Elizabeth did not try to retrieve it. She stepped back as Arthur bent double against the rail. His breath was harsh, his face agonized and draining quickly to an ashen grey. He slid downwards, his legs folding beneath him. The sound he made was brief, ugly, not even a cry for help, but an attempt to draw a last convulsive breath before he lost consciousness.

Elizabeth stared. She hardly noticed that Honor and Riley were beside her. She did not move to help them as they crouched over Arthur. She knew, when she met Honor's frightened gaze, that he was already dead.

The book which Edward had given her lay a few feet below her. It was undamaged. Its green cover and gold lettering stood out clearly against the dark red of the carpeted stair.

40

Edward had acted instinctively when he had learned that her husband was dead. Then the doubts had begun. There were the children – Arthur Pengelly's child, and Agnes, a six-year-old stranger. Elizabeth and the hot sun in a barleyfield were only memories among many other memories: the stench of death in fields of mud, a crocus flower and Marianne, her hair like fine gold. His image of Marianne was fading, as his picture of Elizabeth had done. The most intrinsic details of eyes and face, the nature of a smile, became shadows, which flitted briefly through his mind, too swift to catch.

Was the present, then, all that he could be sure of? His arms on the broad shiprail, the grey sea far below, the noise of the engines? But he had Elizabeth's letters – he felt for them in his pocket – and her last letter of them all, saying Arthur Pengelly was dead.

There were no indications in there, no commitment, no please come. Just the facts of the accident, the newspapers' speculations about the fortune she would inherit, the endless legal formalities. She was tired, she said. And, to the end, no hint that she wanted him to come.

It was autumn in the bush. The far blue light was clear and empty over the Queensland plains. Agnes was running among the pet lambs in the field. Katherine ran behind her, her arms spread wide, crying to be noticed and for her sister to wait.

Elizabeth, hot in black silk, shaded her eyes with her hand to watch them from the doorway.

Amy had written when she heard of Arthur's death. 'My dear

326

Elizabeth, you must come to us.' And, depressed by the aftermath of it all, Elizabeth had finally bent under the months of strain and taken a ship for Queensland.

The bush landscape and Amy's and her husband's calm acceptance of everything that had happened had worked a tranquillity on her. She turned from the door as Amy came into the sitting room. Elizabeth held out the letter in her hand, it was from Honor. 'Riley has gone back to carpentering. He thinks, with the endowment on them, he will start his own workshop.'

'You were more than generous to them, Lizzie.'

'Carpentering was his real trade,' mused Elizabeth. 'You know, it never occurred to me to question what he really wanted.'

'And what do you really want?'

Elizabeth turned back to the veranda, torn between the needs of the two small figures in the paddock and a deepening certainty inside her. The longing to return to England had become an almost physical ache. 'I must think how it would affect the children. They were born here. They are Australians.'

Amy came to stand beside her. She put an arm round Elizabeth's shoulders. 'We've been apart a long time. But I've known, since that day you told me about Agnes, where your heart really lies. You'll be a wealthy woman when the Importing Company is sold. You can do just as you please.'

'If I go, it will be on my own terms,' Elizabeth said defensively.

Amy smiled and let her hand fall. 'You're a lot like Mr Cavendish. Tom says, once a stockman, always a stockman. He has such a thorough knowledge of the farm and the country, he knows instinctively how to manage the shepherds and the men on the station. He would be miserable doing anything but what he knows.'

Elizabeth, unsure that the persistent strain of stock-rearing in the blood of Tom Cavendish was relevant, looked at Amy questioningly.

Amy went to the door. 'Once a teacher, always a teacher,' she said. 'You're a schoolmistress, Lizzie. You'll never get it out of your system. And you can do it as well in England as Australia.'

'I'm nearly forty,' called Elizabeth. Her anxiety conveyed itself to Amy, who smiled, knowing that she was not thinking of her capacity to teach.

'A feeble excuse.'

'How shall I know?' Elizabeth said desperately.

Amy put her head back round the door. 'You will know when you see him. But you must make up your mind what it is you want, Lizzie. Time is running short.'

Elizabeth paced up and down in the sitting room. She heard voices on the front veranda. She had fled indoors when Amy ran to tell her that a lone rider was approaching the station. It would be one of Mr Cavendish's acquaintances, Elizabeth reasoned, a passing bushman, a neighbour. She strained her ears. There were sounds of laughter, footsteps coming into the house. She ran to the mirror. How old she looked. Her figure had thickened. Her skin was browned by the wind and the sun.

She caught her glance in the mirror. The anxiety and hope in her eyes shocked her and she moved away and stood by the fireplace, her arms hugging her body. The voices in the next room came nearer, and then the door swung open.

'You have a visitor,' said Amy, tense with the uniqueness of the occasion.

The broad and dignified woman by the fireplace was a stranger. Her face had coarsened. Her hair was streaked with grey and neatly smoothed against her ears; gone were the copper lights. The whole impression – the mourning dress and stillness of her figure – was curiously unreal.

Elizabeth came slowly towards him, her hand outstretched. Her smile, hesitant at first, warmed to his own smile. 'Hello, Edward.' Her voice broke a little with nervousness, or emotion, he could not tell.

Their hands met in a formal handshake. Her clasp was firm, but she quickly let his hand fall. Edward's throat felt dry and he could not speak. As their gaze met again he saw that Elizabeth's eyes shone with tears.

'I shall go and order some tea,' said Amy Cavendish. 'You must be parched, Mr Munro, after your long ride.'

Edward cleared his throat. 'Yes. That would be most kind.'

Amy left them alone. Elizabeth crossed the room to a sofa. 'Do sit down.' He sat stiffly on a chair by the fireplace. 'It's all very strange,' said Elizabeth, voicing his own thoughts.

'You've no idea how much store I set by your letters.'

'And I yours,' she said gently.

'I could not be sure you'd get my letter, to say that I was coming. They told me at the Pengelly Importing Company where you'd gone.'

'You've had a long search,' she said. Her words were a statement of fact rather than an attempt at apology.

'They told me you were selling your house in Sydney.'

She nodded. 'My real home was always in Yooma. And I could not bear to stay in Sydney with all its associations.'

So she would go back to Yooma. Of course, he should have realized. There was the school which she had built, and the friends which she had written to him about.

'You mean to return –?' he began. He swung round at the disturbance by the doorway. A child came running in from the veranda and halted abruptly by the door. She was small and dark, and Edward recognized her at once from her photograph. The child's first words froze on her lips as she saw the stranger in the chair.

'Come in and greet Mr Munro,' said Elizabeth. 'He has come to visit us all the way from England.'

The child held out her hand and bobbed a curtsy, as if it was a performance which she had been practising.

Elizabeth's gaze met Edward's anxiously. 'This is Agnes.' Her glance dropped to the bowed head of her child.

'I'm very pleased to meet you, Agnes,' Edward said. She looked up at him and, without shyness, Agnes smiled.

'And this –' said Elizabeth as a second child appeared in the door, smaller and tear-stained, in a dirty frock, and with a wail of 'Aggie wouldn't wait for me.' 'This is Agnes's sister Katherine.'

'You don't have to be pleased to meet Katherine,' said Agnes, regarding her sister with scorn.

'Oh, but I am.' Edward was looking, not at the child, but at Elizabeth, who looked quickly away. 'If you only knew how pleased I am to see you all.'

'It's a long way to England,' said Agnes. 'Thousands of miles.'

'A very long way,' agreed Edward.

'Mama says the sun does not shine so much there as it does in Australia.'

'Oh, sometimes it shines. And then it is very pleasant.'

'Good,' said Agnes with satisfaction. 'Because Mama and me and Katherine are going to live in England soon.'

Edward's self-possession faltered. His heart began to pound against his chest. 'Is that true?' He looked at Elizabeth for confirmation.

'It's true.' Elizabeth's smile was calm, but in her eyes, for a moment, there lingered that spark of excitement which he remembered. And this time she did not look away.